Becoming HER Series

BOOKS ONE THROUGH THREE

K WEBSTER

Cover Designs: All By Design (http://kristi609.wix.com/allbydesign)
Photo: Dollar Photo Club
Editor: Mickey Reed (http://www.mickeyreedediting.com/p/freelance-editor.html)
Formatting: Champagne Formats (http://thewineyreader.com/champagneformats/)

ISBN-13: 978-1514623602
ISBN-10: 1514623609

K WEBSTER

Becoming LADY Thomas

BECOMING HER SERIES

Dedication

Dearest husband . . .

You'll always be my reason.

A heart well worth winning, and
well won. A heart that, once
won, goes through fire and water
for the winner, and never
changes, and is never daunted.

-Charles Dickens-

Prologue

Elisabeth

Sixteen Years Old

THE CRICKETS CHIRP IN A melodic cadence as I walk along the edge of the woods behind our house. Father has been asleep for nearly an hour now, which is why I've chosen this time to sneak out. My younger sister of three years, whom I share a room with, Ella, was also asleep, which made my breakout possible.

A snap of a twig to the left of me in the dense forest startles me from my thoughts and I pause.

"Hello? Anyone there?" I hiss toward the darkness.

I'm greeted with an eerie silence that causes a shiver to skitter down my spine. Tugging my shawl higher up my shoulders, I continue my trek to the old barn on the edge of the property. I knew this wasn't a good idea, but I needed to see him. Before he left me for university in London.

Snap.

"Who's there?" I demand, my voice quivering.

When I'm met once again with no answer, I grab hold of my dressing gown and begin to trot at a quick pace toward the dark building that hulks at the top of the hill. It won't be long. Just another few steps.

Suddenly, a cold arm snakes around my waist, and before I can cry out in horror, the accoster's other hand slaps over my mouth. The scream that was poised to leave my throat stays lodged there as I whimper in fear. But the moment the person inhales me just below my ear, I know.

It's him.

My William.

"Shhh, pretty girl," his voice soothes me. "I'm here."

He presses a soft kiss on my chilled-from-the-night-air flesh. This time, a shudder for a whole other reason wiggles its way through me. The moment he releases me, I turn in his arms to face him.

"Miss me, Lissa?"

Instead of answering him, I run my palms up the lapels of his jacket and grin at him. He dips his head to mine and softly kisses my lips. I'll never tire of his taste—a hint of lemon and mint leaves. Something ignites from within me and I deepen our kiss.

"Let me make love to you, sweet girl," he begs between kisses.

God, how I want to. But I'm a little frightened. My older sister, Edith, tells me that it hurts. She says that it feels like a metal poker has been warmed in the fire and pushed forcefully into your body. I'm not sure if she knows this from experience or if she's protecting me much like a mother would.

Our mother died from cholera several years ago, and ever since, Edie has treated me as if I'm a child. *Her child.* Thank goodness she leaves for university soon as well.

"Please," he whispers as he slides his hands to my hips.

My body aches, especially in my midsection, almost as if the emptiness could be cured by his touch. Could tonight be the night? The night I lose my virginity to the love of my life?

"Yes," I murmur back. Even though my words are approval, I'm still terrified.

He rests his forehead to mine and stares at me with eyes as blue as the sky. "Lis, I love you."

As he says his words, he pulls my hips closer to him and I feel his hardness poke me in my belly. A nervous giggle erupts from me.

"I'm scared," I finally manage to tell him.

He takes hold of my hand and guides me toward the barn. "I know you are, darling. But I promise you I'll take care of you. I'm going to marry you when you turn eighteen. You will drop the Merriweather name and become a Benedict. This—our making love—will only strengthen our bond until then."

His words make sense, and I mentally clutch on to them as we walk.

Not even ten minutes later, we're lying on the bed on the loft of the barn. Long ago, we made this our place.

"Your lips, Lissa," he groans and sucks one between his teeth before continuing. "Your lips are like the finest of delicacies. I could feast upon them for hours."

A whimper escapes me as he pushes my dressing gown up at an agonizingly slow pace. My mind screams at him to hurry, but my lips quiver in silence.

"I've wanted this for so long." His voice is needy, and I want to please him.

My mind blanks as he drags my knickers down my thighs and to my knees. It's as if he's going slowly to drive my mind to the brink of insanity.

"Just hurry," I rush out as I kick out of them.

He flashes me a handsome smile and my pounding heart gradually returns to normal. This boy, only two years my senior, has stolen my heart. His hand slides up my bare thigh, and when his pinkie barely flutters over the thatch of hair between my legs, I begin to cry.

I'm not ready.

I want to be ready, but I'm not.

"William," I murmur with a wobbly voice.

His mouth steals mine and he kisses me in a way that coaxes me—makes me yearn for more again. But when he breaks away to unfasten his pants and drop them, the anxiety threads its way back through my veins.

He seems so large, and I'm unsure how he'll fit into the space that barely seems to hold just my middle finger. But he appears to be so happy—so thrilled to be doing this with me. Surely I can endure it long enough to please him.

His hands find my knees and he parts them. Even though the barn is enclosed, I can still feel the chill of the night air on my sensitive flesh. At the sensation of the tip of his penis dragging along my opening, though, I sob harder.

"W-William. S-s-stop."

Blazing, blue eyes meet mine and his brown eyebrows pinch together in confusion. "Lissa, I thought you wanted this. Us."

I do. God, how I do. I just don't want it right now.

I finally find my voice and tell him firmly, "Not now."

A growl bursts from him, and my usual playful William seems lost behind the eyes of the angry one before me. Smashing my eyes closed, I wait for the inevitable loss of my virginity.

But it doesn't come.

"Bloody hell, Lissa!"

I open my eyes to see him yanking his pants up over his erection. His eyes aren't ones of love; they're ones of disapproval. My heart aches to think I ruined our moment.

"William," I sob, "I'm sorry. Please, let's try again."

The look in his eyes is one I cannot bear to ever see again. I'll do anything wipe it away.

He shakes his head in disappointment. "Maybe when you're older. Besides, I'm not aroused anymore. The moment is gone, Lissa."

Will we ever get it back?

Chapter One

Elisabeth

Four years later . . .

"PUT THE KETTLE ON, ELLA. They'll be here soon," I instruct as I peer out the window. Father's coach is nowhere to be seen, but I know they'll be here at any moment.

A clatter in the kitchen draws my attention from the window to my younger sister. Her pale-pink frock is the fanciest she owns, saved only for special occasions. And today is most certainly a special occasion.

Our sister is coming home from university.

My William will be home from university.

I watch her slender hand turn the faucet on as she begins filling the kettle. My sister is beautiful with her long, blond hair always elegantly twisted into a perfect chignon. She reminds me so much of my mother.

"Do you think he'll ask for your hand in marriage? Tonight?" she questions.

A smile plays at my lips as I think about his last letter.

Dearest Lissa,

I cannot wait until the day I see you again. The letters have not been able to fully express how much I have missed you. But I promise you, as soon as I return, I am going to make you my wife. I love you until the end, sweet girl.

Your William

"I don't know. Gosh, what if he doesn't think I'm pretty anymore?" I ask as I bite my lip.

My sister, who's now taller than I am, envelops me in a hug. "You're the most beautiful of them all," she giggles. "I mean, I've never seen anyone with your shade of red hair—the color of the finest cabernet. You're like royalty."

I roll my eyes but secretly revel in her compliment. The last time I saw William, I was but a young girl. My breasts hadn't even fully developed, and I was timid.

Now?

Now, I'm more than ready. I spent four years touching myself in the dark, imaging that it were him. Four years mentally and physically preparing myself for him. That night before he left for university, the dynamic in our relationship changed. A wedge that had never existed before was suddenly there. And even though we've spent four long years writing letters that professed our love back and forth, I knew that it would take a physical union to fully eradicate that wedge.

It is long overdue.

"I see them!" Ella shrieks as she points out the window behind me.

My heart does a flop when I see my father's coach bouncing along the gravel path down the hill. I know that Ella is thrilled to see our sister Edith, whom we haven't seen either in four years, but I don't have room to be excited for her. My heart pounds around in my chest with the need to see *him.*

God, how I've missed him.

Nervously, I wipe my palms along my jade-colored petticoat. Edith used to tell me that green complemented my scarlet hair. Ever since, I've always been drawn to the color.

"Ella, hurry and set out the cakes. They'll be famished from their journey," I instruct.

Thankfully, she heeds my direction and begins placing the plates on the table. I'm lost in my thoughts of hoping he'll still find me attractive when I hear my father's booming voice in the front room.

"In the kitchen," I call out.

Moments later, my father's robust frame fills the doorway. "Lissa, sweetheart. How thoughtful of you to organize this for our return," he praises as he waves a hand toward the table.

Grinning, I bask in his praise and lift my eyes only to lock eyes with *him.*

My William.

Words fail me as my gaze skitters down the tall, filled-out form of the boy I fell in love with, who has now become this—*this man.*

"Sweet girl," he murmurs before stalking toward me and pulling me into his arms.

Lemon and mint fill my nostrils as tears burn my eyes. Oh, how I've missed this man. When his lips find my neck, I suppress the moan that threatens to rip from me. It wouldn't be appropriate to allow him to do the things that are running through my head right now, in front of my family. But later?

Later, I want him to do them all.

"I'm going to make you mine," he promises against my ear before leaving me to stare after him.

My eyes follow him as he hugs Ella. Age was good to him. Through his trousers, I can see that his thigh muscles are broad and hard. I want to run my tongue along them and—

"Good afternoon, sister." Edith's prim voice snaps me from my wicked thoughts.

I attempt to cool the crimson that burns my cheeks and greet her with faux joviality. "Good afternoon, Edie. You look stunning as always."

My words are the honest truth. Where Ella is gorgeous in her innocent beauty and I'm different with my unique appearance, Edith is regal and exquisite. My older sister has silky, dark-brown hair that she keeps in a loose braid down her back. Her eyes are wise and knowing.

Both of my sisters outmatch me where beauty is concerned. But as my William turns and gazes at me so hungrily that I nearly melt into a puddle on the kitchen floor, I know that it doesn't matter. Nothing matters aside from how he feels about me.

"You're mine," he mouths to me.

"Ella, this cinnamon cake is delicious. You're an excellent cook like your mother always was," Father praises with a smile.

Ella grins back at him and pride fills me. At seventeen, she's grown into such a wonderful woman who will make a nice young man happy one day.

"So, Lissa," Edith says with a narrowed gaze. "Now that I'm back from university, do you think you shall enroll? Or do you have plans to be a homemaker with no home?"

An annoyed grumble comes from William as I scramble for something to say. Thankfully, he steps in.

"Actually, Edie, I came here tonight to ask for your sister's hand in marriage. I've loved her since we were children. Franklin has known of my intentions because before I left for university, I asked his permission to marry her. Now that I'm a man with a degree, I can finally take care of her as my wife."

My eyes fly up to his and he winks at me. This. It's finally happening. Ella lets out a squeal of delight, but Edith seems agitated. Lifting her nose in the air, she reaches a hand over and squeezes Father's hand.

"Do you want to tell her, Father? Or shall I?"

He curses under his breath and both Ella and I gasp. Everyone's attention falls to my father.

A frustrated sigh rushes from him as he quickly stands and storms over to the liquor cabinet. I send William a confused look, and his jaw clenches angrily. I'm not sure what's happening, but it doesn't appear that it is going as planned.

"What is it?" I murmur to my father, whose back is turned to me.

We all watch him as he fills a glass with bourbon and then proceeds to down the entire thing.

Finally, he turns toward us and his grave eyes find mine. "Dear girl, I nearly lost the farm."

Our home.

Where our mother birthed all three of us.

"I don't understand," I tell him.

He runs a palm through his salt-and-pepper hair. "I went into debt paying for Edith's tuition. The economy isn't what it was, and we've fallen on hard times. My debtor, Lord Thomas, recently came to collect his debt. Our farm."

Edith must know of what he's telling us because she seems unsurprised. William, on the other hand, is furious.

"Go on," I urge.

Another ragged sigh. "I was ready to give it all to him. We'd find a new place to live maybe in London or somewhere else, but then—"

Edith cuts him off. "But then Lord Thomas saw our family portrait, the one we had painted before Mother died, and he struck a new deal."

Father snatches the bottle of liquor and pours himself another glass. "He's offered to cancel the debt of the farm. No strings attached. But"—he groans and downs his drink—"he wants to marry one of my girls of his choosing."

What?

"N-n-no. That's not possible. This can't happen, Father. William and I are going to wed," I sputter out.

My father frowns. "I'm sure that will still be the case. But until Lord Thomas makes his decision, my hands are tied. Edith is the sure choice because of her age and education, so you needn't worry. This will all sort itself out soon."

A tear rolls down my cheek, and I glance at William for help.

He slams a fist down on the table, causing all of the dishes to rattle. "This is ridiculous, Franklin! Lissa is going to be mine and I don't care if I have to put her into that coach and leave this damn town without your approval. I've waited too long to wed your daughter only to have her taken right out from underneath me now. Tell him no deal. I can meet with my parents—see about taking out a loan with them. You don't have to arrange for one of your daughters to clear your debt. We can fix this."

His words give me hope, and I reach a hand toward him. He takes it and brings my knuckles to his lips, kissing them chastely.

"Yes, Father. The tuition can't be that much," I agree.

Father's eyes flit over to Edith who purses her lips together but nods.

"You see, Lissa, our father has acquired more loans than that of university tuition," Edith explains. "In an effort to recover the monies quickly, he placed some rather large bets and lost. The amount of money our father owes Lord Thomas is ridiculous. He'll never be able to repay it in his lifetime."

I frown, but William explodes. He bursts from his chair and swipes his dishes onto the floor. Glass shatters everywhere, and I stare at him in horror. We gasp in surprise as he stalks over to our father and grabs him by the lapels on his suit.

"Listen here, Franklin. Elisabeth will be my wife no matter what. So do what you have to do to get that prick to choose Edith. If you allow my Lissa to go with him, so help me, I'll kill you with my bare two hands."

This time, I fling myself from my chair and over to them. "William, stop it! Right this instant. We'll make this right, but killing my father is ignorant. Now, come with me. You need to cool off. We'll take a walk."

He sends one more hate-filled look toward my father before he releases him. I've almost managed to pull him to the door before he turns and points a finger at him.

"Make sure it's Edith he chooses, because if he doesn't and he chooses the woman I'm in love with, I will make good on my promise to take your life."

Chapter Two

Jasper

I CLOSE MY EYES AND THE portrait from the parlor instantly materializes. I've been obsessing over her for six goddamned weeks. Ever since I stepped into the home of Franklin Merriweather, hell-bent on taking everything he owns for repayment, I've been fixated on her.

The one with eyes as green as the grass on a warm summer day.

The one with a tiny smile that seems to hide secrets—secrets I want to know.

"Lord Thomas," my butler Gerald calls out from the doorway of my study, "shall I pack the coach for your travels this evening?"

As much as I want to steal away to go claim my prize, I know I mustn't be so hasty. Good things come to those who wait. And she will be worth the wait—this much I know as fact.

"No, Gerald. Please, get some rest. I'm about to retire as well. We'll set off at daybreak. I want my fiancée tucked away in her suite by this time tomorrow," I sigh with reluctance.

He nods and closes the door behind him.

Burying my face in my palms, I once again recall the portrait. Franklin Merriweather may not be very proficient in gambling, but the man has excellent genes. Those girls, a perfect mix between their mother and father, are all beautiful in their own right.

But only one caught my attention. In the portrait, she was no more than fourteen years of age. I know now that she's most certainly of age. And even if she weren't, I'd take her anyway. Images of her naked, lying on my velvet duvet, flood my mind, and I feel my cock begin to thicken with desire.

How many times will I have to find release with my hand until she's the one I'm sunk deep inside of?

Soon after Mr. Merriweather and I signed our deal, I took solace in those of local prostitutes. Each one was paid well to please me. Each one was chosen because of their crimson locks. But none were able to satisfy me. As I fucked them hard, all the while pretending it was her, I knew I would never be satisfied.

That is, until I have my prize.

Her father revealed to me that she was a virgin. I had to excuse myself from his presence to get my cock to settle after his proclamation. To take such a vision's innocence thrilled me beyond repair.

The woman has mangled my mind with her coy smile and scarlet locks. It's only fair I mangle her innocence as well. My cock is as hard as my mahogany desk from just thinking about her tight body ripe for my taking. After unfastening my trousers, I slide my hand into my drawers and fist my length.

Again, she's forefront in my mind as I stroke myself. My God, how will I control myself around her when I finally do have her? I know it won't be easy for her to accept the arrangement her father and I have agreed upon. It doesn't make it any less binding though. She'll be my wife and I'll feast upon her perfect body whenever I shall so please.

She's almost mine.

"Elisabeth," I groan out as thick, ropy spurts of my climax wet my pants. I'm sure Gretchen, my housekeeper, loves washing my soiled trousers each day. But I pay her well, so she never so much as gives me a sideways glance.

They're all under my thumb. Funny how powerful wealth can make a person. The things it makes people do.

This time tomorrow, I shall set to seducing the woman of my literal dreams. She won't be Elisabeth Merriweather for long. Soon, she will be mine.

Lady Thomas.

Chapter Three

Elisabeth

"LISSA, HOW DO I LOOK?" Edith questions as she spins around in her cream-colored petticoat. She's every bit an angel sent from Heaven.

Lord Thomas would be a fool not to choose her. I can see that she's spent many hours perfecting her makeup while I spent the morning with William.

My poor love. It took some time to cool him off yesterday. But after a long walk and an afternoon spent kissing and cuddling in our barn, he finally relaxed. He didn't pressure me to make love but, instead, enjoyed his time simply being with me. It was perfection. And this morning, we had breakfast with his parents.

That, however, did not go as planned.

According to them, our whole township is on hard times. Their savings has been depleted, and therefore, they cannot help our cause.

My William, though, devised a new plan—to make me less desirable than that of my two sisters. He instructed me to not wear makeup and to choose one of my simple frocks I sometimes wear when working in our field. I was told to not wear jewelry, aside from the bracelet he gave to me, or perfume.

He wanted me simple.

So now, as I gush over my older sister, I can't help but glimpse at my own reflection. I've pulled my hair into a tight bun and affixed a frown on my face. Compared to Edith, I'm a moth. An utter mule in comparison to her thoroughbred appearance. Her dark hair has been curled into tight kinks that hang down her back, which lies open due to the daring design of her dress. If I were a man, I would most certainly choose her.

"Father is waiting in the parlor," Ella murmurs from the doorway. "He sent me to fetch you both. Lord Thomas is here as well."

When I turn to regard my younger sister, fear seizes me. She's spent some time dolling herself up as well. It worries me that she appears to be more than that of her seventeen years. What happens should he choose her instead of Edith? The thought sickens me.

"You look much older than your age," I chide as I rush over to her.

Her lips form a pout when I set to braiding her long, blond hair. I want her to appear to be more childlike than she does at the moment. Ella has a chance at a normal life, and I won't allow her to be thrown out with the rubbish.

"Maybe I want to get married," she whines, knowing my stance on the matter without my saying anything.

Shaking my head, I yank the black ribbon from my bun and tie off her braid. "You will, dear sister. Just not to Lord Thomas. This isn't your debt to settle."

She pins me with her blue eyes. "It's not yours either, Lissa. Nor is it Edie's. Father did his, and it's only fair that I'm able to do my part for this family. You're the one who has a chance at a wonderful life with William. He adores you. That's where you belong. Not with some debt monster."

Tears spill over her cheeks, and I quickly pull my handkerchief from the pocket of my dress to dab at them. Her nose turns red as she cries, and I can't help but be thankful that it makes her appear younger. Edith is most definitely the one he'll choose now.

"Come, girls. Let's not keep Lord Thomas waiting," Edith tells us firmly as she leads the way out of the bedroom.

Ella sighs but gives me an encouraging smile before following our sister. My heart does this wicked thing where it pounds rapidly in my chest. We'll get through this. The man will choose Edith and it will all be over.

I hurry from the room to catch up with my sisters only to find they are already greeting our unwanted guest.

"Where is your sister?" he asks Edith in a deep timbre. The depth of his gravelly voice sends a quiver of fear pulsating through me.

"I'm here," I blurt out as I defiantly lift my chin to meet the eyes of him.

Him.

Lord Thomas.

Chocolate-colored eyes meet mine and my lips part open in surprise. I didn't expect him to be so . . . so achingly handsome. His overgrown, dark hair is styled on top of his head in such a way that I wonder if he even fixed it at all. My fingers twitch at my sides with a sick longing to touch it. When his eyes fall to my lips, they narrow. In a nervous move, my tongue darts out to moisten them.

The room spins, and I suddenly wish I'd had a moment to eat something before he'd arrived.

"You must be the precious Elisabeth," he greets, his voice a grumble that makes its way into my bloodstream.

I don't like that it feels as if he's infecting me.

With what?

Him.

It makes me dizzy and lightheaded, and the room tilts again as I reach for anything to steady myself on. He takes a step toward me, and in a desperate move, I grab his arm as if it's an anchor in a turbulent sea.

"Yes, but if you'll excuse me, I should go lie down. I'm not feeling well at all," I whisper, ignoring the warmth radiating from his arm.

He leans in, and I close my eyes as his scent takes its turn invading me against my will. Unlike William, who smells sweet, this man smells different. His scent is dangerous. Intriguing. Decadent. The way my mouth waters in his presence is further proof of my being ill.

When my knees buckle, he slips an arm around my back and pulls me against him, and I'm completely lost in him. His chest is hard through his suit.

"Where is her bed?" he demands.

Ella answers first, because maybe my father and Edith are shocked at my sudden sickness. "This way."

I gasp when he scoops me into his arms and strides effortlessly down the hallway. Once he makes it into the room I share with Ella, he kicks the door closed before striding over to my bed. How he knows that it's mine is beyond me.

"I'm sorry to ruin your afternoon, sir, but please rejoin my family. I'll stay here," I tell him breathlessly.

When he releases me, I push away the shudder my body threatens to take at the loss of his touch. Then his gaze finds mine and it's one of interest, much like how a cat would paw at a dazed mouse. I don't like that I feel as if I'm his prey.

"Lord Thomas, please join us for some tea," Edith chirps as she pokes her head inside the door.

His attention snaps to her, and I watch as his eyes run down her perfect body before waving her off dismissively. I should feel horrified that he's turning her away to focus on me, but I can't help the thrill that surges through me.

"Go on without me. I'm going to take care of her," he declares.

The declaration scares me because I don't miss the double entendre. Edith nods curtly before closing the door again, leaving me alone with this man. Then his eyes find mine and he grins at me.

My chest seizes with some unexplainable feeling, and it's as if I cannot breathe.

"Elisabeth, what is this you're wearing? Did you have intentions on fooling me as to not choose you?" he questions with a smirk on his full lips.

I can't help but regard them as he says his words. It takes a moment to clear my head before I unwillingly drag my vision away from them to stare at him.

"I'm wearing a dress. And we both know Edith is the perfect choice," I assure him.

He skims his gaze along the naked flesh of my neck and down toward my breasts, which are heaving wildly. I feel as if I'm an animal trapped under his claws and my only way of escape will be if I say the proper words. One false move and I'll be doomed.

"I beg to differ."

Our eyes meet once again. His look is sharp and unyielding.

"But she's so beautiful, and with her education—"

He interrupts me. "She's not you."

My eyes widen at his words and I sit up on my elbows to glare at him. Anger floods through me. Here I've done everything in my power to appear the less favorable choice and he wants me anyway. It's as if he's doing it just for the sport of it.

"Excuse me?" My lips form a firm line as I glower at him.

"You heard me properly, Elisabeth. It's you who I want. I made my decision weeks ago. And now—now that I'm in your presence—I'm one hundred percent certain you will be mine."

I gape at him in horror. What about William? Our future?

"No," I blurt out before I can stop myself.

His features become furious. And while they should terrify me, something sinister coils from deep within me. He is even more handsome while angry.

"No isn't a word I'm accustomed to hearing. No isn't a word that even registers in my brain. You will be my wife and you will be coming back to London with me this evening."

This evening? "Absolutely not. Please, sir, take Edith. She's more than ready to banish my father's debt by becoming your wife. You're a fool for not realizing how beautiful she is. Besides," I tell him with a pout, "I am already taken."

Whereas he was furious earlier, he seems outraged now. "What is this you speak of? Who do you think you belong to?" he hisses out angrily.

"His name is William Benedict. I have loved him since I was a small girl. Now that he's back from university, I'm set to marry him. Not you—not some man I've only met today," I snap.

His arm flinches, and from the dangerous look in his eye, I suddenly fear he'll hit me. As he raises his hand, I close my eyes and wait for the impending blow. But he doesn't hit me. Instead, his hand curls around the back of my neck. With surprising strength, he hauls me to him. And I'm shocked when his lips smash against mine hard enough to nick my bottom lip.

I go to slap at him, but his free hand steals my wrist as he lowers me back down onto my bed, never losing the connection of our lips. My mind refuses to kiss him back, but my lips respond by parting and allowing him further access. The growl he empties into my mouth sends a shiver through me that gets lodged in my pelvic area. His kiss is rough and unrelenting, so different from William's soft, worshipping ones.

William.

I slip my fingers into the man's hair and yank him from my lips. "Stop."

But he doesn't stop. No, he pushes toward me again, unfazed by the way I pull at his hair, and kisses me harder. The way his soul attempts to climb inside me through our kiss both frightens and thrills me. Every hair on my body stands on end, and I can't help but realize how alive I feel.

So wanted.

So desired.

My body squirms in a needy way that embarrasses me. I'm William's, yet here I am, enjoying—yes, *enjoying*—the way this man is kissing me so powerfully. It's as if his kiss somehow consumes my soul.

"Are you wet for me, dear Elisabeth?" he murmurs when he breaks our kiss for a moment.

"What do you mean?" I gasp. My words are innocent, but I know exactly what he means. Between my legs, I'm throbbing for this handsome man to touch me. The very thought is a betrayal toward William, and that sickens me.

"Coy is a very sexy look on you," he grumbles before he briefly takes my lips. "But I'm not stupid. I can see that my proximity affects you. Your tight cunt is wet, isn't it?"

I shake my head in disagreement even though the act is a lie. My knickers are damp because of him. Though William and I have had plenty of steamy kisses, never has one made me borderline insane like the one I've shared with Lord Thomas.

"Lies," he chides playfully. "If that is the truth, I'll leave you now. Let you run along to your peasant boy."

I frown at him.

"Your father has a terrible poker face as well. I bet"—he grins—"you're as wet as you've ever been in your entire existence."

My blood boils with rage because he's right. "Wrong. Now, please, let me be. I don't want you. This isn't my debt to repay. Surely there's another way for you to negotiate with my father."

He rests a palm on my belly and I swear my dress nearly catches fire from the heat of it. I'm frozen in fear when he slides it lower and lower. I want to shout for my father. I want to hit him and make him stop. But something inside me quietens the voice. Something inside me wants to be touched by him.

"Ah," he growls, "I bet I could make you scream my name just by touching you here."

The moment his finger connects with a certain part of my body through my clothes, I nearly buck off the bed. While I've always been curious, my fingers have only probed within me—not on the outside. The place he touches me now seems so magical as it pulsates pleasure through every nerve ending in my body.

"W-what are you doing to me?" I whimper. My breathing has become fast and erratic as his finger owns that part of me.

"I'm doing whatever I want," he answers simply.

I know I should stop him from the way he is touching me with practiced efficiency, but my mind is blank of all instruction. All I can think about is how his finger causes stars to blink behind my now closed eyes. Why is my body betraying me?

"Stop," I beg, my voice nothing but a whisper. But as I raise my hips to chase his moving finger, we both know that my plea is a lie.

"I won't stop until you find your release," he murmurs back.

His voice washes over my skin, and the out-of-reach sensation finally obliterates my senses. I want to cry out, but instead, I bite down on my lip as insane, never-before-felt pleasure rages through me. My body shudders wildly out of my control as I ride the waves pulsating through me. When he removes his finger, I hate the feeling of loss.

What have I done?

I'm too confounded to open my eyes. What he just did to me feels so dirty yet so right. I hate that I feel so relaxed and content now. My thoughts begin to clear when I feel his warm hand slip under my dress, I pop my eyes open.

He watches me fiercely as his fingers skim up my bare thigh.

"What are you doing?" I demand angrily. And even though I loathe the fact that his hand is under my dress, I can't help but want him to touch me more—to give me another gift like the one he just gave me.

"Was I right? I think I was," he tells me smoothly when his index finger slides over my knickers. "You have drenched your poor undergarments."

My cheeks burn with embarrassment at his words. This man just says whatever is on his mind. He's horrible. When he pushes my knickers aside, I gape at him, my mouth wide open.

One finger.

He owns me again with one finger as he breaches my wet opening. The way he enters is slow but demanding. His finger stretches and fills me more so than my own ever did.

"Goddammit, Elisabeth. You're absolutely dripping with want for me."

I wait eagerly for him to work more of his magic, but he slips it out of me before I can protest. Then he raises the offending hand in front of me and I see that his finger glistens. When he opens his mouth, I watch in fascination as he darts his tongue out and tastes my essence. I want to be shocked, but I'm quickly learning that this man is bold and daring. He doesn't have the boundaries normal people have.

"You taste like a honeysuckle," he reveals. "Such a sweet flower with a delicious center. My tongue is jealous of my finger."

I'm powerless against his unusual words as I stare hopelessly at him.

"Fifteen minutes. That's all you need to gather your personal things. We're leaving. I cannot wait another second to claim you as mine."

As he stands abruptly, the haze he brought upon me lifts along with him.

"Wait!" I call out, "You can't do this. You cannot just claim me. I'm not yours to claim!"

His tall frame stiffens as he hears my words. Because of the way his suit fits so perfectly, my mind wonders what he looks like underneath. But I don't have any time to examine the thought further because he stalks over to me and places a palm on either side of my head on the bed. Once again, I freeze up and all thoughts turn into unimportant bubbles that float away.

I try not to inhale his masculine scent that is now mixed with what must be mine. Together, it smells too good. Sinful. His lips press against mine again, and this time, I don't hesitate to let him kiss me. I get a taste of something different, which I realize must be me.

I taste good. Just like he said.

Chapter Four

Jasper

SHE'S PERFECTION, JUST LIKE I knew she would be. The moment I laid eyes on her much older flesh than that of the portrait, I was bewitched. Her poor attempt at making herself appear to be demure and unappealing was futile and ridiculous. Instead, she only made me want her more. The older sister reminded me of one of the whores I've taken to bed on many occasions, while the younger one was just a child.

It was the middle one I wanted.

Needed.

The middle one, named Elisabeth, was the one who would be mine.

When she touched me before she nearly fainted, I knew I would never be able to resist her. It was in that moment, the moment I watched her pale features grow even whiter, that I knew she would always belong to me.

My thoughts were further justified when she allowed me to kiss her and, furthermore, pleasure her body. Everything else faded into the background while I drove her to new heights of ecstasy. The woman has no idea what I can do to her.

As she squirmed with her orgasm, my cock ached to be inside her. I was so sure it was going to tear through the fabric of my trousers in an effort to get to her. Thankfully, I was able to tame the beast and somehow managed to leave her on her bed.

Now, I must inform Mr. Merriweather of my selection. But I've barely made it down the hallway when the older sister steps into the hallway in front of me, her lust-laden eyes drinking up my appearance.

"There you are, Lord Thomas. I thought I could speak to you for a moment," she purrs. "Privately."

I know of her kind. She's not an innocent like her two younger sisters. By the way she speaks to me, I know that this woman spreads her legs for anyone who'll show her the slightest of affections. Again, she reminds me of my past whores.

"I'm afraid I have some business to attend to, dear. I shall be leaving for my estate shortly," I tell her firmly.

Her eyes widen in shock at my blatant dismissal. "Wait!" she tries in desperation as she saunters over to me.

Then she grabs my cock through my trousers and I raise a questioning eyebrow at her.

"I can see that you're hard. You like what you see. I could make you so happy," she promises.

Any other man would slide an arm around her waist and let her make good on that promise. I'm not any other man.

"Miss, I'm turned on because of the exquisite thing in the other room that is now packing her things. She'll become my wife, which means you'll soon be my sister. Now, please remove your hand before I forcefully remove it for you."

Tears well in her eyes, and for a moment, I wonder if she'll slap me. Instead, she lets go and rushes into the room with Elisabeth. Shaking my head, I start toward the parlor, where Mr. Merriweather is waiting, but then I hear shouts coming from the bedroom. Something crashes, which sets my desire to protect what's mine on fire. So I bolt toward the door and fling it open.

Edith has her hand raised as if to slap Elisabeth again. I say again because my honeysuckle is cowering in the corner of the room, a red handprint adorning her cheek. The sight of her smacked flesh causes me to explode.

Storming toward Edith, I snatch her raised palm and twist it painfully behind her back. She cries out because I'm seconds away from snapping her wrist into two. When Elisabeth's gaze meets my murderous one, she shrinks back even farther into the corner as if she's afraid I'll hurt her too.

I'm only protecting her.

"What is the meaning of this?" Mr. Merriweather roars from the doorway.

I release Edith and turn toward the older man, ready to clobber him if blows come to blows. "This woman believes she can take out her jealousy and wrath on my fiancée. If she has any sense about her, she'll leave my sight before I slap her as she's slapped Elisabeth," I growl, my chest heaving.

Mr. Merriweather shoots Edith a disapproving glare. She's had enough sense to cry in remorse at her actions.

"Come, Elisabeth. We're leaving now," I bark out and hold my palm out to her.

She startles at my tone but tentatively reaches for my hand. Once I've secured it inside mine, I tug her to me. With my free hand, I gently stroke the swollen flesh of her cheek.

"Are you all right?" I question, my gaze never leaving hers.

Her eyes search mine for some answer I don't have. Finally, she nods.

"Father," the youngest girl says in an urgent tone, "William is here. He's not pleased."

William.

The bastard who wants what's mine.

"William?" Elisabeth questions with a wobbly voice.

"We're leaving now," I snarl and drag her along with me.

I've barely made it out of the room when I nearly slam into the brick wall that must be the infamous William. His eyes drop to our joined hands before he pins me with a mutinous glare.

"Let her go, goddammit! You're not taking her anywhere!"

I feel Elisabeth start to tug away from me, but I squeeze her hand tighter. "She's mine now, so you'll be best to run along. This is none of your business."

His nostrils flare angrily, and I sense his upcoming move perhaps before he even realizes what he's going to do next. Not giving him any leeway, I release her hand and swing my fist upwards until it connects with his jaw.

The crunch is sickening to most, but not to me. I find satisfaction in the way my hand screams in pain while knowing that the pain I inflicted is much worse. Once I set my mind on something, nothing will deter me from my path. And at this moment, this fucking Neanderthal is in my way.

He crumples to the floor, groaning in pain. Elisabeth falls to her knees and sobs.

"Elisabeth. We're leaving. Now," I bark at her.

She flinches but ignores my orders as she attempts to comfort the man on the floor.

"Have you lost your mind?" Mr. Merriweather gasps behind me.

Whipping toward him, I clench my teeth together. "No, I'm just a very serious businessman. But you, sir, have lost your daughter."

Without another word to any of them, I slip an arm around Elisabeth's waist and scoop her from the floor. She struggles and screams, but I'm much stronger than she is. It isn't until I've made it outside with her and shoved her into the coach that I speak again.

"Your life here is finished. Your home is in London now," I tell her as I climb in after her.

Her eyes are puffy and red from crying, but she doesn't attempt to escape. I can see the resignation in her eyes.

"Pritchard, home!" I order my driver.

With a jolt, the horses rapidly pull the coach away from the old farmhouse. I expect her to wave to them or at least look out the small window. But she does nothing of the sort.

Instead, she clasps her hands in front of her and stares absently at them. Because of our struggle, a section of her hair has come loose and is now dangling down the side of her face, partially blocking the sight of her.

The ride back will take several hours, so I unbutton my top coat and shrug out of it. Once I've tossed it on the bench in front of us, I set to rolling my sleeves up. The coach is as hot as the flames of hell and I'm tempted to strip down to nothing. I opt, rather, to just remove my bow tie and stopping there.

"You'll grow used to me, dear Elisabeth," I tell her as I swipe the strand of hair behind her ear.

Without looking over at me, she finally speaks. "Lissa."

Lissa?

Hell no.

"I like Elisabeth more," I murmur. "Or, better yet, maybe I should call you honeysuckle."

When her breath hitches, I smirk. The woman is so damn easy to rile. She wears every emotion on that pale skin of hers. If she's angry or embarrassed or turned on, the flesh turns pink. It's her tell, and I'm very perceptive.

"In fact," I growl as I squeeze her thigh through her frock, "I'd love to have another taste."

She grabs my hand and pushes it back into my lap. "You'll not be having another taste. What we did—what I did—was deplorable. I don't even know the first thing about you, yet here I am, letting you steal me away to do God only knows what with me."

I chuckle at her words. "You put up a fight, if it's any contest."

Her head snaps to face me and her green eyes blaze with fury. "Clearly, not much of one. I let you kiss me. Touch me. Take me from my family and my love."

The way her lips pout again has my cock roaring back to life. With a flash, I grasp her chin and pull her to me. A terrified mewl falls from her perfect lips, which only further punishes my cock.

"Let's get something straight, Elisabeth," I mutter close to her mouth, the heat of her quick breaths spurring me on, "You didn't let me do anything. I took what I wanted. Just like always. One doesn't become as wealthy and powerful as I am without seizing life and taking ownership over what he wants. Now, I want you more than anything. So when I want something, I will take it. Every goddamned time. Got it, honeysuckle?"

A tear rolls down her cheek, but she nods. Leaning forward, I press a chaste kiss to her lips.

"See? Just then, I wanted to kiss you, so I stole a kiss. It will always be like that with us because that's the kind of man I am. I see. I want. I take," I tell her simply.

Another tear. "So, you're going to take my virginity against my will?" she questions with a quiver in her voice.

Slamming my eyes shut, I briefly imagine how fucking amazing it will be when I do push myself into her hot body. The growl that rips from me is purely animalistic in nature.

"If I so please. However, I have a feeling you'll give it to me very, very willingly," I grumble.

She shakes her head in protest.

I smirk at her. "Want to place a wager?"

Her eyes widen when I pull away from her to regard her playfully. "A wager? What do I get if I win?"

"You really think you won't beg me to fuck your tight, virgin cunt by the end of a fortnight?" I ask in astonishment. This woman has no idea of my abilities.

"Actually, I believe the only way you'll get in there is if you force me into it. I'll always love William. You won't ever take that away from me."

Her words set my soul on fire. If I hadn't been so hell-bent on getting her out of there, I'd have stayed to kill the oaf to keep him from meddling in my life.

"Are we betting on this?" I ask with a raised eyebrow.

She bites her lip and nods. "Yes, but I'll set the terms."

"We'll compromise on the terms," I tell her.

Her shoulders hunch in dejection, but she nods once more. "Fine. If you take me against my will, you must extinguish the debt from my father and send me home. And after a fortnight, if my virginity is still intact, you'll let me leave. There will be no strings attached."

I smile. "And when I win this wager?"

She scoffs. "You're not going to win. But, if under some circumstance I lose my mind and you do win, I'll drop it forever. You can make me your wife and I'll never speak of William or my past again."

I'm not sure why I'm considering her bet. I don't have to participate. The deal with her father is as binding as any contract. But she's so cute with her defiant flare that I have the need to amuse her with my agreement.

"It's a deal. Now, let's seal our deal," I say before I kiss her hard enough that she will soon forget her name.

Chapter Five

Elisabeth

HIS LIPS ARE ON MINE in an instant, before I can stop them. For a brief moment, I felt confident in my abilities to stand strong and oppose his advances. Yet now, while he seals our deal with a heated kiss, all confidence takes a flying leap out the window. He manages every time to intoxicate me with his presence. The air inside the coach was already stifling, and as we share this kiss, the temperature seems to rise many more degrees.

His hands find my hips, and I gasp in surprise when he hauls me over into his lap, dragging one knee across him so that I'm straddling him. He's merely kissing me and I'm already getting lost in the confusion that is him. Why is it that my body rejects what my mind demands when in his presence?

Sweat trickles between my breasts, and I almost wish he'd rip the dress from my body just to cool me off. He doesn't go to that extreme, but he does push it up my thighs. He hardens between my legs, and I pant as it rubs me through my wet knickers. I'm already fast losing this bet.

"Mmm," I moan against my will.

His mouth owns mine and shows no signs of stopping. When he grabs my hips and pushes me harder against him, I cry out. I'm not sure what to even call him, and this sobers me instantly. I tear away from him and swallow gulps of air.

"What do I call you?"

A name falls from his lips before he roughly takes my mouth with his.

Jasper.

The way his length rubs the place he drew out so much pleasure from earlier has me rocking against him. I want to feel it again—the sensation from before that was so foreign yet so delicious. While in his arms, it's now all I can think about.

"I want to be inside you, darling, more than I have ever desired anything in my entire life," he murmurs as he kisses me.

Traitorous thoughts of him pushing his thickness into me flood my mind, and surprisingly, that turns me on even more. I want to be embarrassed at the way I'm writhing in his arms, but the desire to find that pleasure again wins out.

"Make me see stars again," I whisper against his lips.

A groan of satisfaction comes from him, and his hand slides under my dress. I yelp when he pushes a finger deep inside me. Then his palm massages me in the spot from before as he probes from within me. It's dizzying. Exotic. Addicting.

Shamelessly, I ride his finger. I urge him with my body to touch me exactly where I need to be touched. It doesn't take long, for my body to deliciously tighten as my release nears. I'm caught in the web that is him.

"Jasper," I moan, the name unfamiliar to my lips, as the stars blind me.

All sensations are lost aside from the gratifying one that seizes my very being. When the contractions of my inner womb subside, I pull away to look at him. His finger is still inside me, and he smiles crookedly at me in smug satisfaction.

"It would seem I'll be taking this"—he wiggles his finger—"before nightfall tomorrow. When shall I begin calling you Lady Thomas?"

The moment he slips his finger out, I slap him hard across his scruffy cheek. A sting instantly burns my palm, but I glower at him through it.

"Never. I may let you pleasure me, but you'll never own me. I'm afraid I just used you for my own personal gain. I intend on winning this bet and driving you mad in the process."

This statement wipes the idiotic grin right from his face.

It's been several hours since we arrived at his manor in London. I managed to keep my features cool and unimpressed as he guided me into the enormous estate. Everything about it spoke of luxury and old money. Each person I was introduced to was friendly and polite. But I refuse to allow myself to grow comfortable.

"We've prepared a meal for you and Lord Thomas," Gerald speaks through the door of my new prison.

"I'll be right down," I promise so that he'll leave me be.

Once I'm sure he's gone, I let curiosity get the best of me and open the armoire. Inside, it's stuffed full of expensive fabrics—dresses and petticoats I could only ever dream of wearing. I run my hand over a corset and can't help the smile that forms on my lips. I've never had the opportunity to dress up for anything. The dresses I did own were hand-me-downs from that of my older sister. A part of me wants to be pretty.

For him.

My skin flushes, and I sit back down on the bed. Guilt consumes me because I'm thinking about Jasper and his magical wizard hands instead of my William, who is probably grieving for me with a sore jaw.

Who have I become?

I don't deserve William. He waited for me for four long years only for me to be whisked away by some rich, pompous arse.

A handsome, pompous arse.

I fan myself with my hand and lie back on the bed. The towel I wrapped myself up in after my bath falls open, and a breeze from the open window swirls in, chilling my flesh.

Can I really win this bet against Lord Thomas?

I'm not ready to lose my virginity to him yet.

No.

I'm not ready to lose my virginity to him *ever.*

Closing my eyes, I remember the way he owned a part of me that nobody ever has. I also remember the way William was planning to take my innocence so long ago. There is a difference I've been ignoring. Jasper made me want to make love by pleasing and teasing my body. William was ready to shove it right in without any pleasure on my end.

My God, why am I comparing them?

There should be no contest. William is my love, not Jasper.

Sitting up, I make a decision. Tonight, I'm going to make myself so irresistible to him that he'll barely be able to contain himself. I'll make him want to take me. With this thought, the realization that I'll be setting myself up for hardship no matter what floods through me. If I win, that means Jasper will have stolen my innocence against my will. If he wins, that means I will have given it up willingly.

Either way, he'll have taken me.

Jasper.

The idea of him being inside me, causing me to feel more of what he teased me with earlier, sends ripples of excitement running through me. He doesn't have to know I am curious about how he would feel. That I desire it more than I'll ever admit.

In fact, I'll drive him to the brink of insanity, all the while claiming that I hate his very being. He'll go mad and take me. And then I can go home to William.

I'll be tainted.

A frown plays at my lips. Would William want me anymore if I've been used by another man? I'm unsure.

It doesn't matter though. I'll be free of a loveless marriage. Father's name and debts will be cleared. It's simple, really.

I take my time dressing even though I've already been summoned for supper. Nearly an hour later, I'm dabbing on a squirt of one of the many vials of perfume I discovered in the washroom when the bedroom door swings open.

"Dammit, woman. I've been waiting for too damn long. If this is some petulant game you're playing—" he roars, but his words die in his throat upon seeing me.

"I'm sorry," I tell him innocently. "I got a little caught up in playing dress-up."

His dark eyes have fallen to my chest, and I feel my skin heat up. The corset I'm wearing pushes my breasts up, giving them the most breathtaking cleavage they've ever had.

"My God," he growls. "You're absolutely stunning."

I can barely breathe in this thing, but with his hungry gaze, he steals the only breath I have left.

"I, uh . . . Thank you."

After stalking toward me, he invades my space as he places his hands on my hips and pulls me to him. "I want you so incredibly much, honeysuckle. My cock aches to plunge into your tight heat. Please let me have you."

I gulp but press my palms against his chest and push him away. "No. You and I both know it's not going to happen."

As I retreat, he encroaches on me. I don't stop until the wall behind me prevents me from going any farther. His hands slide into my hair, which now hangs in loose waves down my back. Tilting my head up, he captures my lips with his. I can taste liquor on his tongue, and I wish for a drink of my own, because in my sober state, I'm not sure I have the nerve to keep him away. The desire to block out everything but him is strong.

He breaks away after a heated kiss and stares down at me. "Dear Elisabeth, it's going to happen."

I shake my head, but when he dips his head down and suckles on my neck, I lose all sense of reality. The room spins as I give in. I give in to his touches and caresses, the way he cups my breasts through my dress, the way he teases my earlobe with his tongue and then teeth. I'm moments away from begging him to do his worst when my stomach grumbles loudly.

He begins to chuckle. "Honeysuckle, we need to get some food in that belly. You're going to need the energy for what I plan to do to your body later."

The wind breezes through the room again and causes me to shiver. I'm unsure if it's the chill of the air or the heat of his words. One thing is certain. I'm affected by him whether I like it or not.

"Come." He smirks before grabbing hold of my hand and pulling me out of the room.

As we walk down the ornate hallways, I can't help but wonder if I would feel the same way had there never been a relationship between William and me. Would I easily let this man into my heart and into my bed?

I think I would.

And that horrifies me.

We make our way into the opulent dining room, and Jasper drags a chair out for me to sit. Once we've been seated, Gretchen sets to dishing out foods I've never even seen before. Everything I sample is much saltier and richer in taste than I'm used to. And I find myself guzzling the wine to wash down the unusual flavors.

Gretchen eventually clears the table aside from our wineglasses. Dinner consisted of surprisingly pleasant conversation, mostly of Jasper telling me about some of the sights worth seeing in the city.

I'd almost forgotten I was here against my will until he spoke again.

"If William loved you like you say, why didn't he marry you the day you turned eighteen?" he questions with a narrowed gaze, as if he's truly trying to work out the reasoning in his head.

His words catch me off guard, so I drain my wineglass while I decide on how to answer him.

"Um, good question," I spit out bitterly. "He had his 'reasons'."

He raises a dark eyebrow at me but wisely doesn't speak.

"What if I don't want to talk about it?" I ask.

"If you're going to be my wife, I must know things about you. This is something that piques my curiosity. I wonder how it is that someone would let someone like you slip through his fingertips. You're a unique and polished ruby I was lucky enough to stumble upon. I'll never let you slip away."

I want to remind him that I have no plans to be his wife, but I instead find odd comfort in his words. The day I turned eighteen without a word from William, I was beyond stung. I was heartbroken. It wasn't until a few days later that I received his letter.

Dear Sweet Girl,

I know you were hoping for an engagement ring. This is better. I've included a bracelet that promises I'll be loyal to you. That I'll marry you after I finish my studies and can provide properly for you. This bracelet is far better, I assure you. What are two more years, love?

William

I blink the tears away once I've recited the memorized letter to him and find that Jasper is watching me with clenched teeth.

"That was it? Some ridiculous notion that you needed to wait for him to graduate?"

Nodding, I lift my hand and swipe a stray tear from my cheek. Even though the letters kept us in continuous communication, the love I had for him had dimmed that night in the barn before he left. I spent the next four years pining over the idea of him. And when he arrived yesterday, I was spellbound by his presence. Intrigued with the way he had changed.

Yet I still had the same uncomfortable feeling I'd had in the barn all those years ago.

Jasper reaches over and takes hold of my hand. "Honeysuckle, I will have a ring on that finger within four nights' time, I can assure you of that. In fact, I might even pay to have the jeweler rush the design of it. I cannot bear another moment without it on that elegant finger of yours."

He squeezes my hand, and I award him with a smile. I imagined I would seduce this man into taking me, and now, here I am, enjoying his company. I didn't tell anyone, not even Ella, of the heartache I'd felt when he sent that letter. Yet I told this stranger.

"I want to hold you, Elisabeth."

For some reason, I want him to hold me too.

Chapter Six

Jasper

HER EYES ARE SO INFINITELY sad. It pains me to see the heartache. That bastard of a man thinks he can push her away for four long years only to return and have the right to wed her. Yet I, having only known of her existence for only a couple of months, would be willing to give up everything to be with her. Luckily, I don't have to give up anything. I just have to make sure she doesn't leave me.

I made a deal with the scarlet-haired devil.

But she's nothing more than an angel in my eyes.

"Please, let me hold you," I tell her as I stand from the table.

Her hesitation is brief, but she eventually nods her approval and allows me to pull her to her feet. I want to be a gentleman and offer her my elbow so I can escort her, but when she stumbles slightly, I realize she may need more than an arm.

"Dear woman, are you drunk?" I question with amusement.

When a giggle bursts from her, the smile on my face is immediate. Her green eyes find mine and shine with an emotion I want to see more of. She almost seems happy—here with me.

"I don't think I can walk," she whispers conspiratorially.

Now, I'm tickled. "Well then, I shall carry you, honeysuckle."

Her cheeks blaze, but she slides a hand up my chest, preparing herself to be picked up. I don't hesitate at all and scoop her into my arms. Even with all of her clothing on, she's still light as can be. I'll have to get her to eat a little more if she's going to mine—I need her to have curves and more to grab on to.

"How old are you, Jasper?" she questions as I stride down the dimly lit hallway.

Briefly, I glance down at her inquisitive eyes before speaking. "Thirty-three."

Her mouth forms an "O," but she doesn't say any more. I'm over a decade older than she is, but it doesn't matter. Age has never deterred me from anything. I took this business over from my father when he passed away when I was only eighteen years of age. Men who owed my father suddenly thought they had been given a free pass when he died. Unfortunately for them, I was tougher than my father and had something to prove. I gave them absolutely no leeway and collected in some form on every debt that was owed.

Now, fifteen years later, I have a reputation that states that I'm not a man to be messed with. The word in this town is that, if the debt is not honored, I will take what is owed without hesitation. Whether it be a life or a daughter or a farm. I. Will. Take. It.

"Where are we going?" she asks as I open a door at the end of the hallway.

I flash her an easy smile. "We're going into my quarters. If I'm going to hold you, I want to do it in my bed."

Her eyes widen, and I see the fear in them.

"Honeysuckle, don't fret. I won't hurt you. It will be more comfortable there. My bed is far larger than the one in the guest room."

Seeming satisfied with my answer, she rests her head against my shoulder. I don't miss the fact that she inhales me. The thought of her wanting me as much as I want her thickens my cock.

Once I've entered the room and closed the door behind me, I saunter over to the bed and set her down in front of it. She watches me with interest when I begin to pull my top coat off. I take the time to neatly fold it and drape it over the chair beside the bed. Pretty soon, I've removed my bow tie and started on the buttons on my dress shirt.

In her drunken state, she stares at me unabashedly. The fact that she seems eager to see my chest delights me. To tease her, I slowly remove the crisp, white shirt, my eyes ever watching her. For effect, I let it drop to the floor.

Her eyes lift to mine. "What are you doing?" Those pretty, green orbs stay on mine for a moment before she's staring at my chest again.

"I'm getting comfortable so I may hold you. You should do the same," I tell her gruffly as I take a step toward her. I expect her to retreat as she's done before, but instead, she lifts her chin and faces me bravely.

"I'll need help untying the back." She turns and tugs her hair over one shoulder to reveal the open back.

Her snow-colored skin invites me to mark it up. One day soon, I shall leave "love notes" from my mouth all over her body.

Reaching toward her, I grasp the end of the ribbon she managed to tie tight by herself while dressing and pull it toward me. Her petticoat loosens as the ribbon slips through the eyelets. Once I've loosened it enough, I push it down in a gentle way down her body. After the dress makes it over her hips, it falls to the floor in a heap.

"Comfortable yet?" I ask. Dipping down, I place a kiss on her shoulder.

She shivers but shakes her head. "I can't breathe well in this thing. Can you help me out of this as well?"

I'm glad she cannot see my features at the moment because the grin on my face is that of a schoolboy—so eager and excited, such a far cry from my normally cool demeanor. As I unhook each fastener of her corset, I wonder how in the hell she managed to get into this thing by herself. Perhaps Gretchen helped her. If it were Gerald, I would have to murder him with my own two hands. No other man shall ever touch her flesh again. She belongs to me.

I free the last fastener and the corset drops to the floor with her dress. Taking a step back, I nearly curse aloud from the sight. This vixen of a woman isn't wearing any knickers or other undergarments. She sat through dinner with her pussy open and waiting, and I was a fool for not having picked up on her exotic scent—a fool for not having climbed under the table and feasting upon the dessert that is her.

As if she knows that her body teases me, she takes her time crawling up onto the bed, baring her ass at me. Everything in me screams to grab hold of those hips and yank her to me—to bend her over this bed and fuck her into oblivion. The sane part of me—the businessman—remembers that we have a deal. She'll have to want me to make love to her. I'll need to hear her beg before I grant her my cock inside her.

"You're a tease, Elisabeth," I growl as I tug my trousers down. After stepping out of them and my shoes, I climb after her onto my massive bed.

The evening air has taken a chilly turn, and a gust breezes in from the open window. I clutch the thick blanket at the bottom of the bed and pull it up over us.

"This is awkward," she murmurs. Her hands are neatly clasped over her belly and she won't make eye contact with me. I suppose someone as inexperienced as she would think that lying naked in bed together would seem awkward.

"How do you suppose we rectify that?" I muse aloud.

She shrugs her shoulders and exhales a nervous breath. Enough of this nonsense.

"I'm going to taste your nipple," I tell her boldly.

She begins to protest, but as I slip under the covers and suck it into my mouth, she cries out in surprise.

"Jas—that—oh—my—"

Her words are cut short when I take a soft bite of her flesh. She tastes like perfection—so sweet. As I tease her breast with my mouth, I squeeze the other one with my free hand. My honeysuckle writhes against my touch. The whimpers of pleasure that come from her body cause my cock to grow thick and hard.

"You're supposed to be holding me," she whispers.

"Where shall I hold you?" I question against her nipple as I start sliding my hand along her belly. The moment my finger grazes the hair on her cunt, she freezes. "Here?"

She doesn't speak. Instead, she begins to breathe quickly. I'll take that as permission. Lifting my head up as I lazily stroke her clitoris, I grin at her. Her eyes are lust laden.

"Honeysuckle, does my finger feel good there?"

Biting down on her lip, she nods once.

"Do you know what will feel better?" I ask with a raised eyebrow.

Her head shakes from side to side. Instead of answering right away, I slowly kiss her pale skin as I inch my way down her belly. The breaths coming from her are erratic with occasional kitten-like mewls. This woman wants me whether she wants to admit it or not.

When I reach the scarlet hair between her legs, I inhale her.

So fucking sweet.

"What are you doing?" she murmurs.

The blanket has drifted along with me, so when I lift my head, I can see her peering down at me with a mix of horror and excitement.

"Darling, I'm going to draw an orgasm from you with my tongue."

Her eyes go wide at my proclamation. But as I blow a breath of hot air on her pussy, she slams them shut. Then I take hold of both of her slender thighs and part her open for me. The sight is breathtaking—her body just begs to be tasted and fucked.

I run my thumb along the slit and am pleased to find her wet with arousal. Seeing her juices glistening on my thumb has me deciding to have a little sample of her there first before I finish with my task of pleasuring her. With a dip of my head, I bring my tongue between the lips of her southern region and run it upwards, lapping up her essence.

My God, she's heavenly.

"Oh!" she wails, her fingers tangling into my hair.

Her clear enjoyment encourages me, so I set to licking every inch of the flesh between her legs. My tongue punishes her in a delicious way, and I groan in pleasure when she shamelessly pushes my head against her—needing more from me. Using my thumbs to open her up to me, I thrust my tongue into her cunt.

So tight.

So fucking tight.

The walls of her pussy clench around my tongue, and for a moment, I wonder how she'll ever be able to take the size of my cock. I bury my face deeper into her, my nose connecting with her clit, and she loses her mind.

"Don't stop!" she shrieks and holds me in place.

As if I would ever stop. I will never stop.

"Oh, God!" she chants over and over again as my tongue fucks her.

Her body suddenly seizes and she screams my name out as she shudders against my mouth. My cock weeps with pre-come as I nearly explode my orgasm all over the bed. With some shred of self-composure, I manage to hold back though.

"W-what are you doing to me?" she stammers.

Slipping my tongue out, I lift up and grin at her. "I'm making sure you'll never want to leave me."

She gapes at me, her cheeks crimson from the release I gave to her. "You're really good at that," she admits.

I crawl over her naked body and find her lips with mine. Kissing her deep, I let her taste the honey I'm addicted to. My cock slides along her wet cunt but doesn't enter.

"Do you feel how badly I want you?" I question when I break away from our kiss.

Her bottom lip pouts out and she nods. "I'm not ready for that," she tells me with tears welling in her eyes.

The sudden rush of sadness breaks something within me. My cock curses my brain because it already knows I have no plans of taking her.

"It's all right, honeysuckle. I promised I would hold you. What I just gave to you was a treat, nothing more. I didn't expect anything in return. From the moment I laid eyes on you, the desire to taste you has been overwhelming."

She blinks her tears away, and a smile tugs at her lips. "Well, maybe I could make you feel good as well."

"I don't doubt that you could, but—" My words are cut short when one of her hands grips my length between us. I slam my eyes shut because it feels so goddamned good to be touched by her.

"What do I do?" she murmurs as she strokes my cock.

"That. Exactly that," I hiss through my clenched teeth.

Her hand is incredibly soft as she fists me up and down, sometimes slow and sometimes faster. There's no rhythm to the way she handles my cock, but I don't care. All that matters is her and the fact that she wants to return the favor.

"Elisabeth," I groan when my climax explodes from me, drenching her belly.

She still clutches me, but her movements halt as I become flaccid. Lazily, I open my eyes and peer down at her. Her eyes are shining with pride, and I nearly become hard again from the sight. She's so beautiful and innocent.

"Did it feel good?" she questions.

I dip down and steal her lips before answering. The kiss is a hasty one. “It felt better than good. It was unbelievably perfect. You’ve ruined me for any other woman.”

“I think you’re ruining me too,” she admits with a whisper.

And even though she seems horrified by her words, I’m fucking ecstatic.

Chapter Seven

Elisabeth

I WAKE WITH A START IN a dark room. A heavy arm lies draped across my bare belly, and I momentarily panic.

What have I done?

The night before is hazy in my mind, but I'm sure we didn't make love. My body, however, is sore from the orgasms he gave to me—especially the one from his mouth. My flesh begins to burn from the embarrassment of my memory.

At the time, there were no bounds to my lack of modesty. Now, as I reflect back, I feel ashamed at how easily I gave myself to him. I remember pushing his face against my center, needing more from him but unable to find the words. He gripped my hips, though, and dived deeper, somehow understanding my needs.

I have to get away from his intoxicating scent—his muscled, naked body—and clear my head. All of my plans to seduce him dissipated and I allowed him to seduce me instead. This man is much more versed in sexuality than I am, and I feel as though he has the upper hand. As if he knows my thoughts, his hand slips over my breast and he pulls me closer.

It saddens me that I was so easily able to walk away from William and right into the arms of Jasper. Yet he feels sort of perfect pressed against my back. I have the urge to close my eyes and snuggle closer to him. Everything about him seems right. Different. Something I want more of.

But the guilt consumes me.

William is most likely pining away for me. Grief stricken as he wonders where it is Jasper has taken me. All the while, I keep offering myself like some sort of cheap prostitute.

A tear escapes and rolls down my cheek.

What do I do?

I need to get away from this man who smells sinfully delicious and clouds my every thought. Maybe after a night in the other room, away from him, I might be able to clear my head. Deciding that that's my best option, I begin a slow creep away from him. I've almost made my escape from the giant bed when an arm hooks my waist and tugs me back down.

"Where do you think you're stealing off to in the middle of the night?" he growls against my hair.

My heart thuds loudly in my chest as I scramble for an excuse. Finally, I just tell him the truth. "I need to think. Alone."

His palm slides over my bare breast and he thumbs my nipple. "You'll never be alone again. You're mine, Elisabeth."

A shiver courses through me—partly because of the way his hot breath tickles my ear and partly due to the meaning of his words. It only serves to remind me that I'm an unwilling participant in this sham of an arranged relationship. I'll always be some prize in his eyes—some payment for a debt. The thought sickens me.

"What if I run away?" I murmur. The idea has been one I've toyed with. William and I could travel to some lesser known town and build a new life there.

My plans for escape are halted when his hand trails along my chest and circles around my neck. Then his thumb strokes the way my blood pulses erratically through the artery there. I gasp in shock when he squeezes just tight enough to let me know the strength in his hand.

"I'll catch you," he answers gruffly. "And if I have to use resources to find you, I'll expect some sort of repayment."

I gulp and slip a hand around his wrist. His grip is firm and unyielding. "What sort of repayment?"

He sweeps his lips across mine before he answers. "Well, considering I know for a fact you're penniless, it would come in the form of a punishment."

My eyes widen in the dark. His silhouette is visible, and he reminds me of some evil demon from Father's Bible.

"Punishment?"

He squeezes my neck again—just slightly, not enough to take my breath away. My heart pounds rapidly in my chest as I wonder what form of punishment he means. When my sisters and I were growing up, Father didn't punish us. We were good girls and never needed anything other than a stern word. The prospect of a physical punishment terrifies me.

I'm still considering his words when he releases my neck and rolls me over onto my belly.

"I could"—he pauses for effect—"spank you."

I gasp when his strong hand palms my bottom. "Spank? Like a naughty child?"

He chuckles in the deep voice of his that warms my insides and runs his thumb along my crack. My body betrays me because I moisten at his touch. Heat floods my cheeks in horror that he might discover that his threats are turning me on.

"Honeysuckle, if you run away from me, I will find you. And I will spank you."

Swallowing down my fear, I squirm to get away from him, but he holds me firmly in place with his hand.

"Are you attempting to run away from me even before the threat leaves my tongue?" he spits out in anger.

I pause at his words. His voice leaves no room for argument, yet a part of me wonders. If I crawled out of this bed, would he actually strike me? Worse yet, would I enjoy it?

The way my pelvis aches has me thinking I would.

Needing to get away from him, I tug away from him once more. "This is insane. I'm a grown woman—"

Slap!

Fire stings my arse at being spanked. He actually spanked me!

"What have you done?" I demand in shock.

As the sting subsides, my desire to attempt to escape his clutches grows stronger. But as I move again, my poor bottom meets the same fate.

Slap!

"You blithering arse of a man!" I screech.

I feel as though I should be crying at the force with which he whipped me, but instead, my nerve endings blaze with something altogether different.

Curiosity.

I want to know why my nipples have pebbled at his abuse.

Why my body is once again wet and lubricated.

I need to know why it is I'm secretly wishing he'd slap me again.

"Honeysuckle?"

"What?" I snap.

"You liked it, didn't you?"

"No," I lie. "You horrible man. I did not like it."

His thumb slides along my crack, past the unmentionable area, and breaches the opening that is, in fact, dripping with need. I gasp at the intrusion—both hating and loving its presence.

"I bet I could make you come all over my thumb simply by spanking that sweet bottom of yours," he growls.

Before I can argue that I would never get off by such an atrocity, he slaps my bottom again. My inner walls reflexively clench around his thumb and I see stars in the dark room.

"Th-that—what are you doing to me?" I stammer out.

Instead of answering, he swats me again, this time taking a moment to massage the tingling flesh after. His thumb remains unmoving, and I wonder if it's because I have it in a vise grip. My muscles are tight, attempting to ready myself for the next swat I'm unwillingly looking forward to.

"Elisabeth, I'm punishing you."

My mouth parts and I go mad with sick thoughts. What sort of person gets off on this sort of thing? Clearly, I do, because with the next swat, I come apart.

Hard.

Stars of every color burst into the darkness as my entire body shudders wildly out of control. Every muscle in my body screams as I tense up in an effort to hold on to the orgasm. His thumb becomes incredibly lubricated as I lose myself to the utter senselessness of what he just did to me.

I liked it.

No, I loved it.

I'm a horrible person.

When his thumb pops out of my body, I cry out from the loss of it. He runs his palm up my back, his thumb dragging a trail of wetness behind. My body becomes languid and I begin to drift off. When he lies down beside me and pulls me against his body once again, I don't fight it.

I give in to it.

I enjoy the warmth his body blankets mine with.

I revel in the erratic pounding of his heart, which matches mine in rhythm, against my back.

I wonder if I might actually like the new person I've become in his presence.

Not Lissa.

Not the boring middle sister with the plain appearance against that of her gorgeous sisters.

Not the put-off fiancée for four long years.

No, right now, I am loving this new me.

Elisabeth.

Soon to be Lady Thomas.

Honeysuckle.

The very naughty woman who's naked in bed beside this very naughty man.

"Miss Merriweather?" a voice questions, waking me from my slumber.

It is morning, and I meet the kind eyes of the housekeeper, Gretchen, as she peers in through the cracked door. My flesh is still naked, and I'm horrified that she's seeing me in this state. Heat floods my cheeks as I yank the blanket over me. With a brief glance of the bed, I notice that Jasper is no longer with me.

"Yes?" I squeak out finally.

"Breakfast is ready. Lord Thomas had a business meeting this morning and is tied up in his study. His instructions were to make sure you were properly fed," she explains as she pushes through the door holding a tray.

I smile because the smell of cooked meats and eggs wafts over to me, which causes my belly to grumble. "Thank you, Gretchen."

She settles the tray beside me on the bed. "I see that you've taken to Lord Thomas quite easily," she chuckles boldly.

Snapping my head over to her, I stare at her with my mouth open in shock. "I, uh, I don't really have a choice."

The woman is older, and with her kind eyes, easy smile, and greying hair that's been pulled back into a neat bun, she reminds me of my grandmother on my mother's side. Aside from her bold words, I like her.

"Sugar," she smiles and pats my shoulder, "you have a choice and you made it. In my honest opinion, I think it's the right choice. He's a good man, and I've never seen him act this way around any woman. You're special to him."

I chew on my lip before speaking. "He acts differently?"

Her brows furrow together. "Normally, he's so poised and serious. Lord Thomas is a focused businessman driven by money and power. Everything he does is an effort to further grow his estate and legacy. And while he's always paid us well and treated us as if we were family, he still guards his heart. But with you, he's different. His eyes shine with happiness. The dear boy is completely smitten with you."

I smirk because, for once, I feel as if I have the upper hand when it comes to him and me. She's provided me with valuable information—I'm more than a pawn in his little game. I'm something he truly wants and enjoys.

As I begin eating, she chatters on about the estate and places she thinks I might enjoy, like the garden and the library. But when she mentions that I mustn't enter the east wing, my curiosity is piqued.

"Child, I just told you not to worry about it," she scolds as I finish up my food.

I frown at her. "Why can't you just tell me? You're my only friend."

My words play on her heartstrings like I hoped they would, because her features soften. She quickly glances over at the door before taking a resolved breath.

"His study is in that wing," she whispers. "But he also has a meeting room where he conducts his business. Lord Thomas has a dangerous profession. Most days, I worry about his safety. Fortunately, most men are terrified of him—he can be quite the intimidator when necessary. Young women don't have a place in that wing, and it will serve you well to remember that."

I nod in agreement at her as she collects the tray. "I think I may find a novel to get lost in over in the library later," I lie.

She beams at me on her way out. "It's absolutely stunning in there."

I smile back as she leaves me be. The clattering of the tray slowly fades with each step as she returns them to the kitchen. Once I'm sure she's gone, I fly out of the bed. There's no way I'm going to wear the dress I wore last night to go on my spying mission. So I decide to throw on Jasper's button-up shirt over my naked flesh. Since he's so much taller than I, the shirt nearly reaches my knees. It smells like him, and I fight the urge to inhale the masculine scent.

After slipping out of his bedroom, which just so happens to be near the east wing, I pad quietly down the hallways until I hear muffled masculine voices behind a doorway. The cool, measured, deep voice that talks over one voice until it is silenced must be Jasper's. Even though I can't hear the words, they are powerful—so him. The conversations are hushed until one of the men begins shouting. I press my ear against the cool mahogany to see if I can make out the words.

"I need more time," the man bellows.

More hushed words from Jasper.

"You're a raving lunatic if you think I can come up with that much money by tomorrow morning!"

This time, Jasper raises his voice, but I still can't understand what he's saying.

When I hear stomping on the wood floors, I am about to retreat, but the door is suddenly flung open. Since I am pressed against it, I stumble right into the arms of the person who opened the door.

A man not much older than William with a mess of black curls steadies me by my elbows. When my green eyes meet his nearly black ones, I quiver in fear. While Jasper may have stolen me away from my family, deep down, I know he has a good heart. However, as the brow of the man before me furrows and his eyes skim my inappropriately dressed body, I realize he is pure evil. His heart is as black as a starless night.

Everything seems to move in such slow motion. The calculating grin of the one before me. The familiar, possessive growl of Jasper. And the out-of-place deep chuckling from behind me.

I'm in so much trouble.

Chapter Eight

Jasper

THE BLITHERING FOOL WAS ALREADY idiotic enough to think I would grant him an extension on the debt he owed me. But to touch my woman—my sweet, Elisabeth—without my permission? That is inexcusable.

"Remove your hands from the lady and depart from us before I forcibly drag you from my estate," I snarl in my most menacing tone.

Mr. Caulder hesitates for a moment before dropping his hands and tossing a smug grin over his shoulder at me. "Such a sweet, fragile thing. Is she yours? You might be careful in this crime-ridden city. A flower such as she could easily get smashed into the filthy streets."

A threat.

Seeing red, I am about to obliterate this goddamned fool with my fists until all that remains is a heap of swollen, broken, bloody flesh and bones. His warning fuels my desire to take his life right here in this room. My knuckles crack as I ball them into fists, readying myself to kill him.

"You, sir, certainly have a death wish. How about I escort you from the premises?" a familiar deep voice thunders from the doorway.

My oldest friend.

The great Earl of Havering.

Affectionately known as Count Alexander Dumont.

Mr. Caulder laughs in an evil manner but wisely allows Alexander to show him the way out. Once the door clicks in place behind them, I turn my attention to my Elisabeth.

"I, uh—" she stammers, but I silence her when I raise my hand.

"What are you wearing?" I hiss, my fists still balled in anger.

As she looks down at her small, bare feet, I take the moment to peruse her body. Scarlet, wild, and wavy hair hangs down in front of her breasts. She's chosen my discarded shirt from yesterday to dress in. Her slender legs are uncovered, which means that fool saw what is mine.

He'll definitely die by my hand and soon.

"Did you want that man to take you and have his way with you?" I roar.

Her green eyes fly to mine and she glares at me. "Of course not. How could you say such a thing to me?" Behind the anger, she appears to be stung by my words, a slight quiver of her bottom lip being her tell.

I shake my head at her. "Honeysuckle, men like that use and abuse women."

"Like you use and abuse me," she snips out.

This time, I'm the one hurt by her words. "Get out. I don't want to see you over here ever again. Do you understand me?"

Her eyes flood with tears and her nose turns pink. My heart aches, but she must realize how dangerous my work can be. Men like Mr. Caulder would damage my honeysuckle beyond repair just to get back at me. She can't ever be in their presence. And because of their meeting, death is certain on his part. I can't take any chances with men like him.

"Elisabeth, this wing is forbidden," I tell her in a low voice, "and should I see you so much as step one pale foot into the hallway of this wing again, I will punish you. You like playing the damsel in distress, locked away by some monster. I will become that monster. Are my words clear enough for you?"

Her eyes widen in horror, and I swallow down the satisfaction. I need her to fear the unknown because being seen by any of the men I do business with is a risk to her safety.

She's still gaping at me when I stride over to her in a few short steps. A gasp rushes from her when my chest brushes against hers. The fact that, even though I scolded her, she still wants me has me smiling smugly at her.

"I hate you." Her words drip with venom.

I slide a hand behind her neck and crash my lips to her hers. Her hand slaps at my chest as she fights my kiss. She's a stubborn woman and won't open her mouth to me. But when I slip my free hand under the dress shirt and run a finger down the slit of her pussy, she moans and gives me the access I demand to her mouth.

"You don't hate me," I murmur between kisses.

Her lips are swollen and ripe for nibbling. The sweet spot between her legs grows wetter and wetter with each bite.

"I do," she argues unconvincingly.

Both of my hands find her plump arse and I lift her body. With an instinctive and mutual need, she wraps her legs around my waist. Our lips and tongues are a flurry of entanglement as I stride with her in my arms over to the wall. Once her back connects with the surface, I grind my cock into her bare pussy through my trousers.

"Oh, God!" she cries out in pleasure.

"Don't call for him," I growl, "because what I want to do to you is sinful."

Her moan is decadent and alluring as I push against her, needing my trousers gone in the worst possible way. If only the fabric could disappear and I could slam into her. The need to tear through her tight innocence is an addictive craving in which I need to indulge. Knowing I'll be the one to make her bleed that first time as I forever make her mine nearly causes me to come in my pants.

"Honeysuckle, I want to make love to you. Please," I beg, which is unfamiliar for me.

She tears away from my lips to regard me with glowing, green eyes. "No."

I glare at her. "What do you mean? You're soaking my trousers because you want it as badly as I do."

Her cheeks redden in embarrassment, but she stays firm to her words. I hold her stare as I slowly rock in a circular motion against her body, rubbing her sensitive area in exactly the right way.

"S-s-stop," she tells me with lust-filled eyes before sucking her lip between her teeth.

I pause my movement and raise an eyebrow at her. Her eyes fly back open and she wiggles against me.

"Why do you pretend?" I question as I ignore her verbal wishes, granting those that are nonverbal by rubbing her again.

"I don't pretend," she pouts breathlessly. "I'm here because I have to be. Not because I want to. I'll never give you what you want."

She flutters her eyes closed and bites down on that luscious lip again. I can tell by the way her body tenses that she'll orgasm just from how I am pressed against her.

"Maybe I'll just fucking take it anyway," I snap as I thrust with force.

A pleasure-filled moan erupts from her throat, but her eyes pop open at my words. "But you'll fail. I'll win if you do that. Are you ready to let me go so soon?"

Her tone indicates that she might be disappointed to have to leave me. The thought of her gone sends maddening thoughts rippling through my head. It will be the most difficult task I've ever encountered, but I will keep from entering her against her wishes. I need to get through that stubborn heart of hers and make her realize she wants me as much as I want her.

"I'll never let you go, honeysuckle. You're mine forever."

My words barely leave my lips before she comes apart wildly in my arms, the orgasm tearing through her with the force of a storm. This woman, whether she likes it or not, feels physically and emotionally for me. She'll need more convincing, however, to make her brain understand what her heart feels.

A plan begins to bubble in my head—one that would help her come to the conclusion faster. Pushing away my thoughts, I admire her post pleasure glow.

"Do you feel better?" I tease when she finally opens her eyes.

She smiles sheepishly at me. "I still hate you." Her words are playful, though, and I certainly don't believe them.

"If this is how you react to me when you hate me, then I will be fucking ecstatic to see how you'll behave when you love me."

Love.

The idea is as foreign as begging for sex.

"It would appear I arrived in time for the grand finale," Alexander chuckles beside me.

Both Elisabeth and I whip our heads in his direction, neither of us having noticed his stealthy arrival. Sneaky bastard.

"Honeysuckle, meet me in the garden in an hour. I'll escort you for a stroll," I instruct and press a chaste kiss on her plump lips before carefully sliding her to her feet.

She nods and scurries off out of the room. Alexander has wisely chosen to admire a painting rather than watch my half-naked woman as she exits.

"Honeysuckle? Boy, brother, do you have it bad or what?" he laughs as he turns to regard me with a teasing grin.

I shake my head at him. "She's to be my wife. I've negotiated a deal for her."

His dark eyebrows fly up in surprise. "A deal? She certainly seems happy to have been purchased as your fuck toy."

I growl at his words. "She is not a fuck toy. Elisabeth will be my lover. My partner. My other half. In due time. Now, please don't talk of her disrespectfully or I'll break your nose."

Alexander, having known me since we were children, brushes off my threat. "Fine, Jaz. I'll leave your woman alone. It surprises me that you haven't already made her your lover. What's the hold-up? Did I literally interrupt your first fuck?"

I squeeze my eyes shut. "It's a long story."

A chair squeaks and I open my eyes to see him getting right comfortable.

"Luckily for you, I have plenty of time, brother."

A groan rumbles in my chest, but I join him in the seating area and sit across from him. "I made a deal with her after the deal I made with her father. She was beautiful and innocent—I simply wanted to humor her," I reveal and close my eyes again as I remember her determined, green eyes as she negotiated the terms of our deal. "Turns out, I must not take her virginity against her will should I want to keep her. And if she can remain a virgin for a fortnight's time, then she will be free to go."

I pop my eyes back open and look at my friend. His eyebrows are narrowed thoughtfully as he listens to my story.

"So, where in all of this do you get to keep her?"

A breath rushes from my lungs. "If she gives herself to me."

Alexander's lips form a pleased grin. "I'd say she was pretty damn well close a few minutes ago."

Groaning, I shake my head at him. "She says she hates me. My Elisabeth is a stubborn woman, and I worry she'll do whatever it takes to deny me, no matter how her body responds to me."

He frowns as he thinks. Alexander has always been a problem solver—even if it falls on the impractical or unethical side of things.

He'll always find a solution. Right now, I'll take either as long as he can figure a way to convince her to stay.

"I seem to be a little confused, dear brother. If the debt has been paid and she clearly wants you, why is she playing some child's game? To what is she so eager to run off?" he questions.

Anger flares in my chest. "Not what. Whom. She was set to marry some pigheaded fool before I came along. Everything about him stinks. The man pushed her aside for four years while he and her sister were at university. He expected her to be waiting when he came back. Unfortunately for him, I saw the angel and swooped in, knowing she wasn't something to ever pass up. I'll do whatever it takes to keep her as mine."

Alexander's eyes widen as he leans forward in his chair, resting his elbows on his knees. "Wait. You said he ran off to university with her sister? Do you think they had relations? Is she as pretty as Elisabeth?"

Not at all. Elisabeth's beauty is unmatched.

"I doubt that any man could ever look at another after being with Elisabeth. And Edith is pretty, I suppose, but she's no Elisabeth," I assure him. "Even when she threw herself at me, knowing full well I was interested in her sister, I thwarted her advances easily."

A sly smile forms on his lips. "What if I did some digging? I could find out if they were ever, at any point, involved behind Elisabeth's back. And if they weren't, I have ways of proving that they were. Do you want me to work my magic? Spin a story if I have to so that Elisabeth is devastated and runs right into your open arms?"

His idea is pure genius even though I know it will come at a cost.

"I trust that, if anyone can make this work, it would be you. And what debt would I owe you?" I ask. I have more money than I could ever spend. The problem is that so does Alexander.

With my dear friend who's always been as close as a brother, it never is about money. Usually, it has something to do with his father—the prick of a man who has never treated Alexander properly.

"Oh, Jaz, don't think of it as a debt. Think of it as a favor. We're brothers and we do these things for one another." He smiles. "In fact, I have an idea that just might do."

I nod at him. My answer is already yes. I'll do whatever it takes to keep my Elisabeth.

"Father insists that I settle and find a wife. You and I both know I'll never attach myself to one woman. However, it might suit both of us for me to handle your problem and then take your problem off your hands. If this Edith is as forward as you say she is, I might be able to convince her, at the right price, to be my faux bride. I'm certainly not opposed to blackmail if the opportunity arises," he chuckles.

"What about William?" I ask. "You can't kill him. If he's innocent of your theories, you cannot take his life. That would only drive Elisabeth further from me."

"Jaz, I'll sort it out. In this day and age, anyone can be bought for the right price. Trust that I'll come through. You do your part when it comes to helping me persuade Edith into agreeing. I'll need a witness of someone with status such as yours of the authenticity of our union to help convince my father. I may call upon you for your help as this plays out."

Hope finally floods my system. "Of course, Alexander. I'll do whatever you need. I think we have ourselves a deal."

Alexander and I shake hands out of formality, but our word is as good as any legally binding document. We're just two brothers doling out favors for the other.

Chapter Nine

Elisabeth

I HATE HIM.

Actually, I don't hate him, which really makes me hate him.

God, he is so confusing!

Earlier, he was rotten with the lash of his tongue as he threatened me from ever setting foot in the east wing. It only fueled my desire to traipse around naked in front of his clients simply because I know that it would drive him mad.

After I left, I took my time bathing and dressing. I have never been one to make myself up, but around Jasper, I want to be beautiful—even if it is for the pure reason of toying with him.

As I walk down the hallway toward the door to the garden, I catch a glimpse of my reflection in a long mirror. With my ruby-colored hair twisted up and only a few curled tendrils escaping, I appear to be more elegant than the woman I was who arrived just yesterday. The emerald, puff-sleeved dress I'm wearing today perfectly complements my hair color and eyes. It will drive Jasper wild—especially how, much like last night, the corset underneath lifts my breasts until they're practically spilling out of the top. I hope that evil penis of his hardens at the sight.

The thought of his penis causes my neck and cheeks to burn with embarrassment. Considering I hate him, I sure think about him a lot. Especially a naked him. Now, my ears burn too.

"Thinking about me?"

I spin on my heel to face the thief of my thoughts. He's still wearing the charcoal-colored top coat, matching vest, and trousers. The white button-up is crisp and unwrinkled despite our earlier romp in the east wing. I'm appalled that my mouth actually waters at the sight of him.

"I was thinking about freedom," I bite out.

His eyes darken as they fall to my mouth. My lips turn up on one corner in a half smile as I remember the dark rouge I discovered and stained my lips with. The color intensifies the pout on my lips, and by the way he appears to want to devour them, I'd say he likes the color.

"You'll never be free," he growls.

I stiffen and then frown as he stalks toward me, but I refuse to back down from his intimidation. When his strong hands grip my hips, I yelp in surprise. Just like every time he touches me, my body flares to life—responds to the way his thumbs caress my hipbones.

"Honeysuckle, don't you see? You're a prisoner to my affection. A slave to your own mutual craving. Together, we are shackled by two hearts that only beat with vigor when the other is near. Now that you've had a taste, you're every bit a prisoner as I am to the love that bubbles under the surface of our cat-and-mouse games. You may think you'd be happier elsewhere, but your heart would never beat the same—you would die from a broken, empty ache in your chest. My own heart fulfills that ache and makes you whole. Stop turning a blind eye to our love that could be and let fate chain you to me as it should."

His words silence me, and I mull them over. While they're

highly presumptuous, I can't help the way my knees buckle at them. I sigh in relief when his hands tighten around my hips to steady me. Each time I'm away from him, I plan all of these ways to keep him at a distance, yet when he's in my presence, he infects my soul. His scent snakes its way in through my nostrils and dizzies me. I lose all sanity because my mind focuses on one thing.

Jasper.

"May I kiss you, sweet Elisabeth?" he questions.

The need in his voice causes my womb to throb in reciprocation. When he's sweet, he's utterly irresistible.

I smile shyly at him. "Since you asked so nicely, you may, Jasper."

He wastes no time before his lips attack mine, certainly sucking the color right from them. I lose myself in the way he tastes and slip my hands up his chest and into his thick, brown hair. My lips part open to allow him to kiss me deeply, as I know we both want him to. He takes the invitation and engages his tongue with mine. Jasper is an incredible kisser, and everything else but him disappears while we have our moment.

Just when I think we'll kiss until we suffocate, he tears his mouth from me and rests his forehead on mine.

"Honeysuckle, shall we go for a stroll in the garden before I lose control and do something we'll both regret?"

His hot, breathy words don't frighten me—in fact, they excite me. I'll never disclose to him that wayward thought.

"I'm rather looking forward to it," I say with a smile.

His grin matches the one on my face as he breaks away from me and threads his fingers with mine. Together, we walk until we reach a door that leads outdoors. As soon as he opens the door, a breeze envelops us and we step out into the garden. Today, rain is inevitable, but it's still rather warm despite the lack of sunshine.

"It's beautiful," I gasp as my eyes take in the sight. It is unexpected that a poised, stoic man such as Jasper would have such a garden hidden away.

The garden is more or less a courtyard surrounded by four walls. Even though it is enclosed by the estate aside from the lack of roof, it is rather large and full of life—plant life, that is.

He releases my hand so that I can touch a fully bloomed azalea bush. The flowers are delicate and stunning with their bright color. I could enjoy them all day. Bending forward, I inhale the unique scent of them.

He chuckles as I flit about to each plant and flower and blubber on about their beauty. When I see a bench under a small tree bearing yellow fruits, I rush over to it and sit down. The sweet air fills my lungs, and I know that, tomorrow, I'll choose this spot to read a book. I want to get lost in this garden and never leave.

"Shall I lock you in here, prisoner?" he jests with a smile.

I scrunch my nose at him and refrain from sticking my tongue out. "Don't call me that."

"Do you prefer," he asks as he sits on the bench close beside me, "honeysuckle?"

My eyes follow his gesture to a plant beside him—a seemingly messy one displaying unusual yellow, delicate flowers. He plucks one of the flowers and tugs out the center part. When his tongue darts out, I part my mouth open and watch him taste it.

"Mmm. So sweet. You're still sweeter." He smirks as his dark eyes lift to mine.

Heat floods my cheeks and I look away only to glance right back at him. "Can I taste?"

His eyes blaze with a need I don't understand, but he nods. Then he repeats his actions and holds the sweet part up to my mouth. I lean forward and run my tongue across the end. It indeed tastes rather delicious like he claims.

"I like honeysuckle," I grin. Visions of myself stretched across the bench while reading and suckling on the flower fill me with happiness.

"I love honeysuckle," he remarks without humor.

My eyes find his, and I frown at him. I know we are talking about the flower, but his words have a double meaning. The thrill that shivers through me signifies that I like the double meaning.

"Where did you find this plant?" I question in an effort to change the subject. "I'm from the countryside and we don't have anything of the sort."

He scowls and turns away from my gaze. "It was given by an out-of-town traveler—someone not from our country. He owed me, and luckily for him, I accepted this unique plant as payment."

I feel as though he's not being forthcoming with the rest of the story. "And?"

His head snaps over at me. "And nothing."

I hold his gaze for several moments. "Jasper, this story upsets you. I'm not some dense woman who doesn't know anything. I'm beginning to be able to read you, and this story stings you in some way. If I'm going to be your wife, you should tell me everything."

As soon as the last words leave my mouth, I jerk a hand up to my lips as to prevent any more odd things from spilling out. Why did I say that to him?

He takes hold of my hands and leans forward. The kiss that brushes against my lips is sweet—thankful, even. And it tugs at my heart.

"Honeysuckle," he breathes against my lips, "you're perfect. And you're very perceptive."

I smile at his compliment, but it falls away when he sits back. I already miss his hot breath mixing with mine.

"The traveler and I had become quite close despite our dealings. He was a professor, always researching something new. His research took him all over the world and thrust him further and further into debt. Instead of being firm with the eccentric man like I am with all of my other business dealings, I cut him slack. He wooed me with his gifts, like the plant, and I turned a blind eye."

A smile plays at my lips. "So he was a friend to you."

He snaps his head over to stare at me with a harsh look. "Indeed, he was. And on his way to visit me one day, he was murdered here in London, just one street over. He'd been carrying an ornate lamp and a bag full of spices from India. Someone killed him to take his gold-plated lamp, which he no doubt was bringing to gift to me."

I gape at him. Even though he's angry, I can see the hurt in in his eyes. He loved this man.

"What was his name?"

This time, his lips break into a wistful smile. "His name was Gus."

Something in me hurts for him, and before I can stop myself, I tangle my hands into his hair and kiss him fiercely. My kiss is meant to put a salve on the burned heart in his body, to soothe the ache. It pains me that he lost someone so dear to him and is still visibly upset by it.

He allows me to control the kiss and moans his appreciation into my mouth. For the first time, I feel connected to him in an emotional way. Clearly, we have no problems with physical attraction. But as we kiss, for the first time ever, I allow myself to truly accept that I could be his wife. And that I might actually like it.

When I finally tear myself away from him, I feel an invisible tethering beginning to form between us. With each passing moment away from my family and William, I feel more like I belong here with Jasper.

He takes my hands and smiles at me. "Dear Elisabeth, would you do me the honor in accompanying me to dinner tonight?"

My heart patters in my chest. "Jasper, I would love to."

This time, he beams at me, and I'm almost blinded by the breathtaking beauty of it. His face lights up with a vulnerability he has yet to reveal to me. He truly does want to be with me. And even though he acquired me through that of a deal gone bad, he's happy to have me. That much is plain as day.

Maybe it is time for the girl I once was to be put to rest, for me to embrace the woman I've become.

It feels right.

Chapter Ten

Jasper

I PULL MY TIMEPIECE FROM MY pocket and check the time yet again. Ever since Elisabeth willingly agreed to a dinner date with me, my stomach has been in knots. My plan to woo her is working. And while it was a plan, every part of my endeavors to endear her to me have been genuine. The woman has been in my life for only a matter of a days, yet I know without a doubt I do love her.

Flipping the timepiece over, I read the inscription. Gus brought it back with him from France.

JAZ, FIND YOUR PASSION AND SEIZE IT.

At the time, I smiled politely as I accepted the gift with the unusual inscription. However, now, as I think about Elisabeth, I understand what he meant. I have worked my entire life to build my empire, but it has never fully satisfied me. The passion was never there—I was only fulfilling a fate my father had passed on to me.

Elisabeth is my passion.

The moment I spied her red hair and knowing, green eyes in the portrait in their family home, I knew. My life would be about her.

I took Gus's words of advice and seized my precious honeysuckle.

She's my passion, and I'll never let her go.

Once the minute hand on the clock slides into place, I quickly pocket the timepiece and stride toward her bedroom door. I've been waiting for the past half hour just steps from her doorway—eager to see her again.

My knock is brisk, and she takes her time answering. The animal inside me desires to fling the door open and find her. But the lover in me wants to give her a chance to come to me on her own. To give us a chance.

A soft click signifies her opening the door, and I hold my breath as she comes through it. My eyes instantly find hers, and I grin.

"Took you long enough, woman. The attempt to be a gentleman is a difficult task with your lack of haste."

She tosses a playful smile my way. "While I like the gentleman side of you, the domineering side is quite endearing as well."

The wink is my undoing, and I pin her against the wall.

"You like when I press my cock against you, honeysuckle?" I growl as I dip my head to her neck and nip at the flesh.

A gasp rushes from her. "Maybe."

Maybe?

"If you want me to taste that tight cunt of yours again until you're screaming my name, tell me what I want to hear. Do you like it when I press my cock against you?"

"Yes," she murmurs.

I grow impossibly hard against her simply from one word. Knowing that, in her turned-on state, she might say yes to anything, I am tempted to ask her if I may make love to her. However, something inside me yearn for her to want it without any smoke or mirrors.

"Good girl. I promise you that, after dinner, I will fuck that part of your body with my tongue until you beg for my cock instead."

She whimpers and my self-control wears thin.

"Come. Let's go indulge in the meal Gretchen has prepared for us."

I tear away from her and clasp her hand. It takes some tugging, because my God, I think she'd rather me make good on my promise, but I finally manage to drag her to the dining room. When I finally take her, I want there to be no hesitation on her part. I want her to beg and scream for it.

As we reach the table, I pull a chair out and help her sit down before taking my own seat. The glow from the candles on the table flickers against her pale face, stealing some of her innocence—much like I plan on doing tonight. A slightly wicked look plays at her features.

We eat in silence, our stolen glances at each other a form of foreplay. With each morsel she places into her mouth, my cock throbs for her. By the time we finish our meal, we're mutually aroused to the point that I'm seriously considering taking her on the table.

"What would you like to do now, honeysuckle?"

Even in the darkened room, the blaze on her cheeks is visible. "I, uh, would like to get out of this constrictive clothing."

My cock thickens at her words. She's shyly finding a way to get naked.

"Do you need some help?" I question with a raised eyebrow.

"No. Uh, let me freshen up first. I discovered a robe earlier. I'll wear that and meet you to, um, to talk."

She's so goddamned adorable while stumbling over her words.

"Unnecessary. Let me take you to my room now to 'talk' and I'll undress you with my teeth."

Her hand sets to fanning herself at my words, which makes me grin at her.

Unfortunately, she shakes her head. "You are incredibly impatient. I'll be there in a short while. I can assure you the wait will be well worth it."

I groan at her insinuation but nod briskly. She bursts from her seat with a grin that owns my heart and shuffles away.

"Twenty minutes," I call after her, "and then I'm coming for you."

Her sweet giggle fills a part of my soul I never knew was empty.

Who knew twenty minutes could seem like fucking forever?

A knock on the front door startles me from staring at my timepiece as I will the minutes to tick by faster. I only have four more to wait. But who would be visiting at this time of night? Furrowing my brow, I stand and stride over to the door. When I open it, I'm face to face with Alexander, who is wearing a mischievous grin.

"I did it."

His words confuse me. "Did what?"

"I located them. Turns out, William does have a dirty little secret. And Edith is not as plain as you made her out to be, quite beautiful actually, but she does have a ruthless edge. In fact, I'm quite certain that, once I present her with my offer, she'll leap at the opportunity."

I scowl at the mention of William's name. "Could this not wait until tomorrow?"

He shakes his head. "No. In fact, I conveyed to William that I would be informing Elisabeth of his secret. He was adamant that he be the one to tell her. All I did was grease the wheel and send it careening down the hill. Once he speaks his piece, then you, my friend, can swoop in and rescue your dear damsel in distress."

My eyes widen at his words. "He's coming here?" I hiss.

"Yes, brother. Give it time to play out. You needn't hasten the process. It's happening. Elisabeth will be yours after his confession,

I assure you."

The thought of William even speaking to her boils my blood.

"Once this blows over and you're married to her, I want you both to come back to Havering with me. I'm sure I'll have convinced Edith by then as well. Together, we'll spin the tale for my father while you honeymoon by the River Beam. It won't take long, and then I'll send you on your way. Remember, you owe me this."

I grumble, but I know I will do that of which he asks. "I won't allow her to speak to him alone. He might attempt to steal her away."

"She won't go with him. That much I can tell you," he swears.

His grim look makes me fear what it is William is planning on telling her. I wanted her to forget about him—not break her heart in the process.

"What happened?"

He is opening his mouth to tell me when another knock raps at the door. This one is much softer.

I shoot him a murderous glare. "Don't put it past me to kill him with my bare hands."

Alexander squares his shoulders and prepares himself to back me up if need be. With one fist clenched, I wrench the door open. Then I sigh in annoyance to see a disheveled woman with wide, frightened eyes.

"Edith. What brings you here?" I demand with gritted teeth.

Alexander nudges me with his elbow and I remember his agenda—and my part with that.

"Please, come inside," I reluctantly tell her.

She sniffles but walks inside. When the light from the entryway reaches her, I can see that her eyes are puffy and red from crying.

"What is it? Are you hurt?" I question.

As she shakes her head, another tear rolls out and she glances at Alexander. "No. I wanted to speak to my sister."

I could go mad because four minutes have long passed and I am supposed to be deep inside of my future wife. Instead, I'm conversing with these two fools.

"Not tonight. You may come again tomorrow and see her. Do you need money for a room at the inn?"

She won't stay under my roof. If Alexander wants her so damn much, he can take her to wherever it is he's staying.

"Please, Lord Thomas, it's rather urgent," she begs tearfully.

I'm about to shut her down again when Alexander speaks. "Edith, your sister will soon have a life here. A life that shouldn't involve you and will not include William. Your family is poor now and your degree worthless without a husband to support you. I propose that you and I marry for business reasons."

Her eyes widen, but she quietly waits for him to finish.

"In order to inherit my family empire, my father wants assurance that I'm married and settled. As my brother here knows, I will never settle. The idea of sleeping beside the same dull woman each night has me wanting to slit my wrists. But taking over and inheriting my father's money does excite me. If you marry me strictly for business purposes, I will provide financially for any interest you desire. You will have the finest clothes and foods. I'll even pay for secret lovers."

She's long dried her tears as she listens with rapt attention. "Sounds enticing."

I scoff at her words. "Moments ago, you were wailing about your sister, and now? Now, you're ready to hop into the coach with Alexander?"

This woman is a calculating bitch.

"I think that Countess Dumont is a fitting title," Alexander snarls and pins me with a glare.

Edith's eyes widen and a slow grin forms on her lips. "You're an Earl?"

He raises an eyebrow in smugness. "A rich one."

"It seems so simple," she murmurs. The excitement rippling from her is palpable. She's thrilled for this insane opportunity.

"That it is, sugar. That it is. Would you kindly follow me into the study and I'll draft a contract?"

She reaches a hand for him and he takes it. "Lead the way, kind sir."

Unreal.

Elisabeth's sister is nothing more than a well-paid prostitute.

And she sickens me.

Chapter Eleven

Elisabeth

THE CORSET IS TIGHT, AND the moment it falls from my body, I gasp for some much-needed air. Normally, I'm not one to wear them, but since they've been included in my wardrobe here at Jasper's estate, I find it rude not to wear what was given to me.

Tiny butterflies have been fluttering in my belly since the moment I admitted to myself that I do want to make love to this man. Jasper might have taken me under the wildest of circumstances, but I'd be a fool to deny the obvious chemistry we have together. My family—William—are quickly becoming second place to the man who has easily stolen first.

Jasper.

My goodness, the way he looked tonight at dinner. Dark eyes visually devouring every surface of my body, focusing on my lips or the way my breasts would jiggle as I spoke. And even though I know that the man wants my body—to take my innocence away—more than anything, I feel as though he does love me as he says.

I always thought that what I felt for William was love. And maybe it was to a certain degree, but now, I realize I idolized the idea of him. Fascinated over what we could be. Yet with Jasper, my heart beats out of control in my chest whenever he is near. I become flushed and needy for his touch. My heart yearns to hear his romantic words—to feel his gentle yet firm caresses.

My eyes fall on the mirror in my room and I smile at it. The smile is one of mystery, and I appear sexy. For once in my life, I don't feel like the girl waiting with bated breath for her man to come back and marry her. For once, I feel desired beyond humanly possible. Sexier than any woman on the planet.

I feel wanted.

Desired.

Needed.

Loved.

Now, the smile turns into a happy one. The pure bliss on my features is surprising. Who knew that, only days ago, I was dreading my future? Yet now, I want to forget the past and run hand in hand with Jasper toward it.

I want to make love to him.

I want him to own me with his body and his soul.

I want to be his and only his.

I'm about to slip the cashmere robe over my naked flesh when I hear a noise at the open window. Turning quickly, I gasp to see William of all people climbing through.

"What are you doing here?" I hiss.

His eyes darken as he blatantly stares at my breasts. After yanking the robe from the bed, I shrug into it and tug it around me so that I'll end his free show.

Once our eyes finally do meet, his are filled with sadness. Something in my heart feels bad for him. I raise my eyebrows in question, and he lets out an exaggerated sigh.

"You're so beautiful, Lissa. I've missed you so much," he says in a low voice as he takes a step toward me.

Lissa.

Funny how I forgot about her.

The name of a girl.

Instinctively, I retreat a bit and repeat my question. "What are you doing here?"

His eyebrows pinch together as if he's angry with my words. "Dammit, Lissa. What's happened? You've changed. You're so different."

I purse my lips before I finally speak. "William, it had to be done to spare my father's farm. You and I both know this. Your being here tonight only makes things harder on the both of us. I'm sorry, but I think you should leave before Jasper finds you."

A possessive growl rips from his throat as he stalks over to me. I stumble back, but he captures me with his strong hands on my biceps.

"Don't tell me he's brainwashed you already. Don't deny that you love me anymore."

I bite on my lip and his eyes fall to them. It reminds me of the way Jasper looked at them earlier today. However, when Jasper was eating them up with his eyes, I felt satisfaction and desire. Now, with William, I feel awkward.

No fluttering butterflies.

No blushing.

No need to fan myself.

"William, things are over between us. I'm so sorry. It has to be that way."

His grip tightens, and for a brief moment, by the angry look in his eyes, I wonder if he'll shake me. Instead, he relaxes his grip but glares at me.

"So he finally got to fuck you instead of me getting to. That's why you're so messed up in the head over him. I should have known you would spread your legs the first chance you had—just like your sister."

The sting of his words is immediate, and tears well in my eyes. "Let me go."

He releases me, and the moment he does, I slap him hard across the cheek.

"Don't ever say such terrible things about me or my sister again. Leave my presence before I have you removed by the man you speak so ill of. He would never talk to me as you just have," I bite out.

His eyes narrow, and he brings his face close to mine so that, when he says his words, they spittle all over me. "I slept with her over and over again at university. A man has sexual needs—needs you were supposed to fulfill as my future wife. Whenever I missed you, I would sink into her and pretend it were you. But, Lissa, know that I didn't take her virginity. Your sister sleeps around a lot. Apparently just like you do."

I have no words for him. The betrayal is too much. And while I should be more hurt over William's having slept with my sister, I'm devastated that she would do that to me.

She's my sister.

My flesh and blood.

"I hate you. And for the record, I have not made love to him. Yet," I snarl with tears rolling out over my cheeks as I raise my hand to slap him again.

This time, he grabs it before it connects and pushes me against the wall. His lips are on mine in an instant, muffling my scream. Then I hear a door swing open before William is forcibly ripped from me.

My chest heaves wildly as I meet the dark, furious eyes of my Jasper.

"Jasper!" I cry and reach a shaky hand toward him.

His eyes shoot me a quick apology before he begins smashing punch after punch into William's face. Blood bursts from William's nose, and I nearly faint from the sight of it.

"Jasper, stop!" I scream. "Please, stop!"

It isn't like William doesn't deserve it, but I hate to see the feral, murderous look in Jasper's eyes. I want my sexual, domineering, yet sweet beast to come back to me.

"Let him go. He's not worth it," I sob. "Jaz, please."

He stiffens at my words and the raised fist doesn't connect with William's face again. Instead, it drops to his side and his shoulders slump. William takes the moment to stumble his way back toward the open window. Wordlessly, he escapes into the night and out of my life.

I've never been happier.

Jasper appears to snap out of his haze, because his shoulders lift back up and he turns to take in my mess of a face.

"My honeysuckle," he whispers before prowling over to me and taking both of my tear-stained cheeks in his palms. "I saw red. Him, kissing you. It was too much. You're mine, Elisabeth."

I nod emphatically. "I am yours. Always. Now, kiss away his taste. I only want you on my tongue for the rest of my life."

His growl spills into my throat as he kisses me hard enough to bruise my lips. My tongue meets his with urgency—a need to connect and forget the past. This man, my Jasper, tastes delicious and perfect.

He is mine and I am his.

As we kiss, his hands slip into my hair and he tugs at it, tilting my head back. Then he breaks the kiss and dips down to my neck. I moan with each desperate suck he takes on my flesh. He's marking me, and I want more. I want him to mark every part of my body and my soul.

"I need you in my bed, honeysuckle. My cock aches to fit inside you—to be completely whole with you," he murmurs against my skin.

"Yes. Take me, Jaz."

The words barely leave my mouth before he scoops me into his arms. I gasp at losing ground under my feet, but I also snuggle into his chest. Then my fingers find his hair and I lovingly stroke at his scalp.

I wonder why I fought this pull for so long. Destiny brought us together. Fate already had plans for us. This was the work of a higher being. It was only a matter of time before I caved and gave in to what was meant to be.

"I have a gift for you, dear Elisabeth. All day, I have wanted to bestow you with it, but I wanted to wait for the right time. Can you wait a while longer and let me present the gift to you before we make love?"

His eyes are tender as they shine with adoration. I would give him the world right now if I could.

"Of course. The wait will be worth it, remember, Jaz?"

He grins a lopsided smile that flips my tummy. The man is achingly handsome.

"Honeysuckle, I love it when you call me Jaz."

I beam at him. "Jaz, I love it when you call me honeysuckle."

His lips find mine for an uncoordinated, chaste kiss as he walks, but it still warms my heart. When we make it into his bedroom, he sets me to my feet beside the bed.

"Stay here," he instructs.

I watch as he disappears into his dressing room. While I wait, I unpin my hair and set the clips on the table beside the bed. My mess of crimson curls fall piece by piece until I've undone it all. I'm sure that, to anyone else right now, I seem an awful sight.

But to Jasper?

I know he sees me as beautiful and perfect—even with my hair looking the way it is while I'm wearing a simple robe.

"Close your eyes," he says in a thick voice as he reenters the room.

My eyes take in the fact that he's removed his waistcoat and shirt. His feet are bare, and he is standing in only his trousers, which hang low on his hips. The lines in his chest that define the muscles are utterly worthy my tongue. When my eyes fall to the dark smattering of hair that follows the V-shape of his lower stomach muscles right into his trousers, a needy mewl falls from my lips.

"You can look at this for the rest of your life. Right now, though, I need you to close your eyes." His grin is smug, and I feel my cheeks redden at being caught.

"Don't take too long. I was getting rather aroused, mister," I tell him saucily before snapping my eyes closed.

His growl satisfies me that my words had the effect I had intended.

"Elisabeth," he murmurs and takes my hand, "I have loved you from the moment I saw your portrait. In that moment, I felt as if I'd been given a glimpse into the intricacies that are this universe. It was as if I caught a vision of a perfect future. But it was one I would have to work for to achieve. Honeysuckle, I'd do it all over again just to have you here with me."

Once he pauses, I peek my eyes open. Immediately, tears spill over to see him so vulnerable on one knee and a shimmering ring between the thumb and finger of his free hand. When he hesitates before sliding it on, I nod with approval.

"Honeysuckle, will you be my wife? Of your own free will? Will you let me make love to you every day until we both are buried in one grave together as one? Will you bear my children and my last name? Will you let me love you like I was born to do?"

I sniffle at his words, nodding after each question. "A thousand yesses, Jaz." Then my eyes widen as he pushes the ring along my finger—a perfect fit. "It's gorgeous," I sigh dreamily.

The ring he chose is appropriate. It's a large ruby encircled by smaller emeralds. Most women wear diamonds for their marriage, but I feel special and different with this well-thought-out ring—the ring he had especially designed for me. When I turn it over, I notice the clever heart etched around the engraving.

J&E

"It doesn't compare to your beauty, but it was as close as I could get." He smiles sheepishly at me.

"Thank you," I tell him before quirking my eyebrows up in a teasing manner. "Now, I suggest you take my innocence and make me yours before I change my mind."

He rises to his feet in such haste that I'm nearly knocked over. The giggle that bursts from me earns a swat to my bottom. I've learned that those swats are the good sort of punishment.

"Honeysuckle?" His voice rumbles through his chest and tickles mine, which is barely touching his.

"Yes?"

"Your name is Elisabeth."

I scrunch my nose up in confusion. "I know that."

"I wanted to remind you because, in a few minutes, I'm going to make you forget it and the only one you'll know how to say is mine."

Chapter Twelve

Jasper

THE WORDS.

She finally said the words.

My honeysuckle. My sweet Elisabeth wants me as much as I want her. She has willingly agreed to be my wife. A carnal desire to beat on my chest and shout to the world that she is mine overwhelms me, but I school those urges. Right now, there are more important things to tend to.

Her.

She smiles beautifully at me with expectation and hope. It worries me that her loss of virginity might be painful, but the thought of taking her and making her mine overshadows it. We'll get through it together. I'll be there for her every step of the way.

My hands find the sash to the robe and I easily untie it. Elisabeth is a perfect gift and I've finally been honored with the privilege of opening her.

She.

Is.

Mine.

I hear her gasp when my thumbs graze across her hardened nipples. Her entire body quivers with the anticipation of our union. Sliding my hand down, I touch her through her thatch of hair and locate her pleasure button. The moment it connects, she whimpers.

"I want you so wet for me, honeysuckle. I want you to drip with your arousal so that, when I slide into you, you'll feel no pain—only pleasure. Can I tease your body and worship it like I want to?"

She nods and threads her fingers through my hair.

"Do you want my tongue on that sweet cunt of yours—tasting and lapping up the very essence that is you?" I croon as I lower myself to my knees.

"Yes, Jaz. I want that again. I like what you do to me with your tongue."

Her words are sexy and they make me crazy for her. I want to own her with my mouth. Show her that she'll never need food or water again. Just me. Just my tongue on her pussy.

"On the edge of the bed," I growl out my order, needing to taste her now.

My girl doesn't hesitate or ask questions. Instead, she stumbles back and does as she's been told. I watch with greedy eyes as she lies back and places her heels on the edge of the bed as well. Then her knees fall apart and she opens herself to me. The trust she has in me to take care of her overwhelms me. I'd die to protect her and will never let her go.

Scooting closer to her, I dip my head to her gorgeous cunt and inhale her. Her scent is unique and belongs to me—more alluring than any rose or lily.

"I want you to touch your perfect breasts while I feast upon you," I instruct.

She murmurs that she will and begins to knead them. The sight is fucking beautiful, and my cock throbs painfully to be inside her.

Using my thumbs, I open her up and admire the pink, tender

flesh. The sight will never be boring. I'll never tire of seeing it.

"Jaz," she begs.

I don't need any more instruction on her part. With vigor, I dive into her.

Tasting.

Sucking.

Nibbling.

I'm lost in the act of pleasing her beyond words. I drive her nearer and nearer to the edge of her own sanity simply with the magic my tongue creates. When I feel that she's about to lose it, I slip a finger inside her tight body. And when she's ready, I push another into her. Her body stretches to accommodate the intrusion.

"I'm—"

Her words are lost to a carnal scream of desire that sounds delightfully like my name. I groan as her cunt clamps around my fingers, enjoying the way I own her body with them.

"Now, Jaz, please," she begs once her body has calmed.

I ease my fingers out and stand before the goddess that is mine. Her hair is a wicked mess of flames spread out on the bed beneath her. My cock bobs in place, eager to join our party.

"Honeysuckle," I murmur as I step closer to the bed until my knees touch the side of it. My cock rests on the hair between her legs. "This will hurt. But I promise you, darling, I will do everything in my power to take that pain away. Do you trust me?"

She nods. Then her eyes flicker with fear, but it's the only sign of hesitation.

"Once I start, I won't stop. I'll fuck you into the next century. You'll scream and bleed and beg, but I won't fucking quit until I fill every inch of your cunt. Are we clear?"

A whimper.

"Ignore the pain and embrace the meaning of this. Our bodies will join in a way no marriage contract will ever touch. This will be the marriage of our souls."

I expect her to cry. To beg. To plead for us to put it off.

Not my honeysuckle.

Not the vixen I've created.

"Stop your blubbering and take me. Now, Jasper."

Her words are bossy as hell and they make me crazy with need.

"Yes, ma'am," I growl as I grab my thick cock.

She squirms, spreading herself as open as she can for me. I drag the tip of my weeping cock through the hair on her pussy and tease her opening.

So.

Fucking.

Wet.

Considering she's a virgin, I should go slow. Allow her to adjust. Prepare her body for me. But I won't. The sooner we break through that barrier, the sooner we can dive into the pleasure. No sense in drawing the pain out.

I line myself up and push into her with a forceful thrust.

Her scream is loud as her innocence is obliterated. The stars in my vision are of pure bliss at the way her body clenches around mine. She sobs but doesn't try to stop me as I rock into her.

"Faster, Jaz," she whimpers.

My eyes find her determined, tear-stained ones.

And I thrust and pump and pound into her until she's no longer crying, until she's moaning my name instead. Her hands are all over her swollen breasts in an effort to maximize all of her pleasure. As I fuck my love, I find her throbbing clit and massage it.

"Jasper!" Her shriek is one of approval. She writhes in ecstasy as I take us both to the edge of our orgasms.

I'm not sure if I can wait for hers, but her body pleases mine when it fiercely clenches around my cock, indicating her inability to wait for me either. I lose all sense of the world around me but her as I burst my seed deep into her.

I don't stop thrusting until every last drop has been emptied.

Then my cock becomes flaccid and I slip out of her, uncaring that the evidence of our lovemaking spills out.

Sliding an arm underneath her, I haul her up the bed and lay my head on my elbow so I can look at her. "I love you, Elisabeth."

Her eyes shine with mutual affection. "I love you too, Jasper. That . . . that was incredible."

I smirk at her. "My intention was to put a spell on you. Have I succeeded?"

A small giggle erupts from her. "Yes. Undoubtedly so. If what we just did was a part of your wizardry, I'll fall victim every time."

God, she's so fucking cute.

"I shall call for a priest in the morning. Another night that you aren't my wife won't pass," I tell her firmly.

Even though she's happy, a frown plays at her lips.

"What? After our mind-blowing lovemaking, you hesitate to marry me?" I question. My heart races at such a prospect.

"No, uh, it's just that I thought maybe my family—"

I cut her off. "I'm your family now. We'll have a reception later to commemorate our union, but you'll be my wife before sunset tomorrow."

She bites her lip as one of her eyebrows rises. "Under one condition."

Condition?

One *fucking* condition?

"What?" I amuse her with my question.

A smile tugs at her lips and her cheeks blaze. I know this look. I know without words what it means. She doesn't have to say anything, and I'm already climbing over her. My once again hardened cock lies between our bellies as I kiss her deeply.

"Jaz," she whimpers when my length drags along her pussy until it presses against her opening.

With a thrust, I take her again, this time without resistance. My tongue tangles with hers as we try to devour each other's souls.

"What?" I grunt again as I mate with my other half.

"That. That was the condition. This. You. Kissing me. All of it."

I pull away from her to stare into her green eyes. With our noses grazing and our eyes locked, we again find the utmost pleasure in each other. Together.

This time, after I've emptied myself into her, I don't break away from her. This time, I fall against her, certainly stealing her breath. I want her secure beneath me at all times. I want her physically connected with me at all times.

I want my Elisabeth.

My honeysuckle.

At. All. Times.

"Jasper, you certainly know how to please a lady."

I find her ear with my mouth and gently kiss the lobe. "It would appear that you, honeysuckle, are not the hearts-and-flowers type of lady. You prefer tongues and fingers."

She gasps in mock horror and playfully spanks my arse. I'll have to pay her back for that one later.

"I spend my entire lifetime accumulating all of this wealth and I find the one woman on the planet who would prefer to run naked and feed only upon me. The only woman who could care less about riches and power. How did I ever get so lucky?" I tease.

Her fingers thread in my hair, and she sighs in contentment. "Jaz, it wasn't luck. I was destined to become Lady Thomas. But now that I've hooked you forever, the corsets are getting tossed into the bin. I'm keen on this whole naked idea you pose."

I chuckle as I find her lips again. "So we'll become poor, naked fools blind to the world and only seeing that of each other?"

"Sounds pretty blissful to me," she laughs.

As I devour her mouth with mine, I agree.

Any world. Any scenario that has Elisabeth in it is pure bliss. Heaven.

I'll never let her go.

She.

Is.

Mine.

"I love you, honeysuckle."

Epilogue

Nearly five months later . . .

Elisabeth

"GRETCHEN, YOU'RE FEEDING ME TOO well. Nothing fits anymore," I pout.

Her knowing eyes find mine. "Is that so? Funny how the only place you've gained any weight is in that belly of yours. Are you sure you aren't with child?"

The thought of being pregnant with Jasper's baby thrills me. A flutter of excitement ripples through me.

Could I be?

The last menstrual period I had was before I met Jasper. It certainly could mean I was with child.

Chewing on my lip, I open my robe and peer at my naked flesh in the long mirror. Gretchen has busied herself with packing our luggage for our honeymoon and isn't concerned with the way I inspect my swollen stomach.

Running a palm over my belly, I pray that a little one is inside me. My breasts have been tender to the point that I've had to push Jasper away from them on many occasions. He swears they've grown in the last few months. I've written it off to all the salty, rich foods they feed me here.

But maybe?

Jasper's deep voice rings out as he enters our bedroom. "Gretchen, can you leave us for a moment?"

She scurries out of the room, but my eyes remain affixed to my stomach's reflection. He steps behind me and buries his nose in my hair.

"Are you trying to kill me, honeysuckle? Becoming hard in the presence of an old woman is embarrassing. You know I can't keep my hands off your naked flesh, yet here you are, presenting yourself like a delectable fruit ripe for tasting."

I grin at his reflection. He's every bit as handsome as the day I first laid eyes on him. Then his hands slide around me and he clasps them against my belly. As he rests his chin on my shoulder, it happens.

It.

Happens.

Our wide eyes meet each other's and tears well in mine. I drop my gaze down to his hands, which are now lovingly splayed across my belly. Then it happens again and the tears spill out, splashing on his hands.

My usual butterflies that flutter in my belly have been replaced. The movement is eerie. Foreign. But so beautiful.

"Is th-that . . ." he stammers but trails off.

It is.

I run my hands over his and rub my thumbs along them. "Jaz, we're going to have a baby."

The movement startles us again and we both chuckle.

"Mine," he growls as he gently squeezes my belly.

Turning my head, I graze my lips against his. "Ours."

The End.

Acknowledgements

Thank you to my husband for supporting me with your words of encouragement. You're the best and I love you dearly!

I want to thank the beta readers on this book, whom are also my friends. Nikki McCrae, Wendy Colby, Dena Marie, Elizabeth Thiele, Lori Christensen, Michelle Ramirez, Shannon Martin, Amy Bosica, Holly Sparks, Sian Davies, Ella Stewart, Ella Fox, Aurora Rose Reynolds, Maggie Lugo, Kayla Stewart, and Elizabeth Clinton, you guys provided AMAZING feedback. You all gave helpful ideas to make the story better and gave me incredible encouragement. I appreciate all of your comments and suggestions.

I'm especially thankful for the Breaking the Rules Babes. You ladies are amazing with your support and friendship. When I hear about catty and nasty street teams, I chuckle. I know our group is nothing but sweet, loving women that care for one another. I'm truly blessed to have you all in my life!

Mickey, my fabulous editor from I'm a Book Shark, thank you putting on your historical hat and swatting me with your editorial rod when I would stray too far into the modern. I can't thank you enough for how awesome you are! Love ya!

Thank you Stacey Blake for working your gorgeous magic and for being such a great wino friend. Love you!

Lastly but certainly not least of all, thank you to all of the wonderful readers out there that are willing to hear my story and enjoy my characters like I do. It means the world to me!

K WEBSTER

Becoming
COUNTESS
Dumont

BECOMING HER SERIES

Dedication

To my husband . . .

Even when you're insufferable, you're still hot.

'Tis love that makes the world go round, my baby.

-Charles Dickens-

Prologue

Edith

A CONTRACT.

To marry the Earl of Havering.

And he's utterly sinful to look at.

Tall. Thick, dark hair. The beginnings of a beard.

It only took one second to make the decision. One tiny second to decide that I didn't care if I spent the rest of my years in a loveless marriage. Love was for the weak anyhow. Look how things turned out for William and Elisabeth.

Love is a farce.

But money?

Power?

Sex?

Those are all very real and palpable. Considering Father nearly lost our farm and continues to struggle to make ends meet despite having sold his daughter off to the highest bidder, I'm in no hurry to rush back.

Nothing remains for me back at the farm aside from Ella.

The vision of my younger sister, with her wispy, blond hair and kind, blue eyes, makes my heart clench painfully in my chest. She's an innocent and always will be. Ella is the type of girl that will marry another farm boy and be perfectly content with a simple, poor life.

Not me.

I've always required finer things. While at university, I learned this when a professor of mathematics, Sven, showed me what the world had to offer. He was teaching abroad while his wife and children stayed in Spain. Even though he came from money, teaching was his passion.

I was his passion.

Many nights, we shared a bed in his expansive home in London. Many nights, he lavished me with expensive gifts and wines. Many nights, he feasted upon me as if I were a world-class delicacy.

But when *she* showed up with the children?

He discarded me like I was a used-up whore.

I'd loved him.

Just like I'd loved William.

So I thought.

However, love is ridiculous and nothing more than a fleeting feeling. In both instances, I thought I was in love. Looking back, I simply needed their companionship. Their bodies pressed against mine. Their mouths worshipping my body.

Now, as I dip the quill pen into the ink, I smile.

For the rest of my life, I will have the best of everything. Wealth, power, a gorgeous faux husband, and whichever lovers who strike my fancy. Love won't have a place in my life—messing things up as it's done in the past.

"Are you having second thoughts, *love?*"

His voice sends a thrill through me as the pen holds still over the paper.

"Not at all, *dear.*" I flash him a conspiratorial smile. Heat washes over my skin when he rewards me with a lopsided grin.

"You're a rare find, Edith. I am one lucky man."

I know we're talking about my eagerness to agree to his deal, but his words still make my heart pound.

He is lucky.

I am one of a kind.

"When shall we marry?" I question as I rewet the end of the pen in the ink and then scrawl out my signature.

Edith Lorelei Merriweather

The moment I sign, he snatches the paper away from me and scribbles his own.

Alexander P. Dumont, Earl of Havering

"Tomorrow." His word is simple, but I gape at him.

"Y-y-you don't want to do that in front of your father? To make it more real for him?" I stammer, surprised by his answer.

He shakes his head as he fans the paper to dry the ink, his eyes never leaving mine. "You will soon discover my father sniffs out lies better than any hunting hound. That is why we need to marry and settle into a routine that will convince him before we return. Once I believe we are ready to return to Havering, Lord Thomas and your sister will come with us to bear testimony of our marriage and faithful love."

I briefly snap my eyes closed at the mention of her. I'm not sure she'll ever want to go anywhere with me ever again, considering what I did to her.

"Are you sure we can't go alone?" I ask, reopening my eyes.

Steel-colored ones find mine, and he glowers at me. I square my shoulders and hold his gaze.

"You've signed the document. The deal is done. We do things my way. End of story," he snarls.

I blink my eyes at him and wonder just what I may have hastily gotten myself into. "What if things don't go your way? What if, when we get there, I tell your father everything?" I taunt. "What if I change my mind?" Some sinister part of me wants to know what will happen if I decide that this life of his isn't for me.

His hand strikes like a cobra and catches my throat. Even though he doesn't squeeze, terror floods my veins.

"Things *will* go my way. You will *not* tell my father. And you *won't* change your mind," he growls.

My lip trembles, and his eyes drop to them for a moment before glaring at me again.

"But what if?" I'm a glutton for punishment.

"Then I'll kill you," he says simply as he releases my throat and begins folding the contract. "Accidental of course. Obviously, you don't understand the importance of this matter. I suggest you clear that foggy head of yours and show up to the chapel tomorrow with a better attitude. It would be tragic if I lost my fiancée on the eve of our wedding."

What.

Have.

I.

Done?

Edith

Almost six months later . . .

"BLOODY HELL, WOMAN," VICTOR GRUMBLES as he stills within me.

My hands are tangled in his hair, and when he stops, I pop my eyes open to glower at him. "What?" I hiss.

But as I go to remove my fingers, I know.

I did it again.

The gigantic ring Alexander gave to me on our wedding day seems to get tangled in Victor's hair every time he makes love to me. This time, the hair is really twisted around it. I slip my finger out of it and watch with amusement as it dangles there like some sort of head jewelry.

He pouts as he pulls out of me and begins fussing with his locks. The man really does act like a woman most days. His hair is his most prized asset, and the fact that we nearly had to cut it last time just about had him in hysterics.

"Shall I get the scissors?" I taunt.

He green eyes fly to mine, and I swear he might cry. Suddenly completely turned off by him, I slide out of the bed to dress. We had a good couple of month run, but I'm done.

"I can't get it out!" he shrieks in a high octave.

I sigh heavily and ignore his whining while I slip my robe on. Finally, after having watched his struggles enough, I storm over to him. With one quick movement, I snatch the ring and rip it from his hair.

"You bitch!" he roars, this time sounding more like a man.

I bite back a giggle as I stare at my ring, which still clutches a rather large chunk of his hair. I'm about to ask him to leave so that I may be alone, but he bursts from the bed toward me. He surprises me, so I don't have time to react before he backhands me across the cheek. I'm momentarily stunned before I find my senses.

"Get out!" I scream at him.

The man is outraged now, though, and won't hear of it. This time, he closes his fist and hits me hard in the belly. Stars dance in my vision as I gasp for breath.

"A-Alexander!" I cry out between ragged sobs.

Victor has left me doubled over as he finishes pulling on his clothes.

A thump against the wall has me thanking the heavens that he's heard me and will come to rescue me from this sissy barbarian.

"Alexander!" My muffled moan rings out through the paper-thin walls.

More thumping.

I should have known. He isn't going to save me. At the moment, he is deep inside some whore—just like every evening.

When I taste blood, I raise my fingers to my lip and see that it has been split from the blow to the face. My eyes lift, and I find that Victor is nearly dressed. Maybe, if I can bite my tongue for a few more minutes, he will leave me and I can crawl back into bed to nurse my wounds.

Thump.

Thump.

Thump.

"You two have a fucked-up marriage," Victor bites out as he turns to stare at me in disgust.

Until now, I've been quite pleased with the arrangement. I've only had to visit with Alexander for supper each night so that he can bore me with more details of his home and family. Like a good wife, I smile and take notes.

"Just leave," I sigh and point to the door. My body aches from his abuse and I can't bear to look at him anymore.

I'm shocked that, instead of leaving, he stalks over to me and his palm closes around my throat. I slap at him, but he hauls me toward the very wall Alexander is fucking his whore against.

"He'd probably love for me to take his little problem off his hands," he snarls, and spittle lands all over my face.

All of this because of his ridiculous hair.

People are insane.

When he squeezes tighter, I try to pound on the wall behind me to get Alexander's attention. Likely, he'll choose to ignore me much like he does all the time. My fist connects with the wall, but as I attempt to hit it, I realize that Victor's grip around my neck is making me weak.

"What? Are you trying to let him know you need help? Here," he snaps. "Let me assist you."

He pulls my throat forward and proceeds to bash my head against the wall. I'm beginning to lose consciousness as I silently cry for a life I've always hated that is already ending.

Life never has been fair.

As my eyes fall shut, my thoughts find a memory of William.

A knock on my door startles me, and I rush over to answer it. I'm not surprised to see a brooding William standing on the other side. His broad shoulders are squared, and he appears to be angry.

"What?" I question and place my hands on my hips.

"You're a witch," he growls as he approaches me. "Why would you send that letter to my room?"

The letter.

I smile seductively at him. I told him all of the naughty things I wanted him to do to me. Since he was trying desperately to hold on to his virginity for Elisabeth, I thought I would relieve him of some of his pain.

"I simply stated the truth, William. If you want to make love to me—to sink your cock into someplace tight and hot—I'm your girl."

He groans as he rubs his palms through his hair. When his blue eyes finally meet mine, though, they're blazing.

"She can't ever know. This can only happen to fulfill a need. I love her—not you," he tells me coldly as he approaches.

I can hardly believe he loves her.

"Let's make this quick. Lift your dress and bend over that chair." He points toward the seating area in the kitchen.

I'm shocked at his bold words but do as I've been told. When the door slams behind me, I jump at the sound of it.

The moment I bend over the chair and lift my dress, I feel his palms on my arse. They're warm as they scorch a trail of heat along my flesh. The sound of him undoing his trousers echoes behind me, and in the next fiery second, he hastily enters me, the sting of the burn taking my body over.

"Ahh!" I cry out at the sudden intrusion.

I snap my head over my shoulder to watch him as he takes me, but the look on his face frightens me. The menacing scowl indicates his disgust for me. The thought has barely formed in my head before he grabs a handful of my hair and shoves my face down onto the table.

"God, you feel so good," he grunts.

I wait for him to touch me. To offer me pleasure. Anything.

All I get is the rhythmic thrusting and his testicles slapping the part of me that aches to be touched. I almost feel as if I could climax from it when he abruptly pulls out of me and spurts his hot orgasm on my arse.

"Um, maybe we can go lie down in my bed," I murmur as it drips from the curve of my bottom and runs down my thighs.

His laugh is harsh. "And what? Let me hold you? Fuck off, Edith."

I'm stung by his words, but I blink back the tears that threaten as I peer over at him. My dress falls back down while he's busying himself with his trousers.

"Maybe you could love me instead?"

His blue eyes find mine, and he shakes his head. "Never. You'll never be her."

I chew on his words and have the desire to spit them on the floor at his feet. He turns on his heel and strides toward the door. As he opens it, he flashes me a grin so hot that my knickers nearly catch fire.

"Same time tomorrow?"

With a move that makes me hate myself a little more, I nod.

"Edith!" A deep, familiar voice snaps me out of my daze.

My head is no longer being slammed against the wall.

Alexander. And he's charging toward us like a bull—a very beautiful bull. I blink away my dizziness to admire the way his muscles twitch and tighten as he stalks toward us. He's wearing nothing but trousers and an enraged glare.

Victor sees him at the same moment I do and releases me. He doesn't even have an opportunity to defend himself before Alexander smashes a fist into his face.

The sickening crunch of bone and flesh satisfies me to my very being.

Alexander, my hero.

I should stop him. I should attempt to pull him away from the man he's crushing with each powerful blow to the head.

But I won't.

I can't.

I'm enraptured in the way he is defending me. His wife. Something niggles its way into my empty heart. I feel, for once, cared for and protected.

A high-pitched squeal rings out from the doorway. "Alexander! You'll kill him!"

My eyes lift to the blonde with huge breasts. A white sheet barely covers her curvy body as she attempts to call my husband off from beating Victor into the wood floor. She sickens me. Even though he's my husband for appearances purposes only, something upsets me when I see her. The events of the evening crush down on me, and I burst into tears.

I, Edith Lorelei Merriweather, am crying.

It doesn't happen often.

Alexander tenses, and the fist that is poised quivers. He snaps his head to look at me and snares me with his feral look. His chest heaves with exertion, and blood drips from his clenched fist.

"Alexander, maybe we should call a doctor," the blonde suggests.

He ignores her and studies my appearance. His eyes land on my lips, and he rises to his feet. With three short strides, his arms are around me.

"Are you okay?"

I nod against his chest, but the tears won't stop. It feels safe here, tucked against him. Warm. Right.

"I-I-I'm s-sorry," I stammer out.

For what? Getting beaten by some womanly man?

A growl rumbles in his chest. "Shh, I'm here now."

I want him to lift me in his arms and carry me to my bed—to crawl in behind me and hold me until I'm long asleep.

"What about me?" the blonde demands behind him.

His voice takes on the edge that first frightened me on the eve of our wedding. "What *about* you?"

I hide away my triumph at having been chosen over the gorgeous tartlet and let my husband take care of me like he vowed to do not that long ago.

Chapter Two

Alexander

IT HAS BEEN HOURS SINCE the innkeeper cleaned up the blood-stained floors but I keep dragging my gaze over to the spot where I lost my fucking mind. I want to relive the moment—to feel the way his nose crushed from the blast of my fist.

I want to make him pay for what he did to her over and over again.

The authorities had come and taken him away. Bribery goes far in this city. Throw a handful of silver coins in the policeman's face and the problem is swept under the rug. It also doesn't hurt having your best friend being deeply involved with every single person with any sort of clout in this godforsaken place. With Jasper's influence, my nearly killing that idiot went away. Simple enough.

What didn't go away was the mood that filled both Edith and I afterwards. There's a thick cloud hovering over each of us, and I don't like it one fucking bit. Gone is the easiness of our agreement. It has been replaced with confusion. I feel as if the foundation of our relationship has been fractured. Neither of us has spoken but I can feel her blaming me for what happened.

She damn well should blame me. What sort of fucking fool agrees to marry a woman and still allow her to have endless amounts of lovers? Guilt niggles at me. Apparently I am that fool. My intention was for it to be easy. A business relationship. I wasn't supposed to have feelings for her—feelings that I don't even know how to comprehend.

I'm not attracted to her.

Keep telling yourself that.

My mind drifts to earlier when she fucked that arsehole. I couldn't get her out of my head and with every moan he drew from her, I wanted to slit my goddamned wrists to escape the taunting of her voice. Sure, I had driven into the blonde over and over again, but it was Edith's name that was sitting on my tongue. And when I slammed my eyes closed before I came, I imagined her haughty raised eyebrow and that mouth of hers. The blonde was a vessel. It wouldn't be the first time I got off with my wife on my mind while I fucked my lovers.

It's a goddamn mess.

She's my wife. I should be allowed to have her any time I damn well please. But is that what I want?

The thought of another man coming into her room ever again infuriates me. I cannot allow it any longer. In fact, we're leaving this wretched city in the morning. I'm ready to take her to safety and introduce her to my family.

She whimpers in her sleep and the fierce need to protect her overwhelms me. It shocks me but I don't hate the sensation. I rise from my seat in the corner of the room and stalk over to her bedside. With each breath she takes, I watch her. Her dark locks are still wet from her bath and I have the urge to twist my fingers into them. Dark lashes jut out over her naturally rosy cheeks and I decide, in this moment, that she is very beautiful. Why else do I think about her continuously?

Another terrified sound comes from her lips as she sleeps. I want to comfort her but I'm not sure I even know how. With a deep sigh, I kick off my shoes and crawl into bed behind her. She's warm and appears to be so tiny without all of her frilly clothes on that she normally wears. I do what feels right and wrap an arm around her.

How could I have ever put her in such a dangerous situation? What if he had killed her?

The thought causes bile to rise in my throat. I squeeze her tighter to me and inhale the lovely scent of her hair. If someone were to come in, they'd see me acting like her damn husband.

I *am* her damn husband. It's high time I begin acting like it. Especially if we set off to see Father tomorrow.

Not long ago, after we signed our agreement, she had mouthed off at me and wondered what would happen if she were to confess our sham of a marriage to my father. I'd gone off on her and told her I'd kill her myself to keep the secret.

It was all a lie though. A lie she believed—a lie I *needed* her to believe to make this work.

Truth was, however, I would never lay a finger on Edith. In fact, the moment I had delivered my threat, I instead wanted nothing more than to take her mouth with mine—to taste the woman that agreed to be my wife so easily.

But I was blinded by my contract to her—I didn't want to mix business with pleasure. After we'd gone off to the inn where I'd reserved two rooms, we parted ways until our wedding the next evening. Once we had our ceremony, however, I realized just how difficult that would be—not mixing the business with pleasure—and I nearly destroyed it all in one evening.

"You may kiss your bride," the officiant says blandly. I had called for him last minute and apparently he has better things to do with his time, even though I paid him handsomely for his services.

Edith lifts her wide, brown eyes to mine and I see the hope in them. I'm snared in her gaze—a gaze that says she believes this marriage may evolve into something more than a contractual bind-

ing of two people.

And that simply cannot happen.

Too much is at stake.

My inheritance for one.

The other is her heart. I'm simply not a man that falls for one woman and stays there. I enjoy the company of a lady in my bed but by dawn I will have grown bored of her. They're for my pleasure without unnecessary ties securing me to them. If I allow myself to kiss her—to taste the mouth that I've learned can be quite saucy—then I'll lead the poor girl on.

I can see it in her eyes.

She is the type to become attached.

The moment I sink into her and find my release, I'll be ready to roll over and forget her. It cannot be that way between the two of us. We're married now and we have an act to uphold. If she were to be clingy, or worse yet, jealous of my other lovers, she may divulge our pact to my family.

Keeping her at a distance is what needs to be done.

Dipping down, I press a chaste kiss to her forehead. When I pull back and smile curtly at her, I see the tears swim in her eyes. The moment is brief before she plasters on a fake smile and storms from the chapel.

Welcome to married life.

By the time I reach the doors to exit the building, I see her hiking her dress up as she hustles across the street to a pub. I groan and check my timepiece. The whore I paid for will be waiting in my room soon.

Running a palm through my thick hair, I make a decision. I'll cheer the poor woman up and the whore can wait. I'll pay her doubly for her time.

"Edith!" I call out but she ignores me as she slips inside the pub.

By the time I have made it indoors, I see her sitting at the bar telling the man her order. I stride over to her and sit in the stool next to her.

"Celebratory drink, Countess?" I question.

I bark out my order while I wait for her to answer. It doesn't come though. I've gone off and married a woman that's slightly mad.

Leaning toward her, I drop my lips to her ear. "I'm sorry if I upset you, Edith. This is a business relationship if you'll recall, not a real marriage."

She nods and turns to regard me. Our faces are inches apart and hell if I don't have the urge to kiss her like I should have at the chapel. My eyes fall to her lips and I stifle the groan that nearly overtakes me.

"Let's drink. We'll celebrate this marriage—our business deal," she says with a false smile. The act turns her pretty mouth into something flat and insincere. I'm not fond of this smile.

Hours later, we've overindulged on liquor and I can't stop wondering what she tastes like—her mouth, her breasts, her cunt. I would imagine she's sweeter than honey.

"When may I call upon my first lover, Alexander?" she questions with a hiccup.

My half grin drops as I imagine another man enjoying the mouth I've spent all night obsessing over. If fucking outrages me. "Not tonight," I tell her gruffly.

Her lips fall into a pout and I feel my cock become erect.

What if?

I tangle my fingers in her hair and pull her to me. Both of us stare at the other for a long moment, neither of us willing to make the first move. Before I do something I shall regret, I bring my lips to her ear and I draw the lobe between my teeth. She lets out a tiny gasp and her hand covers mine that's in her hair. We become statues for what feels like eternity as I tongue her ear. It's evident we both desire more. I'm willing to forget the whole stupid contract for one night. Could we both put it behind us tomorrow and carry on like usual?

"There you are, Alexander!" a shrill, familiar voice rings out. "I have been waiting at the inn for hours."

The whore. I've used her on many occasions because she sucks cock really fucking well. But tonight I don't want her. I want something new.

I want Edith, my wife.

But Edith has sobered in my arms and is pushing herself away from me. "Your lover is here," she spits out in disgust as she retreats.

I gape after her as she stumbles toward the door in her haste to leave. A man steadies her near the door and I see the interest he has for her in his eyes.

"Do you want me to suck you off in the alley or in your room?" the whore questions as she reaches me and slips her arms around my neck.

My eyes are still on Edith. She glances once at me and then smiles at the man on her arm. Together, they stroll out of the pub toward the inn.

I could go after her.

Stake claim on my wife.

Or, I could count my blessings at having avoided what could have been a huge mistake.

"The room will be perfect, dear," I murmur to the whore. My lips connect with hers but my eyes are on the dark-haired woman I can still see through the window.

Edith rolls over in my arms so that our chests touch, jerking me from my thoughts, and I stare at her. Even asleep, she manages to intrigue me. I want to know what it is that she thinks about all day. Do I ever cross her mind? Does she ever wonder what it would be like to make love to me?

I slide a palm up to her cheek and stroke her gently. This

shouldn't feel so comfortable. However, I find myself relaxing and losing consciousness as I hold this woman.

My wife.

When did things change?

Chapter Three

Edith

MY ROOM IS DARK BUT I sense that it is morning. Every bone in my body aches and the memories of yesterday flood me. I curl into a ball on my bed, seeking warmth further under my covers.

In a happy marriage, a husband would comfort his wife. However, in my marriage, I comfort myself apparently. For once, I simply want to be held by someone that loves me. It would seem that my punishment in this life for what I did to Elisabeth will always prevent me from having what I desire most.

To be loved.

"Edith," Alexander's deep voice calls from the doorway.

I pretend to still be sleeping. I'm not ready to deal with him today. Yesterday, he valiantly rescued me from Victor. For a moment, I assumed maybe he cared for me. But then, he sulked in the corner and stewed about the entire ordeal. Never once did he ask me to talk about what happened. I was left to manage on my own.

The floor creaks as he steps into the room and strides over to my bedside. The bed squeaks when he sits beside me. My heart flutters at his proximity and I desperately attempt to calm it down.

"Edith, dear, we're leaving."

This certainly gets my attention and I twist to face him. His brows are furrowed but I can still see them in the room that is becoming less dark by the second as the sun rises. I try not to notice how handsome he looks with his dark hair styled in a floppy way on his head. He has dressed fancier than his usual attire and it reminds me of our wedding.

To keep from staring at him all morning, I draw my attention from him and over to the window.

"Where are we going?" I rasp out. My throat is still sore at the abuse I suffered at the hand of Victor.

I startle when he swipes a finger over my forehead and pushes my hair aside. "Havering. It's time, Edith. I'm ready to present you to my family as my wife."

We never discussed leaving today so I'm slightly alarmed at his proclamation. "When?"

"In two hours. That should allow you enough time to have breakfast with me and pack a suitcase."

I'm still reeling from his plan to take me to Havering. I cannot argue though for the simple fact that I agreed to this. Six months ago, I assured him I could be his partner in this unusual scheme.

"I shall hurry, Alexander. Can you see to it that I get some tea?"

He smiles at me. "It will be ready upon your arrival to the dining room."

A small grin tugs at my lips. When this husband of mine is nice, I sort of lose my head and become mesmerized by all that is him. He grows more handsome and it is in those moments that I crave for him to kiss me.

It was just last week that I had to physically refrain from throwing myself into his arms during one of those rare moments he had me swooning for him.

Ouch!

I found myself sidestepping to avoid the cat that lives in the inn and tripped over my dress. One moment I was in mid-sentence greeting Alexander for dinner, and the next I was on my hands and knees.

"Edith!" Alexander shouts and I hear the scrape of the chair as he gets up from the table and makes his way over to me. "Are you okay, darling?"

I roll over to sit on my bottom and stare up into his concerned eyes. My chin quivers but I hold it up bravely. "I'm fine. I just bruised my knees."

He frowns at me as he squats before me and brushes a hair out of my face. "You must be more careful. I don't want anything to happen to you."

I smile at him. His words are genuine and I believe that he truly cares for me. Oftentimes I wonder if I'm simply a business partner to him. Other times, I know in my heart that he feels some sort of affection for me.

"I will survive, Alexander. It was a simple fall," I giggle.

His eyes light up and he grins mischievously at me. "Let me be sure that you are not hurt. May I?"

My eyes widen when he takes hold of the end of my dress and inches it up my legs. Our smiles are gone as he holds my gaze every agonizing step of the way. I'm not feeling any pain from my fall because all I can feel is my knickers as they become drenched. His thumbs drag along the inside of my legs, transferring his blazing heat onto my flesh, as he pushes up the dress causing me to nearly go insane. I've had many lovers since I married Alexander but not one has made me nearly orgasm from such a simple touch.

"Alexander," I whine when my dress slips over my knees and stops at my thighs.

"Yes?" he murmurs.

"What are you doing?"

He dips his mouth to my knee and brushes a soft kiss on it. My eyes roll back and I stifle a moan that threatens to rip from me. Why must he tease me so?

His lips press against my other knee and I gasp.

When he lifts back up to face me, I see that he's suddenly angry. "Your scent . . ."

His lips are pursed together and he's scowling. "I need to leave. I cannot have dinner with you tonight," he blurts out abruptly.

Confusion washes over me while he rises hastily to his feet. Tears brim in my eyes as I sit on the floor and listen to him stomp out of the dining room.

What is wrong with my scent?

"Lord and Lady Thomas will be joining us."

His words draw me from my memory and I gape at him. "But she hates me, Alexander. You don't understand."

"That isn't any of my concern. What is of my concern is convincing Father that we are married—and happily so. We shall require Jasper's assistance in that quest. It is already decided and they will meet us at the train station in two hours."

I swallow down my emotion but nod. It hurts that he is being so brisk but I have no other choice. I've promised to do this with him and I won't break that promise.

"Would it be possible that we board at a later time?" I ask hopefully. "So that I don't have to unnecessarily encounter her?"

His eyes drop to my lips and he seems momentarily dazed. "Of course. Now make haste."

As he stalks out of the bedroom, I stare after him and admire the view. He may frustrate and confuse me but I never tire of looking at him, especially when he wears trousers that hug his muscled frame so neatly. His arse is one I wouldn't mind seeing in its bare form. Perhaps when we make it to Havering, I will have that opportunity.

I lick my lips and groan.

Good heavens, I need a cold bath now.

Chapter Four

Alexander

MY FISTS ARE STILL BRUISED, and each knuckle is busted from having beaten that idiot to within an inch of his life last night. I'd simply gone mad—much like during the secret cellar fights I used to have with the guys back in Havering. The fights where I would lose control and my fists would guide the destructive path until someone pulled me off my bloody opponent.

To let loose and have the rage flood through me—rage I'd been pretty schooled at containing—was invigorating. Had it been under any other circumstance, I would have felt drugged from the pleasure of the release.

However, it was not under any other circumstance.

No, it was to protect what belonged to me.

Edith.

At first, I was pissed when I heard the noises coming from her room. I wanted to make my whore—*whatever the hell her name was*—scream out my name in ecstasy just to rile Edith up.

But the moment I heard her scream my name in terror followed by the brutal banging against the wall, I saw red.

Bloody fucking red.

The prick was smashing my wife's head into the wall like it was his God-given right. So help me, had I not seen her crying and looking so vulnerable, I would have killed him with my fists. But she needed me. She was broken like never before. I wanted to protect her.

Now?

My eyes skim over her appearance from across the table. Her normal prissy attitude has been replaced by that of a sadder one. One that concludes she's been made aware of her fragility being that she's a woman. Her bottom lip is swollen, and just seeing it causes rage to flare through me.

Now? I *still* want to protect her.

"You're quiet this morning," I say gruffly.

She's peering out the window, watching the scenery flash by. We boarded the train a short while ago and settled into our private sleeping quarters of the car. I paid an outlandish amount to reserve this car for us. I also reserved the one beside us for Jasper and Elisabeth. Upon Edith's wishes, we boarded after them to avoid a confrontation between her and her sister.

"Not much to say," she whispers with her eyes trained on the window.

Ever since last night, after I'd helped her clean up and tucked her into bed, she's behaved differently. Not at all like herself. It rattles me that she's lost inside of her head and I'm not allowed in there with her.

"Want to discuss what happened?"

She shrugs her shoulders but still won't meet my eyes. I'm seconds from physically shaking the words out of her when she finally huffs out her reply.

"Discuss the fact that my gigantic wedding ring given to me by my 'husband' became tangled in my lover's hair? And that, when I teased him about it, he lost his mind?" she snips out. Her bottom lip quivers, but her eyes remain affixed.

"Look at me." My demand seems harsh even to my own ears.

She flinches but shakes her head. "I'm rather happy looking out the window."

I slide out of my seat and launch myself into the one beside her. Her breath hitches in what seems like fear, but the stubborn woman holds her ground and won't look at me.

"Look at me," I growl as I inch my face closer to hers. Her scent invades me, and I inhale the sweet perfume she's taken to wearing lately.

"No, Alexander."

When I slide a palm across her belly, she yelps.

Not in fear.

Pain.

"Are you hurt here?" I demand as I gently rub my thumb over her stomach.

This time, she does look at me. The tears are back, and they spill out. "Yes."

I clench my teeth together and attempt to keep myself from exploding. My fists itch to smash something to smithereens. How dare that monster hurt my wife?

"Show me." I know I sound like an arse, but I need to see.

"But you'll see me naked and . . ." she trails off when I slide the top of her dress over her shoulder.

I noticed earlier that she'd chosen one of her simpler frocks and forgone a corset. Now, I know that it was because she was in fucking pain.

"You're my wife. I'm going to see you naked plenty of times," I murmur. My lips graze the top of her shoulder, and she gasps. I hadn't meant to kiss her there but it felt right.

I can tell she wants to argue, but instead, she slumps her shoulders and allows me to unfasten the back of her dress. Once I've undone it, I slide the material down her arms and let it fall into her lap.

My eyes land first on her pert, bare breasts. I nearly groan aloud when my cock hardens in response. Her chest rises and falls in rapid succession as she watches me watch her. The urge to taste them is overwhelming and my mouth waters accordingly.

I blink my eyes to clear my mind and meet her brown ones. "Where?"

Her small hand slides out of the sleeves of her dress, and she tenderly strokes a place on her stomach. I lean down to take a closer look, and when my ear grazes her nipple, she gasps. The moment I see the green-and-purple bruise the size of a fist on her stomach, I become livid.

"That fucking pig! I should have killed him!"

She whimpers when I lean forward and place a gentle kiss on her flesh—such a stark comparison to my harsh words.

Being this close to her naked body, inhaling her, I become hungry for her. A hunger that never existed to this degree for this woman begins to furl its way through me. When I kiss the bruise again, her hands thread themselves into my hair.

The action is intimate, and my cock begins to painfully ache to be inside her.

I drag my nose along her skin upwards until I feel the curve of her breast. The tiniest of kitten-like mewls escapes with her ragged exhalations. Not waiting for permission, I flick my tongue out and taste her breast. My tongue drags along the pale flesh until it encounters her pebbled nipple.

"Alexander," she hisses as if my name is a curse word.

As I tease her nipple with the tip of my tongue, I notice she tastes sweet like the sugar cubes I devoured as a boy. It is just as I always imagined. Needing more, I suck her into my mouth with an urgency I don't understand.

A knock on our door startles me, and I pop off her nipple.

"Who's there?" I snap.

I'm frustrated that she's frantically sliding the dress back into place. With a sigh, I set to helping her fasten the back.

"It's me—Jasper," the voice answers on the other side of the door. "And Elisabeth."

Edith's eyes widen, and I know she's terrified at the idea of meeting with her sister.

"Hold on a moment," I call out and turn to her.

"I can't talk to her," she whispers. "She hates me."

I slide an arm around her and pull her to me carefully. "It will be fine. Trust me."

She relaxes in my arms as if my words calm her.

"Come in," I bark.

The click of the doorknob causes Edith to sigh raggedly. I hate that she's so anxious about meeting with my best friend and his wife.

"Good afternoon, you two lovebirds," Jasper smirks as he enters.

I nod my head at him. Behind him, he tugs his wife along. Both women avoid the eye contact of the other. Jasper assists Elisabeth into the chair before sliding in next to her. I give Jasper a look that says, *Tread lightly,* and being that he knows me so well, he simply nods.

"Have you told Alfred of your marriage yet?" he asks.

I groan, because even though my intentions had been to send him a letter of my marriage, I hesitated to go forth with it. The letter sits folded in my breast pocket along with the contract Edith signed and our certificate of marriage.

"No. I shall inform him upon our arrival."

Jasper's eyes widen, and his gaze flickers over to Edith. "I'd like to suggest the two of you begin acting like a married couple. Alfred is no fool, Alexander. He will call you out on the authenticity of the marriage. And what about Alcott? You know your idiot brother will be eager to ruin you if at all possible—that's his life goal."

I grumble and clench my jaw. Father will question our relationship, no doubt. And Alcott? That bastard will do whatever he can to blow our secret wide open. We have to up our game before our arrival.

"I guess I don't understand why you would go along with this," Elisabeth whispers, but she doesn't raise her eyes to meet Edith's.

Edith stiffens beside me, and instinctively, I reach over and take her hand in mine.

"I mean, when did you become this person?" Elisabeth asks.

"I forced her into it. Much like you were forced into a marriage with Jasper," I snap.

Jasper sits up straight and pins me with a glare. "Enough, Alexander. And, honeysuckle, they'll work it out just like we did."

Everyone sits in tension-filled silence until finally Jasper speaks again.

"I apologize for being forward, but have the two of you even kissed? Made love? How do you intend to convince your father?"

He's absolutely correct. We're going to have a hell of a time convincing my father. Edith and I never even sealed our marriage with a kiss. I've looked after her, but we've carried on with our lives. Bloody hell! What was I thinking? We should have spent more time with each other rather than with our lovers. Father will figure it out immediately.

"Kiss me, wife," I murmur to Edith.

She turns to regard me with surprise. I can feel the eyes of Elisabeth and Jasper upon us.

"What?" she asks.

"Kiss me. The act begins now. We've had our time of holiday, but now, it's time to work," I inform her.

Her eyes widen. The woman who agreed to this has gone and left the goddamned train, because the one before me seems terrified. Hell, I'm fucking terrified but it needs to be done.

I slip a palm over her cheek and thumb it in a gentle manner. "Edith, it will be okay. Just close your eyes and go with it."

After a moment's hesitation, she slams her eyes closed and parts her lips. The sun shines in, and a few strands of red sparkle in the sea of her mahogany hair. Her face is free of any color, and she is simply beautiful in her natural skin. I've never wanted to kiss her as badly as I do now—now, it's all I can think about.

Leaning forward, I graze her lips with mine and relish how soft they feel. Her breath smells of the sweet honey she added to her breakfast tea. I want to taste her.

Knowing that her lip is injured, I press my lips more firmly to hers, careful not to hurt her, and kiss her deeply. Then her tongue darts out and meets mine. The moment they connect, I'm flooded with the taste of her. Honey. Cinnamon. Vanilla. And her.

I want more of her.

My hand slides into her hair, and I pull her to me. She lets loose a moan that I devour with my mouth as I kiss her. Suddenly, the metallic taste of blood warns me that I've kissed her too hard—that I've reopened her cut.

When I wrench away to inspect her, I see the small trickle of blood, and once again, fury floods through me. That bastard did this to her. Then she opens her eyes and explores my face as if she's trying to uncover why our kiss was so decadent.

I know the answer.

Edith.

Leaning forward, I suck her bottom lip into my mouth and run my tongue over her cut. She whimpers but allows me to clean her with my mouth. There's something carnal about the way I nurse her wound with my tongue.

A clap startles me, and I jerk my head over and see Jasper grinning crookedly at me.

"That. Keep doing that and you'll convince him." He shakes his head. "Hell, you convinced me."

Chapter Five

Edith

THE KISS. IT'S ALL I'VE been able to think about during the entire ride to Havering. Once we concluded our kiss, we had a lovely lunch with Jasper and Elisabeth. My sister and I remained quiet while the men laughed and told stories of their childhood. I even found myself smiling on more than one occasion.

Alexander and Jasper are closer as unofficial brothers than Elisabeth and I are as flesh-and-blood sisters. Perhaps, one day, she can find the heart to forgive me and we can have the friendship our husbands have.

Husbands.

Each time I remember that Alexander is my husband, I want to chuckle. It has been a game for us, but now, we need to focus and become serious if we're interested in making it seem real for his father's sake.

"We're nearly there," Alexander says tightly beside me.

Jasper and Elisabeth recently retired to their cabin and left us alone. We remained in companionable silence until now.

"Are you worried?" I ask, turning my head to look at him. He hasn't left my side since he first came over to me earlier.

His dark eyebrows furrow together, and I see it. This strong, confident man is intimidated by his father. The same motherly instinct to protect, much like I did for Elisabeth and Ella after Mother died, washes over me. I'll see to it that his father has no doubts. I will throw everything I have into this relationship to make him believe.

I tentatively touch the hair on his face. The coarseness of it scratches my palm, and I briefly remember the way it felt against my breast. A warmth floods my veins at the memory of it.

"We'll convince him, husband." I smile conspiratorially at him.

His full lips spread into a grin, and his eyes flash me his appreciation. A woman like myself really could fall for a man like him. She wouldn't even have to try that hard.

"I'm pleased that you're so confident, wife," he teases.

I lean forward and surprise him with a chaste kiss on his lips. The moment I move away from him, he growls and seizes my lips again, but there is nothing hasty about it. He kisses me as if he intends on living there—owning every inch of me with his mouth.

"Why haven't we done this before?" he murmurs between kisses as his fingers tangle in my hair.

I fist his shirt and pull him closer. "You were too busy with your whores."

He grumbles in response, and before I know it, he's dragging me onto his lap. I gasp when he shoves my dress up and pushes my leg over him so that I'm straddling him.

"No more talk about the whores. While in my father's estate, we won't speak of it all. Understand?" he questions harshly.

I release his shirt and glare at him. "Understood."

When I go to slide off him, his hands grip my hips and prevent me from moving.

"Where are you going, wife?"

I shake my head as I stare at him in disbelief. He doesn't want me. He needs me. And not in the way I would like. I'm a partner in his game. I'll do well to remember that.

"I asked you where you were going."

The desire to the slap him is overwhelming, but instead, I throw myself into character. I thread my fingers in his hair and nearly laugh aloud when his eyes widen in surprise. Leaning forward, I kiss him as if he were the sweetest lover in all of the land. I kiss him as if he were the love of my life. I kiss him as if he were to be gone tomorrow.

He is erect beneath my spread legs, and I wonder what it would feel like to make love to him. I'm sure he would be the same overbearing arse in the bedroom that he is outside of it. But would he touch me in ways no other has? Would he be there for me afterwards to hold me? Before I can allow myself to give into the hope of something more, I squash it. These men are all the same.

Just as he really gets into the kiss and rotates my hips so that he can control how I rub against him, I pull away.

"Dear husband," I purr, taking satisfaction in the way his eyes darken at my tone, "this act we're engaging in is quite enjoyable."

"Yes," he agrees before he attempts to kiss me again. His efforts are in vain, because I tug away and pin him with a firm stare.

"It's an act and nothing more. You can count on me to put on a stellar performance in front of your family, but behind closed doors, you can shove your officious attitude up your arse. I know how this ends if you make love to me," I tell him in a matter-of-fact way. "I will fall in some sort of infatuation with you and then you'll discard me for another whore. I'm far too much of a jealous woman to handle that. In fact, I can't be held responsible for my actions if that were to happen. So, if you want to keep up the feint, then I suggest we keep this strictly business like our original agreement."

His jaw works as he listens to my words. I become mesmerized by his lips for a moment before shaking away the weakness.

"Understand?" I throw his word back at him.

After shoving me off his lap, he rises and stalks over to the door. Before he leaves, he spits out his response. "Understood."

"There it is." Jasper grins as he points through the small coach window.

The ride from the train station to Alexander's family estate has taken longer than I imagined it would. Being in close quarters with Elisabeth, who hates me, and Alexander, who is angry with me, has only made the journey seem even longer. Poor Jasper has filled the silence, rambling on about God only knows what—I wasn't listening. Instead, I thought about how thrilled I felt at having made Alexander cross with me. The man believes that, because he's rich and powerful, he'll always wield the upper hand. This afternoon, I showed him that he was sorely wrong in that thinking.

Peering out the window, I catch a glimpse of the estate Jasper pointed at. The enormous home sits proudly on a hilltop, surrounded mostly by trees. It's quite possibly one of the largest homes I've ever seen, and a ripple of excitement shudders through me as I realize that this will be my new home.

When we climb out of the coach, I stretch my legs and inhale the countryside air. It reminds me a lot of home, and I prefer it here over London already.

"I'm rather exhausted from our travels and wish to rest before supper," Elisabeth murmurs to Jasper. That's when I happen to gaze over at them and watch as he strokes her belly.

"Lissa, are you pregnant?" I blurt out.

Her green eyes lift to mine, and she lifts her chin in defiance, as if I'll try to take this away from her too. "I am."

Happiness washes over at me, and before I know it, I've thrown my arms around her. "I'm going to be an aunt. This is wonderful news. Congratulations," I babble out.

She doesn't hug me back as she mutters her thanks. I realize she must feel uneasy with me touching her, so I retreat. I'm once again reminded how I selfishly chose my own wants and desires over that of my younger sister. When I was supposed to look after her, I took from her instead. A bitter memory of what I took floods my mind.

He pushes the door closed and prowls over to me with a look that normally brings me to my knees quite literally. However, tonight I am not interested. Last time we were together, I discovered a letter from Lissa that had fallen from his pocket. While he cleaned himself up from our sexual encounter, I read it without his knowing.

And I was gutted.

She missed him incredibly so. It was a moment of clarity for me. I was able to take a step back and actually witness what I was doing—how I was hurting her and she didn't even know it. The revelation had nearly crippled me. It was so easy to live in the moment while we were at university but the reality was that he had my sister counting down the days until he came back to her. The desire to steal off back to the farm and confess everything to her was overwhelming. That evening, I decided it would happen no more.

But when William came back into the bedroom, he gathered his things and left without a backwards glance. I hadn't had the opportunity to tell him until now.

"Good evening, William," I greet brusquely. My arms are crossed over my breasts and I hold my chin up bravely.

"I need you, Edith." His voice is a growl that works its way through my body. Tonight I am strong though. I'm no longer the weak woman that I was from before. I'll do this for her.

"No more, William," I tell him with a clip in my voice.

He halts his step forward and places both hands on his hips. "Excuse me?"

His tone is harsh even though his mouth is quirked into a lopsided grin. It's apparent that he believes I am teasing him.

"I'm done with you. What we did to Lissa was despicable. In fact, I'm going to tell her everything—"

"You'll do nothing of the sort!" he snarls, his smile long gone. "She mustn't ever know. You will never tell her."

I gape at the man, who even though he's pledged himself to my sister, still chooses to see me each weekend to find his release.

"How I ever imagined I was in love with you is beyond me. You're a bastard, William Benedict."

He roars with obnoxious, hateful laughter. "Love? You? You're a foolish woman, Edith. Did I ever kiss you? No. That, dear girl, is because I could never love you. You have always been a way to fulfill a need, nothing more."

The tears well in my eyes and I bite my lip. "Please leave."

His demeanor changes and his shoulders relax. "Edith, I'm sorry. I didn't mean it that way."

I swallow down a sob and drop my gaze to the floor. When he envelops me in a hug, I sag against him and allow the tears to win over. He runs his fingers through my hair and whispers soft assurances that comfort me. I hate that I'm letting him hold me.

But I desperately want to be held.

Once my tears have dried, he leans back and lifts my chin so that we're staring at each other. I get lost in his crystal blue eyes that mesmerize me often.

"I love this," he murmurs, "Our moments together. Can't that be enough? For now?"

My heart clenches painfully in my chest. "I love this too. I love you, William. But Lissa will be heartbroken."

His brows furrow and I see indecision behind his eyes. Finally, he steels his features and dips his head to mine. My eyelids flutter closed when I feel his warm breath upon my lips for the first time. Mint and lemon invade me.

The kiss is soft and without tongue but it holds promise.

"What about Lissa?" I try again with a slight whine to my voice.

Maybe if he breaks it off with her, we can stop seeing one another in secret. He'll fall in love with me and we'll marry instead.

"Right now, Edith, I want you. I want to be inside of you, on top of you. I want to kiss you while I fuck you."

Tears shimmer in my eyes as I bask in his words.

"Let me love your body, darling," he murmurs before capturing my lips again. This time he kisses me with his tongue. This time, I don't protest when he pushes my dress down and over my shoulders.

When our bodies connect physically, he kisses me urgently with each thrust. It fulfils a missing part deep inside of me. This is love.

"I love you, William," I tell him over and over.

The tears are partly from joy and partly from the pain I am causing my sister. William loves me and not her. It's me that he has chosen.

I cry out when he pulls out of me and spurts his orgasm all over my belly. I haven't found my own release but I don't care. I'm happy to have made progress in our relationship.

"Are you going to sleep over tonight?" I question as he slides off of me. The hope in my voice is evident. It would be the first time to spend the entire night with him. With him holding me. Touching me. Loving me.

He wrenches himself away and tucks his dripping cock back into his trousers. "Edith, I tried. I thought that maybe we could work. That I could forget her."

I sit up quickly and watch in horror as he strides toward the door, buttoning his shirt along the way. "Don't leave," I choke out in protest.

"I cannot throw away what I have with her. I am sorry, Edith. We're done here. I won't bother you again to fulfil my needs. We shall soon be leaving university and surely I can wait for my Lissa. It will make it all the more worthwhile."

"William," I call out to him, "Please stay with me."

My chin wobbles as tears roll down my cheeks.

He doesn't provide me with an answer and instead slips out the door without so much as a goodbye.

Love is an illusion.

The memory feels fresh and I can feel tears brimming in my eyes. Batting my eyes, I turn away from my sister whose heart I broke for him. William. The man that only used me until he could have her. My God, I was such a stupid woman.

"Come. Let's get this over with," Alexander grumbles as he begins striding toward the front door of the home.

I shake off the sickening memories of William and grab hold of my frock to hurry after him. "Alexander, wait for me," I hiss as I struggle to catch up to him.

His demeanor has changed; he seems more rigid. Anxious, even. The first time we see his parents as a married couple, we should at least seem in love—not like he's trying to run away from me.

He doesn't wait for me and bounds up the steps. Right as he reaches for the door, it flies open and a man steps out.

A gorgeous man.

"Alcott," Alexander practically snarls as he comes to a halt in front of his brother.

Instead of greeting him back, Alcott looks past him at me. His eyebrows quirk up in surprise. "Where'd you get this one?"

I gape at him as I reach the porch and stand beside Alexander.

"She's my wife," Alexander snaps at him. "Show a little respect."

Alcott blatantly scrutinizes me, and I want to squirm. But I don't. Instead, I thread my fingers with Alexander's and meet Alcott's narrowed, brown eyes.

"A little on the plain side. Not usually your *type,*" Alcott laughs.

Alexander tenses beside me, but I squeeze his hand to calm him.

"Apparently, his *type* can't satisfy him long enough in his bed to keep him for more than one night. It would appear that this 'plain' woman has more than entertained him both in and out of bed for nearly six months. It would seem"—I smirk—"that I'm exactly the *type* he needs."

He works his jaw, clearly thinking of some brilliant reply, I'm sure, but then Jasper clears his throat behind us.

"Baby brother, can you show us to our room?" Jasper asks from behind us. "My wife isn't feeling well and needs to lie down."

Alcott winces at the juvenile name but nods and turns to go into the house. As he crosses the threshold, he snaps his head back toward Alexander.

Ten seconds.

The man isn't a quick witted individual.

I can see by the nasty look in his eye that he's finally thought of something to say back to me.

"That's an unpleasant cut there on your lip, Countess," Alcott sneers. "It would seem that you're the *type* of woman a man has to put in her place. My brother always preferred to get his way by means of his fists. Can't say I blame him in your case."

I'm shocked by his words, but Alexander seems to have expected them. He roars as he charges his brother and tackles him onto the marble floors of the exquisite entryway. Before anyone can stop them, they roll around, each one trying to get the upper hand to do damage to the other.

"Boys, that's enough," a stiff, regal voice echoes through the room.

As if someone has grabbed both of them by the collars of their shirts and yanked them up, the two men rise quickly to their feet but manage to shoot evil glares at one another.

"Father," they greet in unison.

My eyes find a tall, older version of Alexander. His hair is white instead of the warm, brown hues my husband has.

"Sir, I would like for you to meet my—" Alexander waves toward me. Before he can finish, Alcott interrupts, gesturing to me the same way as his brother.

"*That* is his wife."

The way he says *that* as if I'm some disease-ridden woman stings, but the way their father wrinkles his nose in disgust guts me. I'm not sure why I'm upset that he is evidently repulsed by my presence, but I am.

Alexander stalks over to me and snakes a possessive arm around my waist. I know he's acting for his father, but the fact that he has come to my side soothes the pain of their dislike toward me.

"Her name is Edith and I love her."

Even I can hear the phony tone of his words. I'm scrambling to come up with something that will back up what he's saying when Jasper steps beside me and slings an arm over my shoulder.

"It's quite sickening to watch, actually. All they do is ravish each other at every opportunity. Clearly, they're desperately attempting to rein it in out of respect for you, sir. Hell, the way they're normally all over each other, I'd be surprised if Edith here wasn't already carrying his child," Jasper muses.

Alfred's eyes carefully examine each one of us before he finally nods. "I'll see you all at supper. Your mother will be pleased with this news, Alexander."

He storms off to wherever he came from, but Alcott sends us both a scathing look before motioning for Jasper and Elisabeth to come with him.

Once we're alone, I turn toward Alexander. "What's wrong with you?" I hiss.

His dark eyes are liquid fury as he regards me. "I told you this would be fucking hard. You don't know how those two are. Father would prefer to hand over his empire to Alcott, I'm sure. Stick to the plan and we'll be just fine."

"Alexander, I was sticking to the plan. You're the one who went fanatical. Can't you just ignore them? Don't let them get to you. We're partners. Husband and wife. We can do this, but we need to stop acting like we're two players with different agendas on the same team. It will have to be us against them. Always."

His features soften before me, and I sigh. The poor man is so used to holding his ground against his family who are hell-bent on bringing him down. For once, he has an ally. He may be an insufferable arse, but he's my insufferable arse.

And I'm not going to sit idly and watch those two try to ruin him.

Chapter Six

Alexander

THE FAMILIAR ANXIETY FROM BEING home begins to infect my veins. There's a reason I travel so much and stay away for months at a time. My father and brother are intolerable.

"It will have to be us against them."

Her words find a way into my heart and give me strength. The two of us may be bound by a contractual agreement and a certificate of marriage, but the idea of having someone to combat them alongside me is refreshing. I draw concentration from it.

In the past, I would have unleashed my anger at the two of them in the cellars. The cellar fighting ring I created is a place where young men could take their problems out on another person with as many problems as they had. We had few rules and lived to beat the stew out of the other. I was known as The Beast by the other men. It's been way too long, and my fists, after having beaten Edith's lover's fucking skull in, itch to smash the flesh of another. A memory assaults me and I'm nearly crippled by it.

"You nearly killed him," Winston snaps, startling me from my

daze. I stare up at him in confusion.

"Who?"

"Fucking hell, don't play the part of a fool. Ten minutes ago, you were bashing that poor fellow's head into the dirt. He wasn't an equal opponent for you, Alexander. Why did you go so rough on him?"

Guilt trickles its way through my veins. Darby was his name. The kid home for holiday from university in London. He'd come out tonight to fight and have a good time. Not to get his nose crushed and lose teeth.

"I, uh, I lost my cool," I grunt.

Winston glares at me. "It's because of what he said isn't it?"

I spit into the dirt and run a hand through my soaked with sweat hair. "No."

"You lie poorly. It has everything to do with what he said."

A heavy sigh rushes from me as I stare up at the dark night sky littered with twinkling stars. He's right. Darby set me off and I saw bloody fucking red.

"Everyone in town knows your father hates you."

He had meant to rile me up. Truth is, everyone in town does know my father treats me as his less favorite of his two sons. The wild card. The son with no care to mold himself after the stoic man. It has always been a tender subject in my family. Darby had no right to rub salt in the wound.

But he didn't deserve to get killed for it. Had Winston not yanked my arse off of him, I would have bashed his face in until he died. End of fucking story.

And then what would have happened?

Father truly would have had his reasons for hating me then. He and Alcott could have a fucking hell of a time discussing all the ways I never measured up.

"Why don't you get away for a while? Don't you have that friend over in London? Perhaps you could spend some time with

him. I understand your troubles," Winston tells me with a shake of his head. "My father is a terror to deal with as well. And had I not gotten Suzette pregnant, I would have already left this small town and headed for the city. I care about you, Alexander. You're losing your wits about you as of late. Please tell me you will leave before you do something regrettable."

I shake off the memory as we approach my section of the estate. The next morning after bashing Darby's face in, I left and chose to travel rather than fester and submit myself to the mental abuses from the terrible twosome that are my brother and father.

"In here," I say gruffly as I open the double doors that lead to the wing that solely belongs to me. I have a grand living area with high ceilings and a stocked bar. Several rooms and washrooms line the hallways. And my favorite part of it all is the study. Of course, it remains locked and nothing of business goes on in there. But it contains everything that makes me happy.

Weights.

Gloves.

A bag for hitting.

"This is all yours?" Edith questions. "It's stunning."

"Ours," I remind her as I usher her into the master bedroom.

"Right," she says breathily.

The comforts of my room envelop me. It's been awhile and I've missed this damn place. Especially my bed.

After shrugging out of my waistcoat, I toss it onto the folded blanket on the end of the bed and then unbutton my dress shirt. When Edith sees me undressing, her eyes widen.

"What are you doing?" she asks.

I let my shirt fall to the floor and smirk at her. "We have a bit of time before supper. I thought you could pleasure me until then."

The look on her face is downright comical as she goes from pleasant to fucking insane. "Did you not hear a damn thing I said on the train?" she snarls. "Behind these doors, nothing happens. Got it, mister?"

I chuckle darkly at her. "If I wanted to force the issue, I would. Luckily for you, I'm not fucking interested."

Now, her brown eyes moisten, and she looks away from me. "You're an arse."

"An arse who, despite your words, you wish lavished you with praise. I'm sorry, Edith, but if I wanted to fuck you, it would be out of your control. You're lucky to have someone like me to have chosen you. Lest you forget that, just six months ago, you were wreaking havoc on the lives of all of those around you? I chose you because of your lack of morals. Not your beauty. Not your body. Not your wits or your fucking education. I chose you because you're as ruthless as I am."

Her head whips over to me, and she loses her damn mind. After rushing toward me with both fists balled, she attempts to beat me with them as if they could actually exact damage on my muscled frame. Easily, I seize her wrists and twist them behind her. A yelp bursts from her as she meets my eyes with a glare that could obliterate anything in their path.

"I'll be worth something to someone. You may think I'm scum, but I'm not. Someone will love me one day." Her words carry a vulnerable edge as tears well in her eyes.

I should comfort her and apologize for having said words I didn't really mean. But my stubborn arse won't let me. No, I only add fuel to the fire.

"It won't matter. You belong to me, and therefore, I won't allow anyone to love you. I'll kill anyone who tries."

Her mouth pops open in shock, and I feel the urge to kiss those lips.

"Does that mean you plan on loving me?" she questions, hope lacing her words.

I drop my mouth to hers but hesitate before our lips touch. Her breaths come out hard and fast. She's so close I can almost taste her.

"I'll never love you. I don't have that ability. But, nevertheless, you belong to me, so I won't be letting some other fool have you, either."

She struggles to escape my grasp, but I grip her tight enough to bruise her wrists. We both gasp when the door to my master bedroom flies open and Alcott bursts in as if the chump were actually going to bust us out. Not wasting a second, I smash my lips to hers and release her wrists. My wife knows the rules of the game, because her hands slide up my bare chest and around my neck. Even though our kiss is for show, there is truth to it.

Gripping her curvy arse, I pull her to me. I let her feel the reaction our kiss has on me. The needy moan that leaves her only serves to make me grow even harder. If I have to fuck her in front of the idiot, I will.

I groan at the thought of being inside this infuriating woman. She is not even close to the prettiest woman I've encountered, yet she allures me more than any other has. She is not sweet or doting or even fucking friendly. She's borderline crazy.

Yet.

Yet I desire to sink my cock into her.

I know she's a good lover, because for six months, I had to listen to her moans. Moans other men had drawn from her. Moans that had me coming as I fisted my cock on the other side of the wall.

Then the door slams shut and I grin against her lips. We've just won this round against Alcott, and I want to celebrate with my wife. But just as I begin leading her to the bed, she breaks away from our kiss. I'm outraged when she slaps me across the face.

"You're a monster," she spits out at me.

I growl in response and toss her onto the bed. "A monster *you* married."

My hands find the bottom of her frock, and I push it up her thighs. God, her milky white skin needs to be marked. By me.

"Don't touch me."

Ignoring her words, I dig my fingers into her thighs and haul her toward me, careful not to touch her where that bastard bruised her. She's angry, but there's no fear in her eyes. The woman is a fucking fighter—I'll give her that.

"The moment I touch you, you'll melt in my hands, dear wife," I tell her smugly as I urge her knees apart.

She doesn't resist and, instead, meets my stare. "You'll never please me like that of my past lovers," she taunts. "Victor had a way with his fingers and—"

I see fucking red again at the mention of his name.

Leaning over her, I smash my hand over her mouth to shut her up, and my other hand slides between her legs. I'll be the best lover she's ever had. Those men have nothing on me. Fucking nothing.

"Did he touch you like this?" I growl as I stare into her furious eyes. When my hand rubs over her knickers, she whimpers. "That arse had woman hands. Was he soft and gentle when he touched you? Or," I murmur as I slip my hand under the fabric, "was he rough? Did his fingers feel firm and leathery like mine?"

Her eyes flutter closed, and I watch with smugness as she shamelessly bucks against the way I touch her. When my middle finger pushes into her wet opening, a moan begs to be released from her mouth, which I still have covered with my hand. I want to hear it. Letting my hand slide away, I replace it with my mouth as I fuck her with my finger.

She's drenched and completely aroused at my touch despite her attitude. Her body clenches around my finger, and my cock aches to replace it—to feel the way she grips it.

"Alexander." My name on her tongue is a prayer.

The possessive feeling of ownership I have over her fills my soul. I can't bear the idea of another man even looking at her, much less touching her. She's my wife.

"No more lovers," I murmur as I own her cunt with my fingers. "You'll only come by my touch until the day you die."

"Same goes for you, mister. I'm far too jealous to share," she tells me firmly.

Her words cause me to pause. I cannot make promises I'm not certain I can keep. It reminds me of the one woman that thought she had been able to hold on to me.

"When are you going to make an honest woman out of me?" Nicolette asks as she tugs her dress back down over her arse.

I shove my cock back into my pants and shake my head at her. "It isn't like that for us."

Tears well in her eyes but I don't feel sympathy for her. In the very beginning, I told her I had no interest to do things the proper way. I wanted a good time. She was that good time. But once I was done, we would move along. She was a friend with sexual advantages but nothing more.

"It can be," she urges.

I snatch up my waistcoat and fold it over my arm as I retreat back through her bedroom window. "It won't be, dear. If you're still unmarried when I come back, shall I call upon you again?"

Turns out, I could call upon Nicolette whenever I had wanted. And after that initial conversation, she seemed at ease with our simple relationship based purely on sex and nothing more. I hadn't cared at all about Nicolette the way I do about Edith.

Edith is different.

"I'm going to fuck you, wife. You're going to wear the afterglow of our union to dinner." Changing the subject has always worked well in my past. I don't want to promise Edith anything and I certainly don't want to dwell on the reasons as to why I believe she's different than all of the other women.

She whimpers when I curl my finger and hit her in a spot only my finger can find. "God!" she screeches and comes hard, her entire body shuddering wildly.

"I'm going to fuck you now. Understand?" I question as I lift up to observe her. Her cheeks have reddened from her orgasm, and a pleased smile plays at her lips.

"Understood. But I meant what I said." She frowns. "I can't share you, Alexander. I'll go insane if you take on another lover after me. I've lost my head for far less before, and I'm warning you—it won't be pretty."

I contemplate her words. Can I handle it when she becomes unhinged the moment she finds out I've slept with another woman? It is inevitable that it will happen. But my cock aches and I know I'll convince myself of anything just to get inside her.

Women have always been my demise. This one included.

"Only you, Edith," I lie. "It will only be you from here on out."

The smile on her face is breathtaking, and for a moment, I wonder if I can hold true to my word. It will be easier on the estate because, unlike London, there aren't women ripe for the fucking milling about. Maybe I can do this.

"Make love to me," she murmurs in way that helps finalize my decision.

With a nod, I pull away from her and stand beside the bed. As I work to get my trousers and shoes off, she begins sliding her knickers down her thighs. The moment I get a glimpse of the dark hair between her legs, I can't contain myself.

"On your hands and knees," I command, my booming voice echoing off the walls.

I should let her remove her dress, but I can't wait any longer. So, the moment she assumes the position, I shove the frock up her back and enter her with force. Her scream is laced with part pleasure and part surprise. Then she gasps when I begin thrusting in and out of her, my fingers digging into her hips to guide her to my pace.

"I want to kiss you," she murmurs.

"Later. We're going to come together first," I grunt.

After slipping a hand around her, I find her swollen clitoris and start working it as we fuck. It doesn't take long until she's screaming my name as if I'm a fucking god. I get lost in the amazing way she grips my cock and am soon coming deep inside her.

I've never come inside a woman. Ever.

So why the fuck did I just do it?

A possessive thought wickedly swirls in my head. Because she's my wife. If she becomes pregnant, then it will only further prove the validity of our marriage. In fact, every time I fuck her, I shall come inside her. I want her belly swollen with my child in less than a year's time.

She collapses onto the bed, and I watch with pleasure as my come drips from her. If I didn't have other things to do at the moment, I would push my fingers back into her and hold all of it inside her so that she'll indeed get pregnant.

"Will you come lie down with me? Hold me?" Her face is hopeful, and I hate that I must crush her in this instant.

I lean forward and hastily kiss her forehead. "I'm sorry, dear. I have business to attend to."

Big, fat tears glisten in her eyes before they roll down her cheeks. "What sort of business?"

Shaking my head, I slip my trousers on and then pad toward the door. "Not yours." I don't mean to come off as harsh—simply matter of fact. I've spent far too long hiding parts of myself from everyone. Just because she's my wife, I'm not keen on delivering everything about me on a silver platter. I'll keep her in the dark as I do everyone else.

I'm a selfish man.

I ignore her sobs as I stalk toward my study.

Chapter Seven

Edith

TWO HOURS.

For two hours, I've watched the clock on the wall slowly tick away as I waited for him to return. I finally gave up and bathed. Once clean, I felt renewed. The heartbreak he so carelessly bestowed upon me was left along with the suds in the tepid water.

I'm horrified that I so easily gave myself to him. That I assumed that this was different. That, finally, someone wanted me for more than just a place to come.

But, alas, Alexander is like the rest. Just like William and Sven.

I'm so foolish.

Thoughts of Sven's dark, wavy hair and smoky brown eyes assault me.

He drags a slender finger between my bare breasts and I let out a small chuckle when he dips it into my belly button.

"This is my favorite part of you, lover," Sven says in his thick Spanish accent and presses a kiss on my nose. "Simply beautiful."

I sigh and palm his cheek. My professor and I began flirting when I first became a student of his. But now, months later, we're completely devoted to each other as lovers.

"I want to be your wife. You tell me you love me all the time. Why not marry me? I want to have your children," I pout.

His eyes darken and his lips press into a firm line. I've upset him.

I slip my fingers into his hair and pull him to my lips. "You love me too."

He smiles at my words. "I do love you. That is why I'm going to taste every inch of your flesh. Tonight when we make love, I'm going to make you come over and over again until—"

Someone pounds on the other side of his office door, interrupting him.

"Who is it? It's late!" I hiss at him as I scramble to redress.

Sven tugs on his clothes and yanks up the blanket from the sofa we were lying on. He still hasn't answered me but he seems worried. Surely, if it's the dean from the university or another employee, he can explain to them that we're in love. It will all work out.

"Sven," a female voice shouts, "It's me, Margareta."

"Goddammit," he huffs out.

I throw him a questioning look to which is answered with an apologetic one as he unlocks the door. The door immediately flies open and a stunning woman with long flowing brown hair glides in. She's carrying a baby with chubby cheeks on one hip and tugging along a small child behind her.

"Who are you?" she questions, looking straight past Sven at me.

"I, uh, I'm his—" I start but Sven interrupts me.

"Darling, this is my student. She required some additional tutoring but was just leaving."

His words are dismissive as he takes the baby from her. "My son, I've missed you."

I gape at him but my heart shatters when he leans forward and kisses the woman on the lips—lips that were moments earlier promising to do very naughty things to me.

"Who is this, Sven?" I ask in a shrill tone. I want to hear the words from his mouth even though I know exactly who this woman is to him.

He scowls and shakes his head slightly at me. I feel a threat in his stare. "This is my wife, Miss Merriweather. I'll see you in class tomorrow. Good evening."

His wife. Of course. While we were together and she was so far away, it were almost as if she were a fantasy. Never had he mentioned her name or even spoken much of his children. It was always just the two of us. And he always professed his love for me. I had imagined I would come first if it ever came down to me against her.

Clearly I was wrong.

As the door closes behind me, I know that I was his toy. Nothing more.

That night crushed me. I had spent three days in my bed sobbing and nursing my broken heart. He had cast me aside for something better—his family. A family I had known little about. It still sickens me that he made so many empty promises—that he told me over and over again that he loved me.

It was all a farce.

I was used as a place for him to get off until his wife came back. Much like William used me until it was time to go running back to Lissa.

And Alexander?.

I'm sure he has his own wicked scheme up his sleeve. This time, though, I won't sit idly and watch it happen. My heart isn't his to use and abuse.

A knock at the door startles my thoughts, and I smooth out the frock I redressed in before answering.

"Oh, hello, Alcott," I say flatly. I'm in no mood to grace him with a smile, as that would take too much effort.

"Countess." He nods and holds both of my suitcases up. "I figured you might need these. Father prefers everyone to dress accordingly for dinner. And that frock belongs in the bin."

My lip quivers at his statement, and his callous smirk fades away.

"My words were in jest, dear." He smiles in a genuine way that takes the sting away. "I honestly was trying to be nice by bringing you your things. To make up for the way I behaved earlier."

Now that he's smiling and being pleasant, I cave. "Thank you. I'll make sure I'm presentable."

He flashes me a flirtatious grin, and I roll my eyes at him.

"What? I'm trying here," he chuckles.

"I think I like you better when you're not," I tease back.

His eyes widen when he's shoved to the side as Alexander enters the room.

"Moving in on my wife?" Alexander snarls. "So typical, Alcott."

Alcott scoffs at his brother. "Hardly. See you both at dinner."

The moment the door slams behind him, I turn to glare at Alexander. Sweat drips from his hair, which has fallen in his face, and a scowl has stolen his features. If I weren't so angry at him, I'd think he was absolutely delicious-looking.

"You may unpack our things while I bathe," he says blandly as he pushes his trousers down on the way to the washroom, giving me a beautiful view of his arse.

When the door closes behind him, I want to scream in frustration. Instead, I swallow down my hurt and curiosity about where he's been. Then I scoop both suitcases up and bring them over to the bed, where not but three hours ago my husband used me like a plaything.

I'm nauseated by the very idea of it.

He takes his precious time in the washroom while I unpack my stuff. I leave his in the suitcase. My arse of a husband can unpack it his damn self.

Once I've placed all of my makeup onto the vanity, I sit at it and take the time to artfully paint up my face so I shall be breathtaking. Alcott thinks I'm plain—well, he can eat his words right along with his supper, because I plan on making him feel like a fool.

It's apparent that, in this family, you have to always have your claws bared. They're hell-bent on literally screwing you the moment you let your guard down. Well, no more. I'm not going down without a fight.

I peer at my reflection, satisfied at the change in my appearance after I've applied the color to my face. The rosy dusting on my cheeks makes my cheekbones seem higher, and I wink in the mirror. My full lips are now as crimson as the blood I'll shed if those bastards try to mess with me. A smile plays on them as I think about bloodying up a certain man in the room next door.

My hair has become a mess, so I twist it into a chignon and pin any strays in place. In a mere minutes, I've completely transformed into a woman of elegance. A woman who fits in at this estate.

A countess.

After a quick search through the armoire in which I hung my dresses, I decide upon my most expensive dress and then put it on. The silky, black material hugs my body in all of the most flattering ways, and the corset I choose lifts my breasts in an eye-catching manner.

The Dumont men can go to Hell, because I know I look amazing.

I'm smoothing my dress out when the washroom door swings open and Alexander fills the doorway. The plush towel is tied dangerously low on his hips, accentuating the way his pelvic muscles point downward in a delectable "v," and water droplets remain on his sculpted chest. He's taken the time to shave his normally overgrown face, and I'd be lying if I were to say that I were immune to how handsome he is when he's clean-shaven. My breath catches at the sight, and I am immediately angry at myself.

He used me.

I'll do well to remember that.

"Like what you see?" He smirks as he saunters over to the armoire. "I could give you more of what I gave you earlier."

"I hate you," I seethe.

He chuckles without humor at me as he searches through the large mahogany piece of furniture for his clothing. "Where are my clothes?"

This time, I'm the one smiling in sweet revenge. "In your suitcase. Next time, call the maid, because I'm certainly not one. Last time I checked, I am the Countess of Havering, married to a pompous earl."

He curses under his breath as he storms over to the bed and begins rifling through his clothing. I observe with pleasure as he searches for this things. Once he's found everything and starts dressing, I go to exit the room, but his words stop me.

"Where are you going?"

I turn and stare at him incredulously. "I have business to attend to," I say, spitting his own words back at him.

He fastens his trousers as he stalks over to me. His dress shirt is open, and my eyes once again skitter across his chest before making their way to his furious gaze.

"You're not going anywhere without me. We have an act to uphold, and your going anywhere without me will appear to be suspicious."

"Oh, I can act. Just like when I acted as if I were turned on by the way you touched me, dear husband. Honestly, I was bored. As you fingered me, I wondered what it is we'd have for supper. I thought about whether or not your brother were a better lover."

His steely eyes narrow and he becomes enraged. I wonder for a moment if he'll hit me like that bastard Victor. Instead, he slips a palm around the back of my neck and crashes his lips to mine. My breath is stolen from me as he kisses me deeply. And while the desire to push him away is strong, the warmth he pulls from my body only draws me more into the kiss.

I slide my palms over his pectoral muscles and skim my thumbs along the ridges of them. He's quite possibly the fittest man I've ever been with. As his cock grows hard between us, I hate the fact that, if he were to ask me to bed, I'd go willingly. Finally, he breaks our kiss and rests his forehead against mine, his coal-colored eyes searching mine for answers.

"You're an insufferable woman. I'm pretty sure you're insane."

His words hurt, but I don't let it show. "And you're no prize chicken yourself," I bite out.

This time, his lips softly meet mine, and I nearly sob at the sweetness of this kiss. No man kisses me unless it's passionate and a means to making love to me. But Alexander? He's kissing me as if I'm precious to him.

When he practically jerks himself away from me, I stare at him with questions dancing in my head. He grits his teeth and shakes his head before he finishes dressing. Apparently, he doesn't know the answers either.

"You'll arrive in the dining room on my arm. No negotiations," he murmurs as he adjusts his bowtie.

Even though his words infuriate me, I'm still lost in our kisses. This man makes no sense to me. I hate him, yet . . .

I don't.

I simply don't.

In fact, I crave more of him.

I crave the urge to slap him and then let him fuck me senseless.

"This way," Alexander grumbles as he ushers me into the exuberant dining room.

The table is extremely long, enough to fit at least fifty people. One end has been set with plates and tableware for our supper. There, three people turn to regard us as we enter.

"Alexander!" a female voice chirps upon our entrance.

"Mother," Alexander greets warmly as he releases my hand to stride over to her. His entire persona has changed upon the presence of this woman.

I follow behind him and wait to be introduced. As he hugs her in her chair, my eyes skitter over to Alcott, who is gaping at me. I wink at him in a way that says, *Take that, you smug bastard,* and he grins. With a slight nod on his part, I'm awarded with his approval. I'll take it. Maybe Alcott isn't as bad as I originally thought.

"Who is the vision you've brought to supper?" she asks with a smile once he releases her.

"My wife," he replies gruffly.

I'm about to swat at him to remind him we're supposed to be convincing his family, but his mother beats me to it. She rears her fist back and socks him in the belly, which causes me to gasp. Her action has Alcott bursting with laughter.

"You went off to London and got married? Without telling your mother?" she scolds.

"Mother, meet my wife, Edith. Edith, meet my mean-as-a-snake mother, Maude," Alexander groans. I don't miss the affectionate tone in his voice though that contradicts his words. He loves her and that has my heart clenching in my chest.

I reach my hand out to shake hers, but she holds her arms open. Her gesture causes an ache in my chest as I long for my own mother. Tears well in my eyes, so I hurry and throw myself into the hug to hide my emotions from her. She smells sweet, like peonies.

"You're a beautiful treasure, dear Edith. We're honored to have you in our family," she whispers into my ear.

A tear rolls out as she strokes my back. I already love this woman. One hug and I don't care if the rest of the family members are nothing but self-gratifying monsters. Maude is the true family jewel, and I cannot wait to learn more about her.

"Please sit beside me, darling," she coos as I pull away. And as any mother would, she notices my being upset and flashes me a look that promises that everything will be okay.

I swipe the tear away and sit in the seat Alexander has pulled out for me. She reaches over and takes my hand, squeezing it in a reassuring way. Her touch is almost hot, and I'm once again reminded of my mother, especially in her last days, when she was so ill.

"Jasper and Elisabeth won't be making it for supper tonight," Alfred informs us. "It appears your sister was feeling exhausted from your travels."

I nod and steal a glance over at Alexander, who has found his seat beside me. He's watching my exchange with his mother with interest.

"Nicolette, we may carry on with dinner," Alfred booms over his shoulder toward the door to the kitchen.

Alexander sighs beside me, and I shoot him a questioning look. He won't meet my gaze, though, because he's too busy sending death looks to his brother, who's wearing a pleased grin. What in the world did I miss?

"Edith darling, we're going to plan a celebration. It simply isn't fair that I missed my eldest son's wedding. We'll hold an elegant reception tomorrow evening. All of our closest friends and family will join us," Maude tells me in a firm tone as she finally releases my hand.

I nod in agreement, but my attention is drawn away from her when a gorgeous woman steps into the dining room carrying two bottles of wine. She's followed by two more older women who are holding trays. Her dress indicates she's the help, but she may as well be royalty, because she doesn't belong in the clothing.

My eyes are drawn to her rather large cleavage, which is bust-ing out the top of the black blouse of her uniform. The top two buttons have been undone, and something about the way she carries herself rubs me the wrong way. Her pink lips curve into a grin when she sees my husband.

Back off, princess.

"Nicolette," Alexander greets with a grumble.

She saunters over to his side, completely ignoring me, and sets the bottles on the table. "Alexander, you look good—*really good.* I've missed you."

With every sugary-sweet word that pours from her mouth, I feel my talons extend. There's clearly a history between these two—*before me*—over which I'm already feeling jealous. They may have some sort of history, but he's mine now.

When she leans down and hugs him, dipping her breasts in front of his face, I lose control.

"Good evening. I'm Alexander's wife," I seethe between clenched teeth.

She jerks back up and stares at me in shock, as if she's seeing me for the first time. Alcott's sniggering from across the table reminds me that I don't, in fact, like him.

"Oh," she says as she eyes me, her blond curls bouncing. "I haven't heard one thing about you." She places a hand on Alexander's shoulder and squeezes it. "Alexander, I had no idea you had settled down. If only I had known you were ready to settle. I would have . . ." her voice trails off with a hint of remorse.

"I'll have some wine now, please," I tell her coldly, reminding her of her place in this house.

Her cheeks redden, and she whips her head over to Alcott as if to ask how to respond to me. He shrugs his shoulders and smirks. I think I like him again.

"Yes, of course," she murmurs in an embarrassed tone.

Alexander glances over at me and shakes his head in disproval. I don't care though. The *maid* should step away from my husband before I push her away.

"I was just in the garden the other day, and the lemon trees were yielding the most beautiful batch of lemons almost ripe for the picking. Perhaps, Edith, tomorrow, we'll pick them and use them in our décor for the reception?" Maude questions, drawing me away from my desire to claw Nicolette's eyeballs out.

Her sweet tone is almost that of how my mother's used to be. She always had an uncanny ability to dissolve arguments between my sisters and me. An ache in my chest seizes me as I regard the woman who reminds me so much of my mother, whom I miss dearly.

"That would be lovely, Maude. Lemons remind me of home. We had many fruit trees in our orchard in the fields behind our house. My sisters and I would get lost for hours picking fruit. A lemon-themed reception sounds perfect, actually." I smile.

She takes my hand again, and something in the way she clenches it makes me think she's proud of my letting Nicolette be. Just like mother would be.

"Darling, call me Ma. Maude is much too formal for you to call me. We're family now," she says with a grin.

With tears filling my eyes, I nod my understanding. We are family, and I somehow already love this woman I've only been with for a matter of minutes.

Chapter Eight

Alexander

PRIDE FILLS MY CHEST WHEN Mother asks Edith to call her Ma. I was temporarily frustrated with her behavior toward Nicolette, but it soon subsided the moment Mother calmed my wife. It fascinated me that Edith, such a strong-willed woman, so easily gave up her fight when it came to my mother.

And my mother, who turned her nose up to every woman who's ever entered my life, seems entirely stricken with Edith. I cannot be any more pleased with the arrangement.

Conversation flowed easily and I found myself utterly intrigued with all that Edith had to say about her life on the farm, her time at university, and some slightly embellished times she and I had together. She was selling her part as my wife quite well. Hell, even I was buying it.

In fact, I wanted it all to be true.

I found myself watching her lips as she spoke, and craving to touch them with my own. When she would laugh, I would close my eyes and revel in the sound of it. And whenever she would touch my hand and draw me into the conversation, my skin would buzz to life.

Edith had managed to enchant not only my family, but me as well. Here we had spent so many months with me ignoring her—never taking the time to get to know her—and this darling of a woman had been there the entire time.

God, I'm such a fool.

No wonder Father always thought ill of me.

Tonight, however, even he appears to be smitten with her wit and charm. I can't help the feeling of pride that washes over me. Edith, my wife, is singlehandedly bridging a gap between my father and me simply by her being herself.

"Shall we have a drink and a smoke in the billiard room?" Father suggests to Alcott and me upon our finishing our supper.

"I think that's a lovely idea, Alfred. Edith and I could use a little one-to-one time. We'll be here while you do your business." Mother smiles at him.

He stands and gives her a peck on her cheek before leaving with Alcott on his heels. Mimicking my father, I rise and lean forward to kiss my wife for show. But when she beams beautifully at me, seemingly pleased at my desire to kiss her, I know that it isn't an act on her part.

The woman with the viper mentality has a vulnerability that shines through every now and again. And though it may be brief, I see it.

I want to see more of it.

Dipping down, I bypass her cheek and brush a soft kiss on her lips. A small sigh escapes her, and I smell a hint of the vintage wine in which we indulged at dinner. The desire to devour her pouty lips is strong, but I would never disrespect my mother. Instead, I pull away and bring my lips to the shell of her ear.

"You're absolutely stunning tonight, Edith. I haven't been able to take my eyes from you most of the night. My hands are eager to caress your sensitive flesh that's hidden under your dress. I'm practically watering at the mouth at the very idea of sampling what

I had the opportunity of pleasuring earlier this afternoon. Dear wife, please let me make good on my promises behind closed doors later," I whisper, my hot breath undoubtedly tickling her ear.

She turns to observe me as if to uncover any hidden tricks. I'm certainly not toying with her in this moment. I very much want to devour her sweet body.

Her eyes flutter closed when I bring my lips to hers once again. The kiss is short and sweet, but with a stroke of my thumb on her heated cheek, I nonverbally convey that I mean every word.

"I'd love that," she murmurs as I pull away.

Behind her, Mother watches us happily. "Now, go away, son. She's mine for the next hour. Then you can carry on your husband duties later, when not in the presence of your mother."

Edith's cheeks blaze, and I shake my head good-naturedly at Mother. My wife doesn't have the honor of knowing my feisty mother just yet, but she soon will.

After a nod to both of them, I stride from the room and down the long corridor toward the billiard room. Before I enter the next room, someone reaches a hand from an open doorway and grabs hold of the lapel of my waistcoat. My fists clench, ready to punch the attacker. When my eyes meet the sultry, blue ones of Nicolette, I relax because she is of no threat to me.

"Alexander." She grins as she tugs me into a pantry lined with jars of food. "I've missed you for so long."

I narrow my gaze at her as anger floods my veins. Alcott and I are going to have a serious conversation about this, because I'm almost certain he has something to do with her employment at our estate.

"How's your father?" I question.

She releases me and folds her arms under her breasts, which causes them to spill out even more. Normally, my gaze would be drawn to them and I'd have my cock pushed into her before even considering the repercussions. But now, being that things have changed between Edith and me, my actions remain paused.

Nicolette and I go way back to our teen years. She was my first kiss. The first woman to put her mouth on my cock. And the woman to whom I lost my virginity. I think, deep down, she's always thought we'd marry one day despite my telling her otherwise. It doesn't help that I toyed with her along the way. Whenever I was feeling lonely or needed to fuck, she was there to service my needs.

But now?

Now, I'm not interested in anything she has to offer. Nicolette is missing something Edith has. And if I'm honest with myself, it has nothing to do with their outward appearances. Nicolette doesn't even carry a small spark in comparison to the blazing personality that is Edith.

Edith infuriates me yet turns me on.

She is crazier than any loon at the asylum, yet I want to keep her as mine.

My wife is average, if you will, in comparison to this exquisite blonde before me, yet I still desire to be with Edith and not Nicolette.

"Father lost his property. The taxes were too much of a burden on him and it was all repossessed. Your father asked how he could be of service to my father. But he didn't want to incur any more debts and instead only asked that he employ me so that I may have a solid roof over my head and food to eat." She frowns after her explanation.

I blink thoughts of Edith away and regard Nicolette, who now has a tears in her eyes. "I'm sorry to hear that," I murmur.

Apparently, Alcott isn't to blame for her sudden appearance, so I drop my guard. She must sense my release of tension, because she throws her arms around my neck. Her lips attempt to find mine, but I turn away.

"Nicolette, that's enough," I bark out. My words are stern, and she gasps as if she's been stung. "I'm a married man now, and it's inappropriate for us to even be alone, much less your being all over me."

"How could you, Alexander?" she demands. "We were supposed to marry! And now? Now, you've gone off and married some plain bore of a woman."

I know she's hurt, but it is the course of our life.

"It's done, dear. There's no changing it. And quite frankly, that 'bore of a woman' has done nothing but entertain my thoughts and my heart for months. I'm quite fond of her. Excuse me. I must be going," I growl.

"Fond, maybe. But love? You can't love her like you love me."

I clench my jaw and spit out my response. "I don't love you."

She attempts to kiss me again, but I push her away easily, as she's a slight woman. Her tears aren't silent as I stalk out of the pantry and toward the billiard room. I hope that Mother and Edith don't hear her hysterics, because I don't want to explain the situation.

"You'll always come back to me Alexander. You always do."

Her last words send a shiver of uncertainty through me.

Unfortunately, she's right.

Can a man really change his ways?

Drinks with my father and brother weren't of interest to me. After my talk with Nicolette, all I could think about was seeing Edith again. To convince myself that I could, in fact, become a changed man.

Now, as I reenter the dining room with them, I'm certain that I can.

Edith tilts her head back and peals of laughter bounce throughout the room as she's entertained by something my mother has said to her. The sound brings a smile upon my lips, and I have the desire to make her laugh more often. When she truly lets herself free of the stiffness she usually hides behind, she's quite a beauty.

I nearly groan aloud as I watch her lick the cream from her spoon. She's quite fond of her sweets after dinner and I am quite fond of watching her devour them. In fact, that was one of the first times I had truly noticed her in a sexual way.

I'm boring her, much like every evening. However, the woman needs to prepare to meet my father. And knowing all that she can about my past and my family will only assist her for their meeting.

"And Alcott went to boarding school in—" I start but am interrupted by her eyes widening.

"Sorry to bother you," the innkeeper chirps as she enters the dining room. "But, I made the absolute most delicious teacake that I insist you both try."

I grunt out my thanks as she sets down a lemon dessert dusted in sugars and then leaves us be. With my spoon, I scoop out a piece of the dessert and catch a glimpse of Edith that causes my dick to go hard.

"Oh my," she moans with closed eyes as she licks the food from the spoon. "This is absolute perfection, Alexander."

I'm gaping at her with my own spoon poised at my lips. Her dark hair tonight has come loose from the pins and stray hairs dangle around her face, making her look less put together and a lot more stunning than usual. I have the urge to tug it all loose and run my fingers through it. And then—then I want to kiss her mouth that is the cause of many dirty thoughts running through my head at the moment.

Why in the fuck do I have the urge to kiss Edith of all people?

I shovel in the bite of the cake to distract me from my thoughts and scrunch up my nose in disgust. The dessert is way too sweet for my liking.

"I've had better," I growl.

Her eyes pop open and she eyes me incredulously. "You're mad! This is the most delicious thing I have ever tasted, Alexander. I could lick up every morsel and never be satisfied for I would always crave more."

Now, my dick is throbbing from her words. All I can do is stare at her mouth and envision it were me she wished to taste instead. She shakes her head and spoons another bite into her mouth—a mouth that I'm suddenly noticing and really fucking wanting. Full pink lips press against the utensil in her valiant effort not to miss a crumb and I have to tear my gaze from them.

"I understand why it is that you have so many lovers," I smirk and shove my dessert across the table toward her.

She grins at me as she pulls it over to her. "Oh, do you now?"

"Your mouth."

Her cheeks blaze and she ignores my comment. Instead of responding, she devours the dessert and I hungrily stare at her while she does it.

"Countess? Shall I wait for you in your room?" a husky, masculine voice booms from behind me.

Anger flares in my chest because I know this man is calling upon my wife and her mouth. A mouth that by contract belongs to me. A mouth I should indulging upon.

"Are we finished for the evening?" she questions as she stands.

Her lips are once again pursed together primly and indifference is painted all over her features. Clearly, I stupidly allowed my cock to think I actually wanted this woman.

"Yes."

Problem was, I did want her. And that evening when the fool was fucking her, I tossed and turned in my own bed with my pillow wrapped around my head in an effort to tune out her moans. Moans that had my cock thick and ready to go. In the end, I stroked myself until I came and dreamt about that sweet mouth of hers.

"Edith, I'm feeling quite tuckered out from our day. I think we should retire for the evening." My memory has me wanting to drag her back to our quarters while ripping her clothes off along the way.

At that time, back at the inn, I had chosen not to have her. However, tonight, I will be having *all* of her. I wink at her in a way that I hope she interprets.

She bats her eyelashes at me and nods, fully understanding the meaning behind my words. "Of course, darling."

I begin walking toward her as she and my mother stand. But my attention is drawn from her as Mother's face turns white and she wobbles.

"Mother!" I gape in horror as my mother crumples to the floor.

Edith is the first to crouch beside her. "Ma! Are you okay? What's wrong?" she sobs. Hysteria builds in my wife's voice, and I can't say that I don't feel the same way.

Father and I flank the other side of Mother almost immediately after Edith.

"Alcott, call for Dr. Nubert," Father instructs as he scoops her into his arms.

She comes to and looks around in confusion. "W-what happened?"

Father's jaw clenches as he holds back emotion on his normally steeled features. "You fainted, sweetheart. How are you feeling? Your skin is warm."

Her mystification dissolves as color resumes on her cheeks. "Oh, Alfred, I must have just had a dizzy spell. I'm sure I'll be fine. I would prefer to lie down though."

He begins to stride from the room with my mother in his arms, but she swats at him.

"Alfred, put me down. I'm not a porcelain doll to be carried around as if I'm fragile. I can walk."

My father growls with a possessive protectiveness I no doubt inherited. "You most certainly will not walk. I'll carry you to bed. The doctor can see you from there."

"I'm sorry, children. Edith, please join me for breakfast on the back porch in the morning. Invite your sister and we'll enjoy the sunrise together. The view there is magnificent," Mother chirps in her usual tone.

Since her demeanor is back to normal, I release the breath I was holding as I stand. "Goodnight, Mother. Edith, come, darling."

Father leaves the room with my mother, and Edith stares after them, still sitting on the floor. When she finally looks up at me, her face is stained with tears.

"Will she be okay?" she questions with a wobble in her voice.

I reach down with both hands, and she accepts them with her own.

"She'll be just fine. My mother is a fighter through and through. Where do you think I got my winning personality from?" I tease as I pull her to her feet. "Certainly not my father."

A small giggle escapes her as I sling an arm over her shoulder and tug her against me. It feels right to have her close to me.

"She's a lovely lady. I'm so worried about her," she murmurs as we walk.

The fact that she speaks so fondly of my mother unlocks something inside me. I want her to love my mother and my mother to love her. It's upon this moment that I realize I am truly delighted to have Edith as a part of my family.

Our stroll back to our wing is quiet, and with each step toward our bedroom, I find myself growing with desire to make love to her.

Not fucking like earlier.

Lovemaking.

It's out of character for me, but I want to kiss her decadent lips as I thrust into her tight body. I want our bodies to remain connected as our souls bond.

The moment we enter our room, my thoughts are interrupted by sniffling.

"What is it, Edith?"

She lifts her head to gaze at me with tears in her eyes. "She reminds me of my own mother. When she fainted, I thought about how my mother became ill with cholera and was taken so quickly from us. I'm horrified that maybe God is punishing me for what a wretched woman I've been and taking out the people I love as retribution for my actions."

I tug her to me and shake my head. "Dear, you aren't being punished. Besides, I have it on good authority that you're far from the wretched woman you claim to be. I think you're quite unique and you're all mine."

Her lips turn up into the smallest of smiles. "You can be rather sweet when you want to be."

Leaning forward, I graze my lips across hers. "If sweet is rewarded with your smiles, then I shall be nothing but sugar and candy while in your presence."

A sigh momentarily rushes from her before I seize her lips. I taste her, and she tastes every bit as delicious as the candy of which I spoke. Then her mouth parts and she meets my kiss with fervor of her own.

My cock thickens between us with each whimper that escapes her throat. When she jerks away with haste, I groan in frustration and have the urge to attack her lips again.

"Alexander," she says softly. Then her cheeks redden as if she's embarrassed to say whatever is on her mind.

"Speak, woman. I have many events planned for us this evening. Events where my mouth is the appreciative audience and your body is the deserving star."

Her eyes slam shut as she considers my words, but they fly back open when she resolves to say what's on the tip of her tongue. "You hurt my feelings earlier today," she rushes out in a whisper.

That bottom lip of hers, which I so crave, quivers uncontrollably. Dipping down, I still it with a soft kiss to it. After I kiss her, I pull away to look into her eyes.

"How did I hurt your feelings, lovely?"

Now, she chews on her lip before speaking her words. "You

fucked me as if I were your toy. And then you left me. I felt alone and unwanted. My heart broke, Alexander. You broke it."

I stare at her, incredulous. "Did you not enjoy our lovemaking?"

She frowns, "There was no love being made. Yes, you pleasured me. But did I enjoy it? No."

My brow furrows at her words. Not once has any lover of mine not enjoyed what I gave to them. Why is it that Edith claims she did not?

"But you came from my fingers and then again with me inside you. How is it that you didn't enjoy yourself?" I ask in astonishment. I'm completely dumbfounded by her words.

"You're missing the point. We didn't connect. It was purely physical. I desire more from you, Alexander. I absolutely need to feel wanted and loved by you," she admits.

I stare at her as her face morphs into a resolved expression. It took a minute for her mind and body to stand behind the words of her heart. After lifting a hand to her cheek, I stroke her gently.

"I'm not sure that I know how to make this connection of which you speak," I confess.

This time, her lips quirk up on one side, and I'm reminded of the feisty woman with whom I began this journey. Edith is so multifaceted, like that of a perfect jewel. I do believe I've uncovered one in a million.

"Well, I had hoped we could figure it out together," she says seductively as she hooks her hands into the collar of my waistcoat and pushes it off my shoulders.

It falls to the floor in a crumple, and I cock an eyebrow at her. "What if I'm not exactly a master at this lovemaking?"

"The mere fact that you're willing to try is enough, husband."

Chapter Nine

Edith

HE NARROWS HIS GAZE AND scrutinizes me as if my words hold another meaning than that which I've said. Finally, he relaxes his features and presses a kiss to my forehead. When he pulls away, his normally hardened features seem soft.

"I'm sorry if I treated you in an ill manner this afternoon. I assure you that wasn't my intention, love. You're special to me. Precious, even. I don't understand it because it is out of my normal character. As you well know, I'm a man who can hardly be tethered to one woman. Yet, with you, I feel as if I'm drawn to you like a fly to honey. Your magnetism allures me in a way that confuses me. But I crave it nonetheless."

His words thread themselves inside me and latch themselves on. For once, I have hope for something more—something authentic for myself. That tiny sliver may as well be as thick as a sailor's rope, because I desperately hold on to it as if it will save me from drowning in my own misery.

"You're beautiful, Edith," he murmurs as he drags his fingers along the front of my breasts, over my dress, and down my sides to my hips. "You have a natural, simple beauty about you, but when you dress like this, you're absolutely exquisite."

I let his praise wash over me and reward him with a smile. The man can be quite a romantic when he wants to be. I'm starting to understand why he was the ladies' man prior to our coming to Havering.

He's now a one-lady man.

My man.

"I didn't think you noticed," I admit with a small smile. "Alcott noticed at dinner, but it seemed that you looked right through me instead of looking at me."

He growls at the mention of his brother. "He'll do best to not notice you ever again. You're mine, Edith. Mine."

My skin flushes at the possessive way he claims me with his words. I lift my hands to the buttons of his dress shirt and begin undoing them. His hands simultaneously tug at the ribbon on both sides of my dress. As soon as he unties them, the material loosens and sags away from my body. Then I drop my arms to my sides and the dress falls to a heap on the floor.

"This corset will be the death of me," he grumbles almost angrily.

But I know he isn't angry. Far from it. He's turned on by the sight of me in it, and that turns me on. I feel my arousal dampen my knickers and wish to rid my body of them.

"Sounds like such a simple death," I muse.

He chuckles as his lips find my neck. "There is nothing simple about this corset and you in it."

I gasp when his hands find my arse and he squeezes gently. My knickers are ruined by the way he suckles on my neck—it causes my body to drip with need. When he pulls away and begins working the ribbons on the corset, I watch his face. Determination furrows his dark eyebrows together as he sets to further undressing me. The moment the corset falls away, his eyes widen and his lips curve into a half smile.

"Your breasts are absolute perfection, Edith."

I smile and tease him. "Perhaps, if you hadn't been in such a rush earlier, you could have properly enjoyed them."

"I'm an ignorant man, dear. Please allow me to make up for my foolish ways. I want to mark your pale flesh. I want your breasts to be bruised and tender from the delicate assault I plan on inflicting with my mouth."

As if to prove his words, he kneels before me and wriggles out of his shirt. Once he's tossed it to the floor and awarded me the view of his sculpted chest, he grabs hold of my hips and hauls me to him.

Pulses of desire course though me at having him in such a position that he seems to be worshipping my body. The moment his lips connect with the skin of my belly, I whimper. As he sprinkles soft kisses along my abdomen, his hands find my breasts and he cups them reverently. When his thumbs skim over my hardened nipples, I cry out.

"Are you wet for me, dear Edith? Do you want me to pleasure every inch of your body?"

I thrust my breasts into his face and thread my fingers into his thick, brown hair. "Yes. Do it. I need you to love my body with your mouth."

His tongue flicks out and he tastes one of my nipples. The sensation is almost too much to bear.

"I cannot pleasure you the way I want from the floor, wife. Remove your knickers and shoes. I need you bare and open to me. I'm simply holding on by a thread from ravishing you completely," he murmurs, his hot breath tickling me.

When I don't move, he grabs my knickers and yanks them down.

"Oh!"

"Oh is right," he growls. "Now, get naked and onto the bed."

I kick out of my shoes and then flash him a saucy grin as I sashay over to the bed, giving him an irresistible view of my arse, which is wiggling just for him.

"Goddammit," he curses. "Could your body be any more perfect?"

I smile at his praise and crawl onto the bed. Lying down on my back, I steal a glance at my husband. He's pushing his trousers down, and his erect cock bobs heavily out. My pelvic area physically aches with need as I know that, soon, he'll fill me to the hilt with his sheer size.

When he reaches the end of the bed and hoists himself onto it, I nearly melt from the anticipation of him touching me. This man, my husband, is the most exquisite man I've had the pleasure of being with. His body is simply a piece of artwork with its chiseled lines. I could easily view it for hours and be wildly entertained.

He smirks. "Something funny?"

I give in to the giggles of imagining him on display for my own personal viewing. "N-n-no."

His eyebrows pinch together as if he's angry, but his lips draw up into a breathtaking smile. "Woman, you lie. You're laughing at me. What is it? You haven't seen a cock as impressive as mine before?"

His words only serve as fuel to the fire of my laughter, and tears roll down my cheeks.

"You're in trouble now," he growls playfully as his body pins mine.

His strong hands grip my wrists, and he holds me firmly against the bed. I can feel said impressive cock pressed against me, and I can't help but wriggle against him, hoping it will push its way inside me.

When his lips capture mine, the laughter melts away. The kiss is powerful and possessive. I relish in the way he tangles his tongue with mine as if they were always meant to dance this way. All jokes are tossed aside as we lose ourselves in each other.

"Make love to me," I gasp between kisses.

He's heavily pressed against me, so the moment he lifts some of his weight, I slip my legs out and wrap them around his hips. My husband isn't one to waste a moment, and within seconds, he pushes his massive cock with one hard thrust into me.

"Alexander!" I scream at the joyous sensation of being stretched fully by his thickness.

"My God, your body fits like a glove," he hums against my lips.

I love the way he crushes me with his strength. It would be my desire to stay connected with him this way all day without another care in the world.

One of his hands cradles my cheek as he pounds slowly into me. "Dearest Edith, I like this—this lovemaking of which you speak. I feel my soul tethering itself to yours. The very idea of being tied down used to terrify me, but right now, in this moment, there's not another soul on the planet I would choose other than you."

A tear rolls out as his words cut open my heart and insert themselves inside. It is my hope that his words are true and honest, because I so desperately want to believe in them.

"This feels right, Alexander," I whimper as his thrusts become harder. "How were we so lucky? Two people lost in a world only to find solace and companionship in someone just as fractured as they are. I think destiny has played a hand in our union."

My words are stolen from me as I feel the delicious beginnings of an orgasm. Then it clutches my abdomen and explodes throughout my body. I buck up from the bed as I lose myself to it. Nothing exists in our world but him and me.

"My love," he groans as he bursts his own hot climax into me.

His thrusting slows to a halt, and he lifts slightly to regard me with sexually satisfied eyes. But behind the satisfaction lies something else. An emotion I feel with every ounce of my being.

Dare I say that the emotion is love? I want to ask him but I don't dare sever the moment of our blissful union. I've had many lovers in my lifetime, but nothing compares to the way Alexander encompasses me fully.

He's my ending. My happy ending.

I—Edith, the horrid home-wrecker—have somehow found myself with luck and captured the beautiful man before her.

"Is it unusual that I find myself wanting to remain locked within you, only staring into your eyes for the rest of the night? Does it make me a perverted fool to want to keep my cock seated inside you even as it relaxes?" he questions with a grin that does me in every time.

"We must be unusual birds, the only two in our flock, because I don't find it perverse at all. In fact, I find it highly arousing. My body tingles at the prospect of you sleeping with me tucked beneath you. I feel quite safe and protected in your arms."

He dips down and places a kiss on my nose. "I'll always protect you, Edith. We may have begun this marriage as a sham, but there is nothing false about my feelings for you. Tomorrow, I hope that you have the most breathtaking reception for our wedding, because you do, indeed, deserve that. Allow my mother to spoil you as I know she will. And then I shall spend the rest of my life spoiling you as I wish. You're mine to cherish, my precious jewel."

Thoughts of his mother once again bring tears to my eyes. "Are you sure Ma is going to be all right? I'm sick with worry about her."

His stare becomes firm as he looks me over. "Darling, she will be more than okay. I promise. Nothing is going to happen to her. Mother is as tough as they come. She's the paste that holds this broken family together. Without her, my father and brother and I would have parted ways long ago. We stay, though, because of her."

My eyes flutter shut when his lips find mine again, and he kisses me as if to solidify his promise with it. I cling to it, because once again, I hope that his words are true and I can trust in them.

If Alexander ever becomes bored of me like his past lovers, I'll die. Plain and simple.

"I can feel myself growing hard inside you. How is it that I'm already eager to make more of this love with you? Under normal circumstances, my body requires rest. Alone. But now, I want to take you again and then I want to rest with you in my arms, dear. You've bewitched me, I believe. However, I'm your willing victim."

I giggle as he begins thrusting at an agonizingly slow pace within me. "Husband, you best be hastening your speed. Because, if you keep it up with your teasing, you'll be a victim for sure—a victim of having been smothered by a pillow."

He slams himself into me hard enough to make me scream his name again. "So my sweet wife loves the slow but she also loves the hasty fucking as well? Am I right, love?"

My words are garbled as he takes me roughly. He's right. I'll take him any way and at the moment, I'm quite content at the way he owns my body.

When I don't answer him, his mouth finds my earlobe and he nips at it with his teeth.

"Yes, Alexander. I like it when your lovemaking is turbulent as well. Take me hard," I instruct as my nails dig into his shoulders.

The moan that rings out into the room is almost embarrassing when he forcefully sucks my neck into his mouth.

"I'm going to impregnate you with my children," he announces unexpectedly.

I'm too far into the throes of passion to do anything other than nod emphatically. "Yes," I agree and then give in to another all-consuming orgasm.

The thought of becoming a mother has always been a dream of mine. But hearing it aloud that he, my husband, wants me to be pregnant with his child washes through me, and I'm cloaked in the joy of his proclamation.

He grunts and unloads more of his seed into me. As he settles and relaxes, he once again makes no moves to sever our physical connection. Unlike my lovers in the past, he slides his arms beneath me and hugs me tight. My hands slip into his hair and I hold him to me.

"Don't ever let me go," I murmur as I begin to drift to sleep.

His voice is thick with sleepiness but firm. "I'll never let you go. It isn't an option. You're mine until the end, Edith Dumont."

Chapter Ten

Alexander

THE SUN HASN'T RISEN YET, but I'm awake. And watching her. After last night, I'm completely enthralled with the way she's managed to seize my heart. If someone had told me a couple of days ago that I'd be falling for the vixen of a woman with whom I started this journey, I'd have laughed.

But now?

Now, I can't take my eyes from her. It satisfies me to watch her breaths softly come out and see the tiny smile that twitches at her lips from time to time. I'm not sure what's made me this way—so eager to devour every detail that is her.

At some point in the middle of the night, she must have removed the pins from her hair, because now, it lies wild and unruly beneath her. The desire to tangle my fingers in it as I make love to her is strong.

What is it about this woman that draws me in so?

"Mmm," she whimpers in her sleep.

The sound sends swirls of want directly to my cock and it thickens in response. During the night, we made love countless times, yet now, I still crave to be inside her. The woman has simply infected my brain, and I can't say that I'm complaining one bit.

Sitting up on my elbow, I drag a finger across her bare breast and circle the nipple in a soft manner that doesn't wake her. Her body must be exhausted from our exertions. I take pause with my movements and wonder if I can stay true to her and not sleep with other women. I know I've promised her this, but it seems against the very fabric of who I am.

Her lips pucker into the cutest of pouts. It's as if she's clued in to my very thoughts. And as the craving to kiss her threatens to rip me in two, I know. There's no way I'll ever want another like I want her.

That is simply fact.

It's guaranteed that I won't let another man even so much as look at her—especially Alcott. It will be a man's death wish if he is to gaze upon what's mine.

I would kill a man for this woman.

That is also fact.

My feelings for her are overwhelming to me and they grow stronger by the second. Dear God, I hope she feels the same way for me.

"Alexander," she murmurs as she turns toward me.

I expect to see her big, brown eyes, but she's still sleeping. An alpha response to the knowledge of the fact that she dreams of me too possesses me, and I nearly growl in satisfaction.

My hand finds her hip and I glide my thumb across the bone. Soon, I hope to see her fatten up with pregnancy. I want the evidence of our love all over her body, especially in the form of a largely swollen belly.

Do I love her?

I think that, on some level, I already have for the past six months. It's as if I always knew deep down that it would come down to this—our being inseparable. And that's how it will be because I don't want her to leave my side. In fact, if I had it my way, we'd stay in this bed forever.

"I believe I love you, dear Edith," I whisper so soft that she can't hear.

But in her slumber, I ascertain that she does hear, because her lips twitch again in that smile I've grown to adore.

My cock begs for me to wake her up, but I don't want to. I want to freeze the moment at hand and bottle it up for eternity. This must be the wedded bliss Jasper of which speaks so fondly.

I'm lost in my thoughts when a petite hand grips my cock. When my eyes fly to her face, I find her grinning at me. She blinks slowly, as if to rid herself of her sleep, and I have a new favorite moment—watching her wake up.

God, she's so beautiful.

"Good morning, dear wife." I dip down and kiss her lips with a peck before lifting back up so I can look at her.

"Is it morning already?" she questions in confusion but never stops the fisting of my cock.

"Indeed, it is. In fact, the sun shall rise soon."

At my words, she jerks up into a sitting position. "Damn! I promised your mother I'd meet her for breakfast before daybreak," she shrieks.

She's about to spring from the bed, but I grab her arm and haul her to me. Her legs instinctively straddle my hips, and the worry melts away. Something else takes its place.

"Someone is quite awake and frisky this morning," she giggles as she rocks her hips, causing her pussy to rub against my cock.

"Woman, if you have any desire to meet my mother today, I suggest you stop your teasing and fuck me," I growl.

Her eyes narrow as if she has something up her sleeve and my eyebrow raises in question.

"You want me to fuck you, hmm?" she purrs.

Everything about that sentence drives me to the brink of insanity. I need to be inside her nearly as badly I need to breathe.

"Can a countess properly fuck an earl, or will it always be the other way around?" I taunt.

She throws me a sexy wink before grabbing my cock. I watch with hunger as she aligns herself with me and sinks down onto my length. It feels borderline sinful to have her sitting on me, me deep inside her. Her breasts are on full display, and I gaze at them in awe.

"What do you call this?" she questions as she begins circling her hips in a teasing pattern that makes my cock throb.

I'm at a loss for words when she tosses her head back and cups her own breasts. With each rhythmic rocking of her hips, I feel myself about to come.

"Mmm," she moans as she rides me as if I'm her favorite horse.

"Countess, you fuck like a goddess. You make me insane for you. It is through my own carnal thoughts that I assume I'm the one who owns you as my wife, yet as you perform your magic on me, I swear you're the one who owns me."

I am useless as she fucks me into oblivion, so I slip my thumb between her thighs and stroke her clitoris, which I find beneath her thatch of dark hair. It is warm, throbbing as if it requires my touch. The very idea that her body responds to mine ignites the selfish desire to possess her, and I once again take over the reins of ownership as I pleasure her.

"Yes!" she cries out.

Her body shudders as she clenched around my cock, and it causes me to explode inside her. Then we both groan out in unison as we come together. When the high of our bliss finally subsides, I grab her biceps and tug her to me. I want her plastered against my chest.

"Stay," I beg as I stroke her hair.

When she sighs, I know she wants to. "I can't. I already promised Ma. The rest of the day, though, can be about us. If you want to stay in here, we'll stay in here. If you want to go for a walk or have lunch by the river, I'm certainly happy with that idea as well. I'm yours after breakfast."

Her lips find mine and she kisses me as if she wants to assure me she isn't going to be gone for long.

"You're mine always," I grumble once she breaks away.

She rolls her eyes as she climbs off me. I see a flash of her pussy as it drips with my release, and I'm half tempted to drive myself back into her.

"You're such a man," she says in faux annoyance.

I sit up on my elbow and watch as she saunters toward the washroom, her arse jiggling slightly with each step. "A man you love," I chuckle.

She flicks her gaze over to me, and her cheeks turn red. Then she bolts into the washroom and closes the door behind her.

What did I say?

The punching bag swings back toward me, and I pummel it some more with my fists, which are wrapped in the cloths I use for boxing. I've lost myself to my actions so much that I don't realize that someone has entered the room until a voice speaks.

"So this is what you do," Alcott chuckles. "What? The wife make you angry? Need to take it out on the bag instead of Edith to keep up appearances? We all know your wedding is a farce."

I whip my head up and sweat flings off my hair with the action. "Our wedding is not a farce, and I would never strike my wife."

"I'm only teasing, brother."

But he's not and we both know it.

"Why are you here?" I snarl.

"I wanted to discuss a matter of business with you," he begins. "Since, clearly, you're sticking to your story about Edith and you being happily married, then we need to discuss alternatives."

"Alternatives to what?" I grumble as I begin punching the bag again.

"To your inheritance, of course."

I pause and stare at him, incredulous. "Father is doing quite well, it would seem. I won't be inheriting anything for probably another ten years or more. Why is it that you're so concerned about my inheritance? Do you wish to off me in my sleep and run away with my bride?" The very idea of him touching my wife has me clenching my fists.

"Edith? No. Offing you? Maybe?" he says in jest. His dark orbs twinkle with mischief, and I'm reminded of when we were children—when I actually liked my little brother.

"Get to the point, Alcott. What is it that you want?"

"I'm weary from waiting on an inheritance on which I may never have my hands. I am still young and have my life ahead of me. I don't want to wait on this estate for half of my family to die. Instead, I want to go abroad, much like you did, and enjoy the world. I've even approached Father about lending me some money to start my own business in London. However, he's made it clear that my place is here on the estate and to not bother him again about the matter. So it is my desire to create my own future, because the one destined to me as a second-born is bleak."

I fold my arms across my bare chest and glare at him. "How does this involve me? I just told you I'm not receiving my inheritance for at least another decade."

He smiles. "I overhead Father speaking to Mother about gifting you and Edith some of your inheritance early so that you may start a home of your own. It is in honor of your wedding that they would bestow such a gift. My request is that you lend me a portion to start my company. You could be the sole benefactor, and once I begin making my earnings, I could pay you back with interest."

His desires seem genuine, and I ponder his words.

"So, that's what this is about? You're not set on destroying my marriage to Edith to ruin me in front of Father?" I question in disbelief.

He frowns at me as if he's disappointed. "Brother, you think so ill of me. I'm not as cold and calculating as you would believe. I have desires and wishes for my future much like you do. It is my hope to find a wife to love and bear my children one day. I think I deserve a happy life, too, despite my birth order. Staying on this estate until the day I die makes me feel as if I'm a caged animal when I was born to run free."

"I suppose that, if Father were to gift me the money, we could make arrangements for you to borrow a portion of it," I agree with hesitation. "But if this is some ruthless trick, I swear to you, Alcott, I'll kill you. I'm finally at peace with my life now that I've found Edith. I love her, and I don't intend on losing her or my rightful place in this family."

His face breaks into a grin. "No tricks up my sleeve, Alexander. Thank you for your generosity. I promise to not fail you, and you'll soon have the return on your investment plus a healthy interest payment." Then he gives me a nod and strides from the room.

Is it possible that, finally, I may relax in this life? That, finally, I have more than I could ever ask for? Something deep inside, though, begs me not to let my guard truly down. Everything seems too perfect—Alcott's attempting to befriend me, my parents' accepting Edith so easily, and my loving Edith.

What happens if it all comes crashing down on me?

The very thought of losing Edith causes rage to bubble in my chest. I proceed to pound the bag as if I could absolutely beat my insecurities into submission.

Chapter Eleven

Edith

"YOU MISSED THE SUNRISE," MA chides as I step out onto the porch.

My gaze travels along the expansive deck that overlooks the river and eventually lands on Ma and Elisabeth, who are sitting at a small table. Elisabeth avoids my gaze as she sets to stirring her tea as if she doesn't even realize I've arrived.

"I'm sorry. I, uh, was tied up with Alexander," I stammer out.

When I finally meet Ma's stare, she's beaming at me. "That boy has a way of demanding one's attention. You should have known him when he was two and then again when he was in his teen years," she chuckles.

I grin, imagining a small boy with a mop of messy, brown hair, wearing suspenders, and tugging on his mother's dress as he begs her for a lollipop. It reminds me of his words—that he wants me to bear his children. The very thought of sweet, little boys who look just like Alexander running around is almost as satisfying as it actually happening.

Almost.

Now, I crave the real thing more than anything.

"I do apologize," I say as I sit between her and Elisabeth. "Lissa, we missed you at supper last night."

She finally looks over at me and nods. "I was ill. Do forgive me."

When she looks back down, I sneak a glance at Ma, who is observing our exchange. I feel as though this breakfast will be uncomfortable, and it's confirmed when Ma bluntly calls out the obvious unease between my sister and I.

"My sister, Magdalene, and I were very close. In fact, I helped deliver her first child when her husband was away on business. She was my confidant and my friend. Even after we both married, we spoke often and drove our husbands mad with our incessant giggling." She smiles at the memory. "But then, one day, we had a disagreement. She accused my Alcott of forcing himself on her daughter. My boys were as rowdy as they come, and I can always sniff out their lies, but Alcott was adamant that he wouldn't do such a thing to his cousin. As it turns out, my niece was seeing a boy of whom her father didn't approve. When they caught a glimpse of a man sneaking out her window, she threw herself into hysterics and claimed it was my son. Of course, they had her examined by a doctor and discovered she was no longer a virgin. They had taken her word without considering there could be an alternative story."

Elisabeth and I are both completely enraptured in her story, and we wait for her to continue.

"Our families were divided. I stood by my son's word and she hated me for it. Two years went by and we didn't speak. When I would see her in town and attempt to approach her, she would glare at me and take off in the other direction. Eventually, I gave up on attempting to clear my son's name."

"So, you lost your sister over a misunderstanding?" I blurt out. I know that Elisabeth hates me for what I've done, but not ever speaking to her again breaks my heart.

When I risk a glance at my sister, I find her eyeing me warily. So I smile at her in such a way that begs for forgiveness. We hold each other's gaze until Ma speaks again.

"Nearly, darling. It wasn't until my niece turned up pregnant by the boy her family disapproved of. The very idea that she was carrying the child of a simple man who worked at the mill despite their own family's higher social class was the talk of the town. I felt bad for them and sent my sister a letter. In the letter, I reminded her that we were still sisters and, if she needed someone to confide in, I was still here."

"What did she say?" I question.

Ma purses her lips together. "She wrote back and told me that she was thankful for the sentiment and the offer but she had to decline. There was also a small apology stating that her daughter finally came clean and confessed that the boy from the mill was her only lover. Alcott never touched a hair on her body, much like I already knew."

"So you two forgave each other and worked through your problems," I state with hope filling my voice.

Ma glances at Elisabeth and then at me. Her eyes fill with tears before she blinks them away. "No, that was not the case. I'd been planning to visit her in an attempt to rekindle our relationship. It was as I was packing that I was informed of the fire."

I gape at her, and when I turn, I see Elisabeth doing the same. Out of habit, I reach across and take my sister's hand to comfort her. She accepts my hand, and I squeeze it.

"Dear girls, the fire consumed her entire family. Later, it was determined the boy from the mill was so distraught that her family had refused to let her marry him. In an effort to eradicate them so they could run away together, he burned their estate to the ground. But he hadn't expected my niece to be inside, as she was supposed to be waiting for him at his home. At the last minute, she had gone to warn her family and was taken by the fire as well. The boy from the mill took his life that night. It was all a tragedy."

Elisabeth and I can no longer hold our sobs in. She clutches my hand, and it reminds me when I had to hold both her and Ella for countless nights after our mother died.

"My point, beautiful girls, is that no grudge is worth holding on to. I loved my sister, and events put a wedge between us. But they weren't events that were more important than the love we shared. We made mistakes, but in the end, I still loved her. And I know she loved me. Our last moments were stolen from us, and I'd do anything to get them back. Elisabeth, I'm sorry for what Edith has done to you. It may seem unforgiveable, but it's not. She is your sister.

"Edith is very much in love with my son, much like you are with Jasper. The William you told me of earlier was just as much to blame. I know that the betrayal you feel from your sister is too much to bear. Believe me—I was in your shoes. However, it is mud in the water now. You two still have the rest of your lives to mend this relationship. Soon, you'll have babies, and it will be important to have your sister's support. Please promise me that you'll learn to forgive and let love back into your heart."

Ma is simply an angel.

I turn toward Elisabeth and tearfully state my piece. "Dear sister, I am so sorry for what I did to you. It was awful, and I'll always feel the guilt of it in my heart. But know this—I never stopped loving you. After Mother passed, I wanted to protect you and care for you like she had. Clearly, I fell short and lost my way. Please give me another chance. I'm not the same person I was during those times. When Mother died, a piece of my heart became jagged and ugly. Alexander has helped mend my heart. I want you to know that I am truly sorry and I want nothing more than your forgiveness, Lissa."

Elisabeth sniffles and dabs her red nose with her handkerchief. "You broke my heart, Edith. I looked up to you."

I nod. "I know and I'm so sorry."

She purses her lips together but finally flashes me a small smile. "I have been bursting at the seams with wanting to tell you all about this pregnancy. It was my hope that we could shop together and find things for the baby. Each time I go to speak to you, I have to remind myself I'm angry with you, and then I'm only angry with myself. I'm tired of fighting. I want my sister back."

The words are barely out of her mouth before I leap from my seat and launch myself at her. We hug like we used to and cry like a couple of babies. When our sniffling subsides, I slide my palm over her swollen belly and feel my niece or nephew like I've been dying to since the moment I discovered she was pregnant.

Her baby moves in her belly and we giggle. Then I finally break away to take my seat and see that Ma is no longer smiling. Her face is ashen, and her mouth is slightly hanging open.

"Ma!" I scream as I collect her in my arms when she begins to fall from her chair. "Lissa, get help!"

Elisabeth scurries off as I hold Ma up from falling into the floor. Tears stream down my cheeks as I mutter reassurances to her.

"Stay with me, Ma. Wake up!"

Several moments later, she flutters her eyelids and blinks them open. "Darling," she purrs as she lifts a shaky hand to swipe a stray hair out of my face. "Why are you crying?"

I squeeze her to me and sob into her chest. "You fainted again. What is going on with you?"

She pats my back but doesn't answer. We stay glued to one another until we hear a collection of stomping feet toward us. I'm suddenly pulled from her as Alfred takes her in his arms. Then I find myself tight in Alexander's embrace. He's recently bathed again, and he smells like the lavender soap that we found in the washroom. His scent comforts me and I snuggle my face into his chest to inhale him.

"Shhh. Don't cry beautiful," he coos as he strokes my hair.

His presence is soothing, but my worry for Ma doesn't dissipate. "What's wrong with her, Alexander? We can't lose her too!"

"We're not going to lose her. Alcott, alert me of the doctor's findings. I'm going to take Edith to our room—she is a bit distraught," he calls out over my shoulder. Then he slides an arm beneath me and scoops me into his arms.

I rest my cheek on his shoulder as he carries me to our room. I'm lost in thought as he walks and don't completely rid myself of my daze until he sits me down on our bed.

"Did you eat anything?" he questions as he crosses his arms over his chest.

Warmth surges through me as understanding hits me. This man cares deeply for my wellbeing. His mother is ill, yet here he is fussing over if I've eaten or not.

"I managed a little," I lie.

He cocks a dark eyebrow at me. "Edith, the corner of your mouth twitches when you fib. You'll never be able to trick me. I'll bring you something to eat. Until then, get comfortable and lie down."

I scrunch up my nose at having been caught.

He chuckles. "Do as you're told, woman."

Before I can argue, he strides from the room, his laughter echoing down the hallway with him. If he weren't so good-looking, I could be angry with him for being such a smug arse. Luckily for him, I've seen him naked and I know that his cock has the uncanny ability to make me forgive him.

The moment I'm alone, I shed myself of my clothes and climb on top of the bed. I'm lying on the bed, tracing patterns along the duvet with my finger when Alexander reenters the room carrying a tray. When I hear the dishes rattle, I glance up and see that he's glaring at me.

"What?" I question with concern. My thoughts immediately go to Ma.

"You. I can't think straight around you—especially when you distract me with your naked flesh. You've afflicted my mind, wife."

I smile at his words and sit up as he places the tray on the bed. It's filled with pastries and fruit. We both chuckle when my stomach growls at seeing the foods.

"I passed by Alcott on the way back, and apparently, Mother is doing well. He was on his way to the garden with a large basket to fill it with lemons for her. She'd already created a rather long list of chores he is to complete before our reception this evening. If he weren't such an insufferable idiot, I might have felt sorry for him," he laughs. Then he sits down beside the tray and watches me as I begin devouring a small cake.

"I'm glad she is well. I hope the doctor will treat her accordingly for her symptoms," I tell him with a worried tone. "It isn't natural for her to faint so often."

He nods in agreement as he picks a strawberry up by the green stem and brings it to his lips. My chewing halts, and I swallow my food down as his lips surround the fruit and he bites into it. A small, pink dribble of juice rolls down his chin, and I do exactly what feels right. Leaning in, I drag my tongue along his stubbly face and lick him clean.

When I pull away, his eyes are clouded and seemingly angry.

"What?" I ask with feigned innocence. The bulge in his trousers indicates what I've done is far from innocent.

"Lie back. Now," he growls as he picks up another strawberry.

With a cocked eyebrow and a smirk on my lips, I do as instructed. His eyes peruse my body, not missing an inch of my flesh. When they land on the small pelt of hair at my pubic bone, I spread my knees apart and award him the rest of the view I know he wants to see.

"My God, woman." His voice is gruff and one would almost think annoyed. But I know better. He's very much aroused by my body.

He brings the strawberry down to my belly button and trails it all around in circles with no pattern. It tickles, yet it also turns me on. I feel myself becoming increasingly wet as I wish for him to bring the fruit lower. I'm not exactly sure what I want him to do with it, but this teasing is simply not enough.

"Alexander," I whine.

He lifts a dark eyebrow up in question. "Yes, sweetheart?"

"Stop—don't stop—yes, stop—oh my goodness," I gasp and snap my eyes closed when he drags the tip of the strawberry between my legs. It barely nudges against my clitoris, and I see stars.

He chuckles in a deep timbre that vibrates down my thighs and to my core. Then, when his mouth finds the inside of my thigh and he begins kissing me toward my center, I nearly become unhinged.

"Alex—ahhh!" I cry out when his tongue replaces the berry.

"So goddamned sweet," he murmurs as he tastes me.

Everything disappears aside from the way his tongue owns this part of me. My hands have long since tangled themselves in his hair and are tugging and pushing him to continue the delicious assault he's begun on my body.

When I finally can't take any more of the tantalizing tasting, I succumb to a shuddering climax, all the while repeatedly screaming his name out. The moment I relax after having come down from my high, he pulls away and grins at me. His lips and chin glisten with my arousal, and I swear to God I might come from the sight of it.

"Darling," he tells me with a mischievous tone, "I think I shall spend the rest of the day feasting upon your decadent flesh. I want my lips and tongue to learn every inch of you. My hope is that you'll be sore and achy from the pleasure I want to give you but somehow still crave more."

His words work their way deep into my womb and have the exact effect he desires. He thinks he'll have to pleasure me to get me to crave him. Well, he's incorrect in that thinking.

I'm already hopelessly addicted to him.

Chapter Twelve

Alexander

"YOU LOOK LOVELY THIS EVENING, Edith," I praise as I enter our bedroom. Earlier, I left her to dress while I fetched the gift I planned on giving her for our reception. I also have a couple of surprises for her.

Her face lights up when she sees me, but she frowns when she looks back down at her dress. "Thank you."

I can't hide my smile as I carry the box behind me. "I bought you something."

She lifts her eyes to mine and rewards me with another breath-taking smile. "You did?"

Pulling the box in front of me, I walk over to the bed. Then I set it down. "Open it."

"Oh, Alexander, you shouldn't have," she gasps as she approaches the box. With tentative hands, she grabs the ends of the black ribbon and tugs. Once the ribbon has been loosened, she pulls off the lid. "What is this?" she whispers.

She knows what it is.

"I thought we could renew our vows, darling. We're quite different than we were when we first said them. My feelings for you have grown into something special and unique. It would be my honor to vow to care for you in front of our family."

I watch with a grin as she takes the cream-colored gown from the box. When Mother informed us that we were going to have a reception, I wanted Edith to be the belle of the ball. This gown is proper for a wedding—and fitting for a bride as beautiful as she.

"It's exquisite," she murmurs as she inspects the detailed beadwork.

The dress cost a fortune to have it rush designed, but it didn't matter. All that matters is it's here now and she'll wear it.

"It pales in comparison to your beauty, Countess."

She flashes me an embarrassed smile. "Where'd you put that fellow I first married? Maybe we should find a thick chain and shackle the door so he doesn't ever come out again."

I toss my head back and full-belly laugh. "He's still around. I'm pretty sure you'll want to keep him because he's the master with his tongue."

"Oh, then, by all means, we'll keep him too. He just won't be allowed to speak. His place will be right between my legs," she purrs as she slides a hand up the lapel of my waistcoat and into my hair. "But this guy? He's the one I want to spend the rest of my life with."

Dipping down, I attack her lips with mine. She tastes like honey from her midday tea, and I can't help but want to devour her.

"Maybe I don't want to share," I growl and then chuckle against her lips for the mere fact that I'm jealous of myself.

She giggles and tugs away to stare at me saucily. "Then maybe you need a little more practice doing his occupation. Once I feel you're a master, we'll get rid of him."

"Alexander Phillip Dumont! You're not supposed to see her in the dress! Now, get!" Mother chides from the doorway.

Reluctantly, I release my wife and step away from her. "Mother,

I'm not a child and we're already married," I groan.

Edith is properly amused as my mother swats me out of the room.

"Goodbye, my love," I call out before the door is slammed in my face.

"Goodbye, my love," she returns in a muffled voice through the closed door.

I grumble as I stalk down the hallway to search for Jasper to ask if the other part of my surprise for her has been fulfilled yet. I'm passing by one of the empty guest rooms in our wing when a voice from within calls to me.

Confused as to who would be in the room, I halt my steps and enter the room. "Nicolette?" I question as I walk inside.

The door clicks behind me, and I swivel around to see the naked blonde batting her eyelashes at me.

"Oh, Alexander, don't tell me you haven't missed this."

My eyes aren't even tempted to glance at what I used to be so familiar with, so I easily hold her gaze with an angry glare. "What in the fuck are you doing, woman? It is the evening of my wedding reception and you dare throw yourself at me? I should have you terminated from our employment and kicked onto your arse for presenting yourself this way to me!"

She gapes at me in horror but rushes for me. "I know you've missed the way I would suck this"—she grabs my flaccid cock through my trousers—"until you were dry. I could do it right now to relieve some tension."

"Let go of me," I snarl.

Her lips quirk into a feisty grin, and she squeezes me. "We could be quick. Our little secret, Alexander. Nobody would have to know."

I'm about to physically shove her away from me when the door clicks open and Alcott peeks in. His features harden once he sees our position.

"It's not what you think," I grumble and this time I do push her away.

Before she stumbles too far away, she slaps me across the face then runs past Alcott and out of the room.

"What I think is that you aren't in love with the countess. What I think is that, had I not intruded, you would have done some regrettable actions, brother. Please tell me why it is that Nicolette was naked and grabbing your cock," he snaps.

I run my hands through my hair and grip at it. "Oh, what do you care? You think now you'll prove to Father once and for all that I don't love Edith? It's a fucking lie, Alcott. I love her so goddamned much, and I won't let you or Nicolette stand in the way of my happiness with her. Do you understand me? Breathe one word of this to her and I'll rip your head off and dump it in the river. Edith is my life, and I cannot lose her. Are we clear, brother?"

He's furious—his jaw clenches in rage. "Crystal clear. But let's get one thing straight. I don't give a rat's arse about proving anything to Father. As of earlier, I thought we'd come to an agreement, you and I, that had nothing to do with him. What I do care about is your hurting Edith. She's the best damned thing that's happened to our family. So you, brother, watch your head, because if you break her heart, it will be yours floating down the river."

I sling my hand toward him, and he flinches as if I'll hit him. "Deal. Make the deal, brother. I won't hurt my wife and you never speak of what Nicolette has done. I'm not at all interested in that maniac of a woman. And I want father to release her of her duties to our estate in the morning. I won't have her meddling in my affairs and pining after me when I very clearly have a wife I love and adore."

Alcott scowls but slams his palm into mine. "You know what a deal means to the Dumonts. Don't betray me."

"Likewise, brother."

I scan the guests who have all taken their seats on the lawn of our estate and are facing myself and the officiant as we wait for Edith to emerge from the house. When I see an older man and young, blond woman seated beside Jasper and Elisabeth, I smile. The other surprise I planned for my Edith has come through. After the vow renewal ceremony, I'll properly introduce myself to her father and youngest sister. I had sent for them because I wanted her family to be a part of her big day.

On the other side of the aisle is my family. Father remains stoic beside Mother, their hands threaded together tightly. I may despise him most days, but his fierce love for her has always been his most endearing quality. Mother, even though confined to her seat most of the day, still managed to pull off one of the most stunning events of this family's history. She catches my eye and smiles broadly at me. With a grin of my own, I nod back my thanks. Of course without us saying anything, she understands our nonverbal conversation well.

My attention is drawn from the crowd to the back door of our estate when it opens and the string quartet begins playing a lovely song. Edith emerges and my eyes widen at how beautiful she seems to grow with each passing second. The moment my wife fully steps onto the porch and the late afternoon sun catches the beads and stones on her gown, my breathing ceases.

I've never seen her more stunning and elegant during our entire time of knowing one another. When her eyes lock with mine, she flashes me a smile full of love and promise. It baffles me how this woman was just as lonely and lost as I was six months ago.

And now?

Now, we're each other's everything.

My attention should be drawn to the distractions all around us. Sounds. People. Smells.

But it all fades into the background. All that remains is her.

A gentle breeze lifts her veil as she comes toward me, sending it trailing off to the side beside her. She's an image of what dreams are made of. And as soon as she is close enough for me to touch her, I reach my hand out, and she takes it without hesitation.

After hauling her to me, I capture her lips with mine and ignore the chuckles from Jasper and Alcott and the gasps of shock from the elders in attendance. They can all keep their mouths shut, because this woman is mine and I shall kiss her whenever I damn well please.

"You're so naughty," she murmurs against my lips with an equally naughty grin of her own.

"You're no angel," I tease. Then I steal one more peck before turning my head to the officiant, who appears to be irritated by my bending the traditional ceremonial rules.

He clears his throat and begins his sermon, but I'm not listening. All I can do is stare into her wide, brown eyes and attempt to somehow thread our hearts together eternally.

Another clearing of the officiant's throat startles me, and I blab out that I will. She agrees, and then we're once again lost in each other's gaze. Finally, he asks for our vows.

"Vows?" I turn my head over to him and glare. Nobody told me that we had to create any of our own. And it's in this moment that I notice the folded slip of paper wrapped around her bundle of flowers.

"It's okay," Edith murmurs as her cheeks redden.

She's excusing me for not having them. For not loving her enough to have come up with some. Which is not fucking acceptable.

I wink at her. "I memorized them."

A sweet smile spreads over her face, and I smile back. I may not have any written vows, but it does not mean I don't have any from my heart.

"Dearest wife, thank you for standing by my side these past few months. We might not have always seen eye to eye or slept in the same bed for that matter, but know that I always cared for your well-being. I was deeply jealous of any fool who looked your way even though, at times, I had a funny way of showing it. If I could take back the early days of our marriage, I would. I would replace them with countless moments of affection. Hours of kissing and cuddling. I would have showered you with the finest of gifts."

She mouths at me to stop. I know that it was all part of our agreement in the beginning, but now, all I feel is that I wasted that time with her. She could have been all mine and I squandered that opportunity. I won't waste another second though. Every moment of every day shall start and end with her.

"Edith, you have been a partner. A friend and confidant. And the most amazing lover a man could ever want. You're my everything, and I vow to forever prove to you just how important you are to me. Please promise to love me forever, because forever, I'll promise to love you."

This time, her eyes shine with unshed tears. Seeing her so vulnerable breaks something inside me, and I need to hold her. Once again ignoring the babbling from the crowd, I draw her to me and kiss her gently.

"I love you, Edith Dumont. My Countess."

At the moment I feel she's been properly comforted, I release her and flick a gaze over at the aggravated officiant before indicating that he may proceed. This causes Edith to giggle, and I flash her a wicked grin.

"Countess?" he interrupts.

She lifts her eyes to mine and smiles. Her words too, it would seem, are from the heart, because she isn't reading from her paper. "Alexander, thank you for choosing me to be your wife. Although you could have had anyone on this Earth, for some reason, you chose me. I'm thankful for that opportunity and grateful that our feelings only grew and intensified for one another over time. I'm not the woman you married anymore. I'm someone better, and I have you to thank for that. Thank you for loving me when nobody else could. I will love you forever too, Alexander."

This time, the officiant gives his blessings for us to kiss. And boy, do we kiss. It's almost too sinful to display in front of all of these people, but we do it anyway.

Edith kisses me back as if we're the only two souls standing upon the lawn. But she also kisses me proudly in a way that tells people watching that she'll always be mine.

Together, we kiss until Mother calls out that it's time to cut the cake.

And then we kiss once more.

Chapter Thirteen

Edith

I'M FLOATING ON A CLOUD.

A lemon-scented cloud.

And I'm in love.

We've been enjoying our reception for several hours now. Alexander keeps getting pulled in the direction of old friends and family members who are all vying for his attention to wish him well on his marriage. I keep hugging my sisters and father or swatting at Alcott for his ridiculous jokes. The very idea that Alexander surprised me with bringing my entire family together with his to witness our joyous renewal of our vows was incredibly surprising. The man is revealing a sweet part of himself that I am quite fond of. I'll reward him later this evening in a way that he'll most certainly appreciate.

My mind drifts to wicked thoughts and that's when I meet the heated stare of my husband. Even though we've spent most of the evening apart, our eyes always find the other's. Each time, Alexander flashes me a grin or winks in a way that promises me pleasure the moment we're alone. His looks are addicting, and I find myself blushing each time our gazes meet. This time, he must recognize the glint in my eyes because his jaw clenches in that angry way that I now know equates to pure, animalistic want.

"I love you," he mouths from across the room.

My heart patters about at his words. Only spoken a few hours ago, his first proclamation of his love to me shattered what was left of the blackened part of my soul, and I felt as if I were whole again. For once in my life since Mother died, I felt as if she would be proud of me.

"I love you too," I mouth back to him.

"Were you talking to me?" a deep voice questions.

Turning my head, I meet Alcott's twinkling, brown eyes. "No, you loon. I was talking to my husband. You're a mess. Don't you have some other woman to bother?" I tease.

He slings an arm over my shoulder and brings his lips to my ear. "I'd like to bother your baby sister, Ella, but for some reason, I don't think you'd like that."

I shove him, and he stumbles away chuckling.

"Damn, woman, I was teasing. She's far too innocent for the likes of me." He winks at me.

I roll my eyes at him. "*Far* too innocent. Alcott, God would strike you down from Heaven if you were even to look at her in a lustful way. Stay away from her, pretty boy, or I'll break your knee-caps." I say this with a sickeningly sweet smile and a giggle, but we both know there is truth to my words.

"Yes, sister." He bows dramatically before he saunters off toward Ella.

That man just goes looking for trouble.

Speaking of trouble . . .

I'm finally free of anyone's conversation, so I clutch my dress and make my way through the crowd, toward the last place I saw my husband. When I arrive at the other side of the room and still don't see him, I nearly give up. But then I hear his voice down the corridor.

Figuring he must be calling for me, I steal off down the hallway and hope we might be able to sneak away from these people and make love.

"Nicolette." Alexander says her name in a deep growl on the other side of a door. Just the sound of her name sends unease crawling up my spine.

"Tell her it's off. Tell her you want to be with me," she says tearfully.

Rage blooms in my heart, and my palm curls around the handle as I prepare to enter the room and stake claim over my husband. But then he murmurs something I can't hear and she begins shouting.

"I saw the way you appreciated my naked flesh earlier! If your brother hadn't walked in, we'd have already made love countless times! It's not too late, Alexander."

Her words rip a hole in my heart. He saw her naked? They were going to make love?

I don't understand.

"Edith?" Alcott questions beside me.

I whip my head in his direction, and tears well in my eyes. "You knew? Nicolette and Alexander? Together?"

He drops his eyes to the floor in shame, and the smile falls from his lips.

No!

"How could you let me go on and make a fool of myself?" I hiss. "I trusted you, Alcott!"

"Edith," he rushes out, "it's not what you think."

So it is true.

He reaches for me, but I shove past him and run for the nearest door that will allow me my escape from the stifling home and give me fresh air. The moment I push through the door, I swallow in deep, cool breaths. Tonight, the cicadas are loud, but they can't drown out the screams of despair inside my head.

I need to get away. Alexander doesn't love me. He still clearly wants Nicolette. I'm nothing but a conquest to him. A trophy. A partner in his sham of a marriage.

My vision blurs with tears, but when I hear the soft neighing of a horse that's strapped to someone's coach, I know what I'll do. I'll escape while no one is paying any attention. There's no way I can look at him while knowing he secretly prefers her over me.

All lies.

After rushing over to the horse, I quickly untie him from the post and climb up the steps to sit where the driver normally holds the reins. Because I grew up on the farm, I know how to drive a coach and immediately snatch the crop up.

"Hiya!" I shout as I whip at the horse to go faster.

He thrusts into action and takes off away from the estate. I clutch one side of the seat to keep from falling out and keep my eye on the path ahead. As we bounce along, the moonlight reflects upon the grass and lights the way. Even though my eyes are swollen from my crying, I can see well enough to guide the horse away from the trees.

God, I'm such a stupid woman. I fell for him hook, line, and sinker.

We've been bouncing along for several minutes, full speed ahead, when I hear shouting. Flicking my gaze over my shoulder, I see that the lights from the party at the house are barely twinkling—they're so far away now.

"Edith!"

A shadow on a horse barreling for me materializes from the darkness.

"Hiya!" I swat at the horse again to make him go faster.

Even though the horse is going as quickly as he can, the coach we're pulling is slowing him down. I soon hear the thuds of another horse galloping behind us.

"Leave me alone!" I scream.

"Never!" *Alexander.*

"Go away!"

"Edith, I love you!" he yells back. This time, he's so close.

When I look over, I see that Alexander, on his horse, is trotting at the same speed as I am. His hair is wild with the wind, and my fingers twitch to smooth it down for him.

"You love her! Not me!" I sob.

"Stop the coach, woman!"

I shake my head and make futile attempts for the horse go faster. Eventually, I give up and drop the reins.

"You broke my heart," I bite out tearfully as my horse slows.

"Edith, it isn't what you think. The woman has an obsession. She keeps throwing herself at me. There's only one woman I love. That woman is you."

As the coach comes to a stop, all that can be heard again are the cicadas and the soft sounds of breathing from the horses. Then my breath hitches when I warm hand slides over mine. I turn and see that Alexander is no longer on his horse—he's standing beside me.

"Come here. I need to hold you," he murmurs as he squeezes my hand.

A resigned sigh rushes from me, and I give him one nod. The truth is that I want to believe his words. And I do want him to hold me.

He doesn't wait for me to change my mind, tugging me right out of my seat and into his arms. Relief floods me as my arms wrap around his neck and his circle my waist. He stumbles back with me in his grip a few steps before letting me slide down his body to my feet. Finally, his palms find my cheeks, and his thumbs graze over my cheekbones.

"I love you, Edith. You have to believe me," he begs. "She means nothing to me. But you? You're my whole fucking world."

I stare into his dark orbs and find only truth.

I find love.

"But she said . . ." I trail off.

"She lies. She's delusional. Yes, she threw herself at me. No, I did not accept her advances. I. Love. You."

I allow his words to wiggle their way into my heart, which was quickly hardening. They soften the edges, and I relax.

"I love you too. I can't lose you, Alexander. You filled a part of me that was incomplete. Without you, I'm nothing," I admit.

His brow furrows, and his lips press into a firm line. "Don't be foolish, Edith. You're a diamond. A fucking jewel—so very precious. You're my everything. Don't ever call yourself nothing. *Ever.*"

My whimper of relief is silenced when his lips crash to mine. I urgently kiss him back. The next thing I know, we've fallen into the thick grass with a thud and he rolls me beneath him.

"My God, Edith. I thought I'd lost you," he groans as he works his body between my legs. His thickness presses against me through our clothes, and I moan out in bliss.

"I'm here," I gasp. "I'm here."

"Forever," he reminds me with a growl as he pushes harder. I may come simply from the friction of our bodies.

"I'm sorry, Alexander. I panicked. Everything seemed too good to be true. I couldn't have handled the humiliation if you didn't want me anymore," I tell him.

His mouth finds my neck, and he sucks the flesh hard enough to leave a mark. "I would die by my own hand before I ever lost you for good."

The very thought of him dying guts me. I need him to be closer to me. "Make love to me. Now, Alexander."

He doesn't reward me with an answer, but his hands do find his trousers. The moment he's freed himself, he pushes my knickers down my legs. When he lowers himself over me, he doesn't give me any warning before he slams himself into me.

"Ah!" I scream out into the night air.

My body is already wet for him, and the way he stretches me

is almost too much to bear. Then his lips find mine again, and he pounds into me hard enough that I know the grass is staining the back of my beautiful dress.

But I don't care.

If I could find a way to bottle this moment up and live in it, I would.

"Harder," I beg him.

"I want to stay like this forever," he growls, voicing my exact thoughts.

We grunt and pant and fuck like two wild animals until we're both unraveling in each other's arms. It feels like an eternity of bliss whereas in reality it is probably only a few passionate moments. Finally, Alexander breaks the seductive trance we've been suspended in when he comes deep inside me and collapses on top of me.

"You're perfection, sweet wife," he murmurs against my neck. "This is where we belong. Together."

When he lifts up to look down on me, I smile at him. "I love you, Alexander Dumont. You're mine."

"And you're mine, Countess. I'll love you until I'm ashes in the dirt. Then I'll love you even more."

His words flood my soul, and I close my eyes. "Take me home, husband. I'm ready to begin our forever."

He thickens as he begins a slow thrusting inside me and his lips hover over mine. "Edith, our forever has already begun. It began the moment I locked eyes with you."

And we lock eyes again, just like the first time.

We sneak back into the party, and Alexander guides me toward our wing. We're nearly there when Jasper shouts for us.

"Alexander!" he says grimly. "It's your mother."

"What about her? Where is she?" Alexander demands.

He motions for us to follow him, and Alexander all but drags me toward his parents' bedroom. When we walk in, several men are around her, fussing about.

I cry out once I see her sprawled out on the bed. "What's wrong?" I shriek as I run toward her side.

Her face is pale, but she's awake. "Oh, darling, I didn't mean to ruin your party. Go be with your guests."

I shake my head at her and squeeze her hand. "No. I'll stay here with you."

"So, what do you think, Dr. Egnater?" Alfred, his voice thick with tension, questions. Dr. Egnater clears his throat and scratches his beard. "I've seen a case similar to this in London when I was there on holiday last winter. They determined that it was called dropsy—a heart condition, if you will."

I gasp and burst into tears. "How will you fix her, Doctor?"

He chuckles, and Alexander growls angrily. "Oh, dear, if it is indeed dropsy, it isn't life threatening. Now, the antidote is a little hard to come by. They treat this condition with foxglove leaves. We'll need to send for someone to get not just the leaves, but the plant. I would suggest you plant some here on the estate so you'll always have access to them."

"I'll leave in the morning to acquire the plants," Alcott says firmly from one corner of the room. I didn't realize he was there until this moment.

"So, she's going to be okay?" I ask.

Dr. Egnater smiles warmly at us. "Yes. Once we have the plants, she can begin her treatments. She'll always suffer from the condition in her heart, but now that we've identified the source of her faintness and weakness, we can take measures to prevent those episodes. I'm afraid, though, she will need to live a life free of exertion."

"Oh, bollocks. I think I'll be just fine," Ma finally rushes out in exasperation. Her voice is weak and shaky.

"Mother, please. Listen to the doctor. He knows what's best for you. Besides, we need you to be well so you can be here for your many grandchildren with which we plan on bestowing you. Edith and I plan on making this a reality very soon," Alexander tells her firmly.

His words cause her ashen face to alight with joy. "Grandchildren." She beams. "Alcott, hurry back with those wretched foxglove leaves."

"And this one," Alexander murmurs against the shell of my ear as he drags his thumb over a freckle on my shoulder, "I shall name Gertrude."

I erupt into a fit of giggles. "Gertrude? Are you mad? And why is it you see fit to name all of my freckles?"

His teeth nibble on my ear, and I stifle a moan.

"Because they're all beautiful and have a life all they're own. They should have names."

I smile at his words. We're relaxing in the hot bath together, and the bubbles have long diminished. When his hand slides over my belly, I squirm as it begins teasing its way down south.

"Mmm," I whimper when his finger grazes over my clitoris.

When his cock becomes stiff against my back, I suddenly want him very badly. However, I still need answers from him before I will allow myself to completely let go.

"Alexander?" I ask as he begins massaging me in an achingly slow pattern between my legs.

"Yes, beautiful?"

"How come it took six months for you to see me?" Tears sting my eyes at my question, but it has often plagued me.

"Come here," he growls, halting his motion.

After twisting in his arms, I straddle his hips and lower myself down onto his cock. But once we're connected, neither of us moves.

His dark eyebrows are narrowed as he studies my face.

"My dear wife, you are sadly mistaken."

I scrunch my nose in confusion. While he took on many lovers—and I did too—I felt as if I had been just a neighbor to him who met him for dinner and nothing more. I could have died suddenly and he wouldn't have taken notice.

"You see, Edith, I always noticed you. Each morning, I knew you loved cinnamon and honey in your tea. I made sure to pay the inn tenfold to make sure those ingredients were always in stock and they weren't to offer them to the other guests. Whenever I would catch scent of the enchanting combination, it meant you were near. I would inhale it and it filled my soul—with you."

He presses a kiss to my lips. "And when I'd see you bring a lover to your room, I would nearly go mad with confusion. Even though it was our agreement, it didn't feel right. I despised every man that looked at you. But the ones that touched you—shared a bed with you—I wanted them gone. It didn't make sense at the time but now I understand. You were mine and I didn't want them to have you."

I frown. "I heard you with your own lovers. You didn't seem at all distracted by the fact I had my own."

His palms grab my arse, and he begins urging me up and down his shaft. It's easily drawing me away from our conversation, and the water splashes out of the tub and onto the floor.

"You misunderstand, dear. I wished they were you. My cheeks endured their fair share of abuse when I insisted upon calling them by your name. I was maddened by the idea that you were next door with someone other than me."

I ponder his words and, for a moment, lose myself to the way he feels inside me, the water adding a beautiful element to our lovemaking.

"I also," he grumbles, "know that you hate venison. Your favorite vegetable is potatoes. And that, if someone were to bring you a dessert at this moment, you'd climb off me and choose it over me."

I giggle because it's pretty much true. I love my sweet treats. Luckily for Alexander, he's my most favorite sweet treat.

I smile. "I never told you any of that."

He flashes me a sheepish grin. "I know, but I observed every detail that is you from the very first moment I saw you."

I ride him a little faster, and our conversation is lost to our moans and grunts. Once we've both come and I've curled myself against his chest, he speaks again while stroking my wet hair.

"Darling, I know that, when you bathe alone, you sing a beautiful song I've never heard before, but it's my favorite. And I know that, when you see an animal, your face lights up and your soul rejoices at the opportunity to connect with the creature. I also know that, when you have a bad dream, you pace around at night to soothe the unease in your mind. I know that, even though you agreed to forge forward with a seemingly wicked plan with me, there was a twinkle of hope in your eyes that matched mine—a twinkle that hoped we truly would find happiness in one another."

I close my eyes and let his words blanket me. When I didn't think he was watching me, he was. It warms me to my core to know that his level of interest in me has always matched mine with him.

His fingers trail down my back, and I shiver in his arms.

"I know that you belong only with me, wife. I love only you, Edith."

"I love only you, Alexander," I sigh, contented.

"Father gifted me with a large sum of money last night," he says quietly.

I kiss his chest. "That's nice."

He chuckles. "It was for us to build a home of our own."

Jerking back, I stare down at him. "What? I don't want a home of our home. This is our home."

His hands slide into my hair, and he pulls me toward him. Then our lips meet for a chaste kiss before he speaks again.

"My thoughts exactly, darling. I'm going to lend it to Alcott instead. This will always be our home. I want our children to grow up here and run wild in the same fields Alcott and I used to play in. We should grow old in this home—together."

The idea of growing old with this man fills me with joy.

"Are you still going to make love to me when we're wrinkly and old?" I laugh.

His face spreads into a mischievous grin. "We'll be the talk of the town because, beautiful, a day won't go by when I won't be inside you. Even when we're old and grey. I hope you have thick skin, because we might become the joke everyone speaks of."

I feel him harden inside me again, so I begin riding him slowly. "We're partners, Alexander. Remember? Now, get me out of this cold bath and fuck me, old man."

His hands pop me on the arse, and I cry out. Then he lifts us out of the cool water and climbs out of the tub. We don't even make it out of the washroom before he has me smashed against the wall and he's driving into me.

"Will it always be like this?" I moan as he takes me.

He grunts and nips the flesh of my neck near my ear. "No, Edith. It will only get better."

Epilogue

Alexander

HER SCREAMING IS NEARLY MY undoing, and I almost break the goddamned door down to get to her. "Edith!" I growl as I fist the knob.

"Son, let the doctors take care of her," Father firmly instructs with a hand on my shoulder.

But the problem is that they're not taking care of her. Dr. Egnater has one foot in the grave, the old man, and he thinks he can help my wife.

She screams out again and then begins loudly sobbing. I can't handle it anymore. After bursting through the door, I push past the nurses and doctor to my wife's bedside.

"Alexander!" she cries out upon seeing me. Her normally put-together face is glistening with a sheen of sweat, and her hair is matted to her head.

"Darling," I murmur before I press a kiss to her chapped lips and take her hand with mine.

"Sir, you should go," the older nurse snaps. "You're distracting her. We really need one more push and the baby will be out. Time is of the essence."

I ignore her and bring my lips to Edith's ears. "Push, beautiful. I'm here. We'll get this baby out together. I know you're in agony, but you've waited so long for this baby. You can do it, my brave Edith."

As if my words ignite her internal fire, she clutches on to me fiercely and screams as she bears down, pushing with all of her might.

"Ahhhh!"

The moment she relaxes, I hear it.

A tiny wail pierces the air, and I drag my gaze from my wife's toward the little voice.

"Earl, Countess," Dr. Egnater says proudly, "congratulations. It's a boy."

A boy.

The nurse quickly wraps our child in a cloth and sets him on Edith's stomach. She and I devour him with our eyes while he cries.

"Oh, Alexander, he's beautiful," she chokes out through her tears.

And he is beautiful.

His crying stops when he hears her voice. I watch in awe when his eyes lock with mine. He regards me in the same way his mother did when we first met. With one look, he asks, *Will you love me forever?*

I answer him aloud the same words I thought when I first saw his mother. "Forever. I'll love you forever. You're mine now."

"May we come in?"

My eyes find Edith's and she nods her head in agreement. Seconds later, Jasper ushers Elisabeth in on his arm.

"We came as soon as we heard you had delivered him," Elisabeth gushes as she breezes in and sits beside her sister. "Oh my, he's absolutely perfect."

"Where's Gus?" Edith asks about Jasper and Elisabeth's baby boy that isn't but a few months older. Elizabeth scoops Xander into her arms and presses a kiss on his forehead.

Jasper chuckles while he stretches out on the sofa in our master bedroom. "Ma has him. One would think he were her own flesh and blood by the way she adores him."

I smile at his response. My mother was born to be a grandmother. I've already had to make her leave every evening since Xander was born so Edith could rest. Each time, Mother cries and tells me I'm a horrible man.

But, every morning, she returns to our room tending to the boy so we can sleep in. I can't say that I'm unhappy about the arrangement. Originally, I had worried I would lose time with my wife assuming the child would need her continuous attention. That was before I considered the mother of all hens that lives under our same roof and her obsessive need to assist us.

"Gus is family. They're cousins," I tell him as I stand from the bed and walk over to him.

Jasper sits up and rests his elbows on his knees, regarding me with furrowed brows. "You do know that these two are going to raise all kinds of hell when they get older being as that they're both boys and close in age. Not to mention, they're our offspring."

My mind briefly flits through times of when Jasper and I accidentally caught the woods on fire and got drunk on countless occasions from old whiskey found in Father's cabinet. There were times when we stole fruit from our neighbor's orchards because we were rebellious little bastards and even though we could afford the fruit, it was entertaining to act as if we couldn't. We were harmless enough, I suppose.

"They'll manage, brother. We certainly did alright for ourselves," I wink.

We both regard our wives for a moment as they chat over whatever it is women chat over. Both of us are smiling when we turn back to look at one another.

"What if you have a daughter?" Jasper muses with mischief in his eyes.

An image of a small girl with Edith's wide brown eyes and fierce personality seizes my heart. No girl should ever be allowed to do half the shit Jasper and I did. Especially no daughter of mine.

"What if *you* have a daughter?" I challenge back.

His face darkens. "I shall lock her away until her twenty-first birthday."

"Do you imprison all the females in your life?"

He glances over at Elisabeth and nods as a wicked grin curls the corners of his lips up. "It would seem that way."

My mind is plagued with thoughts of what having a girl would do to my sanity. At one time, I imagined Edith and I having many children. Now, I'm afraid that we'll have a mess of girls and I'll end up going mad with worry in my attempt to protect them.

"Dear God, I hope we don't have any girls," I groan, mostly to myself.

Jasper stands and slaps me on the shoulder. "Don't fret, Alexander. We'll set to work at dawn on a tower with no windows or doors to house all of your daughters," he chuckles.

His words are in jest but I nod my agreement.

I wave my hand toward the door and raise a brow at him. "Will you accompany me into town and we'll fetch the supplies now?"

He laughs. "Lead the way, brother."

The End.

Aknowledgements

Thank you to my husband for doing that thing with your tongue (you know what thing)! Ha! You'll always be my inspiration and my muse. Keep swatting my ass in the gym in front of everyone and I'll keep having sexy material for my books. You rock my world, babe.

I want to thank the beta readers on this book, whom are also my friends. Nikki McCrae, Wendy Colby, Dena Marie, Elizabeth Thiele, Lori Christensen, Michelle Ramirez, Shannon Martin, Amy Bosica, Sian Davies, Ella Stewart, Nikki Cole, Anne Jolin, Maggie Lugo, Kayla Stewart, Elizabeth Clinton, and Melody Dawn (I hope I didn't forget anyone) you guys provided AMAZING feedback. You all gave me helpful ideas to make the story better and gave me incredible encouragement. I appreciate all of your comments and suggestions.

A special thank you goes out to Ella Stewart and Dena Marie for pointing out some plot issues that I needed to work through. Even though it was difficult to go back and fix these areas, I trusted your words and took care of them! This book wouldn't be what it was without your help. And thanks to both of you and Nikki McCrae for reading through it once more after the changes to make sure I covered everything that needed addressing. You all are too good to me!

I'm especially thankful for the Breaking the Rules Babes. You ladies are amazing with your support and friendship. Each and every single one of you is amazingly supportive and caring.

Mickey, my fabulous editor from I'm a Book Shark, thank you for always going with the flow with each and every one of my books. It is nice to know that you'll be able to handle whatever it is I throw at you. Love ya!

Thank you Stacey Blake for dealing with my blond problems like me forgetting when I've booked you and about a million other things (including my love for Beringer White Zin). You are patient and always take care of my book babies as if they are your own. I appreciate you immensely! Love you!

Lastly but certainly not least of all, thank you to all of the wonderful readers out there that are willing to hear my story and enjoy my characters like I do. It means the world to me!

K WEBSTER

Becoming MRS. Benedict

BECOMING HER SERIES

Dedication

To Mr. Webster,

You were the love I found when I wasn't looking for love.

And when I found this love that I didn't know I was missing,

I grabbed desperately on to it and will never let it go.

You're my forever.

To conceal anything from those to whom I am attached, is not in my nature. I can never close my lips where I have opened my heart.

-Charles Dickens-

Prologue

Alcott Dumont

Five days after . . .

ELLA MERRIWEATHER. THE INNOCENT BLONDE I never pursued because I'd actually respected the wishes of her older sister, Edith. Now, it's too late. Somehow, I blame myself. For if I would have gone after the young woman who had somehow seized my heart with her shy glances and unusually wise, crystal-blue eyes, she would be safe.

In my arms.

When I met her, I assumed my normal urge to conquer and fuck the woman would have possessed me.

But with Ella? *It did not.*

Instead, some other feeling overwhelmed me. The need to protect her. Even if that meant protecting her from the likes of men like me.

And now?

At what cost?

"Edith! Alexander!" I shout as I burst into their bedroom without warning.

Edith's eyes widen in surprise, and Xander is suckling on her tit. My nephew is perfect, and upon his birth, something began to fester inside me. I had a newfound desire to have a child of my own and soon. I'd need to find a wife first though.

"Brother, what is it?" Alexander demands.

My chest heaves because I've been traveling without stopping at an almost inhuman pace to get here to deliver the news.

"It's—It's—" I pant out and double over to attempt to catch my breath.

"What?" they both exclaim in unison.

"Ella. She was taken in the middle of the night."

Edith bursts into tears while Alexander curses. After stalking over to my brother's wife, I lean forward and plant a kiss on the top of her head.

I pull back and stare at her fiercely. "Don't you worry, sugar. I'm going to get her back—*for us.*"

And with that, I burst from the bedroom and make my journey back to London as fast as I possibly can. I'm going to go save my future.

Chapter One

Ella Merriweather

I PLACE A PALM ON FATHER'S forehead and cringe when I feel the heat of his skin. His health has deteriorated over the past few months and I'm worried sick about him. The doctor says that he is on death's bed, but I refuse to believe that. However, as I regard his grey—almost green—flesh and considerably labored breathing, I know. The man who has taken care of and provided for me for almost nineteen years of my life will soon be gone.

Then where will I go?

I suppose I could visit Lissa in London, but ever since she discovered that she is pregnant with their second child, she's busied herself with the preparations for the baby. Little Gus is at the age where he gets into everything. I would only be in the way.

And Edith?

She's written to me numerous times and asked me to come visit. I've yet to see little Xander, but she promises he's gorgeous. Havering is so far away though, and since she and Alexander live with his family, I would, again, feel as if I were an intrusion into their lives.

For as long as I can remember, I have been the one everyone

wants to look after. The baby sister. But now, as I wring a cool rag out and place it above Father's brow, I believe I have finally grown into a woman. I'm coming into my own.

And with this change, I need to embrace the fact that Father will soon die. It will crush me when it happens, but I will expect it. My poor sisters have no idea of his health, but I don't want to worry them. I shall inform them only after his inevitable death, as not to have them fret in their current states.

I stifle a yawn and rise from his bedside. He hasn't spoken in days or hardly opened his eyes. Tomorrow morning, I could wake up and he could be gone.

"Father, I love you. You were always good to us and Mother," I whisper through my tears.

When I bend and press a kiss on his cheek, the tears splash his face. He doesn't even flinch.

"Very well," I murmur as I extinguish the candles in his room.

He lies there very still as I watch him. His breaths continue to be loud and labored, but aside from that, he remains motionless. With a sigh, I exit his room and hurry back into the one I used to share with my sister, Lissa.

Memories of her are everywhere. She and I were much closer than Edith and I. Edith was away for four years at university, so that meant Elisabeth and I spent nearly every waking moment together. When she left with Lord Thomas, she didn't take a single item with her. Nor did she ever return to retrieve them. It was as if she had become someone new and left her old life behind.

I'll never admit it to her aloud, but it broke my heart to lose her. And even though we've seen each other a couple of times since then, I still miss her incredibly so.

My gaze falls upon my reflection in the mirror above the dresser on the far wall. As an adult, I'm taller than either of my sisters and nearly as tall as Father. The weight from my childhood is long gone, and I've become slender and willowy. Wide, blue eyes peer back at me, and I frown. I don't feel beautiful like my sisters; I feel cast aside as the dull, younger sister.

Whilst they are out carrying on with their lives with their incredibly handsome husbands, I'm left here to nurse our dying father. I have no one to talk to. No potential lovers. Nothing. It seems as if I am alone in this rather large world.

I am burdened with remaining in this cage that is my life when I was born to soar among the clouds.

Maybe he'll come for you. There was a connection between you and him.

My thoughts flit to the first time I met the handsome man who steals my thoughts daily. It's been nearly a year since I met him, but I think of him often and wonder about him. I'm sure he's found a wife by now and has a child on the way. Nonetheless, I remember the way he made me feel, and I grasp on to that sensation. It makes me feel alive—like one day, I shall burst from this cage and do great things with my life.

"Alcott, this is my wife's sister, Ella. And her father, Franklin," Alexander gruffly says, introducing us to his brother.

I want to stare at the man before me, yet my skin burns simply from looking at him. It wasn't long ago that William showed up from university and I also felt flushed by the simple fact that he was so handsome. But Alcott? This man is achingly beautiful. My heart hurts from just the mere sight of him.

"Your sisters are pretty, Ella, but clearly, they left the exquisite beauty for their younger sister. How is it that you don't have a lad on your arm aside from that of your father?" he inquires with a velvety-smooth voice that makes my skin prickle with awareness.

Father tenses beside me, and I feel he shall embarrass me with his protective nature. Of course I am correct, because he speaks, causing my cheeks to burn further.

"Son, my daughter isn't eighteen yet. Perhaps you shouldn't be looking at her with a gaze that is dangerous when in a woman's fa-

ther's presence," Father threatens.

I steal a glance at Alcott to apologize for my father's behavior through an unspoken look, and I'm unnerved when I see him blatantly staring at me—as if I'm a small bird and he's a cat ready to pounce.

The sad thing is that I want this gorgeous man to pounce. To paw me and lick me.

When his brown eyes meet mine, they increasingly darken—almost seeming that he has access into my thoughts. Then his gaze finds my lips and I feel lightheaded and dizzy. I may faint at any moment.

Maybe he will catch me.

"Sir," Alcott says to my father while staring directly at me, "I apologize for my forward nature. But your daughter is simply the most perfect being I have thus encountered in this lifetime. Excuse me while I savor her a moment longer."

Father growls, but when Alexander's booming voice interjects, he is distracted from the younger brother. They carry on a conversation while Alcott and I continue with a much more silent one.

"A lad should be so lucky to have a woman such as yourself on his arm." He flashes me a grin that makes my knickers feel as if they may catch fire. When he seizes my hand, I gasp. Then he raises the back of it to his lips and presses a soft kiss there. "I hope luck is with me tonight."

And with that, he releases my hand and throws me a wink before stalking off somewhere else within the home.

I'm left a hot, flustered mess.

For the first time in my life, I am more than just the baby sister in my family. I am womanly and grown.

Good luck to you, Alcott Dumont. I'm most certainly hoping that luck is, indeed, on your side.

My memory fades, but the smile on my lips does not. If life had taken another turn, I could be married to a man like Alcott. A man who seems to wear his passionate nature on the outside rather than hiding it within like I do. Perhaps once Father truly passes, I shall go look for him.

Oh, who am I fooling anyhow? So much time has passed. He is certainly happily married, gracing his elegant wife with his grins that will melt her knickers daily.

My life is certain. I shall always be alone. It might be nice if God could take me when he takes Father. Then I could be with both him and Mother. Now that's a life I would truly want to live.

I quickly remove my frock and don my thin dressing gown. As a chilly breeze enters my room from my open window, I briefly consider closing it. Instead, I opt to climb into the bed and bury myself under my covers, where I can dream of days when my family was whole.

Silence.

I sit up from a dead sleep and scan my dark room. Only the moonlight entering from the window lights my room. Something is wrong. I can feel it.

"Father," I call out, but my voice is more of a whisper. Bumps rise on my flesh as I fear he's finally met his death. "No!" I sob.

After scrambling from my bed, I run toward my bedroom door but slam into a rock-hard frame. My first thought is one of glee as I think maybe Father is well. However, as a strong hand steadies my arm and the scent of lemon and bourbon floods my senses, I realize there is another man in my house.

"Help!" I shriek before the intruder slams a palm over my mouth, silencing me.

Twisting away from him, I tear off toward the open window. I continue to scream, but I know that it is a fruitless endeavor, considering the nearest neighbor is too far from shouting distance. The window is within reach when the strong man's arm hooks around my waist and hauls me to him.

"Sweet girl, it is only me. William."

His gravelly voice instantly calms me. I've known William Benedict since I was a small girl, and he has always protected and looked after me. Once my sister chose to be with Jasper, I knew that William was heartbroken. In some ways, I always wondered if he would come for me and sweep me off my feet. I waited for some time and finally gave the notion up.

But now?

He's here, in my bedroom, with his muscled arm around my waist. This is certainly romantic, and silly, girlish ideas of him kissing me run through my head, pushing away sane thoughts as to why he's here in the first place. Perhaps it was always my destiny to marry the simple farm boy from down the road. Dreams of being with the unattainable Alcott vanish as I try to formulate new ones with William.

"I was frightened," I murmur as my body relaxes in his arms. I feel him inhale my hair and a shiver runs down my spine.

"Darling, no need to be frightened. I have come for you."

A sigh rushes from me, and a smile plays at my lips. "Took you long enough," I tease.

He twists me around in his arms so that I'm facing him. With the moonlight pouring in through the window, I'm rewarded with a view of the man who only became more handsome after he had come back from university. Shadows darken his face, and he almost appears to be angry. I drink in his blue eyes that seem to be on fire with an intensity I have never seen from him before. His cheeks are scruffy from having not shaven in days. He's utterly breathtaking. Not nearly as handsome as Alcott, but certainly beautiful in his own way.

When he sways and brings his mouth close to mine, I realize he's been drinking. I want to push him away and tell him to go home—to come back when he is sober. But as I remain locked in his arms, I don't want him to go. In fact, I want him to press his lips to mine and give me my first kiss.

"Are you still a virgin?" he questions briskly.

My eyes widen at his words. "Of course I am, William. I haven't ever even been kissed—"

I'm interrupted when he slams his lips to mine. At first, the kiss is just our lips interlocked. But soon, with a little urging, he gets my mouth to part open for him. Then his tongue slips in and eagerly tastes mine. I find that I enjoy the taste of bourbon on his tongue—so much so that a needy moan escapes me.

Who knew that my first kiss would be from my sister's old love, William Benedict? Thoughts of the two of us growing old in Father's farm home and rearing several children floods my mind, pushing my silly dreams of Alcott out. With William, this is more of a real dream—this fantasy could happen.

I just knew I would get my happy ending. And somehow, I knew that it would always be with William. I just hadn't admitted that to myself.

"My God," he groans as his hand grips my bottom. He pulls me to him, the indication of his thick, hard arousal evident against my lower stomach. "What I wouldn't give to fuck you right about now."

I break our kiss, his words having startled me. "William, maybe you should go. Return tomorrow when you aren't drunk and I'll cook you a fine meal. Perhaps you could get Father's blessings to be with me. He's very ill, you know—" My words still in my throat when I tug away from him and see the blood on his shirt. "William? Are you hurt?" I gasp and reach back for him. I gingerly skim my fingers all over him, searching for the source of blood, but I'm confused when I don't find one.

The silence.

Father.

"William, what have you done?" I say in the softest voice.

"'Tis time for retribution for what *they* have done to *me.* I shall make them all pay for ruining my life—for taking *her* from me," he snarls, his blue eyes snaring me in their gaze. "And you, Ella. Sweet, virgin Ella are part of this repayment."

I burst into tears and once again dive for the window. As quickly as I conjured up the romanticism of William and me, I swipe them from my mind. The man is a monster, not a husband.

This time when I make it to the window, he shoves me and I land in the shrub outside of it, thorns scratching me through my dressing gown.

"Help!" I scream at the top of my lungs as I try to disentangle myself from the bush.

"Shut your mouth, Ella. Nobody can hear you."

I'm still scrambling to free myself when I hear him land with a heavy thud on the ground behind me. With his hand fisting the back of my dressing gown, he yanks me out of the bush. I manage to claw him across his face before he tackles me into the grass, pinning me beneath him. The sick man is still aroused, and in a vulgar manner, he thrusts against me.

"God, I wish I could fuck you."

His words confound me, and for a moment, I halt in my struggles.

"You'll never touch me," I snap and then spit in his face.

When I wiggle again, his hand finds my throat and he squeezes enough to make me see stars. I grip his wrist, but he's too strong. After dipping his nose close to me, he drags his lips over mine.

"They'll wish they never ruined my life," he threatens cryptically.

I can't breathe, and for a brief time, I relax. Giving in to my imminent death, I close my eyes. Though he relaxes his grip, I'm too weak to fight him off. His palm finally releases me, sliding over the thin fabric of my dressing gown. His painful grip on my breast pulls me out of my weakened state.

"There, there, sweet girl. Don't go dying on me. You'll be worth nothing as a dead virgin. Mr. Caulder wants you in perfect condition. If he weren't paying me a huge sum of money for this, I'd fuck your tight cunt right now and slit your throat afterwards," he growls as he squeezes my breast again. "I wonder if the blood from your neck will splatter all over me as your father's did. Fucking bastard."

He sits up and glares down at me. The sight of him blurs as I hear his confession—that he murdered my father.

"You're nothing but a sick, demented pig. I will find a way to kill you, William. Mark my words—" I'm interrupted when he backhands me across the temple.

Pain and then darkness.

My life is over.

So much for the happy ending.

But at least I'm finally flying . . .

Chapter Two

Ella Merriweather

MY HEAD IS POUNDING, AND I feel nauseated. Today seems like a perfect day to sleep in and nurse my headache, but my sense of responsibility takes over. Father will need to be fed some broth because . . .

Something isn't right.

I struggle to open my heavy lids—to make sense of what is wrong. My skin is cold. Sore. Bruised. In fact, I feel as if maybe I'm bleeding.

Open your eyes, Ella!

I manage to crack one eye open and find that I'm lying on a cold slab of cement in what appears to be a cellar. Fear surges through me as my memories of William killing my father resurface. He killed him and now he's trapped me here!

"Help," I choke out, my voice raspy and soft. I try to swallow, but my throat is too dry. Upon sliding a hand up my neck, I tenderly touch the bruises William inflicted upon me.

I will kill that bastard.

"Help!" I hiss out once more.

I need to free myself from this place and locate the authorities—there is no way he'll go unpunished for what he has done to my family. Dragging myself into a sitting position, I blink away the rest of my unconsciousness and hunt for a way out. The only light comes from a tiny window near the ceiling and also under the crack of what must be the door that leads out of here.

I begin crawling toward the door, but before I have hardly moved, something cold grips my ankle. Tears spill out when I realize I've been shackled by a chain around my foot. Furiously, I attempt to free myself, but the chain is unrelenting.

"Help me! Someone!" I cry out, my voice louder than the last time I spoke.

The scrape of a chair across wood and then heavy footsteps over me sets my nerves on edge. The door abruptly flings open, causing me to jump, and light spills across the floor just out of my reach. When a hulking figure looms in the doorway, I shrink away.

"Please, just let me go. I won't tell anyone, William. I swear," I sob as he prowls toward me. I scramble away until my back connects with a cold wall, ending my retreat.

His hand seizes my arm and he lifts me effortlessly to my feet. I can't see his face, but I can smell him. The scent of bourbon is gone, and the familiar lemony mint odor is back. Tears gush down my cheeks as I cry.

"Don't hurt me, William. This isn't you."

The grip on my arm relaxes, and I cry out when his arm slides around my back and he pulls me against his chest.

"I'm so sorry, Ella," he murmurs into my hair.

I want to scream and shout at him that sorry can't bring my father back to life, but instead, I whimper while he holds me. "Just let me go, William. Please."

He stiffens and leans away. His palm slides over my cheek, and he uses his thumb to swipe away a tear. "My dear, I cannot let you go. I have a deal with Mr. Caulder. When he returns from France, I will turn you over to him to do as he wishes. He and I share a mutual hate for Jasper. It was his desire to use you to blackmail that fucker. I'm promised a great sum of money for my part in this. Little does he know, I would have done it without payment. My hate for your family is deeply embedded into my soul. Killing your father and turning you over to that worm of a man is a means to exact revenge on both Lissa and Jasper for ruining my life."

My tears won't stop as I realize I'm only a pawn in his scheme to get back at them. "William, this is ridiculous. I have done nothing. What will this Mr. Caulder do once he has me?"

I'm terrified of William, but I'm even more afraid from the mysterious man he claims to be partnered up with. Before I can ponder the other man too long and his intentions, William drops his hand from my cheek and storms away from me.

"Wait! Don't leave me!" I shriek, finally finding the full capacity of my voice.

He pauses and grumbles out his response to my previous question. "Dear Ella, I'm sure his plans are evil and deviant. He wanted to be absolutely certain you were a virgin. What he plans on doing with said virgin is of his concern, not mine. You'll stay here until he collects you in a fortnight."

I silently process his words as he slams the door behind him.

It would seem I have a fortnight to convince William to let me go.

The urge to urinate is overwhelming, but I am confused and dazed in the cold, dark cellar in which he has imprisoned me. He won't answer my screams as I plead for him to let me go, feed me, or offer me something to drink. I feel so abandoned.

And Father—my heart aches at the loss.

But my bladder, at the moment, aches more.

I run my hands along the rough wall and attempt to find a place where I can relieve myself. Once the length of my chain yanks at my ankle, indicating the end of the line, I push my knickers down and lift my dress. The moment I get in a safe position, I relax and finally urinate, nearly crying at the sensation of being able to find release. And when the warmth pools around my feet, I try not to gag. The truth is, though, I like the fact that it warms my icy toes.

Damn you, William!

Carefully, I attempt to stand and keep my dress from dragging through the urine. But the moment I stand, a wave of dizziness washes over me at having not eaten in who knows how long.

Blackness.

I blink open my eyes to a pounding in my head. A sob rips from my throat upon the realization that I fainted. Urine and dirt from the cellar floor have saturated the entire back of my dress.

"No! No! No!" I squawk as I scramble away from the disgusting area.

Tears roll down my dirty cheeks as I frantically work to remove the gown. The moment I rid myself of it, I kick it out of the way. My goodness, I stink something awful!

"I hate you, William!"

My screams are in vain, because I don't even hear a sound from above. Curling into a ball, I wrap my quivering arms around myself and attempt to warm up.

I must have fallen asleep for some time, and I wake at the moment footsteps sound above me. My flesh is cold, and I'm shaking uncontrollably. The stupid gown is within my reach, but I refuse to redress in it. However, as the night progresses, I realize I will die without its warmth.

With shaky fingers, I clutch the fabric and tug it toward me. Once it is in my hands, I discover that it is mostly dry. As I put the filthy thing back on, I weep.

Somebody, please help me!

"Food," William barks out from the doorway to the cellar.

I snap my head toward him and squint at the light spilling from it. "William, please," I beg. How long have I been here? Two days? Three?

He silences me when he storms over to me and drops the bowl of food in front of me. "What in God's name is that smell?"

"Th-there's nowhere for me to relieve myself," I stammer through my tears.

"This is some sickening shit, Ella. Are you a damn animal?" he spits out as he stalks over to corner of the cellar, out of my reach. He retrieves something and heads toward me.

If only I could get close enough to grab him . . .

Apparently, he can see right into my head, because he flings a bucket at me. It whacks me across the face and scuttles to the floor. With my cheek smarting in pain, I blink the stars away. Before I can yet again ask him to free me, though, the door to the cellar slams closed.

Defeated, I collapse to the floor and clutch my bruised cheek. But soon, the smell of the food makes its way to me and my stomach grumbles violently. While crawling toward the bowl like the animal he claims I am, I try to convince myself I am surviving.

The moment my fingers make purchase on the food, I dig my dirty hands into it and eat ravenously. I don't even care that what he has given me is nothing but scraps leftover from his own dinner. It is delicious and still warm. And I eat until it is gone, licking the bowl clean afterward.

Five days.

I think.

I'm becoming delusional.

William only comes into the cellar once a day to replace the bucket I use to relieve myself or deliver a meal. I feel as if I've become some unwanted, caged animal. Every time he enters, I beg for him to release me. He's resorted to not talking to me. Each time he comes down here, he ignores my pleas.

It's making me lose my mind.

And I'm horrified at the smells that permeate the small space—smells that undoubtedly come from me. I just want to be free. To see my sisters again. To breathe air that doesn't reek of urine and feces.

I have been sitting against the cold wall that no longer chills my forever-numb flesh and rocking myself back and forth for hours. After my first or second day, I tried singing Bible hymns to subdue the terror in my veins. But once I realized God wasn't coming to save me, I refused to sing another word.

Only I can save me now.

When the door swings open, I immediately rise to my feet. Previously, when he would come down here, I would beg until I was hysterical. I'm tired of begging. Now, I am desperate to try anything.

"William. I want a bath," I tell him firmly.

Ignoring me, he strides over toward my bucket, which is within my reach. The moment he has it in his hands, I grab one side of it and pull it toward me.

"What the fu—" he starts as we wrestle over the bucket containing my waste.

He yanks at it hard, and I quickly release it. I giggle like a maniac when he stumbles and falls on his arse, spilling the contents all over him in the process.

"You disgusting witch!" he roars as he climbs to his feet and charges me.

Instead of shrinking away from him when he is close, I throw my arms around his neck. He stinks worse than I do now, and that causes me to cackle even more.

"You have lost your goddamned mind!" He is no longer trying to get at me. Instead, he's attempting to rush away from me.

I grip him tight around his neck as his fingers bite into my ribs in an attempt to pull me off. When he manages to rip himself away, he hastily stumbles back until he's out of my reach. I expect him to yell or hurt me, but he turns and stalks up the steps.

The sound of commotion comes from upstairs as he no doubt hurries to clean himself. A satisfied smile tugs at my lips. It serves him right for what he's done to me. I must sit for another twenty minutes giggling to myself as I imagine the horrible man attempting to clean my waste off himself.

As he reenters the cellar, I'm suddenly blinded by the light of a lamp. It's the first time in several days I have seen any light. The glow indicates that he's removed his shirt, and my eyes skitter over his smooth chest. If only I could get him to remove this chain. I'm certain I could seduce him into releasing me.

"Ever made love to a virgin?" I purr as he nears.

He growls as he sets the lamp down on a shelf. "I have not."

I'm surprised he even answered my question. "Want to?" I taunt.

"Shut your mouth, woman," he snaps as he produces a key from his pocket.

My eyes widen as I allow hope to seize me for a moment. Will he finally release me?

"You smell like a fucking pig and I'm tired of it." He kneels before me and sets to removing the chain from my ankle.

Before I have an opportunity to run, he rises and grabs my wrist. I'm weak, so he effortlessly drags me behind him up the stairs and out of the cellar. The air is fresh up here, but the lights from the candles hurt my eyes and I squint to shield my gaze from them.

We take another flight of stairs until we reach our destination. I feel warmth from the steam of the bath the moment we enter the washroom. And as the scent of soap permeates my senses, I choke back a sob. Who knew the prospect of a bath would seem more alluring than my own freedom?

"Take off your gown," he demands, staring at the floor as if he's afraid to face the horrors he created.

I take a moment to look him over and find that the man I once adored is nothing more than a monster. A handsome monster with feces on his arms.

I laugh maniacally again upon seeing what I did to him.

"Ella," he warns, his blue eyes finally rising to meet mine.

Upon hearing my name, some of the inner crazy dims. "Say it again," I whisper. The sound of my name sobers me, and I can't believe how it soothes me.

His lips purse into a firm line. "Ella, get into the tub."

I close my eyes and peel the soiled gown from my body. When a rush of breath escapes him, I pop my eyes back open to see him hungrily devouring my bare breasts. Then an idea forms in my head, and I quickly work out my next plan of action. Upon hooking my thumbs into my knickers, I push them down to my ankles. After I step out of them, I shyly lift my eyes to him.

"Are you going to bathe with me?" I question. "You're dirty too."

He groans, which causes my eyes to flicker down to the bulge in his trousers. A satisfied smile tugs at my lips, and I stare him down as I climb into the nearly scalding water. It feels heavenly and immediately begins to thaw my body. Once I've sunk into the water, I almost moan in delight.

"You're so different than they are," he mutters aloud. His eyes skim over my naked flesh as I lather up with the soap.

"Them?"

"Edith and Lissa."

I smile even though it isn't genuine. "I'm very different. You're still dirty," I purr.

"If I get into that tub . . ." he trails off with a sigh.

"What?" I question, feigning innocence.

"I may not be able to control myself."

I swallow the fear of his words and pin him with a knowing glare. "Maybe I don't want you to control yourself."

He swears, and I bite down on my lip to keep from laughing like a maniac once again. "Ella, I have to control myself. If I had my way, you'd no longer be a virgin the moment I entered that tub. But I am to preserve you for him."

Though his words terrify me, I let them roll off as if they don't affect me. Then I hold my breath and dip under the water. The burn of the water envelops me, and for a brief moment, I wonder if I should gulp in as much water as I can. They can't take the virginity of a corpse.

My lungs burn from remaining under the water with my breath held, and I'm about to give up on life when firm hands grip my shoulders and lift me out of the water.

"What are you doing?" he snarls. He's bent over the tub, and I use his position against him.

Latching on to his neck, I pull him into the tub with me. He roars furiously as water spills out over the side. Before he regains his bearings, I'm able to dunk him under the water for a moment. We're a tangled mess of limbs in the tub, and I lose myself to hysterical, crazy laughter.

When he grasps on to my neck and glares hatefully at me, I yelp.

"You're insane. I went and kidnapped a damn lunatic!"

"You made me this way when you killed my father and caged me like an animal!" I throw at him, not backing away from his menacing stare.

I thread my fingers into his hair and attempt to force him back under the water. He's much stronger than I am in my weakened state, easily subduing me. Since I can't kill him, I'll enact my backup plan. I slip my legs around him, hooking his waist.

"Kiss me, William," I challenge.

He settles himself against me and glares at me, inches from my face. Between my legs, he's as hard as the cement floor in the cellar. Even in my disgusting state, I turn him on.

"It could be you, William. I could be yours. I could become Mrs. Benedict and we could run away. Away from all of this. Just you and me," I say in a soft tone that I hope convinces him.

For a moment, I see hesitation in his eyes, so I pounce. This time, instead of trying to dunk him, I pull him to my lips. His lips stay pursed, but the second his mouth grazes mine, he loses control.

"My God, I want you," he grumbles before seizing my mouth with force.

I throw myself into the kiss and allow him access into my mouth. When he dives his tongue inside, I nearly choke on it. This is the man who killed my father. He deserves worse than the same death, but I need him.

I need him to let me go.

"I want you too, William. Since I was a girl. It could be you instead of him. Make love to me," I beg.

My voice doesn't feel like that of my own. It feels far more grown and seductive than it has ever been. Maybe when I free myself of this hell, I'll run away and become an actress.

"But . . ." he trails off as he grinds himself between my legs hard enough to bruise me.

"But nothing. All that matters is us," I whimper, "Just do it. I want you inside my body."

He massages my breast before dramatically wrenching himself away from me and climbing out of the tub. His soaked trousers are glued to his muscled frame, and I want to curse at him for having ruined everything. Had he not been hell-bent on revenge, we could have been together. We could have found love with each other.

But he did not. Instead, he murdered my father.

I rise from the water and step out of the tub. He glances over his shoulder at me and once again gazes at my naked form.

"Goddammit, Ella! You're making this very difficult," he snaps.

I storm past him but not before casting a disdainful glare his way. "I don't even know why I tried. I'm sure Mr. Caulder is a much better lover anyhow, seeing that you couldn't please either one of my sisters."

And then I brace myself for the impending storm that is sure to come.

Chapter Three

William Benedict

SHE'S A WITCH.

Just like Edith.

Just like Elisabeth.

The Merriweather women have an evil way of slipping their tentacles around my heart and clutching it. With Elisabeth, it was love. A pure, simple love between a boy and a girl. She stole my heart with her coy smiles but hidden curiosities. I loved her with every part of me.

And then she pulled away from me. We were to be married, yet she dangled her virginity in front of me like a fucking carrot. I was outraged but mostly hurt. Why didn't she understand that, had we slept together before I'd left for university, it all would have worked out? I would have only had eyes for her.

Instead, she teased and toyed with me, and on the eve of my leaving, she withheld what she knew I desperately needed. I was a man with a voracious sexual appetite but had no way of whetting it. For a girl who claimed she loved me, she tormented me by allowing me to believe we could lose our virginity together. All I ever wanted was her impregnated by my seed and our living a simple life on the farm.

But alas, she refused me.

And I was angry.

However, at university, I began to cool. My studies were important to me, and I wanted to be the best man I could before I came back for her.

Then Edith fucking ruined it all. She all but threw herself at me. The witch harassed me with her forward nature, and my cock wanted what Lissa didn't want to give. Edith offered solace with her body. A place to release my tension and sexual desires. At first, I was horrified that I was considering her, but soon, I found myself in her room and then, moments later, inside her.

Her body was fucking amazing.

She ignited the flickering flames in my soul until they were raging fires. I couldn't put them out. All I wanted was to be inside Edith whenever the mood would strike. She wasn't Lissa—my heart wasn't attached to hers—but she provided me with something else. The woman with a silver tongue allowed me to take what I wanted—what I needed—without receiving anything in return.

It was almost too good to be true. A woman to fuck until I got back to the one I was to marry.

But she became attached. She fucking threatened to tear apart what I had with Lissa. With Lissa, my heart wanted to grow old. Had she given herself to me at sixteen, none of this would have happened!

Edith was sorely mistaken. I could never love her. Why couldn't she see she was merely a dumping ground?

All was well until I came back. My girl had grown into a beautiful woman. Her curves had swelled, and I nearly went mad with the prospect of fucking her at the first possible chance. With each smile, kiss, and touch, Lissa made nonverbal promises to make up for four years before. I was prepared to take what was mine and move on with my life.

And then Franklin, the now-dead arse, made the worst mistake of his life. He involved himself with Lord Thomas. Made a fucking mockery of my engagement to Lissa. That idiot gave his daughter away to a man willing to pay enough.

Then Lord Thomas took her.

He fucking took my woman as if she were a damn trophy.

I lost my goddamned mind. All of my energy was spent trying to come up with tactics on ways to rescue her from him. I was confident in the thought that I would steal her and take her to France.

But the Earl of Havering further ruined my life.

He'd discovered my relations with Edith somehow. Threatened to use them against me. These men all deserved to die—and by my hand. It was only fair.

When Lissa chose Lord Thomas over me, I died.

A part of me was left on the blood of that man's fists after he beat me up and I crawled out the window. Without her, I had nothing to live for.

That night, I drank myself stupid in a nearby pub and complained to any arse who would listen.

One man listened with rapt attention.

Samson Caulder.

He felt sorry for me.

This man took me into his home. He fed my rage with his mutual hate for Lord Thomas. Made me his apprentice. And together, we plotted and planned.

An idea formed.

There was no guilt as he suggested we take the youngest Merriweather girl. There was nothing but the urge to seek justice. Too bad it took a year for the proper conditions to turn about—for her father to become weak and ill. When my parents had so innocently informed me of his illness, I knew I had to move to get her. The man would have fought me for her had he not been on death's bed. Even though Caulder was out of town, it had to be done with or without his help, for it was our plan all along.

This was my justice—ruining their lives in whichever way I could. Ruining Ella.

It was all too simple. I very gladly killed Franklin, which was the easy part. Ella was to be handed over to Caulder, and we were to use whatever means necessary to extort all we could from Lord Thomas. Elisabeth could see if she still loved him when they were without a cent to their name or a roof over their heads.

Would she come crawling back to her true love?

But now that I have Ella in my clutches and the plan is set into motion, something niggles at me. I made the mistake of kissing her perfect, plump lips that night. The idea of taking her overwhelmed me. How wonderful would it be to take the innocence of the youngest Merriweather, who resembles her older sister, Lissa?

The idea infected me. Diseased my mind.

Caulder wanted his virgin.

I was his pawn in a much larger scheme of revenge.

Yet . . .

The witch sank her claws into me. Teased me. Fucking toyed with me.

One sister teased me with her virginity. Made promises she never intended to keep. The second one gave it up easily but wanted my damn life in return. And now, another one dangles yet another fucking carrot?

I'm not the man I was before.

I have nothing to live for—so why not take what I want?

The bitch is practically handing it to me—begging me to take it.

And, my God, I fucking want it.

I want to feel how she cries and squirms beneath me as push myself into her. Her discomfort will be a salve to my heart, which has been raked across the coals. It will feel as if I have garnered some tiny bit of retribution for what this family has done to me—the first of many acts to soothe my soul.

"I don't even know why I tried. I'm sure Mr. Caulder is a much better lover anyhow, seeing that you couldn't please either one of my sisters."

Ella's words stab my heart and reopen the wound I daily attempt to hold together. The bitch just won't let it go.

Caulder will put a bounty on my head for this. Our deal will shatter the moment I fuck this girl. And boy, am I going to fuck her now. There's no backing away this time. I've dealt with her crazy arse for nearly a week.

She wants to become Mrs. Benedict?

Then I will take her. Make her mine. I'll steal off with her and use her body. Exact my revenge every day as I fuck her whenever the mood strikes. She will bear my children. Cook my meals.

Fucking serve me.

Her family has spent the past five years ruining me.

Now, it is time to spend my lifetime ruining theirs—all starting with the insane, dirty girl before me. As she arches her brow in a disdainful challenge, I pounce.

She's mine now.

Chapter Four

Alcott Dumont

JASPER THINKS I'M INSANE.

My brother assumes it's a lost cause.

But my new buddy, old man Gerald, gets me. He understands why I'm doing this, and that is why he is with me tonight. Ever since I came to the Thomas estate, he and I have connected much like a father and son would. I trust the old man as a confidant and friend.

"I'll wait out here. See if I can garner any information," he grumbles. It's late, nearly midnight, but the pub is still open.

I nod my thanks and push through the door. The pub is full of life, which causes the muscles in my neck to relax. I can blend in, ask questions, and not bring much attention to myself.

After sauntering over to one end of the bar, I sit and dip my head. When I feel as though people have become bored with my arrival, I scan the room almost as if I'm looking for a woman to take home with me.

I *am* looking for a woman to take home with me. A certain

blond-haired, blue-eyed, innocent woman.

"Scotch. Neat," I answer the bartender when he asks me what my poison will be.

While he makes my drink, my attention is drawn to a couple of men in one corner. They're drunk and loud, but something about them has me turning an open ear to them. The moment I hear one of them mention Lord Thomas, I stand and slowly walk toward them.

"Are you friends with him?" I question.

The bigger of the two men stands and glares at me. "What's it to you, pretty boy?"

I scoff at him. "I owe that arse money and he won't grant me an extension," I complain. My lie is smooth on my tongue, and the fool believes me, because he slaps me on the shoulder and invites me to sit with them.

"A man who hates Lord Thomas is okay in my book," he booms with laughter.

The bartender drops my drink on the table, and I knock it back before interrogating these men. The bigger of the two men says that he's off to take a leak outside and leaves me alone with the other one who just spoke.

"He's a pussy these days. I hear he took on an apprentice to collect his debts because he's bogged down with a family," I tell him.

He nods and leans forward conspiratorially. "The man is about to pay."

Finally, some fucking information.

"Oh, really?" I shoot him a wicked grin. "Do tell, friend."

"Our boss man is going to fuck up his wife's sister."

Rage explodes within me, but I maintain a cool demeanor aside from the gritting of my teeth. "Too bad you can't fuck him up instead."

The man chuckles. "No, this will be better. Caulder plans on extorting an exorbitant amount of money out of him, but not before smashing that Merriweather girl under his feet. It will ruin Lord Thomas, because not only will he be broke, but I'm sure his wife will hate him as well."

I force an evil smile. "I like this Caulder guy. Does he have her now?"

He shakes his head. "Benedict has her. Took her right out of her bedroom window. The man has her until Boss gets back from France."

This is the best information I've come across in five fucking days.

"Here in London?" I question. Then I not-so-patiently wait for him to chug his drink.

"Yep. On Cosgrove Street. He's staying with her at the abandoned shoe shop Caulder owns. Why are you so interested anyway?"

Smirking at him, I stand from the table. "I've been waiting for the day to see him fall for some time. Maybe this will get me out of the debt I owe him."

He nods and raises his glass to me. "You can guarantee it."

I slap a few coins onto the table and walk out of the pub as if I don't have a care in the world. But the moment I reach the night air, I jog toward Gerald.

"Cosgrove Street. Now," I growl.

"Shall I fetch the coach?" he questions.

"No, too conspicuous. I'll go on foot. Bring the coach to where Cosgrove meets Houghton Avenue," I instruct.

He grabs my shoulder and squeezes. "Be careful, son. That William character is a bad fellow."

I scowl. "And I'm his worst fucking nightmare, old man."

With that, I trot off into the darkness and grip my knife, which is sheathed in the belt of my trousers. Tonight, I'm going to bring her home. But not before killing that arse first.

Ever since the moment we received word that she was taken, I have been mad with the need to find her. The man who has her is a murderer. When the doctor went to check on Mr. Merriweather, he discovered that the old man's throat had been slit from ear to ear. The doctor said that his death had been a quick one.

What horrified everyone, aside from their father being murdered, was the fact that Ella was missing. That arse took her for reasons that were unknown to us until now. Now, as I prowl along the buildings and through alleyways toward her, I know that it was all an act of fucking revenge.

Of course, Jasper and I discussed this idea, which is why I urged him to take Elisabeth to Havering. Getting them out of London was a must, considering that William hates Jasper for having taken his fiancée. Little Gus and their unborn child need the protection only our estate back home could provide.

I promised both Edith and Elisabeth that I'd bring their sister back to them. Now, I'm so close to finding her after five long fucking days. Soon, I'll have the sweet, innocent flower of a woman in my arms. I was drawn to her the moment I laid eyes on her at Alexander and Edith's wedding reception.

Edith expressed her wishes for me not to pursue the woman. At the time, I agreed. However, it was only for the mere fact that she wasn't of age. I also had nothing to show for myself as a man. After I came back to London, I learned Jasper's business. He took me on as an apprentice. And I was almost ready to begin courting her when she was taken.

A scream suddenly snaps me from my thoughts.

Ella!

Bolting toward the noise at the end of the street, I unsheathe my knife as I run to her. I will save this woman. When she is finally in my arms, I'll never let her go. I will spend the rest of my life protecting the girl.

Stupid fucking William will die by my hand.

This ends tonight.

Chapter Five

Ella Merriweather

"WHAT DID YOU SAY TO me?" William snarls.

I give his wet body a once-over. Feigning disinterest, I lift my nose in the air. "I said, William, that if you couldn't satisfy my sisters, you could not come close to satisfying me."

His face reddens with anger as he shoves his wet trousers down to his ankles. When he rises back up, his erect cock bobs in front of him. Suddenly, fear threatens to overwhelm me.

What am I doing?

I am getting myself out of here.

"No wonder." I narrow my eyes at his cock. "I expected something a little larger."

My words cause him to explode, and he pounces on me. I have the instinct to run from him, but that will only send me right back into the cellar. Instead, as he reaches me, I throw myself into his arms.

"I'll make them all pay for ruining me," he threatens, his body pulsating with rage.

I run my fingers through his hair and whimper. "Shh, William. Take me."

His tense body relaxes once he seems to understand I was only riling him up, and he smashes his mouth to mine, kissing me as if he has something to prove. I could care less if he's a good lover or not. This is a means to an escape.

I moan when his large hands find my arse and he lifts me up. Knowing that he wants to hold me, I hook my long legs around his waist. Then he strides from the room with me in his arms and carries me into the bedroom.

"I cannot believe I'm choosing this body over all of that fucking money—over everything," he grumbles as he lowers us onto the bed.

No virgin. No money.

I can do this. It's just William. If I have to lose it to anyone, I'd rather it be him than the stranger to which he planned on selling me. Even if he did murder my father, he is still William from down the road—well, at least in looks. Deep down inside, he's something wicked and evil. However, I'm desperate to leave this place and will do whatever is necessary to do so—even if that means sleeping with the devil.

"Make love to me," I say, goading him.

"God, yes," he murmurs before kissing me hard enough that I can barely breathe. "I'm so goddamned tired of not getting what I want."

At the way his large cock rubs along the thatch of hair on my pubic bone, I begin to feel panic rising. He seems way too big and I've never really explored what I am sure is a small opening.

"Will it hurt?" My question is my only sign of weakness.

He breaks our kiss to look down at me. His features have softened, and I see genuine affection in his eyes—the William I remember from when I was much younger.

"Sweet girl, only for a moment."

Clamping my eyes shut, I bite the inside of my cheek and wait for it. As if he's punishing me, he teases my entrance with the tip of his cock. I'm not aroused—this is going to hurt.

"I'm going to marry you. After we make love, I'm taking you away from here. You'll become my wife—Mrs. Benedict. I will look after you forever," he promises, "and you will be mine. I *deserve* to have you."

I shut his words out and prepare for him to do his worst. An instant later, he slams into me. Fire rips through me and I scream. Forceful thrusting begins, and I keep waiting for the painful moment to pass. But it doesn't.

"So fucking tight," he grunts as I sob. "I deserve this so fucking much."

When his mouth finds mine again, I lie there like a corpse and let him take me. The burn in my southern region is fierce and mind boggling. And as I give in to the hysterics that were threatening to take over, tears stream down my face.

"Th-this hurts," I garble out.

He grunts once more before he pulls out of me. I cry out, almost thanking God for the reprieve. But then I remember that God isn't here with me.

Finally, I peek my swollen eyes open to see him fisting himself until ropy spurts of semen pour from him all over my belly.

"So good," he praises as he falls onto the bed beside me.

I curl into myself and turn my back to him. What have I done?

I saved myself from worse problems—that is what I have done. Now, I just have to figure out a way to run away from him.

"Don't cry, sweet girl. The first time always hurts for the woman. Next time, you might even orgasm," he tells me.

Not answering, I shudder with my tears. When his hand finds my waist, I quiver in fear. I don't want him to touch me. The cellar almost seems more preferable than sharing this bed with this monster. *Almost.*

He begins to stroke my ribs, and eventually, he curls up against me from behind. Then his hand finds my breast and I close my eyes. Bile rises in my throat, but I swallow it down. I pop my eyes back open when he slides his hand down between my legs. I'm still so sore from him that I don't want him to touch me. But he does. In goes his finger, and I shove down the scream that is lodged in my throat.

My eyes frantically search for something to fixate on—anything to distract me from his painful intrusion. Luckily, something on the bedside table catches my eye.

So shiny.

Covered in crusted blood.

A knife.

The knife he used to murder my father.

"I need to make love to you again," he groans as he nudges me with his once again hardened cock. "You're mine, Ella. You belong to me now. There won't be a day that goes by that you aren't ready and willing to take me. I have saved you from him, and now, you will save me from myself."

My heart races in my chest because I don't want to feel the pain again.

But . . .

If I could somehow manage to get that knife.

"Can I be on top this time? It might hurt less," I whimper, letting him hear some of the fear in my voice.

He caves, because I feel him roll onto his back behind me. Discreetly, I reach for the knife and tuck it under the pillow before I sit up. Lust-laden eyes meet mine as he hungrily devours my heaving breasts.

"I can't believe I get to fuck the youngest Merriweather sister for the rest of my life," he smirks.

I have the craving to slap the smug look right from his face. But I do not. No, instead, I find myself winking at the monster and straddling his hips.

"Every day for the *rest* of your life," I purr.

His hands clutch my hips and he guides me over his cock. When he pushes me down over it, my body tenses and I cry out once again. Edith once told Lissa and me that sex felt like being assaulted with a hot fire poker. She wasn't lying.

"Ahh!" I sob as the pain seizes me again. My body has barely adjusted to him when he urges me to ride him. Inside, I am dry and raw.

I bite my lip and shove away any weakness from the way I am hurting. Affixing my best actress smile, I ride the man as if he were my favorite pony.

"Yes, Liss—Ella," he groans and slams his eyes shut.

I feel like my heart is going to explode from my chest. Every nerve ending in my body is alive and exposed as I mentally prepare myself for what I am about to do. Days ago, I wouldn't have considered such a thing.

Yet now?

Now, I know it is necessary.

I'm doing this for Father. For Lissa and Edith. *For me.*

Darting my hand under the pillow, I retrieve the knife and don't think twice before plunging it into his chest with all the force I can muster.

"FUCK!" he roars, and his eyes fly open to meet the wide ones of mine.

I scramble off him and fall onto the floor on my elbows and knees.

He struggles to shake off the shock of what I've done but manages to sit up. His hateful eyes meet mine. "Ella, you bitch. You ignorant fucking bitch! What have you done?"

I'm on my feet in a second and start to run for the door. Surprisingly, he leaps after me and tackles me. His breaths are coming out raspy and labored, but his strength still overpowers mine.

"Ah!" My chin slams the hardwood floor, and for a moment, all I see are stars. The moment they dissolve, I realize I have blood in my mouth from having bit my tongue.

He grabs a handful of my hair and jerks me back. "I am going to kill you," he wheezes.

I twist and turn until I'm no longer on my stomach, splinters tagging my body throughout the struggle. Blood is rapidly pouring from his wound, but it doesn't slow him from backhanding me across the face. Undeterred, I reach for the knife and yank as hard as I can to pull it from his chest. He gasps and collapses on me. His attempt to choke me is futile because his strength is now gone.

Everything goes red.

He killed my father.

He hurt my family.

He caged me.

He took my innocence.

Stabbing and stabbing and stabbing and stabbing.

For seconds or minutes or months, *I stab.*

I stab until my arm is screaming in pain. And when the heavy body on top of me no longer moves, I eventually shove it off me.

"I hate you, William. I hate you," I sob out as I shakily stand and hobble toward the door, but not before spitting on his dead body first.

I'm dizzy as I make my way down the stairs, hurrying to distance myself from the man who took so much from me. It takes me forever to figure out how to unlock the front door, but the moment I burst out into the cold night air, I cry hysterically.

I am free. Finally, I am flying.

Until two strong arms encircle my waist.

And I lose my mind.

Chapter Six

Alcott Dumont

ANOTHER SCREAM PIERCES THE NIGHT.

Almost there.

My lungs smart in pain as I charge toward the shoe shop. I've been running as fast as I can to get to her, but now, I'm practically flying.

As I approach the building, the door swings open and a wild animal of a woman blasts out the door.

A bloody, crazed, naked woman.

Ella.

My God, what did he do to her?

Because she is covered in blood, I worry about what sort of injuries he's inflicted upon the innocent woman. But she is clutching a knife in her hand while she runs, so I understand she is the one who made it out alive.

There's not a doubt in my mind that William is dead.

My first inclination is to grab her before she draws attention to herself. So I get close enough behind her and snatch her in my arms.

She's explodes in a feral, manic fury in my arms and starts slashing at me with the knife. And before I manage to grip her wrist to keep her from doing any damage, she slices my forearm open.

"Ella!" I hiss against her damp, bloody hair, "Ella, it's me! Alcott!"

At hearing her name, she sags in my arms. All fight drains from her, and she nearly collapses.

"He . . . I . . . Cellar . . . Virgin . . . Feces . . . Dead," she babbles through her tears.

"Shh. I have you now, angel," I promise fiercely.

She sobs as I scoop her into my arms and take off. The woman holds fiercely on to her weapon as if she's afraid she'll have to use it again, so I don't dare try to take it from her. I'm exhausted from running, but I won't stop. Not yet. Not until she is safely tucked away at the Thomas estate under my protection.

Trotting along with her slight frame in my arms is a difficult task, but I don't slow until I see the coach waiting for me at the corner. Gerald is standing beside it with the door open and ready. His eyes widen in horror upon seeing the broken girl in my arms, yet he doesn't say a word as he helps me load her inside.

"Back to the estate. With haste!" I bark at him as I climb in after her.

I've barely managed to close the door behind me before the coach fires off toward the estate. When I drag my eyes over to Ella, I can't help but cringe. The poor woman is barely holding on to her sanity by a thread. After I shrug out of my top coat, I drape it over her shoulders.

"Come here," I urge softly as I tug her into my arms.

She doesn't protest as I hug her to me. While I stroke her matted hair, I ignore the way she smells. That fucking arse ruined this girl. The sweet, blue-eyed angel I met a while back is gone. He turned her into this broken mess. If he weren't already dead, I'd kill him.

"I'm t-t-tainted." Her words seem nonsensical to me.

"Shh. Don't speak, Ella. You're safe now. I shall protect you with my life," I promise and then kiss her hair.

I think she passes out because she falls limp in my arms. Staying true to my word, I hold her the whole half hour until we pull up to the door of the estate. Gerald silently assists me in getting out of the coach with her and inside the home.

"Draw a bath. Have Gretchen prepare some food for her," I order as I stride past him toward the wing I've been staying in with Ella in my arms. "And lock this place down. No open windows or unlocked doors."

He assures me that it will be done as he rushes past me. By the time I make it to my room, I can hear him preparing the bath in the washroom.

"Can you stand?" I question.

She nods, so I carefully set her to her feet.

"I'm going to find you a robe—"

"Don't leave me!" she hisses, clutching on to my shirt. Her teeth chatter away as she buries her face against my chest.

At a loss of what to do, I simply hold her until Gerald emerges from the washroom.

"Everything is ready. I'll attend to the rest of the matters now," he assures me before leaving us alone.

I assist her as we walk into the steamy washroom. Scents of lavender hang in the air and mix with the odors coming from the abused woman in my arms. After I've guided her over to the tub, I remove the top coat that's draped over her and help the wobbly girl into the bath. As she sinks into it, she practically moans.

My lips purse into a firm line when I see that her blue eyes are vacant and staring into the now pink water. In a gentle manner, I take the knife from her tight grip and drop it to the floor.

"Do you need help washing yourself?" I ask.

She doesn't answer, so I pick a sponge up and lather it with soap. When I hold it in front of her, she doesn't take it from me.

"Ella, talk to me. What is going on in your head right now?" I question as I begin scrubbing the blood from her body.

It doesn't take long to see that her body is covered in tiny cuts. She has many splinters, and bruises color her flesh. Anger bubbles in my chest, but the man I would take my rage out on is dead. So, instead of getting furious, I focus on fixing this woman.

"I'll have Gretchen remove these splinters when you get out and—"

"No!" she screeches, grasping my wrist. "I don't want to see anyone!" Her vacant eyes are now filled with terror.

"Okay, angel. Don't fret. Mother taught me well." I smile in a way I hope calms her. "I will remove them for you."

She sighs in relief and relaxes, her eyes dropping back to the sudsy water. I continue silently cleaning her, but all the while, I wonder how I'll revive the sweet, doe-eyed girl I met at the reception, which now seems like ages ago.

I fear she'll never be that woman again.

"I think we should wash your hair. Can you get it wet?" I ask.

She nods, so we set to cleansing her soiled hair. After we finish, she turns to me and a flash of the girl I remember sparks in her eyes before the feral one takes her place.

"I killed him." Her voice is quiet but not sad. It's almost as if she's trying to convince me that it is forgivable that she did so.

And it is.

"Yes. I came to that conclusion. He deserved it. You were only protecting yourself."

Tears well in her eyes, and her bottom lip quivers. "I was so frightened."

I swipe one of her tears away with my thumb and bring my face close to hers. "I know, darling, but you're safe now. Do you understand me? Nothing will ever happen to you again."

Her gaze is guarded, and I can see that it hasn't truly sunk in that she is safe now. I will try my damnedest to convince her though.

As soon as I hear the clattering of a tray in the bedroom, I stand.

"Where are you going?" she screeches.

I grab her towel and hand it to her. "I'll be right back, Ella. I promise."

She rises from the water and wraps the towel around her body.

After rushing from the washroom, I find Gretchen and instruct her to bring me a medical kit but leave it by the door. Her worried eyes fly to the washroom door for a moment, and I see her desire to want to go in there and help the woman. But she heeds my direction and shuffles from the room.

"Is she gone?" Ella whispers from the washroom.

"Yes. Come eat something."

She emerges with the towel tied around her. Now that she's clean, I notice that her long, slender legs are dotted with all sorts of markings. An angry, purple bruise coats one of her ankles, and I hate the fact that she has been living in hell for the last five days.

"I'll have Gretchen find one of Elisabeth's dresses for you and—" I start, but she cuts me off.

"No."

I frown at her but motion for her to sit. "Listen, Ella. I only want to help. Tell me what you want and I'll do whatever it takes to make it better. Can you at least eat something?"

She warily eyes the food, but eventually, she sits on the bed beside the tray. With a shaky hand, she lifts a lid on the plate and finds a steaming bowl of oatmeal with fresh fruit. For some reason, I expect her to hesitate, but she dives right in and eats as if she's ravenous. This infuriates me, as I wonder if she starved while she was imprisoned. By the way her skin hugs her ribs, I'd say that she missed far too many meals in those five days.

After a light rap on the bedroom door, Ella drops her spoon and bolts back into the washroom. The poor girl is scared of her own fucking shadow at this point.

"Ella," I call out to her, "it is only Gretchen bringing the medical kit. You can come out and finish your meal."

It isn't until I have retrieved the kit and am sitting on the bed, bandaging up the cut to my arm, that she finally emerges from the washroom. Her eyes are cast downward as she sits and eats every morsel on her plate.

"Would you care for more, dear?" I question.

She shakes her head, and her teary eyes meet mine. "I'm satisfied now."

I don't believe her, but we'll deal with that later. Right now, I must tend to her wounds. Standing up, I retrieve the tray and move it to the bedside table. When I return, I sit near her.

"I'm going to look you over, Ella. Remove some of these splinters."

She shocks me when she tugs the towel away from her body and tosses it to the floor. The girl I've fantasized over for almost a year is naked and in my bed. It is a shame she isn't here for other reasons than of my helping her in her abused state. Dropping my gaze, I hunt through the kit until I find the salve and a metal tool to remove the splinters while she stretches facedown across the bed.

She remains quiet, her arms tucked underneath her, as I search for the wood pieces. I'm completely lost in my task of removing them from the backs of her thighs when the bed starts to shake. Tearing my gaze from what I am doing, I discover she's crying.

"Do you want to talk about what happened?" I question in a soft voice.

Her crying becomes hysterical sobs, and the brokenness that radiates from her crushes a part of my soul.

"Come here," I say as I scoop her into my arms. "You don't have to talk about it. I am only trying to help you."

Her wild, blue eyes find mine and I search them for the girl from nearly a year ago. I need to find her and prove to her that she is safe now.

"Alcott," she cries, "I came back haunted. I'm lost, and my

head is filled with thoughts, none of which are good."

I squeeze her to me and press a kiss to her forehead. "You have survived a horrific trauma, Ella. It is expected for you to have unpleasant thoughts. There is nothing to worry about now."

Her features morph from an expression of despair to one of hate. Then she practically spits out her words. "What about Mr. Caulder? Do you think he shall simply go away?"

Until this moment, I hadn't quite considered past rescuing her. "He won't touch a hair on your body—not a goddamned hair," I growl.

She lifts an unconvinced, blond eyebrow. "And you're so sure—why? He has some vendetta against Jasper, does he not? Now that I've thwarted his original plans, you think he'll sit by idly? Do you think he will ignore the fact that his plan was foiled?"

Rage bubbles in my chest at the thought of this arse attempting to damage her or my family any more than he already has. "Ella—"

"He. Will. Come."

We silently glare at one another. Her pink cheeks are tearstained, but there's resolution in her eyes. I want to argue this matter with her but I'm afraid we'll go all night. Instead, we hold each other's stubborn gazes until I finally speak again.

"We'll leave in the morning and travel back to Havering." My voice is firm and I'm not going to negotiate the matter.

"And then what? He'll follow us there? Attempt further atrocities against my sisters? Against Jasper or Alexander? When will it end, Alcott? I need answers or I'll never be able to ease the anxiety that infects my soul."

I clench my teeth. "I will kill him."

She sneers. The dainty, pure woman is overtaken by something dark and sinister. This woman sends a chill down to my bones.

"*We* will kill him."

I gape at her. "Absolutely not. You will stay here while I handle this. It is not a woman's place to—"

She stops me with a slap across my cheek.

What in the fuck is wrong with her?

What did that bastard to do her?

"It *is* my right, Alcott! I have every right to kill the man who started this!"

I want to be angry with her, argue with her, but right now, the woman is slightly unhinged. It is in both of our best interests for me to calm her.

"Sure, angel. We'll figure something out. I want you to rest now," I say.

Her eyes lose their feral flare upon winning so easily. "Don't placate me."

"I would never. Now, please, let me tuck you into bed. We can discuss the matter further once you've had rest," I tell her softly.

She sighs but crawls out of my arms and under the covers. Once more, my eyes skim over her naked flesh, and a longing begins to fester within me. If only I could have her here, spend my years tasting and pleasuring her. Instead, I'm trying to learn who this new, crazed woman is—attempting to walk on the broken glass between us in a struggle to bring her back to a sense of normalcy.

Once I've situated the blankets, I stand to leave her.

"Where are you going?" she hisses, her voice taking on the vulnerable quality from earlier.

"Darling, I'm leaving you to rest. You *need* rest."

Her face crumples as her body shudders with a silent sob.

"Fuck," I growl. "I'm tired as hell, but if you want me to stay, I will. But we're sleeping—no more talking. You *need* to sleep, Ella."

I take my shoes off and don't bother with removing any of my clothes before I snuff out candles. Once the room is dark, I climb into bed with her. Her slender arm snakes across my chest and she wraps herself around me as if she's afraid I'll steal off in the middle of the night. That's not going to happen.

"I'm sorry this has happened to you, Ella," I murmur into her still damp hair. "I was so close to a point where I felt comfortable in asking to court you. Ever since I met you in Havering, I've been enamored with you. You're beautiful and sweet and incredibly intelligent. I wanted to wait until I had made something of myself so that I would be worthy of you."

She tenses at my words, and her thumb grazes over my nipple through my dress shirt. The simple touch causes my cock to twitch in response. If only things were different.

"Now, all I care about is gluing your broken pieces back together. You're changed and everything in my soul screams at me to fix you. Let me put your innocent being back together again, Ella."

The darkness ripples with her hollow, throaty laugh. "I'm no innocent. My innocence was killed the moment William stepped into my home and slaughtered my father. He took that from me—shattered that piece of me."

I swallow my unease and run a finger down her bare arm. "You're here, alive. Not him. You were strong enough to do what needed to be done."

We both remain quiet for a few moments, and I've almost drifted off when she speaks.

"There is still so much to be done," she whispers so softly that I almost don't hear her words.

My flesh chills at her cryptic statement. I don't know this person in my bed. This is not the Ella I met in my home in Havering.

I allow her to think I have fallen asleep, whereas, in truth, I stare in the darkness as I try to work out what I'll do next. If I have any hope of saving this girl, I need to locate Caulder and rip him to fucking shreds. Then, maybe she can begin to heal.

Then, I can court my fucking woman.

Chapter Seven

Ella Merriweather

I WAKE WITH A START. MY rapidly beating heart calms the moment I realize I am no longer in the cellar. Actually, I'm on my back, Alcott's heavy arm is slung across my middle, his nose is pressed against my neck.

I'm safe.

William is dead.

But Caulder is not. That needs to change soon.

With each measured breath, Alcott tickles me and an unusual sensation skitters across my flesh. It feels as if I crave for him to touch me. How glorious would it be for him to erase the last touches I endured at the hand of William?

It would cure my wild heart, I presume.

As he sleeps, I slide my palm over the back of his hand and guide it south. Once his hand rests warmly against the thatch of hair between my legs, I relax and test my theory. An undiscovered part of me throbs for him—both inside and outside my womb. I'm achy with a longing I don't understand, and it feels as if he holds some remedy that could save me.

Again, I attempt to calm my heart as it flutters wildly for a reason other than fear. Could it be desire? I am not sure. The very fact that Alcott, the sinfully beautiful man I met but a year ago, has his hand between my legs nearly makes me forget all I have endured. His comforting presence distracts me from the pain of my life.

And the mere fact that he never married and is here with me soothes a piece of my soul. Maybe he truly wants to be with me like he so plainly stated so many months back. Last night he certainly seemed keen on wanting to protect and care for me. A woman can hope.

A smile, the first since I was taken, tugs at my lips while I remember when I first met him. I developed quite the crush for the man.

"When you see God, tell him I said hello," a deep voice rumbles from behind me.

I tug away from Father's arm, as he's lost in conversation with Edith's father-in-law, and face the man who spoke. Upon seeing him, my heart catches in my throat.

Alcott Dumont.

We were introduced when we arrived for the ceremony, and our encounter was delicious yet uncomfortable. He seemed to undress me with his eyes and I was embarrassed.

Yet now . . . Now, I want to see more of those dark eyes that appeared to see through me when nobody else hardly noticed my presence.

"I don't understand." I half smile back at him.

He chuckles and crosses his arms over his chest. Very blatantly, his eyes peruse over my figure. As of late, I've bloomed into a woman—a woman he very clearly sees.

"You came from heaven, no?"

My cheeks blaze as I realize he's complimenting me. Apparently, my innocence intrigues him.

"No," I reply and drop my gaze to the floor.

I'm hardly comfortable in my recent womanly skin, and I feel as though Alcott's quite comfortable in that of his manhood. We're as opposite as can be—he with his cultured wit and charm and I with my nerves and naïvety.

"Your sister has tried to intimidate me into staying away from you. She claims you're too good for the likes of me, angel."

My eyes lift to find his humored ones. At first, I believe he's making fun of me. But I soon realize he is entertained by my shy demeanor. I can see he's used to riling people up for sport. And he's quite good at his game.

"Are you bad?" I question, a tiny smile tugging at my lips.

"Mother would say otherwise. Edith, however, would beg to differ. But what matters"—he flashes me a grin that dizzies me—"is what you think? What is it, Ella? Do you think I'm bad?"

When he takes a step closer, I am infected by his scent. Never have I noticed a man's smell—besides that of my own father—before. Alcott smells as if he had rolled around in a lemon field and then drunk tea with vanilla. His presence is alluring, and I find my mouth watering for the man.

"I think, if you go against Edith, you're asking for trouble. So perhaps you are bad?"

He chuckles and takes yet another step that threatens to cause my rapidly rising and falling breasts to tear through the fabric of my dress. "Care to dance, dear? I promise to be good."

I blink up at him. His dark eyes are playful, yet I see the desire in them. He wants me, Ella Merriweather, and his want is transparent.

"I don't know how," I whisper.

He winks and grabs my hand. His hand is warm as it firmly tightens around mine. I follow willingly as he guides me through the throng of people. Most are dancing in elaborate fashion with their fancy footwork and twirls.

I'll never be sophisticated like them or be able to dance the way they do.

I'm overwhelmed and embarrassed, afraid I'll certainly make a fool of myself.

"Don't fret, Ella," he says in a calming voice. "I shall take care of you."

His words blanket my pounding heart, and I trust in them. I trust this man I hardly know, who seems so enamored with me.

"I don't know how to dance like them," I tell him, my eyes cutting over to the others on the dance floor.

When my eyes find his again, I see him devouring my face with his eyes. I flush as they skim over my lips and then down my neck, toward the cleavage spilling from my dress. It is as if I am naked under his gaze, but the idea doesn't frighten me as it should.

"We shall make up our own dance," he tells me when his brown eyes are back on mine.

He clutches my hand, and with his other, he encircles my waist, causing me to shiver at his intimate touch. I notice that the other women have their palms on their partners' chests, so I mimic their actions and look up at him as if to say, What next? *He begins a slow movement, and it doesn't take long for me to sway along with him. We aren't moving much, but it feels as if we're dancing.*

This time, I take the time to inspect his appearance. His dark eyes are locked on mine, and his jaw is set. He pierces me with a hungry stare that makes me heat up in places I didn't know had the ability to warm to such degrees. The man is utterly handsome with his full lips and slight smattering of facial hair. His shoulders are broad, and his grip is strong. I cannot believe I am not melting from being in his arms. Everyone else blurs into the background and it feels like it is just the two of us—like I am the only woman in the room and him the only man.

He sees me like nobody else ever has.

And that scares me.

"Ella, you're so beautiful. How is it that I cannot take my eyes

from you?"

I blush at his words and divert my gaze to the buttons on his shirt. "My innocence has blinded you," I murmur. "If you're as bad as you claim, my goodness draws you in."

His hand breaks from mine, and he lifts my chin with his fingers. "I'm not bad, dear. I am simply poorly understood. So, where does that leave us?"

I chuckle, but my laugh dies when he gently grips his fingers around my waist and draws me closer until our chests touch. He is aroused from a simple dance and I can feel his hardness up against me. My head becomes light, and I feel as though he's crawled inside me. The man is in my head, in my veins, flooding me with his essence.

"It leaves me confused," I whimper. "I'm very inexperienced with men, you see. I have never been looked at, much less courted."

His hand slides around my jaw and into my hair. I flutter my eyes closed and hope for a kiss. How wonderful would it be to have the most handsome man I have ever laid eyes upon kiss me? He may claim to be bad or misunderstood, but I want him to kiss me nevertheless. Does that make me bad too?

"I want so much more than to court you," he growls so close to my lips that I can nearly taste the wine upon his. "I want to kiss you. Ella, I want to touch you. I want to fucking taste you so bad it makes me crazy."

My eyes blink open and I stare into his angry eyes. Why is he angry?

"I have never been kissed." The words spewing from my mouth are childish and immature. I'm embarrassed by them in front of this man.

"May I be your first?" he questions.

Our lips are so close. And as his nose grazes mine, it feels comfortable. Familiar.

"Yes."

The word is barely out of my mouth when we hear the crashing.

"It's Maude! Someone find Doctor Egnator!" a voice shouts.

Alcott blinks away the haze we were suspended in and tears from me without a backward glance as he runs to be with his mother. I stare after him with my finger to my lips, which still taste like him even though we never touched.

I'm dragged from the memory when I hear a clattering from somewhere else in the house. It would seem that the help is preparing breakfast. My stomach grumbles in response.

When I look over at the sleeping man in my arms, I can't help but notice that the confident, young man has been replaced. He's different and tired, with dark bags hanging under his eyes. This man has a few worry lines that are now permanently etched between his eyebrows. After abandoning his hand between my legs, I run my fingers through his thick, dark hair. A few strands of grey peek out near his temples—grey hairs that weren't there this time a year ago.

This man has been through stresses that have caused a change within him. Much like myself. I am no longer the doe-eyed, harmless girl. I have been wronged in an unforgivable way. Hopes of love and marriage, although still there deep down inside, don't flutter through me like they once did. Revenge and anger surge to the forefront instead.

Will I ever get that girl back?

Will I always be this new person I have become?

When he flinches in his sleep, one of his fingers grazes a part of me between my legs that flares every nerve ending to life. I release his hair and slip my hand back over his. Whatever he did was exhilarating, distracting me from my inward thoughts. With my finger, I press against the same offending one and nearly buck off the bed. My sisters never spoke much of sex to me until after they were married. All I really know is what I experienced last night, which was wretched and awful. It was unwanted. Yet, now, something deep inside me furls in a decadent way that has me thinking that perhaps, with Alcott, it would be something otherworldly.

Then I press again and my skin breaks out into a sweat.

This is something nobody ever spoke of—this sensation. I soon find myself massaging his finger so that it rubs me in that delicious area. My body squirms and writhes as I search for something that seems sinful and out of reach.

I gasp when I realize I am no longer doing the work. His fingers are touching me masterfully, yet he still breathes heavy with sleep. My hand slips from his, and I drag it up to my breast, where my nipples have become hard. And I ache to touch them.

I have never before explored my body, and now, I feel oddly curious. With Alcott beside me, I feel safe to try. William was a bastard, but he ripped away the skin that was my innocence, and I am now probing the wound, exploring its depths.

My muscles begin to tighten—as if they aren't sore enough already—and I nearly cry out. As something festers deep inside my womb, I feel as though I will explode at any moment. His fingers are magic as he touches me where no other has.

"Oh," I gasp.

I'm so close. To what? I am not sure. Perhaps the elusive orgasm William spoke of. Just the thought of what we did, he and I, causes bile to rise in my throat. I quickly swallow it down and embrace the feeling of Alcott touching me.

Alcott came for me.

Alcott wanted to court me.

Alcott wanted to kiss me.

"Yes," I breathe out.

So close.

So incredibly close.

His groan reverberates through me, and his erection pokes my leg through his trousers. I can feel myself hurtling closer to the edge of my sanity and I want to throw myself over it. But just as stars begin to dance in my vision, he unceremoniously rips his hand from me as if he were burned.

"Bloody hell!" he curses.

I shriek from the loss of his fingers, and tears form in my eyes. My body is shaking with need, and I nearly scream obscenities at him

"Ella, I'm so sorry. Oh my God, I have no idea what came over me," he apologizes as he sits up on an elbow and looks down at me with concern.

I snatch his hand and attempt to force it to where it felt so delicious and sinful only a moment earlier. "Do it. Whatever it was you were doing, I want you to do it."

His eyes widen before a groan rushes from him. It is almost as if he has given in, but he instead rolls away from me and climbs off the bed. When he turns around to look back at me, his eyes are wildly darting all over the place. His hair is wild and unruly. He's even more handsome now than when he is put together. I crave for his touch.

"What is going on in that head of yours, Ella? This isn't you."

My lip juts out and I pout. "I want you to touch me."

He's already shaking his head in protest. "You don't know what you are saying. He fucked with your goddamned head, woman. This isn't right."

I sit up to rest on my knees, throbbing and wet between my legs. He's wrong. I want more of his caresses.

"Touch me, please," I beg with tears in my eyes. "I need to feel something other than the anger and hate rushing through me. Please."

"No. You need to dress and come to breakfast." His voice is hoarse and thick. My eyes fall to his trousers and I see that he's most certainly still aroused. I'll make him want me just as I made William want me.

"Please," I purr, my begging turning into something seductive and sexy.

But when I slip my hand between my thighs, his eyes bug out of his head. I flinch as I connect with the place that was the cause of my pleasure.

"Ella, stop it."

I pin him with a challenging glare as I work to find the sensation again. My finger slips against my wetness, and I use it to further chase the feeling I so crave. Though his jaw is set and he clenches it furiously, he makes no move to approach me.

"Do you not want me?" I taunt.

He growls in response. "Are you fucking blind? Of course I want you, but now is not the time. You have been through too much trauma. It is too soon, woman."

No matter how hard I try, I can't find what it is I am searching for. My finger aches, and I feel defeated. With a frustrated sob, I fall onto the bed and stare up at him, tears rolling from my eyes.

He smiles sympathetically at me. "In time, dear, I will make you feel things you have never felt before. I will taste you as I once promised. My kisses will begin and end each of your days," he sighs. "However, now is not the time. Trust me, darling. Now, get dressed and I'll come for you in a short while. We can attend breakfast together." He waves toward a dress, presumably my sister's, which has been draped across the chair at the vanity.

I don't respond to him. Instead, I bury my face into the blanket. The floor creaks, signaling his approach to the bed. My body aches for him to join me—to distract my mind from all that haunts me. However, he disappoints me. One simple kiss is pressed against my hair and then he's gone.

Chapter Eight

Alcott Dumont

THE WOMAN IS MAD. CERTIFIABLY crazy. It is in her best interest if I call for a doctor—one who can pry into her mind and fix her. Clearly, I am not that man. I am incapable of understanding what is going on with her.

When I awoke to touching her, I at first assumed that I, too, had violated the woman. But the moment she begged and pleaded for me to continue, I soon realized it was by her own wishes—she was using me to pleasure herself.

My cock still aches, thick and harder than a fucking rock, in my trousers. It was my desire to spread her open and show her exactly how good I could make her feel with my tongue. However, I would have been no better than the predator who stole her from her bedroom.

I will not harm the woman.

And I will not allow her to harm herself.

After a quick, cold bath and having dressed, I stalk back toward the room I left her in. Then I rap on the door and wait for her to answer.

"Ella, are you dressed?"

Silence.

For a moment, I worry that someone has taken her again. Not wasting another second, I plow through the door. She stands at the window with her back to me. The woman is still stark naked, peering out into the street.

"Why aren't you clothed?" I hiss through clenched teeth.

The sight of her milky skin mottled with bruises and cuts seems harsher in the daylight. I want to cover her up and hide what that bastard did to her.

When she turns toward me, I drag my gaze away from her breasts to her face. A frown tugs at her lips as she recedes to her inward thoughts. With a growl, I snatch the dress up and storm over to her.

"Put this on. Now. We cannot have you traipsing around naked. Why are you naked, woman?"

I am completely flustered and unsure how to handle her. Calling for a doctor is of utmost importance.

"No."

My jaw drops, and I gape at her. "Ella, put on the goddamned dress."

Tears well in her eyes, but she shakes her head vehemently.

"Put on the dress or I'll put it on for you," I threaten.

She shoves me the moment I near her with the material. "Get away from me!"

"This is insane! You will dress and you will come to breakfast with me. It is evident that you are upset and distraught from your times with William, but I will not allow you to act like some madwoman. Put the dress on."

When I approach once more with the dress, she screams and rips it from my hands. I watch in astonishment as she tosses it to the floor. Closing in on her, I clutch her wrists and still her flailing arms.

"Why won't you put the dress on, darling?" I question in a softer tone.

She struggles for a moment before her shoulders sag and a wail rips from her. "I-I-I can't. He made me wear that dressing gown for so long. I stank!" Her body is consumed by shuddering.

I pull her into my arms to calm her. "Okay. Okay. Will you at least wear a robe? Please?" I beg into her hair.

She slips her arms around my waist and hugs me as she cries, but I feel the slightest of nods. Progress.

"I shall fetch it for you and escort you to breakfast. Ella, darling, I promise that it will get better. Let me help you." Then I pull away to regard her teary face.

Her cheeks are red from crying, and her bottom lip is dry and cracked. The whites of her eyes are bloodshot, and her nose is pink. Even in her wrecked state, I want to kiss her. Not much in my attraction to her has changed since I met her.

Before I can talk myself out of it, I bring my lips to hers and kiss her softly on her mouth. I need to get lost in her—to extend the kiss and allow it to evolve into something more. To kiss away all of her problems. But I am a man with morals, contrary to my brother's beliefs, which means that, as soon as the kiss begins, I pull away and end it.

Her eyes are no longer feral or sad—they're confused. Hell, I'm fucking confused. I am supposed to be caring for her, not wishing I could lead her over to the bed and pleasure her instead.

"Dress before I do something regrettable," I tell her gruffly and attempt to move away from her.

She widens her eyes but bravely shakes her head. "It wouldn't be regrettable. Why won't you touch me? Is it because I am . . ." she trails off.

I snake my arm around her waist and tug her to me. "You're what?"

"Tainted."

A roar rips from me. My thumb barely traces along the bones in her spine in a soft manner that contrasts the menacing noises coming my throat.

"He took what wasn't his to take? Ella, did he rape you?"

She bites her lip and then shakes her head.

"I don't understand."

"I asked him to."

Her eyebrows defiantly pinch together when I glare at her.

"Why in the ever-loving fuck would you ask him?" I snap but immediately soften because I don't want to upset her any more than she already is. "It was only once and you were under duress—"

"It happened twice."

Twice.

But not against her will.

"Talk to me right now, Ella," I say in a low voice, "You're not making one goddamned bit of sense."

"It was my plan!" she cries. "Okay? Don't you see? I was looking for a way out. I'm no whore!"

I slide my hands into her wild, blond hair and grip her tight. Her breaths come out in angry gasps as we stare at one another.

"You were a victim, darling!" I exclaim. "You could have fucked him a million fucking times and you, dear Ella, would not be tainted. He may have tarnished your soul, but you're still perfect. In fact, all I can think about is kissing those damn lips again."

Her mouth parts as she flutters her eyes closed. Without hesitation, I dip my mouth to hers and I kiss her with every emotion I'm feeling at the moment: fury, sadness, hope, adoration.

A moan spills from her into my mouth, which I devour. I kiss her until she's collapsing in my arms. She holds on to me as if I will disappear at any moment.

"I'm not going anywhere," I growl out when we finally break from our impressive kiss.

My guess is that she's soaking wet for me based on the lust-filled gaze she's staring at me with. The thick erection in my trousers presses painfully against her. Together, we sit in a moment of time we have frozen and simply regard one another.

Her lips, so swollen and pink—I crave them incredibly so.

"Make love to me," she murmurs.

God, how I want to. And oh, how I could. But it simply isn't right. She's too feral—not quite right after her distressing situation. The woman is too fragile, and I'm afraid she'll shatter her already fractured soul. I want to help her find herself before I take her body. It must come with time, not out of necessity to erase the past.

I need her to love me, because when I finally do take her, I will be in love with her. There's no doubt about that. I'm already falling fast and hard. And that is why it is important for me to lay a more solid foundation for our relationship.

"Darling, I want to make love to you so badly it hurts. But, unfortunately, we must resist. You are still afflicted from having been taken against your will and then made to do things you wouldn't normally have done. Had this not all happened and I called upon you to court you, Ella, you wouldn't be asking me to take you to bed after one kiss. Please understand why I am doing this. Not because I don't want to, but because I cannot. We'll know when the time is right. Trust me, dear, for I have never given you a reason not to."

Her shoulders sag, but she nods in a sad, defeated manner. Upon pulling her to me, I kiss the top of her head. She feels right in my arms, and I want to keep her here, where she'll always be safe.

This woman is unlike any other lady I have been with. Ella Merriweather, while once innocent and unknowing of the harmful way of the world, is now fierce and has discovered an inner strength most people will never find within themselves. Her body thrums as it attempts to control this newly revealed part.

As much as I mourn for the girl who was lost the moment William killed her father and did heinous things to her, I know that I must celebrate the woman she has become.

Ella Merriweather is a survivor.

But with this newfound persona, she must learn her boundaries and limitations too. Throwing herself at me is, in her mind, a cure, when, in actuality, it is only putting a bandage on her innermost bleeding wound. I want to heal her, not simply stop the bleeding. My desire is to stich her up with the strength of my love.

"You're amazing, beautiful girl," I growl into her hair.

When her sobs die down, she hugs me tight. My fingers skitter down the smooth skin of her back, and I rest them right above her arse. Though I itch to grab a handful of it, I refrain.

"Darling, our courtship starts now. Let's find you a robe, and then I am escorting you to breakfast. We shall spend the day together, getting to know one another. Will you allow me to court you, Ella Merriweather?" I question and then pull away to look at her.

Her blue eyes flicker with an innocence I remember but thought had long since been snuffed out. As a tiny smile tugs at her lips, I have the desire to kiss it right off her face.

"What if you don't come to like what you learn about me?"

I grin at her and graze my nose against hers. "Too late, angel. I'm far past like. The truth of the matter is that I hope you do not decide you don't like me, for *I* will go mad. There is something between us, and it will only grow with time. It will be something perfect and wonderful—all we have to do is nurture it," I say before I press a kiss to her lips. "And there will be no lovemaking."

When I glance down at her to gauge her reaction, I see that her nose is scrunched up and her lips are about to argue. So, I kiss them to silence her.

"Yet, dear woman. There will be no lovemaking *yet.*"

Both Gretchen and Gerald met my gaze with widened eyes this morning when I escorted Ella, who was barely clothed in a short, silky robe, on my arm for breakfast. Wisely, however, neither of them spoke a word. Gerald commented on the weather and politics while Gretchen asked Ella about her nephews. It was clear we were all dancing around the obvious topic of last night. Several times, Ella became frightened or had a bout of anxiety. Each time, I simply slid a palm over her bare thigh and squeezed it. It relaxed her immediately, and I was thankful I had the ability to calm her.

"Alcott, I need to ask you about some business matters in the study. Care to meet with me now that breakfast is over?" Gerald questions as he sips his hot tea.

My eyes skitter over to Ella, who regards me with terrified eyes.

"I could really use some help with the cleanup. Would you help me, Ella?" Gretchen questions.

I know that Jasper pays Gretchen to do the housework without the assistance of anyone. But I also can see that Gerald wants to speak to me out of her earshot. They are playing a game to subtly make that happen.

Guilt over making the old woman do all of the work wins out and Ella agrees, only with slight reluctance.

"Very well," I say as Gerald and I stand. "Ella, I shall fetch you in a bit and show you the garden. You may find it quite enjoyable there. That is Elisabeth's favorite place to relax."

"I'd like that." She flashes me with a shy smile. This smile, I recognize from before.

I wink at her and take satisfaction in the way it reddens her cheeks. Then we hold each other's gaze until I'm out of the dining area and striding toward the study with Gerald on my heels.

Once he follows me inside and we close the door, I regard the old man. Gerald is a smaller fellow, and one would think he could be broken with a simple embrace. However, he is cunning and wise. I'd never put my strength against his knowledge. The man would cut me down to my knees in an instant—which is why he and I were a perfect team in our endeavor to find Ella. We complemented each other and found a balance that helped complete our mission of finding her.

"The girl is unbalanced," he says gruffly as he sits in the chair opposite the desk Jasper allows me to use for work.

I frown at him. "The bastard fucked her. Not against her will—it was her plan to free herself. Clearly, it worked. She's disturbed by that notion, but I will calm her, Gerald. I will bring her back to me."

He nods his approval. "If she is anything like Elisabeth or Edith, she'll be worth the troubles, I suppose. I want you to be happy, son."

I beam at him. My father, though I love him, has always been regal and stiff. Gerald, on the other hand, feels like the loving fathers Mother used to read to me about in the storybooks as a boy. He is very close to me.

"Thank you, sir. Now, have you heard any word on Caulder or his goons?"

"Not a word, but I don't doubt that we shall soon be investigated. It will be advisable for you to carry a weapon whenever you go out for business. I would suggest you bring very little business into the estate in an effort to protect Ella."

My lips press into a firm line. We will have to be on the constant lookout for those bastards. In no time, they'll be crawling on this estate like fucking rats.

"She desires to end Mr. Caulder's life. I'm afraid she won't settle until it's done," I sigh.

He palms his scruffy face and regards me with raised, white eyebrows. "That is the most horrible idea I have ever heard. Keep her safe, here. Don't let her out of this compound, Alcott. I will do whatever I can to help you dispatch Caulder and his men. Anything. But for the love of God, don't let the girl go. She may have had luck on her side with William. But Caulder is ruthless and cunning unlike William. He isn't blinded by a broken heart. Caulder will stop at nothing, and if he gets her in his clutches, he will damage her beyond repair."

The warning hangs thick in the air, and my breakfast threatens to make a reappearance.

"So be it, Gerald. I shall do my work behind her back. I will need your help in distracting her. Now, let's formulate a plan."

Chapter Nine

Ella Merriweather

THE WIND PICKS UP, AND a slamming door startles me from my daze. My heartrate quickens, but I still it once I realize nobody is here to harm me. Then I turn my attention back to my novel and stretch my bare legs out on the bench.

Out here, in the garden, is the only place I can be free. It is completely surrounded by walls, but the sky is open to me. The small area is overgrown with wild and beautiful plants. A thick, heavy, sweet honeysuckle-and-lemon scent permeates the air, and I gulp in lungfuls of it.

Today, the sun is shining and I can feel my skin cooking from the heat of it. I am almost happy and carefree. Neither Alcott nor the staff says a word about the fact that I bask in the sunlight every day, free of clothing. However, he did insist that Gerald hang some curtains in the windows so I could have my privacy.

The birds chirp in the lemon tree, and I sigh. It is almost a perfect escape from my mind and reality. Since coming to Jasper's estate a week ago, I have spent countless hours of each day out here.

"Ella," Alcott's deep voice booms from the doorway.

Lazily, I drag my gaze over to him and shield my eyes to see him better. "Alcott."

His eyes are downcast, but I wish he would look at my body. Ever since that first night, he has refused to touch me in a sexual manner despite my daily begging. Now, I'm tired of begging aloud for it. I shall simply hope instead.

"I must leave to take care of some business," he says as he enters the garden and makes his way over to me.

I wait for his eyes to peruse my body—to show an interest in me. But alas, he does not. Much to my dismay, he picks my robe up off the ground and hands it to me.

Rolling my eyes, I huff at him but don't don the robe. "What sort of business? Does it involve Caulder?"

Our conversations always loop back to that man.

This time, he meets my gaze with a glare of his own. "No, just business."

I thread my fingers together behind me and stretch. Now I have his attention. His eyes skim down to my breasts, which are on full display, before he drags them back away.

"Care for a taste?" I taunt with a raised eyebrow and a smirk.

He grunts and ignores my question. "I thought we could visit my brother and your sisters in Havering. We could leave in the morning."

I leap from the bench so quickly that he doesn't have time to react or retreat like normal. When my hands find the lapels to his waistcoat, I tug him against my bare body.

"What about Caulder? I'm not leaving until it is done, Alcott."

He goes to push me away, but I clutch tighter. Once he realizes I am not going anywhere, he slips his arms around my waist and pulls me to him. We may not be as sexual as I would like, but Alcott *is* affectionate. He steals me to him for kisses and hugs often, and I look forward to his touch, even if it only makes me wish for more.

"Darling, I'm worried about you. Doctor Morton thinks—"

I cut him off. "Doctor Morton is an idiot. He thinks he can fix me with his potions and tonics. I don't need fixing, Alcott. What will fix me is the day I stab Caulder in the fucking heart!"

Alcott glares at me with a ferocity I should fear—but I don't. Instead, I dampen between my legs and the familiar ache taunts me. Every night, with my fingers, I search for the elusive pleasure button. And each night, I fail. I'm frustrated and angry that he won't ease my ache.

"You can't go around killing everyone, Ella. You're a small, dainty woman for fuck's sake," he snarls.

I sneer at him. "Just one man, not everyone. If Caulder doesn't get what he deserves, he'll only seek out more women to destroy. Do you think I am the first one?"

He stiffens in my arms. "Why can't you just let me take care of it, woman?"

"Because I need this," I sigh. "I need this for my sanity, okay?" My tone melts the glacier between us.

Then his hands find my arse. "You make me want to give you your way."

I smile broadly at him. "So give it to me."

Even though we're talking about Caulder, neither of us miss the double meaning. I have begged and pleaded for his touch, but he continues to deny me, saying it's for my own good.

"Oh, I want to give it to you. You have no idea how badly that is truth," he says, dipping his lips close to mine.

His thumbs slide around to my front and he drags his palms up along my ribs, his fingers leaving a trail of heat in their wake on my back. I'm pretty sure he'll give in this time, and I am further convinced when his lips crash against mine. Through his trousers, just like always, I can feel how my proximity affects him. And when his hands are a little higher, his thumbs brush against the underside of my breasts and I moan into his mouth.

I am seconds away from climbing up his hard body and pleading for him to make love to me against the brick of the garden wall.

"Ella," he grumbles as he breaks our kiss and pushes me slightly away from his body. "You're killing me."

Undeterred, I attempt another tactic. I rub my palm over his length through his pants and his cock bounces to life.

"You don't play fair, angel," he groans without stopping my assault on him.

"Perhaps it is because I'm no angel, Alcott," I purr as I stroke him.

"I will make love to you if you forget all of this mess and come to Havering with me."

His proposed deal causes me to take pause.

He is propositioning me with an alternative to protect me in exchange for giving me what I want. My womb aches at the idea of finally having him—of finally seeing if he can ease the unrest in my head and body. If I can't feel something while with Alcott, I shall be doomed, because I am incredibly attracted to him. If it turns out to be as it was with William, I won't know how to carry on.

And that thought frightens me.

"I'm scared," I tell him with a quiver in my voice. "What if I still don't like sex, even with you?"

His brow rises as he smiles smugly at me. "Not possible, darling. When I finally get to have you, you won't know which way is up because I'll turn your world upside down. I shall play your body as if it were an instrument especially designed for my hands and tongue. Together, we will harmonize and make love to only a song we can create."

I lean forward and kiss his confident lips. "Like when we made our own dance?"

"You couldn't be more correct."

He deepens our kiss, and I lose myself in all that is him. When he showers me with his affections, it is easy for me to forget everything that plagues me.

"Do we have ourselves an agreement? Shall we make some amazing love and then I will take you to see your sisters?" he questions against my lips.

I nod as I sling my arms around his neck and climb him like a pole. Since day one, I have wanted to attack him, and now, I can. I'm finally allowed the opportunity and I cannot wait any longer. He groans, but his hands find my arse and he holds on to me.

"Not here. I am going to make love to you in the bed." His words are lost in my mouth as he walks us out of the garden and through the door into the house. As we enter, he tears his lips from mine. "Divert your eyes," he calls out in warning in case Gretchen or Gerald are nearby.

I giggle like a madwoman and steal his lips again. While he blindly leads me back to the bedroom, we manage to run into only a few pieces of furniture along the way. Within moments, we're next to the bed he lets me sleep curled up against him each night, the door kicked shut upon our entering.

He peels my arms off his neck and playfully tosses me onto the bed. I expect to see a smile, but he peers down at me with a serious look, making no moves to remove his clothes.

"Are you sure about this? Because once we do this, it cannot be undone. I know that, the moment I make love to you, my heart is going to thread itself with yours. If this is simply a ploy to fix your heart and you lose interest, I will be brokenhearted, Ella. Do you understand? I want to do this because I want and care for you. Do you feel the same about me?"

I nod slowly. "Alcott, I'm terrified. I'll admit that. But I have a craving for you I don't understand. It possesses me. A part of me worries I will be disappointed—that it will be like it was with William and that I will never be able to be loved or to love anyone. A part of me worries I am forever broken. However, the other part of me, the one that still has hope for a normal life, knows that this is more than a physical union. That part of me knows that this is a way for your stronger heart to connect with mine and, together, they shall beat as one. You once asked me if I trusted you, and the answer was always yes. I still trust you. I'm ready to go forward with you."

His smile is one of relief, and he begins tearing at his clothes with undeniable speed. Once his trousers are gone, I gape at his cock. I've never simply looked at one. It is an odd-looking thing with its bulbous head and veins. What is even odder is the way my mouth waters to taste it. I truly am insane.

"It is ugly," I tell him with a playful grin.

He smirks as he crawls onto the bed on his knees. His eyebrow rises as he takes hold of it and strokes it. "They're all ugly, Ella. Mine is quite handsome in comparison."

A laugh bursts from me. "Quite confident, are we?"

"I'm confident that you may not think he's a looker but you'll love his tricks." He winks at me as he spreads my knees apart.

My body grows wet for him, and I squirm with warring thoughts of needing to close my legs or letting them drop farther open. Then he drags a finger across the place I've massaged and rubbed for an entire week. Whereas I couldn't produce one inkling of pleasure, his barest touch sends sparks blazing through my veins.

I close my eyes and whimper as I wait for him to enter me. But when something warm and wet slides between the lips of my southern region, my eyes fly open.

"What are you doing?" I hiss when I realize he is tasting me there.

His breath is hot, and it makes me crazy when he answers. "I am going to give you an orgasm you'll never forget, dear. Now lie back and enjoy this."

I cry out when his mouth connects again with the place that throbs wildly for attention. My hands find his hair, and in an embarrassing move, I push him against me there. I need to feel him all over me—inside me.

"Oh!" I shriek as his tongue goes into a frenzy of circling and flicking and sliding.

I'm squirming and writhing as I either run to or from whatever it is he is giving me. Then the sensation from last week when his hand was upon me sneaks up on me and my skin breaks into a sweat as every muscle in my entire body tightens in preparation. I'm terrified yet eager to see what happens next. With every lash of his tongue on my body, I dive deeper and deeper into oblivion. And once blackness steals my vision, I slam my eyes shut.

"Alcott, something is happening," I gasp. It feels foreign and unusual, but I want it so badly.

He doesn't respond, only intensifies his actions.

After one more flick of his tongue, I lose control. My body shudders as if a demon has crawled inside and taken over. I feel like I'm combusting from within and no longer have power of one single aspect of myself. And as quickly as it possessed me, it leaves.

"Alcott," I whimper when he pulls away from the part of me that is still pulsating and sensitive.

His face glistens with my arousal as he flashes me a smug grin. "How was that?"

I close my eyes again and attempt to formulate what it is that happened to me. "It was . . . It was . . ."

"Magic?"

"It was otherworldly."

He chuckles, and it reverberates to my core. I look up at him expectantly.

"Are you ready for more?" he asks.

"Make love to me," I plead.

Sitting back on his haunches, he seizes my leg and draws my foot to him. I gasp when he kisses my ankle. He begins a slow ascent up the inside of my leg, trailing kisses along the way. When he makes it to my pubic bone and presses a kiss there too, a mewl escapes me. This man makes me insane with his teasing nature.

And then he's back on a mission as he tickles the flesh of my belly with his lips. The moment he arrives at my breast and his tongue tastes my nipple, I cry out.

"So sweet," he groans after he sucks and nibbles.

I thought I was wet before, but now, I am positively dripping with want. "Why must you tease me, Alcott?"

He continues his kissing until he has tongued his way up my slender neck and is at my ear. His breath is hot, and it sends shooting flames of desire right back to the place he drew an orgasm from moments before.

"I tease you because it entertains me," he growls, sliding his cock against the hair on my pubic bone. "And because teasing you makes me incredibly hard for you. Foreplay is every bit as important as the final act itself. You'll soon grow to love the teasing, angel."

I absolutely love it no matter how torturous it is.

"Kiss me," I demand.

He makes haste, and his lips are soon on mine. With each seductive dive of his tongue into my mouth, I arch my hips up to his to encourage him to continue what our bodies both want. His cock is slowly thrusting against me, but I desire so much more.

"I need to be filled by you," I moan. It is the only way to articulate what I need.

He groans. "My fucking God, your mouth does me in. Your talk is so foul yet you do it with such an innocent flare."

I slip my legs around his waist and latch on to it. "I want you inside me. I want your thick, ugly penis in my body."

We both chuckle at my words, but as he lifts up to grab his cock, we fall silent. His dark eyes find mine and ask permission. Then I nod, losing myself the moment he begins inching himself inside me.

My body fully accepts him, as I am completely drenched with my arousal. There is no resistance like there was the first time I had sex. This time, with Alcott, he slides right in and I go dizzy with the exquisite sensation of the way he stretches the inside of my body.

"I knew that, the moment I had you, it would be perfection," he murmurs as he dips his mouth to mine. "The moment you showed up in my home in Havering, I knew. I knew you would become mine one day."

I gasp as he begins slowly thrusting into me. The entire world disintegrates around me and all that exists is Alcott, with his dashing good looks and playful demeanor. I'm lost in all that is him and I never want to be found.

It is safe here in his arms, with not one single worry in my head.

Not one single angry, vengeful thought enters my mind.

Warmth and affection and desire fill my being.

"I like this, Alcott. Our bodies seem to be as one," I say in awe as I feel yet another glorious orgasm teasing me from unknown depths.

"Our courtship was short-lived," he grunts as he slides in and out of me.

I frown. "Are you already bored with me?"

He growls and attacks my lips. "No, I am going to marry you, sweet Ella."

His words ignite the climax that was on the horizon, and it obliterates every nerve ending in my body. As he pumps into me, he groans, and just as his body tightens up with his own orgasm, he goes to pull out.

"No! I want you inside me," I whisper as I dig my heels into his arse.

The man must have been holding on by a tiny thread, because in an instant, he is coming deep inside me. His heat explodes into my body, and I revel in the blissful sensation of it. Once we both relax from our ecstasy, he rests on his elbows to look at me.

"A fortnight ago, when William showed up in my bedroom, I actually entertained the thought of becoming Mrs. Benedict. How silly and naïve was I?" I question. "I was lured into a trap and abused by a monster. And now look at me."

He dips down and presses a kiss to my forehead. "Fuck becoming Mrs. Benedict. You will become Mrs. Dumont. I won't let much more time pass without you becoming my wife, Ella," he says in a gravely yet fierce tone, "A year ago, I attempted to do the honorable thing and court you properly. As a result, I sent you right into the lion's den. I could have swept you away back then and made you my wife. Instead, I chose to make a life for myself first so that you would have a secure future with me. I was such a fool."

His cock softens within me and he slides out of me. With it, his come trickles out and soils the bed beneath us. Then he rolls us over to our sides and strokes my hair away of my face.

"Alcott, you are not a fool. You're the best man I know. The moment I laid eyes on you, I was completely smitten by you." I smile and let my eyes flutter closed as he lazily drags his finger along my cheek. "And you came back for me. You found me when nobody else would or could. That makes you a hero in my eyes, certainly not a fool."

Chapter Ten

Alcott Dumont

HOW I RESISTED HER FOR so long was beyond me. But now that I've had a sample—an exquisite taste—I'll never be satisfied. I shall make her my wife upon returning to Havering.

After a full day of rolling around in the bed and learning one another's bodies, she passed out from our excursions. I'm tempted to wake her up with my tongue between her legs, but I must prepare Gerald for our travels tomorrow.

I press a chaste kiss on her forehead and slide out of the bed. Upon grabbing my trousers from the floor, I pull them on and then saunter from the room to find the old man. I find him smoking his tobacco in the den. When he sees my disheveled appearance, he raises a white eyebrow.

"Sir, it would seem you have been indisposed all day. With Ella, I presume? Did you finally give in to her incessant beseeching?" he chuckles.

I laugh and shake my head at him. "That woman will be the

death of me. However, it will be quite a pleasurable death—one would invite death in if that were the way he had to go."

He smiles, but his features quickly fall. "Son, I am afraid I discovered some information."

My playfulness dissipates as I fold my arms over my bare chest and regard him seriously. "And?"

The old man sets his pipe down and sips his bourbon. "Caulder's men are all over the place looking for you. They haven't quite pieced together that you work for Jasper, but they are close to figuring it out. I have ascertained that he has three fellows working for him through my investigations. Two you met the night we obtained Ella. The other is an unknown."

I nod and grit my teeth. "So I need to dispatch three men before I get to Caulder. Has he returned from France yet?"

"He's close," he grumbles. "The moment he received word that his scheme had been foiled, he set back for London. I presume he'll arrive tomorrow afternoon."

Fuck.

"We need Caulder," I say. "It won't be difficult to take the three men out, but he'll only find more to take their places. He'll come after her or someone I care for. I cannot sit back and allow this to happen. We need to figure out where he'll be when he gets back into town. If there were a way to spy on his goons, we might find out that information. However, my cover is blown. Do you think they made you, Gerald?" I question as I run a frustrated hand through my hair.

He shrugs. "I can't be certain. We could always invite them to the estate and take care of them upon their arrival."

I roll my neck and attempt to relieve the stress there. "We need to get to Havering. I can speak with my brother and Jasper—together, we can figure out what to do. Sitting here is unsafe for Ella. Do you know where those men have been spending their time? The same pub?"

He shakes his head. "No, unfortunately. Last I heard, they were staying at the Rose Thorne Inn nearby. The pub next door, Edmond's, is where they spend the most of their time."

I walk over to him and pour myself a glass of the amber liquid. "That's too close for comfort. We're within goddamned walking distance," I grumble. "Nevertheless, once darkness is on our side, we shall set out and discover what we can."

Gerald nods his agreement. "And I will prepare an invitation for tomorrow after you and Ella set off for Havering. I shall take care of the men."

Cutting my eyes over to the old man, I raise my eyebrows at him. "Is that so? The two men I encountered are bigger than I am. You are a fucking cockatoo compared to them. How in the hell do you plan on taking three men out by yourself."

He grins and picks his pipe up. Then he lights the end and takes a puff. "Never underestimate the strength and ferocity of someone small. What we lack in size, we make up for in heart and determination. Many giants have fallen by the hand of a mere, simple man. Didn't you read about them in your storybooks as a small lad?"

I'm already disagreeing with him. "Don't do anything foolish, Gerald. I won't risk your life for this. You have full access to the safe filled with Jasper's weapons. Don't hesitate to use them."

With a slap on my shoulder, he dismisses my worries. "I have lived for seventy-three years and am still doing quite well. You're the one who needs to take the lovesick blinders off and do what it takes to protect the woman."

His words sober me. "It will be done, old man," I grumble. "Meet me in the foyer in three hours. We'll head to Edmond's."

As I trace lines up and down her bare spine, I keep a wary eye on the clock on the chest of drawers. My hope was that she would fall asleep and I could steal off without her inquiries as to where I was going, for she would insist upon going with us.

That just isn't a fucking option.

Now that I have made her mine over and over again, I can't stomach the idea of her being anywhere near harm's way. Even though she has promised to go to Havering with me, I fear that, if she discovers our lead, she'll attempt to insert herself into the mission.

It would be my preference, though, to not have to leave her warm, naked body. I would much rather stay here with her glued to my chest and my fingers dancing along her flesh.

"Do you miss your brother?" she questions softly.

I cringe at the fact that she is indeed not asleep and Gerald will be waiting for me soon. "Sometimes. He and I had a tumultuous relationship until your sister came along."

She smiles—her smiles are ones I don't have to see to know they are there because I can feel them. The room warms and I can almost sense the joy radiating from her soul.

"I miss Edith and Elisabeth. I know they had their troubles, but I am glad they are better now. Do they know of Father's death?"

I nod. "I sent a letter explaining what happened and that you were safe now. I'm not sure how they are handling it, but they know. How are you handling it?"

A tear wets my chest, so I hug her to me and run my fingers through her hair.

"Shh. You don't have to talk about it, angel."

My brave girl swallows her sob and lets a ragged breath out. "I do want to talk about it. Father was a good man despite his gambling problems. He only did what he did for our family. Fate had a turn in all of it, because Elisabeth met Jasper. And Edith met Alexander. But he didn't deserve to die like that."

I roll her onto her back so I can see her tearstained face when she breaks down. "I guess your Father, by his gambling, somehow helped each one of his daughters find love. His death wasn't in vain.

You will carry on his legacy and memories. I will carry them with you, sweet girl."

Her palm finds my cheek and she smiles at me. "Alcott, I never said thank you. But I do thank you for being the one to catch me that night. I was horrified and alone and terrified out of my wits. When you tugged me into your arms, I thought I was done. However, the moment I realized it was you, I had never felt so relieved in my life. I should have been embarrassed or disgusted that you had to see me that way, but I didn't. I felt safe and protected. In that moment, I knew you would look after me until the day you died."

I press my lips to hers and kiss her with the promise that those feelings she had are truth. I'll do everything I can to keep her safe. And that includes this evening.

"Darling, you should rest," I tell her when I finally break away from our kiss. My cock, though, begs for me to touch her more, caress her, and make love to her.

But I cannot.

A plan is in motion.

"You're right," she sighs. "I'm rather sleepy."

I expected an argument or for her to continue to talk, but she rolls over with her back to me. After about ten minutes, her breathing is soft and rhythmic.

Luck is with me tonight.

I slip out of the bed and watch her warily. She doesn't make a peep while she continues to sleep, so I stealthily snuff out each candle in the bedroom after I dress. Within minutes, I'm stalking down the corridor toward the front door.

Gerald is patiently waiting by it. He's pulled on one of his caps to hide his appearance, and now, he tosses one at me. I groan at having to wear the old man's tobacco-scented hat.

"Oh hush, boy. You'll look debonair for once," he chuckles as I reluctantly put it on my head.

I shake my head at him in denial as I accept the sheathed knife he also hands over. Once I tuck it into the back of my trousers, we slip out the front door. We don't take the coach and instead travel by foot, careful to stick to the shadows. Tonight, the air is cool and the tension is thick.

So much rides on us ridding London of Caulder and his goons—my future with Ella, her fucking sanity. We cannot fail.

"I'll go inside, snoop around. You stand watch this time," Gerald instructs upon our arrival.

I grunt in frustration, though it makes sense. The men will recognize me. But Gerald? He may be able to obtain information without their knowing.

As he walks in, I nonchalantly watch him through the window. The old man sits at the bar much like I did the night I found Ella and speaks to the bartender. After a few minutes, he turns toward me and nods his head for me to come inside.

They're not here.

Bloody hell!

I push through the door and stalk over to him.

"What now?" I growl under my breath as he pushes a shot of whiskey toward me.

"Next door at the inn. Poker tournament."

I sling the liquor back and revel in the way it burns my throat. "What are we doing sitting here, then?"

"Patience, son. The tournament has been going on all day. When they take a break, all the men come to have a drink. We shall wait for them to come to us. Less suspicious that way."

Another drink is set down in front of me, and I quickly down that one as well.

"So we wait, old man."

And we wait for at least another hour.

I've knocked back one too many when a presence sits beside me. The fellow smells of pipe tobacco just like Gerald. Hell, he's even small like him.

"I'm looking for a man named Caulder."

The voice—so feminine and soft.

A voice I know all too well.

I lose my fucking mind.

Chapter Eleven

Ella Merriweather

TO SIT STILL AND PRETEND to be asleep was the hardest thing for me to do. Especially when I knew that Alcott was planning on leaving me to follow a lead on Caulder and his men. Earlier today, when I went looking for him after my nap and overheard him speaking with Gerald, I almost went mad.

All evening, I contemplated how I could go on my own reconnaissance mission without Alcott's knowledge. As he so easily slipped out away from me, I had an idea.

Now, as I stare at the mirror, I smile. I've sneaked into Gerald's room and stolen one of his suits. I'm a little taller than the man, but he's not much bigger than I am, so his clothes fit rather nicely. And for the first time in nearly a fortnight, I feel comfortable in clothing. The trousers allow me the freedom I require versus the thick, bulky dresses.

Men have it easy.

No corsets or petticoats.

No hairpins or makeup.

Suspenders and trousers and waistcoats. Easy.

I pick one of his hats up and attempt to stuff my long, wild hair into it. After several tries, I realize I am losing time. Alcott and Gerald have been gone an hour, and I have no idea when they'll come back. If I don't slip out before that time, I'll never get away.

My only option is to cut my hair.

Without my golden locks that hang halfway down my back, I will blend in. The chances of finding Caulder's men and obtaining information on where he will turn up will be much easier. I need to become a man.

I don't hesitate as I storm from Gerald's room into the sewing room. After wrenching open a drawer, I quickly locate a pair of sheers. They look just like Mother's, and a memory of her assaults me.

"Sugar bear, stay still," Mother chides as she attempts to cut my hair straight.

I cross my arms and pout. "I want to go play outside."

She sweeps a stray, blond hair from my forehead and smiles at me. "You can go play outside after *I trim your hair."*

"If you cut it all off, then I don't have to get a haircut for a long time. I want to be a boy."

Lissa gasps from her chair, clearly shocked at my words. She's next up for a haircut, and my ten-year-old sister doesn't like it when I sass Mother—hence her horror.

"Let her be a boy. Father always wanted one," Edie giggles. She sticks her tongue out at me from behind Mother, so I stick mine out back.

"That's enough, Ella Corrine Merriweather! Put that tongue back in your mouth or I'll snip it right off," Mother threatens. But the corners of her mouth twitch as she fights a smile, so I know she wouldn't really cut it off.

"Edie started it," I whine.

Mother finally does smile at me as she presses a kiss to my forehead. "And I'm finishing it. We're going to trim your hair so you can go play. One day, when you're a grown woman, if you want to cut off your hair to look like a boy, so be it. But not while under my roof, sugar bear."

I blink the tears away. God, I miss her. I miss all of them. I'm thankful she's in Heaven taking care of Father now. With a gulp, I swallow down the emotion that was thick in my throat as I realize for once I am not cursing God. As long as he takes care of my parents, he's okay in my book.

Walking over to the mirror in the sewing room, I regard the hair I always kept preened for my mother. She's gone now, and I must do this. Upon raising the sheers, I tug a handful of hair away from me.

"Sorry, Mother," I say firmly as I snip a chunk.

Once it falls to the floor, I become a madwoman with the scissors. I cut and cut until I'm left with very little. Until I'm certainly the prettiest boy to ever walk this city. My blond hair hangs short just under my chin. For a moment, I worry if Alcott will hate it.

But it is only hair, and it shall grow back.

I sweep what's left behind my ears and slip Gerald's hat back on. When my blue eyes find the mirror once again, I decide I do look like a young man. In the darkness, nobody will ever notice. Women don't wear trousers for one thing, and they certainly don't keep their hair this short. I'll blend right in.

Before I leave, I locate the knife Alcott never tried to take from me. It was the knife that killed my father and then later killed William. My hope is to slay Caulder with the same sharp piece of metal. Then I can bury it in my father's grave along with this entire horrible ordeal. My life with Alcott can begin free of worry and revenge.

Moments later, I am slinking in the shadows outside in the street. There is loud commotion coming from the left, so I decide to head that direction. The pub and neighboring inn Gerald spoke of are supposed to be within walking distance. And after a couple of minutes, I round the corner to see *Edmond's* clearly painted on a sign above a busy pub. My hope is that I may slip right in with the many other patrons and seek my information without notice.

Sauntering much like a man would, I make my way through the throng of people toward the bar. I would recognize Alcott and his thick dark hair a meter away—however, I don't see him anywhere. When I notice a barstool unoccupied, I stride over to it and slide down onto it. My heart is frantically beating, but I take several calming breaths to get it to relax.

Nobody has seemed to notice that I am an imposter as of yet, and I thank the heavens that I was able to slip in undetected.

I begin to lose some of my nerve at the prospect of actually speaking with these people in order to find information. For goodness' sakes, I never even practiced a manly voice! I clear my throat and attempt a very manly tone as I turn to the man wearing a hat, his back to me, beside me.

"I'm looking for a man named Caulder," I tell him in as deep a voice as I can. To appear more casual, I lean my elbow on the bar and wait for him to turn around.

But the moment he does, I realize I've made a horrible mistake.

None other than Alcott Dumont, looking very dapper, I might add, in a cap, turns to regard me. At first, he's shocked as he skims over my appearance, but almost immediately, he becomes outraged.

"What in the ever-loving fuck are you doing here? And what is it that you've done with your hair?" he hisses.

I curl my lip in disgust. "You're the one who left me in bed without any explanation. You were going to hide this from me!"

His eyes flicker past me to the door and then back on me. Over his shoulder, he growls to who I now see is Gerald, "We're leaving."

When his hand encircles my bicep and he yanks me off the stool, every part of me itches to slap him. However, I still don't want to blow my cover, and making a scene would most certainly do that.

"Let go of me, or so help me, I'll gut you," I threaten and tap the knife tucked into my trousers.

He widens his dark eyes in surprise, but it's evident in his smirk that he doesn't believe me, although he does release my arm. "It is doubtful that some *boy,*" he sneers, "could hurt a man like me."

"I'm staying, you big ape. Whether you like it or not. We both want to find out where Caulder is. So let's just stay and see what we can find."

He's poised to argue when he once again eyes the front door. "Fuck! Gerald, it's the same men. They've already made me, so I can't risk them seeing me, especially now." His eyes flicker down to me. "I'm taking this *fella* to the back."

Gerald grunts that he will take care of talking to the men.

Alcott glares at me. "You will follow me to the washroom so that we may stay out of sight from those men. If you make a fuss, I'll drag your arse back there. I will protect you, goddammit. No matter what that takes."

I'm stunned into tears as I follow the stalking man to the back. I want to stay, but if he's seen those men before, I don't want anything to happen to him. He leads me through a long corridor, and when we reach a washroom at the end, he angrily pushes through it.

"Alcott," I say softly from the doorway.

When he returns to regard me, he is furious. However, even in his current state, I know he would never hurt me. Not like William did.

"Get inside."

I open my mouth to respond, but he seizes my wrist and roughly pulls me into the small room. The door closes behind me and he turns the lock. My pulse quickens, and for a moment, I wonder if he's angry because he hates the way I look—I am no longer his pretty girl. I can deal with his being upset with me for putting myself in danger, but if he's no longer attracted to me, that will be more difficult to handle. In fact, I won't be able to handle it at all.

"I'm sorry. I just wanted to—"

He halts my words when he closes in on me. Nowhere to go, I find my back pressed against the door.

"Why won't you let me take care of you, Ella? Let me whisk you off and protect you?" he questions quietly, his nose grazing mine.

I can sense the rage rippling from him, but his words are soft and comforting. Then my eyes fill with tears, but I blink rapidly to rid them and take a deep breath to strengthen my resolve.

"Caulder was going to hurt me. Don't you see? William *did* hurt me. He hit me. Kissed me. Spat at me. Called me names. Starved me. Made me crazy!" I shriek. "He fucked me too, Alcott. And had he not, he would have turned me over to Caulder to do the same damn thing!"

His hand slips up my neck and a trail of fire slides up my throat with it. I nearly cry from the gentle way he strokes my jaw with his thumb as if to convey to me how sorry he is about everything that happened.

"I know, but I cannot fucking fathom the thought of you getting hurt anymore. You're mine to adore and protect," he tells me firmly, nudging my nose with his. His scent envelops me, and I want to lose myself in him. "I won't allow it, Ella. I simply won't allow it."

I shake away the daze he put me in. "What?" I gasp. "You can't control what I do. I'm a grown woman and—"

He silences me when he seizes my lips with his. The way his mouth owns mine dizzies me, and I soon forget why it is I am even here. Between our heated kisses, though, he growls and reminds me.

"It appears to me that you are no woman tonight, which makes your argument invalid." He knocks the hat off my head and it falls to the floor as if to further prove his point.

His cock painfully presses against my belly, telling me that, despite his anger, I still arouse him. It thrills me to know that he must find me attractive anyhow, even if my hair is mostly gone.

"Does it turn you on that you want to make love to me when, clearly, I am no woman?" I taunt. The moan that escapes me is all female, though, as he drags his mouth away from mine and scrapes his teeth along my neck.

"I do not want to make love to you. For I am too furious to make love," he snarls against my flesh. His tone dives its way into the depths of my body, and I want to soak in it. "I want to fuck you instead, angel."

I yelp when pulls away from me and twists me in his arms. Then he bends me over the small counter and grabs my arse with both hands.

"You madden me with your persistence, yet I admire that about you," he grumbles as his hands slip around to the front of my trousers and unfastens them. "You cut off all your hair, yet you look incredibly more fucking beautiful, if that is even possible."

His hand slides into my hair, causing me to smile. But when he clutches a handful and tugs my head back, I moan again. The rough manner in which he touches me has my pelvis aching and moisture dampening my knickers.

He tangles his hand in my hair and turns my face to meet his. The moment he slams his mouth to mine, I slip into the fog that is him. Though his kiss is punishing and crude, I crave more nonetheless. It doesn't take long before my trousers fall to the floor around my ankles.

"I'm going to fuck you this way. I really want to whip your arse for putting yourself in danger," he snaps, but when his palm grips my arse through my knickers, I nearly come from the touch.

"Are you going to talk about it all evening, or are you going to make good on your threats?" It thrills me to goad him.

Of course he bites the bait—as I knew he would—and releases my hair. My sore neck is given a reprieve as he pushes his own trousers down. When I feel him dragging my knickers off my arse and along my thighs, I whimper.

"God, you're so beautiful," he praises on a growl low in his throat.

My breaths are coming out fast and ragged as I anticipate what he'll do next. A gasp bursts from me when he pushes me back down over the counter. With my backside bare to him, I feel so delightfully exposed. And he doesn't hesitate to exact his punishment, slapping my bottom with just enough sting to make it hurt but not hurt enough.

"I would bet every dime I had that you're wet, angel. You're probably soaked and praying I'll whip your arse again. Am I right?"

I nod in agreement but yelp when he grabs my hair once more, pulling my head back into the twisted position so I can see him. His eyes are a brewing storm, and I want it to capsize me.

"Tell me what you want. I need to hear the words, darling," he whispers.

The lust-wrapped-in-love way he says them with consumes me. I want all he has to give me.

I wriggle my bottom at him, and he swats me again in the same spot. As fire spreads over my arse cheek, I discover I am becoming increasingly wet for him. Rubbing my thighs together, I attempt to ease the ache of my desire for him between my legs.

"Say the damn words, Ella." His cock is thick and proud as he grinds it against me.

"I want you to whip me and fuck me and own my body! Take me, Alcott. When I'm around you, you distract me with everything that is you. I crave you every second I am away from you. You're addicting, and I'll never be satisfied. Please," I beg.

He whips me again, this time hard enough for me to cry out. But the moment his hand slips between my legs, my eyes roll back in bliss. After his finger enters me, he prods me with expert precision.

"So wet," he coos. "I could do this all evening long, but you know I really want my cock there—stretching you with my thickness. Beg me some more, Ella. I'm not done punishing you for being such a wicked woman."

"Please," I whimper, "Your teasing is pushing me to the brink of madness. I'm sorry I came here tonight. But right now, I don't care at all about any of it. I simply want you."

Groaning in approval, he slips his finger out of me. I mewl in a needy way as he drags the tip of his cock between the cheeks of my arse.

"Do it now," I urge him as I look over my shoulder at him. I make my point by spreading my legs as far as my trousers at my ankles will allow.

Our eyes meet, and the reason we got into this dank washroom notwithstanding, we're both on the same level of need for the other. His dark eyes shine with love and the desire to possess my body. I hope that mine mirror the same love and desire to be taken without hesitation.

His fingers tangle into my hair again and he holds me so I cannot look away from him—not that I would want to. I'll always want to look at this handsome man. He's alluring with his strong jaw and scruffy face—purely delectable with his full, soft lips and piercing, brown eyes.

"Ah!" I cry out as he enters me without warning. My body easily accepts every inch of his cock, and his thrusting begins with haste. When his testicles slap against my clitoris with each pound into me, I lose all sense of reality and my knees shake.

"So perfect. You're so utterly perfect. I'm going to marry you and spend my whole life making sweet love to you," he murmurs in the softest tone.

"Kiss me."

His thrusting halts as he heeds my wishes and kisses me hard against my swollen lips. I want to continue kissing him, but my release is so close. He seems to sense this and wrenches his mouth away from me before he continues his unrelenting pounding into me.

"Come for me baby," he urges. "I want the juices of your orgasm all over my cock."

When his arm wraps around my front and slips under the waistcoat, I whimper. The moment he pinches my nipple through my dress shirt, I lose it. My flesh erupts with a fever only his love can evoke, and I shudder with my climax.

"Alcott!" I cry out as I come.

"Mine, darling. All mine," he says fiercely as he holds me against him, pumping his own hot orgasm into me.

My knees have long since buckled, but my Alcott holds me steadfast and firm. It portrays our relationship, being that he is the strong force that keeps me safe and grounded no matter how shaky the earth beneath me is.

"I have you, angel. I will *always* have you."

Chapter Twelve

Alcott Dumont

THE WOMAN WENT AND LOST her damn mind. Last night, when she showed up at the pub dressed in Gerald's clothes, I was livid. Fucking livid. But the fire in her blue eyes in combination with her sexy new hair had my cock at full mast and eager to be inside her.

How could she have gotten any more exquisite?

Now, as she sleeps—not a façade this time—I drag my finger down her bare spine. With this haircut, I have better access to her neck and back. Last night, I marked her neck up with my mouth knowing she didn't have any hair to hide it. I bruised her flesh by my intense sucking while I made love to her in this very bed.

God, I love her.

"Wake up, darling," I murmur before I kiss her shoulder blade.

She moans in protest but rolls over onto her back. Dipping down, I place a kiss on her nipple. The pale flesh around the pink circle invites me to color it up as well—like her skin was made for me to taste and tease.

"Do we have to leave so soon?" she questions, her voice still thick with sleep.

I flick my tongue out and taste her pebbled nipple while I stare up at her. "Uhhhuhh."

She giggles, which does magical things to my cock. "And here I thought we had time to make love once more before our long journey to Havering," she teases.

After popping off her tit, I don't hesitate to spread her legs open, climb on top of her, and attack her mouth with mine. "We always have time for making love, darling," I growl as I grab my cock and push it into her wet opening.

My girl is always so fucking wet for me.

"Oh, yes, Alcott," she purrs as I pound into her.

Her body is always tight—a perfect fit—each time we have sex. I can't get enough of this woman. She is my everything. I knew it the very first moment I laid eyes on her.

Lifting up as I thrust so I can see her pretty, blue eyes, I tell her, "I love you."

A tear rolls down her cheek, and she smiles beautifully at me. "Alcott, I love you too. You were the prince who came to save me. And I your distressed damsel."

I chuckle at her and peck her nose. "You were distressed, all right. However, the damsel part is questionable," I tease as I run my fingers through her hair.

She sticks her tongue out at me, which I steal way. And several intense moments later, we're spent and relaxed, conjoined and sated.

"Will your mother like me as your wife?" she asks. Her thumb runs over my bottom lip, and I have the urge to bite it.

"Yes, darling. There isn't one single thing not to love about you."

And that's the goddamned truth.

Ella is imperfectly perfect.

"Are you sure you don't want to pack any of Elisabeth's clothes?"

Ella scrunches her nose up, worry that I will disapprove etched on her face. "No, I packed some things Gerald no longer uses."

Once we arrive back to Havering, I am going to have Mother sew her some feminine trousers and dress shirts fitting for a woman. The fact that she refuses to wear dresses after her ordeal is understandable, but I am not sure how much longer I can stand her wearing the old man's clothes.

"Do not worry, angel." I flash her a comforting grin. "I was only wondering before I snapped our suitcase closed."

Her smile is one of appreciation that I understand her and her needs. I hope she knows I would do everything in my power to make her happy. Even if that means becoming the laughingstock of Havering at being the only man married to a woman who prefers dressing as a male.

We've had our lunch and are about to load the coach to leave when an urgent knock pounds on the other side of our bedroom door. Ella peers at me with furrowed eyebrows, but I shrug as I stride over to the door. Upon opening it, I see a frantic Gretchen on the other side.

"Mr. Dumont, it's Gerald. I heard a commotion, and he's in the study with three men. At first, there was shouting and then breaking glass. I'm afraid something has happened to him," she sobs.

I snap my head over to Ella. "Stay here." Then I push past Gretchen, storming toward the study on the other end of the massive estate.

Last night, he invited the men over under the ruse that Lord Thomas wanted to meet with them to discuss a deal to make their boss not ever bother Ella or this family again. Of course the money-hungry men were more than eager to begin dialogues before

Caulder arrived in town because Gerald dangled empty promises at them—told them that working for Lord Thomas pays double what they make with Caulder. The greedy bastards were more than happy to "converse" their options before their boss had a say in the matter.

Gerald promised me he had a plan and told me not to worry.

Now, I'm fucking worried.

I'm a fool for having believed that the old man could handle the men alone.

As I near the study, small noises come from behind the thick door—noises that indicate that someone is inside. However, there is no talking or shouting or any signs of a struggle. Dear lord, I hope he is okay.

I'll need a weapon, but I foolishly ran over here without grabbing one. I am with luck though, as I discover a thick, metal chamberstick on a nearby table. Upon ridding it of the candle, I grip it tight and prepare myself to swing at whomever is on the other side of the door.

With a deep breath, I push through the door and quickly take the scene in.

Two men from the pub plus one other.

Broken glass.

Old man leaned against the desk, drinking whisky.

Our eyes meet, and he nods his head at me.

"Alcott."

"You wily arse!" I laugh. "How in the hell did you manage to take three of these big bastards down?" I'm fucking astonished as hell.

He smirks at me. Smug fucker. "Strychnine. I offered them a drink while I fetched Lord Thomas."

Poison.

"I did not give you enough credit, I'm afraid," I chuckle. "Too bad for them Lord Thomas was never coming."

Gerald shakes his head and smiles. "It was a quick death.

They're already frolicking in the afterlife of Hell. I wouldn't waste your worries on these two. Pritchard is going to help me bury them out back."

I raise an eyebrow at the mention of Pritchard. The old fart mostly drives the coaches for Jasper and sometimes helps around the estate. However, I never saw him as an accomplice to murdering henchmen.

"You continue to surprise me, old man. Where in the hell did you come by poison on such short notice?"

He shrugs. "You know the fenced-off portion within the garden?"

I nod.

"Do not ever go back there, son, for it is a very dangerous place to be. The *Strychnos nux-vomica* tree is the most dangerous of the lot," he say gruffly, "and a smart man always keeps a vial of deadly poison ready for emergencies."

I smirk at him. "I see that Jasper keeps you around for more than just carrying luggage."

He smiles. "Indeed he does, Alcott. Indeed he does."

"Darling, are you ready?" I ask as I pick the suitcase up.

"I am. I shall miss this home, but I do look forward to seeing my sisters and your family. This journey to Havering will be the first of many, I hope," she says wistfully. "It is my wish to travel and see things, Alcott. How wonderful would it be to climb the mountains in the Alps or to see The Eiffel Tower they have begun construction on in France? Even better, how lovely would it be to sink our toes into the sand on the beaches in the Mediterranean? Or have a stiff drink in an Irish pub? Or learn beautiful Spanish dances in Madrid?"

I walk over to her and plant a kiss on her forehead.

"I'm just a silly girl who dreams a lot," she laughs.

However, I don't miss the longing in her voice. My sweet little Ella wasn't born to stay caged up. No, my beautiful bird was meant to fly free.

I shall always give that to her.

"Well, silly girl," I chuckle as I open the front door for her, "I will make all of your dreams come true and more."

She flashes me the happiest of grins over her shoulder as she steps out of the threshold.

And then my world freezes.

My beautiful bird has just been captured.

All I see is a glimpse of inky curls on a man before he twists my future wife in his arms with her back against his chest and a blade at her throat.

"Let her go, Caulder," I snarl. I've never seen the man, but I already know he is who has come for retribution.

The suitcase has long been dropped and both of us men are glaring at one another.

"She belongs to me, you fool. Clearly, William could not handle the task. I, on the other hand, am more than up for the challenge," he snaps. "And she is quite a challenge."

Ella squirms in his arms, but he only tightens his grip on her. My eyes find hers, and I expect to see terror or fear or something indicating that she is afraid for her life. Instead, I see fury and hate and determination all rolled into one.

This angel has been waiting for this moment for nearly a fortnight. If I could save her from this time, I would. But we both know she'll save herself. Even with the figure approaching behind them, I know she will finish the job.

A crackle of a leaf underfoot alerts Caulder to Pritchard's sudden appearance. It is enough of a distraction for Caulder to whip his knife away from her neck and toward his attacker.

"Halt right there!"

I *should* charge for them.

I *should* save my woman.

But when I see the flash of metal as she draws that wicked knife of hers from her belt, I hold steady. With an elegant twist of her body, she angles herself away from Caulder. However, before she fully spins away, she slashes her knife across his neck and gracefully leaps away.

The man never saw it coming.

His own knife falls to the earth while he fiercely clutches his gushing neck. I can see his wild eyes flitting about as he attempts to understand what happened but coming up short with answers. Within seconds, he falls to his knees and then face first into the dirt.

An event that only took seconds to play out felt like eons.

"Ella," I rasp out, still in shock from what I witnessed.

Her willowy figure strides over to me. When she wraps her slender arms around my waist, resting her cheek against my firm chest, I squeeze her to me.

"I was afraid I was going to lose you," I choke out, desperately trying to keep womanly tears from forming. But by God, I almost lost her.

She lifts her head toward mine and presses a kiss to my lips. "But you just found me, Alcott. I am not going anywhere without you." A single tear rolls out, and her lip wobbles. My sweet girl is struggling to keep it together, but she's brave and fucking strong as hell.

My palms find her cheeks, and I deepen our kiss as I swipe more tears away with my thumbs. I need to attach my soul to hers so that she never leaves my side. And when her knees buckle, I gather her into my arms.

"I shall never let you go, dear Ella. You don't have to be so strong now. I will be strong for you until the day I die," I vow in a whisper against her hair.

She sobs for a moment, but eventually, her body straightens as she finds that inner strength that is so awe inspiring. This woman will be more than fine.

"I love you, angel," I growl between kisses, "but remind me never to irritate you."

My attempt to lighten the somber mood produces a fit of teary giggles from her that fill my heart with joy.

She tugs away and narrows her red eyes at me, her tears finally drying. "I think it will be good for our marriage for you to have a little fear of your dear wife. It shall keep you always doting and on your toes."

My future winks at me as she pulls away to lift the suitcase. And while she bends over, I admire her arse in the trousers—they certainly look a hell of lot better on her than they do on Gerald.

"You are slightly unhinged, woman. You know that, right?"

She smirks as she regards me. "I will agree to *slightly.* Now, let's make haste to Havering. I'm ready to become Mrs. Dumont and am way past waiting another minute."

I watch proudly as my sassy fiancée provocatively sways her hips as she saunters past Pritchard, who is now dragging Caulder's body behind a bush. In a brave manner, she lifts her chin in the air, and the wind swirls around her—it is almost as if she draws strength from it. Her adorable, blond hair blows wild around her, and I can't help but notice that she seems free.

My angel.

My beautiful bird.

She's innocent again and very much free. As she was born to be.

Epilogue

Ella Dumont

Four years later

WE'VE JUST RETURNED TO HAVERING after a year of traveling all over Europe. I already miss sampling the different cultures, but I am glad to be back home. It has been far too long since I have seen my sisters and their families.

"Are you still exhausted, darling?" Alcott questions from the doorway.

I roll over to face him. My husband is quite delectable in his suit. While we traveled, he dressed casually as I did. I'm not sure he even packed a waistcoat for our journey. But now, seeing him in handsome attire, my skin prickles with heat.

He reminds me of when we first met—when he was sinfully beautiful and I was hopelessly smitten with him. Not much has changed though. After four years together, I couldn't be happier.

Well, I *could* be happier. In fact, I want to share a little happiness with my husband.

"I am quite tired. How are my sisters and the kids? Will you tell them I shall see them at dinner?" I question before I go forth with what I really have to say.

He smiles longingly. "Edith was chastising Xander for throwing lemons at his sister, Lorelei. Gus and Charles were encouraging their cousin as usual. They miss their aunty but know you're still tired."

"Alcott," I sigh, "I'm sorry that I haven't given you a child as of yet." Even though I am happy to be home, my emotions get the best of me and my eyes fill with unshed tears.

His smile falls and he stalks over to me almost angrily. "Darling, that is not your fault and you know it. The time wasn't right. We, too, shall have our chance."

My heart flops around in my chest like a fish on the embankment of the river at his words. He toes his shoes off and crawls into the bed behind me. When he drapes a hand over my middle, I sigh. No matter how many countries we visited or unusual places we had to sleep overnight, one thing remained the same.

Alcott always held on to me as if I might fly off in the middle of the night.

Despite his worry, I would never leave his side. He may think I'm some bird hating the cage. However, as long as he's a bird too and we're together in this cage of life, I could not ask for more.

He will always be the sky to which I soar.

"I have not been plagued with menstruation for two months now," I admit softly.

His large hand slips over my belly and splays over my pudgy flesh there. I can feel his entire body go tense with hope, which matches the way I feel.

"Does that mean . . ." he trails off in a whisper.

"I think it does," I laugh through my tears. "Well, at least, I hope it does."

He kisses my hair and inhales me. "Darling, I do have faith that

God has a plan for us. And if that includes a little one growing inside you, I will be fucking elated."

I sigh as he rolls me over to my back. His lips find mine and we kiss for a moment.

"And," he says with a smile, "If He does not have a plan for a child, we'll still have a hell of a time trying. I shall never love you any less." His dark eyes are brewing with a storm of love and adoration all directed toward me.

"How did I get so lucky to have you?" I ask.

He closes his eyes and presses a soft kiss to my lips. "I prayed for an angel and he sent me you. It would appear that I am the lucky one."

As we deepen our kiss, I send up a prayer of my own.

Mother, put in a good word to God.

The Alcotts are ready for their baby bird.

The End

The Practical Joke

Every now and again, I like to mess with my beta readers and editor by slipping in something totally random and confusing. While writing Becoming Mrs. Benedict, it also happened to be the sinking of the Titanic anniversary. Of course I had to watch the movie on television and very quickly marveled at their clothes and language—they reminded me so much of my characters. So, thus, an evil plan formed. I wrote this "fake" epilogue and placed it before the real epilogue before sending it off to my beta readers and editor.

Then I waited.

It didn't take long before I got plenty of messages that had me laughing like a lunatic . . .

"THEY'RE ON THE TITANIC?!?!?!"

"NOOOOOOOOOOOO!"

"Kristi, you're mean!"

I thought it was quite funny. And I warned them, when they least expect it, I'll be teasing them again. Just keeping them on their toes . . .

Hope you enjoy the fake epilogue I sent them!

Epilogue

Ella Dumont

April 15th, 1912

"I AM LOOKING FORWARD TO SEEING New York," I sigh as we walk along the deck of the ship.

Tonight, the air is crisp and quite chilly. I lean in toward Alcott, and he kisses the top of my head.

"I'm not finished showing you the world, darling. I shall cart you to every corner of this Earth to impress and dazzle you," he chuckles.

We approach a couple standing close on the bow of the ship. They're very much in love, not unlike us when we married nearly twenty-five years before.

"Good evening," Alcott addresses them.

They turn toward us, and the fellow wraps his arm around the woman.

"Good evening. This is quite a ship," he praises. "They say it's unsinkable."

Both men chuckle as the two of us ladies smile at one another.

"I'm Alcott Dumont, and this is my lovely wife, Ella," my husband greets officially.

The woman is beautiful in her stunning dress, but I see her eyeing up my trousers with confusion. I'm accustomed to the looks of disapproval by people when it comes to my clothing choices.

"I'm Jack Dawson," the young man says, "and this is Rose DeWitt Bukater."

We all shake hands and comment on the beautifully starry night. Finally, after some small talk with the younger couple, we bid our farewells and head toward our cabin to call it an early evening.

"My love for you, darling, is as unsinkable as this ship," Alcott assures me.

I scan the massive beast we are floating upon somewhere in the Atlantic Ocean and admire the sheer size of it. If Alcott's love is as big as this ship, the Titanic, then it must true.

"I'll never let go, Jack." My cheeks redden at having accidentally said the handsome young man's name. "I mean, I'll never let go, Alcott. Even if this ship were to somehow sink and I was lying on a big hunk of wood all to myself while you dangled in the water, I wouldn't let go. I would never pry your dead, frozen hands from my arm and push you into the dark, chilly abyss."

cue "My Heart Will Go On" by Céline Dion

A Note from K

If you enjoyed this book, please check out some of my other books (https://www.goodreads.com/author/show/7741564.K_Webster). I've published over a dozen books in many different genres including: contemporary romance, erotic romance, paranormal romance, and historical romance. My stories are all different and unique from one another. Thank you for taking a chance on my book and I hope to hear how you liked it!

Acknowledgements

Thank you to my husband. You'll always be my hero and best friend. Without your support, none of this would be possible. I love you, Mr. Webster!

I want to thank the beta readers, whom are also my friends. Nikki McCrae, Wendy Colby, Dena Marie, Elizabeth Thiele, Lori Christensen, Michelle Ramirez, Shannon Martin, Amy Bosica, Sian Davies, Ella Stewart, Nikki Cole, Anne Jolin, Maggie Lugo, Kayla Stewart, Elizabeth Clinton, and Melody Dawn (I hope I didn't forget anyone) you guys always provide AMAZING feedback. You all give me helpful ideas to make my stories better and give me incredible encouragement. I appreciate all of your comments and suggestions.

Thank you to my blogger friends that go above and beyond to always share my stuff. You ladies rock!

I'm especially thankful for the Breaking the Rules Babes. You ladies are amazing with your support and friendship. Each and every single one of you is amazingly supportive and caring.

I am totally thankful for my author group, the COPA gals, for being there when I need to take a load off and whine. Y'all rock!

Mickey, my fabulous editor from I'm a Book Shark, thank you for being such a great editor. You've been a great friend as well and I appreciate that.

Thank you Stacey Blake for being amazing. Everything you do is magic and I absolutely love your creativity and sweet disposition.

Lastly but certainly not least of all, thank you to all of the wonderful readers out there that are willing to hear my story and enjoy my characters like I do. It means the world to me!

About the Author

I'm a thirty four year old self-proclaimed book nerd. Married to my husband for twelve years, we enjoy spending time with our two lovely children. Writing is a fun hobby for me that has now turned into a livelihood over the past year. In the past, I've enjoyed the role as a reader. However, I have learned I absolutely love taking on the creative role as the writer. Something about determining how the story will play out intrigues me to no end.

This writing experience has been a blast and I've met some really fabulous people along the way. I hope my readers enjoy reading my stories as much as I do writing them. I look forward to connecting with you all!

Join K Webster's newsletter to receive a couple of updates a month on new releases and exclusive content. To join, all you need to do is go here (http://eepurl.com/bllgoP).

Facebook (https://www.facebook.com/authorkwebster)

Blog (http://authorkwebster.wordpress.com/)

Twitter (https://twitter.com/KristiWebster)

Email (mailto:kristi@authorkwebster.com)

Goodreads (https://www.goodreads.com/user/show/10439773-k-webster)

Instagram (http://instagram.com/kristiwebster)

CPSIA information can be obtained
at www.ICGtesting.com
Printed in the USA
BVHW030218160721
612120BV00009B/101